FALSE

T0243252

FALSE IDOLS

LISA KLINK, PATRICK LOHIER, AND DIANA RENN

 ADAPTIVE BOOKS | SERIAL BOX

AN IMPRINT OF ADAPTIVE STUDIOS • CULVER CITY, CA

Episodes written by:
Patrick Lohier – 2, 5, 9*, 11
Lisa Klink – 1, 6
Diana Renn – 3, 4, 7, 8, 9*, 10
*Co-written

Based on the original screenplay by Marshall Lewy

Visit us on the web at www.adaptivestudios.com and www.serialbox.com

Library of Congress Cataloging in Publication Number:
2017962180
ISBN 978-1-945293-35-1
Ebook ISBN 978-1-945293-43-6

Printed in the United States of America.
Designed by: Elyse Strongin, Neuwirth & Associates

Adaptive Books
3578 Hayden Avenue, Suite 6
Culver City, CA 90232

10 9 8 7 6 5 4 3 2 1

CONTENTS

OPERATION CAIRO

· LISA KLINK ·

Layla faced the mirror and took a deep breath. When she went out there, she had to be effortlessly confident. She certainly looked the part, in a rose-colored Givenchy dress that complemented her olive skin and tasteful diamond earrings. She'd swept her dark hair off her neck into a smooth chignon and her makeup was perfect. She'd been prepping for this night for weeks. *I can do this.*

She stepped out onto the wide marble stairs leading down to the patio. At least fifty guests had gathered for the soiree, standing in groups around the pool or sitting in the gazebo, gazing out at the Cairo skyline under a nearly full moon, as waiters circulated with champagne and hors d'oeuvres. The guests were an eclectic, international group, ranging from a seventy-eight-year-old Belgian duchess to a twenty-something Japanese deejay, with one important thing in common. They were all extremely rich.

Farwadi joined her on the steps. He was a dapper little man in his mid-forties, wearing a tailored, pale gray suit, with a thick mustache and dark, wavy hair shellacked into place. "Are you ready?" he asked her nervously.

She nodded. "Are you?"

He looked out at his guests and tapped a small fork against the side of his champagne flute. The buzz of conversation quieted down and the guests turned their attention to Farwadi. He raised his glass. "Thank you all for being here tonight. I have someone very special I'd like you to meet. My cousin Layla." He tipped his glass in her direction and she smiled in return. "Layla is the youngest daughter of my beloved Aunt Fatma. I know that most of you have heard me tell stories about Aunt Fatma and her wild hat collection." A chuckle from the crowd confirmed this. "She was the only person I loved as much as my own parents. When she married and moved to San Francisco I know it broke my mother's heart. But she had a good life. Six years ago, we lost this wonderful woman to cancer."

Layla thought that Farwadi was laying on the sentiment a little thick, but his guests seemed to be eating it up. He went on, "My uncle has since passed away, and my cousins have scattered around the world. But Layla has always made the effort to stay connected to her mother's side of the family. And now she has moved to Cairo to pursue her interest in Egypt's rich cultural history. I hope I can count on those of you with expertise in that area"—Farwadi looked pointedly at a few of his guests—"to guide her as she builds her personal collection." He turned to her and raised his glass again. "Welcome, Layla!"

"Thank you, Nesim," said Layla. Now several of Farwadi's friends approached her, inspired by his heartfelt speech, eager to connect with his favorite cousin.

"I met Nesim fifteen years ago at an auction in Bruges . . ."

"I met him in Tokyo . . ."

". . . in Moscow . . ."

". . . at my own gallery in Florence. I have some pieces there you might like."

Her cousin had quickly left Layla's side, she realized with some worry and annoyance. As she scanned the party, she spotted Miriam Goldman, a world-renowned collector of ancient Sumerian artifacts. Goldman was a widow in her late forties, with glossy, dark brown hair cut in a short, no-nonsense bob. Layla had seen her home featured in a design magazine.

Layla introduced herself and congratulated Goldman on her latest acquisition. "I hear that you beat out twelve different bidders for the cylinder seal of Ashur." By all accounts, the woman was a fierce negotiator who never backed down from a fight.

"Fourteen, actually. It's a remarkable piece."

Layla leaned in, lowering her voice to a confidential hush. "Wasn't there some debate about its authenticity?"

The woman scoffed. "Rumors spread by my competitors to drive down the price. The seal has been authenticated by three different experts, and I've personally met the archaeologist who excavated the site."

"I don't blame you for being careful," said Layla. "There's a lot of fraud in the antiquities market."

"Yes. There is," she said. Then she smiled and took the younger woman's hands in her own. "I would love to introduce you to my boys."

Goldman led her over to a pair of young men standing by the gazebo. "Marcus, Adrian, this is Layla." When they turned toward her, she saw that they were twins. They were in their mid-twenties and identically handsome, although Marcus had dark hair and Adrian had bleached his a startling platinum blond.

Marcus nodded to her. "Hey."

She returned the nod.

"Would you like a drink?" asked Adrian, as Layla watched Miriam Goldman disappear into the crowd of guests. She had obviously hit a nerve with her comment about fraud.

"Nothing for me, thanks," she told them. The twins seemed friendly enough, but she didn't want to get stuck chitchatting with them. "If you'll excuse me, I need to use the powder room." *That's what rich people call the bathroom, right?*

Layla slipped away and went into the house. It was a unique structure, to say the least, combining stone from ancient ruins with contemporary stucco and tile. Farwadi liked to tell people that the design reflected his modern sensibilities, as well as the history of the Egyptian people, which would always be part of him. She thought this sounded a bit pretentious, but his friends and associates seemed to be charmed.

She found Farwadi hiding out from his own party on a small porch off the kitchen, holding a half-empty glass of what looked like Scotch in one hand and a cigarette in the other. "I quit these years ago," he said miserably, taking a long drag. "Now I've started again."

"Everything's going well," she assured him. "Your speech was lovely."

"I hate this. I hate lying to everyone."

"I know." She felt a twinge of sympathy for the man, even though he had no one but himself to blame for his current dilemma. "But this is what you agreed to."

"I'm well aware of that," he said in a clipped tone.

As Farwadi started to take a drink of Scotch, she snatched the glass from his hand and dumped the contents over the side of the porch. "I need you sober. We still have work to do. I want you to introduce me to the Ghaffars."

He looked surprised. "You don't believe that they're involved in this nasty business? Noor is on the board of ECHO," he said, referring to the Egyptian Cultural Heritage Organization, a group dedicated to protecting archaeological sites from looting and vandalism.

"Yes, and that gives her access to the most well-protected sites," Layla told him. "Where ancient relics have a funny habit of disappearing, then showing up on the black market and selling for millions."

Farwadi stubbed out his cigarette. He grudgingly led her back to his guests.

FOUR WEEKS AGO

Layla didn't know what kind of situation she was walking into as she descended to the lower decks of the cargo ship. She made her way into the hot, cramped galley to find three men with guns, shouting at one another in different languages. Agents Holt and Santos were yelling at the young man in the cook's uniform—a kid, really, no more than eighteen or nineteen—to put down his gun. The kid was clearly terrified. Layla couldn't blame him. Five minutes ago, he would have been going about his business, securing the galley as the MSC *Zephyr* docked in New York Harbor, when suddenly two armed men had stormed in and started yelling in some incomprehensible tongue. For all he knew, the Joint Terrorism Task Force agents commandeering his ship were pirates. So he'd grabbed a handgun to defend himself, resulting in the standoff.

When it became clear that they weren't communicating, Agent Holt had picked up his radio and called in Agent Layla el-Deeb, a language specialist with the Intelligence Division. Rumor had it that she spoke twenty different languages. This was an exaggeration, which Layla herself made no effort to correct.

She approached the two male agents, who towered over her. Layla was five feet four and looked even younger than her twenty-nine years. Her less-than-intimidating appearance sometimes made it hard to be taken seriously as an agent, but now she hoped it might reassure the frightened cook.

"Has he said anything?" she asked Holt, keeping her voice low and calm.

He shook his head. "We tried English and Spanish. No response."

Layla nodded. She knew the cargo ship had come to New York from Mozambique, where a local crew had probably been hired. The official language of Mozambique was . . . she could remember this . . . Portuguese. It was worth a try. She held the young man's gaze as she showed him her empty hands. "*Não vamos machucá-lo,*" she told him. "*Largue a arma.*" *We won't hurt you. Put down the gun.*

He looked at her uncomprehendingly. Shit. So much for Portuguese. What else did they speak in Mozambique? The kid's high cheekbones and ebony skin hinted at East African heritage. There was a good chance he spoke Swahili. Her own Swahili, unfortunately, was limited to an online tutorial she'd taken several years ago. It hadn't exactly covered situations like this. Agents Holt and Santos were watching her, waiting for her to say something. She began slowly, searching for the right words. "*Hatutaki . . . kummeza.*"

The corner of his mouth twitched with involuntary amusement. She'd said something wrong. Didn't *kummeza* mean . . . ? Then Layla had to smile, too. She had just informed the young man that they didn't want to swallow him, rather than telling him that they didn't want to hurt him. If she'd really been thinking, she would have made the mistake on purpose, because it made him relax his guard, just a bit. Sticking to Swahili, she asked his name. "*Jina?*"

"Juma," he ventured.

"Layla," she told him, indicating herself. Then she hesitated, unable to come up with the Swahili word for "gun." So she mimed the action she wanted, kneeling and laying an imaginary weapon on the floor. "*Chini,*" she said, meaning "down." She hoped. Juma watched this, then looked back at Holt and Santos, who still had their semiautomatics trained on him.

"Lower your weapons," Layla told them. "He's not going to shoot. He's just scared." The men hesitated, exchanging a quick look over her head, debating whether to follow her orders. She switched to official FBI-ese. "We need to de-escalate the situation."

Holt considered this, then slowly lowered his gun. Santos did the same. Layla looked back at Juma and nodded. Your turn. He studied the three of them, evaluating their intent, his dark brown eyes still wide with fear. She waited, resisting the urge to prompt him again, hoping that her colleagues wouldn't lose patience and charge in. Finally, Juma knelt and placed his handgun on the floor. "*Asante,*" she said. *Thank you.*

The agents quickly stepped forward. Layla picked up the gun while the men pulled Juma's arms behind his back and zip-tied his hands together. She felt conflicted as they escorted him up to the main deck and off the ship. Being part of Operation Treasure Hunt, as the JTTF had dubbed it, was a welcome change from sitting at her desk all day, translating documents and voice recordings collected by other agents. She knew it was important work, but it wasn't what she had joined the FBI to do. She wanted to be out in the field, digging up evidence and solving crimes.

"Nice work," said Holt, as he and Santos led their prisoner away to join his twenty-two crewmates, lined up on the concrete dock under the watchful eye of the Waterfront Commission police. Layla wouldn't be part of the interrogation team. They had more highly trained agents, and more fluent Swahili speakers, for that. Agent el-Deeb was dismissed.

She stood in the cold rain for a moment, frustrated. Then she walked along the busy dock, curious to find out how Operation Treasure Hunt was unfolding. It was a massive operation, with agents from the ATF, Coast Guard, Customs, and the Waterfront Commission of New York Harbor, all under the supervision of the FBI. The Joint Terrorism Task Force had cordoned off a section of the shipyard and commandeered a terminal building for the operation. Three enormous cranes were unloading forty-foot steel cargo containers from the MSC *Zephyr*, setting them down in the shipyard. Agents swarmed around each container with radiation detectors and bomb-sniffing dogs, searching for those that had been flagged by their agencies. The *Zephyr* carried more than twenty-eight hundred containers. This was going to take a while.

She noticed a crowd gathered around one of the open containers and went to see what they were looking at. Inside the steel box was a huge cache of guns and explosives. Tom Monaghan, Assistant Special Agent in Charge of Counterterrorism in the New York office, stood beside it triumphantly, along with three members of his elite strike team. All male, of course. Most of the high-profile squads in the Bureau still were. Monaghan grabbed a Kalashnikov rifle from the hoard and brandished it over his head, shouting, "Fuck the Muharib!"

A cheer went up from the onlookers, who came from different, often competing agencies, but were united in their hatred of the ultra-violent terrorist group known as the Muharib el-Salafi. The

Muharib had bombed civilian sites in Egypt, Turkey, and, most recently, a Christmas mass in Sicily. Over the past few weeks, Layla had been translating messages from FBI informants in the Middle East, reporting alarming intel about the Muharib smuggling weapons to its agents in the United States in preparation for an attack. The arsenal in the shipping container seemed to confirm those reports.

Layla approached Monaghan, a brawny guy with blond hair and craggy features, which some women, she knew, found irresistible. He'd recently been promoted from Supervisory Special Agent to ASAC. He was management now and was supposed to coordinate operations from his desk. But he couldn't stay away from the excitement of the field and delegated all the boring paperwork to someone else. She wasn't even sure he had a desk. "Congratulations," she told him. "Quite a catch."

"It was a team effort." He gestured to the other members of the strike team, gracious in his moment of triumph. Then he remembered to include the woman standing in front of him. "You were a big help, too . . ." She saw him struggling to remember her name.

"So the reports were true," she concluded grimly. "The Muharib really are planning something in the US. Where was the shipment headed?"

"The address on the manifest is a self-storage place in Pennsylvania. I'll have someone there in case anybody shows up to collect, but it's probably a dead end. This operation wasn't exactly covert." He looked around the dock, bustling with activity. "We have to assume the Muharib will find out we grabbed their toys. At least this shipment."

She hadn't considered this. "You think there are more coming in?"

"I'd bet on it. One thing about the Muharib—they always have a contingency plan. But don't worry. We'll get 'em." He gave her a condescending pat on the shoulder. She gritted her teeth and tried to smile.

An exuberant ATF agent came up to Monaghan and gave him a high five that would have knocked Layla flat. "Awesome work!" he exclaimed.

Layla rolled her eyes and moved off through the maze of steel containers, past several that were being opened and searched. She saw a tall, thin woman dragging a large wooden crate out of one of them and recognized her as Ellen Pierce. Layla had been following her career ever since she joined the FBI. Pierce was one of the few women to rise through the ranks of the male-dominated Bureau. She'd done it by being even more fearless than the guys; leading midnight raids on meth labs and going undercover with a particularly vicious drug gang in New York. Two years ago, she'd become the first female director of the national Art Crime Squad. Sure, one could argue that stolen art wasn't exactly a high priority for the FBI, but it was impressive nonetheless.

"Give you a hand with that?" Layla asked, going around behind the crate and pushing as Pierce pulled.

"Thanks." They slid it out of the container and onto the dock. The older woman extended a hand. "Ellen Pierce, Art Crime."

"Layla el-Deeb. Intelligence." They shook hands.

"Nice to meet you." Pierce nodded to a box of tools on the ground near Layla's feet. "Hand me that crowbar?"

She did, and the senior agent got to work prying open the crate. They heard the slap of another high five as Monaghan took his victory lap, accepting congratulations from everyone involved in the raid. "It's great to meet you, too," said Layla. "But what's Art Crime doing on a JTTF op?"

"Hunting for treasure," said Pierce with a grimace as she prized the lid off the crate. She reached in and dug through the Styrofoam peanuts, then lifted out a fist-sized object wrapped in newspaper. "Terrorist groups like the Muharib sell stolen art and antiquities to raise money to buy all those weapons."

Monaghan heard this as he was passing and stopped to gloat a little more. "You mean, like the ones we just confiscated?"

Pierce ignored him, continuing her conversation with Layla as she unwrapped the layers of newspaper. "Collectors in the West pay top dollar for Egyptian relics. These were on their way to a ritzy gallery in Chelsea." She pulled away the last of the paper to reveal . . . a cheap plaster bust of King Tut covered in gaudy gold and blue paint.

Layla's heart sank for her as Monaghan guffawed loudly. "Yeah, they'll get at least a buck and a half for that baby."

Pierce said nothing as she got a hammer and chisel from the toolbox. She set the bust of King Tut on top of another crate and delicately chipped at the plaster until it cracked. As she picked off the broken pieces, Layla saw what the coat of plaster had been hiding: a long-necked ceramic vase, glazed jade green with a gilded Eye of Horus on one side. "That's beautiful," she said.

"It's a ritual amphora, from around the fourteenth century BC. Probably used to hold scented oil." Pierce turned to Monaghan, holding up the amphora with great satisfaction. "This piece alone is worth at least ten thousand dollars. And there are maybe a dozen more like it in this crate."

"Wow," said Layla, all innocence. "That's a lot of Kalashnikovs."

She heard a barely suppressed snicker and turned to see that two other Counterterrorism agents were watching the exchange. Monaghan flushed, glared at all of them, then strode off. The women laughed. Layla examined the amphora more curiously. "So tell me about this gallery in Chelsea."

Pierce smiled. "I've been investigating the owner, Nesim Farwadi, for the past year and a half. I know he's been smuggling antiquities out of Egypt through his main gallery in Cairo, but I haven't been able to prove it until now. The Muharib thing is just speculation. I mean, terrorist groups like the Muharib do sell antiquities like this, but I can't prove that this particular gallery is connected to this particular group. I wanted to be in on this op because I knew that Farwadi had illegal goods in this shipment." She held up the little vase. "And I sure would love to hear what he has to say about them."

"If you really want to throw him off his game, you should confront him in the middle of his gallery. He won't know how to handle a powerful woman, especially in front of his own customers." Pierce gave her a curious look and she explained, "I grew up in Cairo. Dealing with men like that."

"You should come with me to question him."

"Right now?" Layla felt excitement pulse through her.

"Unless you need to get back to the office . . ."

"No," she said quickly, desperate to avoid her desk. "I have some time."

AS FARWADI AND LAYLA went out to the patio, she took a moment to slip back into the persona of Layla Nawar, straightening her spine and tilting her chin ever so slightly to capture that self-entitled, rich-girl attitude.

Farwadi swept her through the party toward a couple who seemed to radiate importance. "Noor and Gamal Ghaffar," he said, "my darling cousin, Layla Nawar." Layla hoped the Ghaffars didn't pick up on the somewhat sarcastic exaggeration Nesim had placed on the word "darling." If he got any drunker he was going to become a liability.

Gamal Ghaffar was a tall, barrel-chested man with the dignified bearing of an ex-soldier. Layla was aware that he was a high-ranking officer in the Egyptian General Intelligence Directorate, a powerful, secretive organization whose critics often disappeared without a trace. His personal beliefs were notoriously conservative. Layla saw him eyeing her pink dress with clear disapproval. By Western standards, the dress was downright demure, with cap sleeves, a modest neck, and a full skirt that hit below the knee. But it flattered her curves in a way that Gamal apparently found inappropriate for a nice Muslim girl. Farwadi's family was Muslim, so he would naturally assume that Layla was as well. For a moment, she was tempted to tell Gamal that she was actually Coptic Christian, just to see his reaction. He might find that even more horrifying than learning she was FBI.

But Layla was more interested in his wife, Noor. She was dressed in a traditional, loose-fitting abaya of richly embroidered, royal blue silk, with a matching hijab.

"Jehan! Come join us," called Noor. A tall, willowy young woman broke off from the group she was talking to and came over to them. She was twenty-two or twenty-three at most, with high cheekbones and dark, somehow mournful eyes. She wore a long denim skirt and a high-necked, three-quarter-sleeve blouse in an eye-catching lemon yellow, along with a white hijab shot through with gold threads and a chunky gold necklace. Her skin was sufficiently covered to meet conservative standards, but the bright color and gold bling weren't exactly modest.

Noor brushed an errant lock of hair off her face. "Layla, my daughter Jehan."

They exchanged greetings. "Love your dress," said the young woman. "Givenchy?"

"Yes." She saw Gamal's jaw tighten and wondered if Jehan was deliberately provoking her father with the compliment.

It wasn't long before Noor excused herself and her husband to talk to another friend. *Another adult*, thought Layla. She realized that the Ghaffars were pawning her off on their kid, as Miriam Goldman had done with her two sons.

Jehan grabbed her hand. "Come on. Hang with us."

Layla reluctantly let herself be led over to the fire pit, where the younger generation was gathered. The Goldman twins sat on one of the low teak benches by the fire. "There you are. We thought you got lost on your way to the 'powder room,'" Adrian teased. She made a mental note to strike the term from her "rich-girl" vocabulary.

Jehan seemed to be the informal social director of the group. She guided Layla to a seat near a twenty-something Japanese guy with spiked hair and introduced him as Hiro. "You like house music? Rap?" he asked.

"Sure." *Why not*, thought Layla, wondering if she'd be relegated to the kids' table for the rest of the night.

"This is Chloe." Jehan sat beside a pale woman with long, auburn hair and put an arm around her shoulders. "She's been having guy trouble."

"Because her boyfriend's an asshole," offered Hiro.

"He is not!" said Chloe, in a thick Australian accent.

Jehan joined the debate about Neal, the alleged asshole, while the Goldman twins held their own conversation in Swiss German. They were saying something about their house in Bern. Layla quietly eavesdropped as they relived the highlights of the wild party they had thrown while Mueti was away on a buying trip. She realized that these "kids" might not be a bad source of information after all.

"Sounds like fun," said Layla, in German. "Call me next time she's out of town."

They looked at her, startled that she spoke the language. Marcus smiled and replied in English. "I'll be sure to do that."

The words caught Hiro's attention. "Do what?"

"Invite Layla to our next party."

"Definitely!" Jehan agreed, then put a hand on Layla's arm, "But if he gives you something called a supernova, don't drink it. Trust me."

And just like that, she'd been accepted into the group. They continued talking about other parties, from a New Year's Eve bash in Hong Kong to a surprise party in Mazatlán that everyone agreed had been a total disaster. Layla got the impression that these people spent their lives simply going from one party to the next. She wondered if any of them actually had a job but knew that Farwadi's wealthy cousin wouldn't ask.

The conversation turned to future parties, and who would be attending what. Layla was invited to join in all the fun. She doubted, however, that the FBI would approve the expense of a last-minute ticket to China or Brazil. "I'll have to check with Nesim," she said, deliberately vague. "I know he's made a lot of plans."

By midnight, the party was winding down. The older guests had gone home, and the younger crowd headed out to the clubs. "Come with us!" urged Jehan, but Layla begged off.

"I'm exhausted," she explained. "But I'll see you at the Arts Council fundraiser next week." Jehan hugged Layla, then piled into a taxi with her friends.

Finally, the house was empty. Layla retrieved her oversized Chanel handbag from the closet, feeling exhilarated. For a rookie, she was pretty damn good at this. But she hadn't been able to stop Farwadi from drinking. He staggered as he escorted her out to the street, where his driver was waiting to take her home. "Thank you," she told him. "You did a great job tonight."

"Are you happy now? Am I finished?" he demanded.

"No, but it was a good start." When he didn't respond, she prompted, "Understood?"

"Yes," he snapped. He looked out at the Cairo skyline, shaking his head mournfully. "I'm glad Tahia and the children aren't here." He'd sent his wife and kids to visit her parents, so they wouldn't have to participate in the undercover scheme. "All of this feels like a curse on my family."

"What do you mean?"

Farwadi stared at her, as if surprised that she didn't understand. "To lie about them like this. It feels like I've laid a curse on my own blood."

Layla turned and slid into the backseat of the waiting Mercedes without another word to Farwadi. She felt an unexpected flare of anger at the man. He and his family, and everyone at the party, had been blessed with lives of privilege that she could hardly have imagined as a child. She may have grown up in Cairo just a stone's throw from this mansion, but the world of the people she met tonight could not be further from the Cairo she knew, that her family knew. Farwadi had no idea what it was like to be part of a truly cursed family.

Layla had grown up in the Cairo slum of Manshiyat Naser, also known as Garbage City, home to a large number of Coptic Christians, including the el-Deebs. They were a widely despised minority in Cairo, and often the only work they could find was collecting the city's trash, which they brought home and dumped in the streets for their families to scavenge through, looking for any discarded bits of metal or plastic they could sell to the recycling plant or, if they were lucky, scraps of still-edible food.

Layla's father had been a proud man and had forbidden her and her two younger siblings from touching the piles of garbage, but sometimes they spotted something interesting and couldn't resist digging it out. The pervasive stench lingered in their hair and clothes. When Layla arrived at school, she would see the disgust her teacher tried to hide if she got too close. And she heard the whispered taunts of her fellow students during class, *"zabbaleen"*— garbage person. But Layla still went to school, enduring their scorn, every day. Even then, she knew it was the only way she'd ever get out of Garbage City.

Now here she was, sitting in the back of a Mercedes, kicking off her Jimmy Choos. Her phone buzzed. As if he had felt her thinking of their childhood, a text from her brother Rami appeared.

It's a beautiful night here. Spring is in the air. What's it like there?

He was assuming she was in New York, of course. She couldn't tell him she was really in Cairo, or he'd want to see her, which was out of the question during an undercover operation. So she opened the weather app on her phone and looked at the listing for New York. The city was under an onslaught of icy rain that would run through the night.

Stormy here, wrote Layla.

She waited for a few seconds but he didn't respond. That was the extent of their communication, really, a back-and-forth focused primarily on the weather. It had been that way since Layla left Cairo eleven years ago. Rami had been nine years old and obsessed with weather. She found it hard to imagine him now, as a young man in his second year of university. Tuition was free for Egyptian citizens, but textbooks and living expenses weren't, so Layla sent him money when she could. She didn't want him to be the poorest kid in class anymore, to be shackled to his childhood in Manshiyat Naser. She knew she was miles from the slums of Garbage City, but she imagined she could smell the relentless stench. Her mother and her sister Sanaa still lived there. She pressed her palm against the window, wondering what it might be like to see them, or Rami, again. Tears stung her eyes as she remembered Farwadi's words—"a curse on my family."

She leaned forward and told the driver, "I don't want to go home yet. Take me to el-Hegaz Street." It was the main drag of a trendy neighborhood, full of bars and restaurants that would be open late.

He nodded and changed direction. But they'd only gone a few blocks when the car slowed to a stop. "What is it?" she asked.

"Police checkpoint."

Layla's heart automatically skipped a beat. "Did something happen?" Her mind jumped to the possibility of a terror attack.

"Not that I know of." He sounded more irritated than alarmed. "There were some student protests in support of Fareed Monsour last week and the government wants to make sure there aren't any more." She'd been reading about Monsour. He was the leader of the Open Society party, which pledged to expose human rights abuses by the current government and put an end to censorship. With parliamentary elections less than a year away, the party was rapidly gaining support.

They reached the checkpoint. She dug out her passport and gave it to the officer. She couldn't tell if his uniform was police or military. The difference between them seemed to be narrowing these days. No wonder Monsour's message was resonating. The driver handed over his passport as well. Layla resisted the urge to smile and make nice with the man who currently controlled her fate. Child of privilege Layla Nawar wouldn't bother. She put on a vaguely bored expression as the officer briefly examined both passports, then tossed them back to their owners and waved the car on.

Layla asked the driver to stop in front of a bar on el-Hegaz Street. "I don't need you to wait for me. I'll get a taxi home."

"Are you sure? A woman alone at night . . ."

She leaned forward and handed the man a substantial tip. "I'm sure."

The bar was packed with customers. Layla pushed her way through them to the ladies' room at the back and ducked into a stall. She opened her huge purse and pulled out a gray, long-sleeved cardigan, which she put on over her party dress. Then she took out a black hijab and put that on as well. Layla emerged and checked herself in the mirror. She was satisfied that anyone who might have seen her going into the club wouldn't recognize the same woman coming out. As an added precaution, she slipped out the back door. She followed the alley behind the building to the nearest street and hailed a cab. "Sixty-five elFalaki, please."

It was past one a.m. when Layla let herself into the modest, two-bedroom apartment. The lights were on and Special Agent Ellen Pierce was still awake, waiting for her.

The apartment was, officially, an FBI safe house. Pierce was living there while using it as a makeshift field office for the undercover op. "The party went well," Layla told her. "Farwadi did exactly what we needed him to do."

Pierce smiled. "So who did you meet?"

Layla approached a large whiteboard hanging on the wall of the living room. It was covered with pictures of the collectors and dealers they were investigating, linked with different colors of thread, mapping out the complex web of personal and professional relationships between them. "I talked to Miriam Goldman briefly," she said, using a dry-erase marker to put a check mark beside the woman's picture. "And Noor Ghaffar. Also briefly." Another check. She knew this didn't sound very impressive, so she added, "I also connected with their children. Marcus and Adrian Goldman." She wrote the names next to their mother's picture. "Jehan Ghaffar. I'm invited to half a dozen house parties in the next month." She'd wait to bring up the issue of airfare. "The best part is, the kids probably have no idea what their parents are hiding. They'll hardly notice if I disappear in the middle of a party to go search the house."

"Hell, they'll probably show you where Mom hides all the good stuff if you ask." Pierce grinned and surveyed the board again. She was whippet-thin and intense, with a kind of nervous energy radiating off her.

"You want a drink?" Pierce asked, tearing her gaze from the board.

"Sure."

"I think I've got wine. Let's see." She padded to the kitchen, calling back to Layla, "How's it feel?"

"How's what feel?"

"Being undercover."

Layla considered this. "It's . . . weird. And wild. Kinda surreal. It feels almost like make-believe, or playacting. I like it."

Pierce returned and handed her a glass of red wine. She tapped her own glass against Layla's. Layla gratefully sipped the wine. She'd been so immersed undercover that she had forgotten how anxious she felt. Anxiety had become part of her, along with the constant fear of being caught out. But the Layla reflected back at her in the glass looked confident.

She saw that Pierce was studying her, too. "Be careful, Layla."

"I'm careful. I know the procedures."

"I'm not talking about procedures. I'm talking about the slippery slope going undercover can put you on."

"Burnout?"

"No, not burnout, exactly. It's more like . . . inside out." Pierce took a long, thirsty pull on her glass and stepped away from the window. "You get so tuned into your cover, the 'playacting,' and the next thing you know you're not playing anymore. You're in it and it is you."

"I don't think that will happen here. I can hardly even identify with these people. They travel. They shop. They go to parties. Their lives are totally free and pointless." Layla turned. Pierce was seated on the chair next to the evidence board, cradling her glass in her hands and looking at the floor between her feet.

"You think it's different in any other situation? Narcotics? Racketeering? Organized crime? Agents walk in thinking they're gonna be surrounded by bad guys. That they'll always be able to tell the difference. But when you're under you're under. You start to realize you're surrounded by *people*, flesh and blood. Things can get fuzzy. You can lose perspective."

"Did that happen to you?"

Pierce leaned back and stared at the ceiling. She was so thin, all sharp angles and lines. "Maybe. I guess. Yeah. If losing perspective means losing everything. Sometimes you go hunting for something and you lose sight of what you're really looking for."

FOUR WEEKS AGO

Layla sat in the passenger seat as Pierce inched the black Ford Taurus through the dense traffic of West 24th Street on their way from the raid at the harbor to Nesim Farwadi's Manhattan gallery. "Do you get back to Cairo very often?" Pierce asked.

Layla forced a rueful smile. "Not as often as I'd like." Translation: not once since she'd walked out of her family's tiny apartment half a lifetime ago, vowing never to set foot in Cairo again.

But the older woman could see the struggle behind her facade. "I've spent a lot of time in Egypt," she said. "Worked out of the American Embassy in Cairo for almost a year. I like it. But it couldn't have been an easy place for a girl, especially a smart girl, to grow up."

This understanding took Layla by surprise. She answered honestly. "No. It wasn't. Most of the girls in my class dropped out before we graduated to get married."

Pierce regarded her with increasing respect. "And you went off to college in the States. Let me guess . . . Princeton? Harvard?"

"Georgetown."

"Your family must be really proud," said the senior agent.

Layla simply nodded. She didn't want to get into the ugly truth about the endless screaming fights she'd had with her parents. Her father had considered school a waste of time for a girl and started pressuring her to drop out when she was fifteen. "Don't be so selfish," he told her at least once a week, as she returned from school. "You have a duty to your family."

But Layla had dreamed of going to college. Preferably somewhere far away. She had worked on her applications in the school's meager library and scraped together the money for postage. The day she'd received her acceptance letter from Georgetown, along with notification of her full scholarship in linguistics, had been the proudest of her life. It had also been the day she'd walked away from the only home she'd ever known, determined never to return.

Layla broke the silence by getting back to the matter at hand. "So how did Farwadi end up on your radar?"

"I was investigating some questionable acquisitions at the Met. He was never a suspect, but he knew the major players in the art world. All of the high-end dealers and collectors go to the same fundraisers and big gallery openings." She waved a hand to indicate the trendy art galleries on both sides of the street. From the outside, they just looked like office buildings, with no hint of the pricey paintings and sculptures inside. At least, that's what Layla assumed was in there. She'd never actually set foot in this part of Chelsea, much less gone inside the galleries. They'd probably charge her a fee just to breathe the rarified air.

Pierce honked at a Jaguar trying to cut in front of her. "You wouldn't believe these people," she went on. "Penthouses in Manhattan, villas in Florence, private jets . . . It's like one big, international country club, with the super-rich buying and selling million-dollar pieces over a round of golf, or sailboat regatta, or whatever."

"Not really my scene," said Layla. She was currently sharing a small apartment in Long Island City, an hour's train ride from the FBI field office, with two annoying roommates. And that was a step up from the rat hole she'd lived in when she first moved to New York six years ago.

Pierce went on, "The problem is that most of their business is perfectly legit, which makes it tough to spot the illegal sales. I need someone with inside knowledge, like Farwadi, to help me figure out how the underground antiquities market works and who's involved."

Layla nodded. "And now that you have some leverage . . ."

"He'll be much more inclined to cooperate." Pierce pulled the car into a parking spot in front of the Farwadi Gallery and put an FBI placard on the dashboard to forestall getting towed. "Of course, if we threaten him with charges right away, he'll clam up and call his lawyer. We need to ease into it, make him think he can talk his way out of trouble."

"Outsmart the silly police."

"Exactly."

They left their FBI windbreakers in the car and went into the gallery. It was, Layla had to admit, impressive—an open, two-story space with white walls that curved seamlessly around the room, illuminated by an enormous, frosted glass globe that hung from the ceiling by a single chain. Half a dozen people were perusing the work of contemporary Middle Eastern artists, from bronze sculptures to brightly colored abstract paintings.

"This is all the legal merchandise," said Pierce as she peered at a distorted portrait in orange and magenta. "The illegal stuff changes hands in private."

They spotted Farwadi talking to an older Asian couple in front of a large desert landscape. He glanced over at the two women as they entered, in their off-the-rack clothes and utilitarian shoes, and swiftly dismissed them as unlikely customers. He continued his sales pitch as Pierce approached. "The desolate beauty of this landscape conveys both the grief and endurance of the people in the artist's homeland . . ."

His pompous tone reminded Layla of a teacher she'd had in secondary school. When he paused to draw breath, Pierce asked, "Mr. Farwadi, can we speak with you?"

Without the slightest acknowledgement, he turned away from her, leading the older couple toward a painting of white birds in flight against a red sky. "This piece was featured in a show at the prestigious Rampa Gallery in Istanbul."

Layla saw the other woman's jaw tighten. Pierce pulled out her badge and showed it subtly. "FBI, Mr. Farwadi. We need to ask you some questions."

Layla saw a flash of panic cross Farwadi's face before it flushed a deep red. He nodded, struggling to maintain his composure. "Please join me in my office . . ."

He started toward a door in the back, gesturing for them to follow. Pierce didn't budge. "That's all right. This shouldn't take too long," she told him, her voice echoing through the open space. Layla stifled a smile.

Farwadi straightened to his full height but still had to look up at the taller woman. "What can I do for you, Agent . . . ?"

She lowered her volume a notch. "Pierce," she told him, then nodded to Layla, in flanking position to his left. "This is Agent el-Deeb. We're investigating a shipment of art and antiques that arrived in New York Harbor this morning, on its way to your gallery."

Layla saw him tense up. He knew exactly what was in that shipment. She smiled sweetly and gave the man an out. "We think that someone at the port in Mozambique slipped some illegal goods into the cargo container with your merchandise."

He tried to cover his relief at her dumb explanation with a frown of concern. "That's terrible. What kind of goods? Drugs?"

"Stolen antiquities," said Pierce. "Mixed right in with yours."

"We could really use your help to sort everything out," Layla added. She lowered her gaze and forced herself to sound deferential. "That is, if you can spare the time."

He puffed up in response. "Certainly. Let me just tell my staff."

As he went to the back office, the women exchanged a quick smile. The good cop/bad cop routine couldn't have gone better if they'd scripted it. Farwadi returned and they escorted him out to the car. Pierce opened the door for their suspect. Sounding bored, she began to recite, "You have the right to remain silent . . ."

He reacted with alarm, his eyes darting to Layla for help. She simpered and reassured him, "It doesn't mean you're under arrest.

Agent Pierce is just following procedure." Agent Pierce was, in fact, covering their asses, making sure that anything Farwadi might say in the car would eventually be admissible in court. If the case even went to court. Layla had seen enough good testimony get thrown out for stupid reasons to appreciate the senior agent's caution.

Back at 26 Federal Plaza, the agents flashed their credentials at the main desk. Farwadi emptied his pockets into a plastic bin and stepped through the metal detector. When he tried to retrieve his belongings, Pierce held them back. "We'll just keep those for you up front," she said. Then she added with a small laugh, "Don't worry, nobody's going to search your phone."

Only because she doesn't have a warrant, thought Layla. *At least, not yet.*

The gallery owner seemed to grow more nervous as they escorted him into the main office, across the large FBI emblem inlaid in the tile floor, past rows of desks where agents and administrative staff were working.

Pierce opened the door to the more comfortable of two interrogation rooms. The chairs were padded, if a bit threadbare, and not bolted to the floor. She pulled one over to the rectangular table. "Have a seat. We'll get the pictures of those antiquities," said Pierce.

She and Layla left Farwadi glancing nervously at the mirrored section of the wall, which anyone who'd ever seen a cop show would know must be one-way glass.

Outside the door they nearly collided with Tom Monaghan.

"Ellen!" he said jovially. "Thanks for bringing him in."

She stared at him. "What?"

The big agent gestured toward the interrogation room. "Farwadi. The Muharib's money man."

"He's not . . . What the hell are you talking about?"

"Farwadi's name is on the manifest for that shipping container. I checked." Monaghan grinned. He was enjoying himself. "It's like you said. He can get a lot of money for those little green vases. And that means a lot of Kalashnikovs for the Muharib." He shot a look at Layla.

Pierce collected herself and spoke calmly. "You know there's more to it than that. The money passes through a lot of different hands . . ."

He was shaking his head. "Tell you what. I'll let Farwadi explain it to me." He started to move around her toward the interrogation room door, but she stayed in his way.

"Forget it. This is my interview, and my case."

They stood there for a moment, face-to-face. Pierce was nearly his height, but Monaghan had more bulk. He leaned in close. "You made 'your' case part of a joint operation. Specifically, a Joint Terrorism Task Force operation. Which puts you on my turf, sweetheart. I'll handle it from here."

She opened her mouth to object, then closed it again. As the ASAC of Counterterrorism, he outranked her in the JTTF hierarchy. Pierce stepped aside. Monaghan smiled. He gestured toward the door of the observation room. "You're welcome to watch me interrogate the suspect if you like." Then he went into the interrogation room and closed the door.

Layla watched Pierce's jaw work as she fought to hold back her frustration. Without a word, the senior agent stepped into the observation room. Layla followed. It was a long, narrow space that might have been a supply closet at some point, barely large enough for two people to sit at a low table and look into the interview room through the glass. Monaghan was flipping through a case file. Through a speaker on the wall, they heard him say, "Mr. Farwadi, I'm Special Agent Monaghan."

"What happened to . . . ?"

"The lovely Agent Pierce? Called away on another case. You'll be dealing with me from now on." He paged through the file. "Tell me about the Muharib."

Farwadi stared at him. "What?" he managed.

"You know, the people you were going to sell those pretty little trinkets for."

"That's not true."

The big agent leaned closer. "Work with me here, Nesim. This is your one and only chance to get ahead of this mess."

Pierce approached the one-way glass, talking to Monaghan even though she knew he couldn't hear. "That's good. Now start with the easy stuff."

"So . . . back to the Muharib," he said, pleasantly enough.

"Shit," she muttered under her breath.

Sweat appeared on Farwadi's forehead. "I don't know anything about the Muharib . . ."

"We know they're planning something in the US."

"I swear to you, I don't . . ."

"Nesim." Monaghan stood, looming over the smaller man. "We're not going to get along if you lie to me."

Farwadi faced him for a long moment, then looked away. "I don't think I should say anything else without consulting my attorney."

The agent backed off. "Okay. If that's the way you want to play this . . ." He went out into the main office.

Pierce snapped off the loudspeaker in frustration. "Farwadi doesn't know anything about the Muharib."

"How can you be so sure?"

"I know this guy. I've been studying him for a year and a half." She began to pace the cramped room. "And I know how the illegal antiquities market works. There's a long chain of suppliers and middlemen between the poor guy who digs up the treasure and the rich asshole who ends up putting it on his mantelpiece. Everyone in the chain knows the links on either side of them, but not beyond that." Pierce scanned the room for visual aids. She found a pen on the floor and pulled a folded FBI memo from her back pocket.

She smoothed out the paper on the narrow table, blank side up. "On one end, you have a group like the Muharib," she began, and drew an elongated circle to represent the first link. "They're sitting in a sandbox full of ancient relics that they want to turn into cash. So they hire some local guys to dig up an illegal site or go ransack a museum." She drew a second link beside the first, overlapping at one end.

Through the glass, Layla saw Monaghan bring in a cell phone and toss it at Farwadi. She focused her attention back on Pierce. "The hired guys get their hands on something valuable . . . maybe a ritual amphora from the Temple of Horus. They take it to a local dealer they trust." She sketched a third circle, representing the dealer. "He buys it from them, no questions asked, for maybe a couple hundred bucks. Doesn't sound like much, I know, but if they sell enough pieces, it adds up. The money goes through them, back to the Muharib." She drew a line through the second link, back to the first. "So, this dealer doesn't know who he's really bankrolling."

"Although he must have a pretty good idea," said Layla.

"Of course he does. But he doesn't say that when he passes along the amphora to someone else to smuggle out of the country." Pierce put a fourth circle beside the third, their ends overlapping. "The smuggler sells it to another dealer, who sells it to another one, then to another . . ." she said, running a squiggly line all over the page. "Everybody jacks up the price enough to make a profit, and the original provenance of the amphora gets lost along the way." She ended the squiggle in a fifth circle, connected to the fourth. "It finally ends up getting stashed in a shipping container full of otherwise legitimate cargo, on its way to a ritzy art gallery. The gallery owner"—she nodded toward the interrogation room—"makes up whatever story he likes about the fascinating history of the item, and sells it for half a million dollars to some clueless rich guy who puts it on display in the foyer of his penthouse and shows it off to his friends." Her pen dug into the paper as she outlined the last circle, then jabbed it again for emphasis.

They both looked at Farwadi through the one-way glass. He was talking on the phone, presumably to his lawyer, his face damp with sweat. Layla glanced at Pierce, reluctant to make what seemed like an obvious suggestion. "I know you've been trying to put this guy in jail for a while . . ."

"But I should cut a deal with him for information," she finished, with a resigned nod. "Yeah. I know."

Layla followed her out of the observation room and into the main office, where Monaghan was pacing like a hungry lion by the interrogation room door. Pierce approached him. "So much for the intimidation approach."

He turned on her, as if he might actually sink his teeth into her throat. "I suppose you want to offer him a deal."

"Unless you want to try waterboarding him for a while," she said. Layla struggled to keep a straight face. "But he still won't be able to introduce you to the Muharib."

"I know that!" he snapped. "I'm trying to choke off their cash flow."

"So am I!" They glared in furious agreement.

In the tense silence, Layla spoke up, her voice perfectly calm. "Then use him as an informant and destroy the whole fucking network from the top down."

The senior agents stared at her. Then Pierce turned to Monaghan. "Works for me."

"If you want to run him out of this office, you'll do it under my supervision," he informed her.

Pierce hesitated. "Farwadi does have contacts in New York," she said carefully. "But he knows a lot more people . . . important people . . . in Cairo."

"Cairo," he repeated. "No way. There's too much corruption in the Intelligence Directorate. If you try to run a covert op with them, your guy is as good as dead."

"I know," said Pierce. "So maybe we don't have to tell the Intelligence Directorate."

Now he laughed. "One problem with that, sweetheart. It's completely fucking illegal for the FBI to operate independently on foreign soil."

"That hasn't stopped you before." Layla was surprised by her own words. They were true, but flinging them at the ASAC of Counterterrorism was a different matter. Monaghan appeared equally stunned. But that could soon give way to anger. "I translate incoming messages from agents all over the world. Including the covert strike team in Syria. And the intelligence operative in North Korea . . ."

"That's enough," he said, but his voice remained calm.

Pierce pressed her advantage. "We'll keep it simple. Six months, tops."

"Simple?" The big agent barked out a humorless laugh. "Yeah, they all start out like that."

THE ARTS COUNCIL FUNDRAISER was being held in the Coriander Gallery, a large industrial warehouse-turned-studio space. Colored lights played over cement walls and tastefully exposed pipes as speakers thumped out a techno beat. As Layla walked in, she could almost imagine she was in a trendy SoHo club. Not that she'd ever been much of a club rat. At least, not as the studious, responsible Layla el-Deeb. But tonight, she was Layla Nawar, strutting across the room in a low-cut red dress with spike heels to match, drawing admiring stares from men and women alike. She found a group of the party kids, including Jehan, Chloe, and Adrian Goldman, hanging out by a photo display showing the stages of the Coriander's transformation.

When Jehan saw her, she let out a low whistle. "Wow." She took Layla's hand and twirled her around.

"You're looking pretty hot yourself," said Layla. Her new friend was dressed in slim black pants that emphasized her long legs and a decidedly un-conservative black halter top. No hijab. She wore a striking jade pendant shaped like a scarab. "That's gorgeous. Is it new?"

"My mom gave it to me for my birthday." Jehan shrugged, smiling. "I have to admit, the woman knows her bling."

Across the room, Layla saw someone who looked familiar, although she couldn't immediately place him. He was fiftyish, with blue eyes and thick, gray hair, dressed in jeans, a casual tan blazer, and very expensive brown loafers. He wasn't exactly handsome but radiated enough confidence to make up for it. She realized suddenly where she'd seen the man's picture: on Pierce's suspect board. His name was Bennett Rothkopf. And he was connected to a lot of other pictures on that board.

Jehan saw who she was looking at. "If you're into collecting, you should meet Bennett Rothkopf. He has a terrific gallery downtown."

He was talking animatedly with a few other well-dressed society types. But the man standing beside him was different. He wasn't part of the conversation. He had dark hair, broad shoulders, and muscles that strained the tight sleeves of his black sport coat. "Who's that next to him?"

Jehan peered closer. "Don't know. Someone he works with, I think?" She turned back to Layla. "And you have to meet his son James. He works in the gallery, too, restoring art. Kinda serious. You'd like him."

"What's that supposed to mean?" Layla asked, wondering if she'd been letting too much of all-business Agent el-Deeb show. She needed to focus on being more flighty.

She had a good role model in Jehan, who had ignored her question and was now standing on tiptoes, scanning the room from a slightly higher vantage point. "I don't see him," she said. Layla followed her gaze and saw a young, serious-looking Egyptian man heading toward them. Jehan clearly spotted him, too.

"Oh, shit, it's Youssef," she said with a roll of her eyes. "He's a 'nice, respectable boy' who works for my dad. My folks are already planning the wedding." She grabbed Layla's hand and pulled her in the opposite direction. "Come on."

"Where are we going?"

"To meet Bennett," said Jehan, as if this were beyond obvious.

As they approached Rothkopf, the man next to him edged forward, as if to protect him from the two incoming girls. He had olive skin and dark brown eyes, but it was hard to even guess at his ethnicity. Or his age, for that matter. Layla thought she'd figured out his job, though: bodyguard. And not one you wanted to mess with. Rothkopf spotted them and smiled.

"Jehan! Lovely to see you." He kissed her on both cheeks, as the other man stepped back.

"This is my friend Layla."

"Pleased to meet you. Bennett Rothkopf." He extended his hand. Up close, she could see that his blue eyes were flecked with green. She also noticed the deep worry lines between his eyebrows.

"Have you been to the Coriander before, Layla?" he asked her.

"No, I haven't."

"It's a communal space for artists, where they can work on their own projects and be inspired by others." He gestured to the paintings and sculptures in progress with obvious pride. "Art is a powerful form of communication. Sometimes more powerful than words." He spoke with great conviction, and Layla honestly couldn't tell if he was sincere or if this was a performance intended to persuade them to donate more money. Pierce's file on Rothkopf had described him as a self-made man who convinced early investors to believe in him while he was still struggling to pay the rent. Layla could see why. He was a good salesman. Which would also make him a good liar.

They began to hear raised voices from a hallway leading toward the gallery offices—a woman with a distinctly Australian accent shouted, "No! Leave me alone!"

Rothkopf looked up, concerned. "I hope that's nothing serious."

"It sounds like our friend Chloe," Jehan told him. "Don't worry. We've got this." She headed off toward the hallway, nodding for Layla to join her.

From a professional standpoint, she knew she should stay and keep talking to the person who was on her suspect wall. But socialite Layla Nawar would go with her friend.

"It was really nice to meet you," she said to Bennett. "I'd love to see your gallery sometime."

"Come by whenever you like" he said, turning the warmth of his smile up several degrees. "It would be my honor to show you around."

Layla couldn't help smiling back before she turned and hurried after Jehan. They left the main gallery space and found themselves in a long concrete corridor surrounded by small offices and studios. "Fuck you!" came Chloe's strangled cry from a room at the other end of the hallway, followed by a chorus of voices. Layla stopped short as she watched Jehan rush toward the commotion as if she were running into a burning building to rescue a child. It was ridiculous. These people led such charmed lives that a little relationship drama seemed like the end of the world. She knew she should follow Jehan and join the others, but the thought was exhausting.

She turned away from the sound of Jehan's voice joining the fray and was startled to find that she wasn't alone. A handsome guy with tousled brown hair, broad shoulders, and deep blue eyes was leaning against the concrete wall, smiling at her. There was something familiar about him, though she couldn't put her finger on what it was.

"You're missing all the action," he said, and she picked up an American accent.

"So are you," Layla pointed out with a small shrug. "I guess I'm not used to people putting their private lives on display."

He laughed and her stomach did a tiny involuntary flip. "Clearly you're new to Cairo, or at least to this crowd." He studied her for a moment. "I'm guessing you're the Layla Nawar I've been hearing about?" He extended his hand. "James."

"Oh!" Layla took his hand, registering its warmth and softness. Worried she was holding it too long or too firmly, she let his hand drop and smoothed the front of her dress. "James Rothkopf? I just met the other Rothkopf. Your dad."

"I'm the more interesting one." He grinned.

"I'm sure you are," Layla said with a laugh. Now she saw the Rothkopf resemblance. The dimple, the intense eyes, the warmth of the smile.

James peered beyond her down the hall, glanced behind him, and then said, "Hey, do you want to see something amazing?"

"Definitely."

He gave her a conspiratorial look, almost mischievous. "Follow me."

He took her hand and led her, quickly, down the labyrinthine hallway toward the gallery but turned off down a shorter hallway of small studios. Butterflies, faint ones, were stirring to life in her stomach. It was a sensation she hadn't felt in a long time.

James paused at a closed door. Glancing around again, he turned the handle and ushered her inside. He quietly shut the door behind them.

The room was dark, and she felt rather than saw him reach past her to switch on a small lamp. Layla blinked and took in her surroundings. "Are we supposed to be in here?" she asked.

"No," said James. "This is all under wraps for another week."

Layla's heart pulsed fast, keeping time with the distant throb of the music from the party. Along the back of the room were tables filled with pottery that was scarred with gold—as if the pieces had been smashed and glued back together with glittering adhesive. Hanging on one wall was a rack of fabrics, rent into shreds and then re-stitched with gold thread. She walked the perimeter of the room, taking everything in; she could feel James's eyes on her, appraising her.

"What is all this?" she asked.

"You're having a sneak peek at the upcoming Coriander Gallery exhibit," said James.

"Yours?"

"Oh, God no." He laughed. "It's a collective of international artists inspired by the Japanese kintsukuroi technique."

"Kintsukuroi?" She searched for the closest English translation and asked, "Golden . . . repair?"

"Yes! You've heard of it?"

"Vaguely."

James crossed the small room in a few strides and joined her in front of the pottery. "It's this really cool process where cracks are repaired with gold." He reached out to touch a vase, softly, letting his fingers trace a golden line on a crack around its neck, down its curved body to the base. Layla shivered, watching his fingers, and suddenly wished she had a wrap so she could disguise the goose bumps that had risen on her arms.

"The artists in this exhibit were inspired by this centuries-old repair technique," James went on. "They're so talented," he added with a wistful expression. "Look at the precision of the gold inlay here. As a restorer, I know the hours that went into getting this perfect." He let his hand fall away from the vase.

Layla traced the line his fingers had just followed, all the while conscious of his proximity to her. She picked up an Isis statuette—a lightweight copy of a relic, she guessed—and inspected its golden patterns. "So you're a restorer at your dad's gallery?" she asked carefully. "Do you use this technique in any of your work?"

"Are you kidding?" He smirked. "I often think it would be a *relief* to do kintsukuroi. Everything I do has to look perfect. Museums and collectors of antiquities don't want any artistic liberties. They want as close to original condition as possible. But that's why I'm here in Cairo."

"What do you mean?" Layla pressed him.

"Learning from the best in the business, getting access to authentic materials, and improving my craft while helping out my dad," said James. "It's an incredible feeling to repair something ancient so seamlessly that it's completely invisible to the naked eye. Kind of makes me feel like I got away with something each time I pull it off." He smiled at her and she felt her cheeks warm.

He spoke about his work with an intensity that made her ache. She hadn't realized how much she missed talking about work like it mattered. It occurred to her that James Rothkopf was the only young person in the Cairo social scene who appeared to have gainful employment.

"So you work for perfection," said Layla, "but you appreciate flawed objects, like this." She handed him the Isis statuette.

"Not flawed. Historical," he corrected, tracing the gold lines with one finger. "The damage is part of the object, and the gold calls attention to it. When the scars are made visible, the object becomes even more beautiful and unique. With kintsukuroi, you're celebrating an object's history." Gesturing around the room, he said, "These are all things that could have been tossed in the trash, but they survived, and were made better. That's the philosophy, anyway. And I think this group of artists really gets it right." He set the Isis statuette back on the table. "Probably the general public won't totally appreciate all that. I guess I just wanted to make sure someone did." He smiled sheepishly and scratched his head, suddenly looking embarrassed. "Sorry for dragging you over here. Maybe this isn't your thing. I'm sure you didn't come to this party tonight for an art lecture."

"No! No, it's fine. I mean—I like it. A lot." She turned slowly and took in the contents of the room through fresh eyes. Through James's eyes. The collection of ceramics with their spider webs of gold dazzled in the light.

James turned to look at her again, and she felt a warmth spread through her, as if she, too, were suffused with gold. She wondered if he could see her damaged parts, the breaks in her story, just by looking at her. She laughed at the idea. How crazy was that?

The sly grin returned to James's face. "What?" he prompted.

"Nothing." She smiled to herself as he held the door open for her. The secret exhibit must have cast a weird spell over her. Time for a reality check. James was the son of Bennett Rothkopf. He worked in his dad's gallery. He knew the world of relics and collectors, and could be really helpful to her investigation. He was definitely someone worth getting to know—so long as she could keep those butterflies in check.

THE GLASS SLIPPER

• PATRICK LOHIER •

Chaos, thought Layla as she crossed the street and nearly got run over by a cab. The streets of nighttime Cairo were filled with cars, pedestrians, lights, and overwhelming chaos.

Layla followed a maze of side streets using the GPS on her iPhone. She was a little ashamed to be dependent on a machine to navigate the streets of the city she had been born in, but she was beginning to understand that that's what life undercover meant—she might always be a stranger, even in familiar places. Even to herself.

Pierce had given her the iPhone the day after Layla arrived in Cairo, along with a Motorola phone and a relic of a Nokia phone that looked like the missing link between flip phones and smartphones.

Use the iPhone for official business, she'd said. *The Motorola is for whatever you want to use it for, and this phone here . . .* She'd taken the Nokia out of her pocket and handed it to Layla. *You use only for contact with me. This is a burner. This is our lifeline. You got it?*

Got it.

That morning, Pierce had summoned her, by encrypted email, to meet at nine that night. Approaching the safe house required vigilance and discretion, but Layla also walked quickly. She looked forward to Pierce's company and some time in the cocoon of the safe house. It was the only place she felt she could relax her cover.

Layla glanced back, and seeing nothing suspicious, ducked down a narrow, well-lit side street lined with coffeehouses. They were filled, she soon noticed, with men—men perched in rickety chairs, men playing backgammon and dominoes, men smoking *shisha*s, men glancing up and staring. Staring at her. *Shit*, she thought. It was a mistake to have gone this way. She couldn't even blame the GPS. The disruptive wake she left behind her churned. Shaking heads and muttered disapproval. She glanced back and saw two young men in soccer jerseys rise from a table. They walked in her direction. Were they following her?

She'd managed to blow part of her cover by the simple act of walking down the street. It was fitting that they wore soccer jerseys. Both men were built like soccer players: slender, athletic, and, she suspected, fast. It was hard to tell how strong they were but she guessed that she could turn and punch them out or stun them with a couple well-placed kicks and vanish fast enough if she needed to. Just as she debated which of the two she might hit first, she passed three tourist policemen, noticeable in their white uniforms and black berets, standing at the entrance to a café. One glanced toward her as she passed and she thought about asking for assistance, then instantly thought better of it. She didn't want to be on the radar of any police force in Egypt.

A quick glance at her phone showed her that she didn't have far to go. She quickened her pace and the men quickened theirs. She turned the corner, onto a quieter commercial street lined by shuttered storefronts and brightly lit signs. What street was this? She considered taking a detour, to throw the two men off. She looked back at her phone and saw that she was going to be late. Her annoyance gave way to impatience.

THE GLASS SLIPPER

She came to an intersection and spotted a shop across the street. Beyond the propped open door, Layla spied an older woman behind the counter. She turned and darted across the street.

"*As-Salam-Alaikum,*" she said to the woman behind the counter.

"*Alaikum-As-Salam,*" nodded the woman, smiling. She looked to be in her late fifties or early sixties, with wisps of gray hair visible at the edges of her hijab. Hers was a friendly, soft, and welcoming face in a night crowded by strange men.

Layla slipped inside. The aisles were jam-packed with merchandise, but no one else was in the store. It reminded her of a Manhattan bodega. She walked fast to the back and lingered for only a moment, too anxious to turn and look at the entrance, her eyes darting this way and that until she spotted it, a narrow doorway without a door, stairs leading down into darkness. She didn't turn when she heard footfalls and a man murmur *As-Salam-Alaikum* at the front of the store and the storekeeper's friendly response. She lunged into the darkness. At the bottom of the stairs she turned on her phone's flashlight and looked around. Shelves lined with overstock goods and wares, boxes of laundry detergent, canned food, bags of rice, and boxes of cereal. She spotted what she was looking for: a big metal door. She darted through it and closed it quickly behind her. She headed back toward the lights of the street. Once she reached the sidewalk, she ran.

The two men were nowhere in sight, and she slowed to a light jog. She buzzed the intercom outside the safe house building and waited for Pierce to answer. She buzzed again and waited. Finally, she retrieved the key from her purse and let herself into the lobby. Upstairs, she listened at the door. Where might Pierce be at that hour? She had never thought about where Pierce might go for her own downtime. Hearing nothing, she used the second key and started to open the door when she heard footsteps in the hallway behind her. She turned, startled, as Pierce brushed past her into the apartment.

"You're late," she mumbled, stalking into the kitchen. Layla saw her throw a brown paper bag into an open kitchen cupboard and snap the cabinet shut.

What the hell? thought Layla as she shut the door behind her. "So are you," she said.

"Well, let's get started then," said Pierce. She headed for the two evidence boards, tidying things up for the night's briefing, straightening photos and securing pieces of tape with her thumb.

They'd made some progress, and had broadened and refined the nebulous cloud of Farwadi's social network a little. Layla felt excited and completely wiped out. Between the late nights partying with Jehan and the rest of the young socialites and the constant playing at being someone else, there were few opportunities to meet with Pierce to take stock and gauge the progress of the investigation.

Pierce turned to her.

"What else've you got?"

"I talked to Miriam Goldman briefly," Layla said, using a dry-erase marker to put a check mark beside the woman's picture. "And I'm in contact with Abello, Chen, and the Roys."

Pierce taped the photos of those targets up next to the others on the first board. A second board was a kind of parking lot of hypotheses, questions, and a few dead ends, all labeled as such.

"How 'bout these?" said Pierce, pointing to photos on the far left of the evidence board. "Ghaffar? Tanaka?"

Layla eyed the cluster of about ten photos.

"Noor Ghaffar was with Miriam Goldman at Farwadi's . . . I've met Tanaka's son, but connecting with the father might be a challenge."

"How old's the son? Is there any possible involvement?"

Layla frowned. Kiyoshi Tanaka was a rich Japanese real estate mogul. Hiro, his son, was a jet-setting deejay, passionate connoisseur of rap, and maybe one of the oddest people Layla had ever met. He could be anywhere in the world at that very moment: San Francisco, St. Petersburg, Delhi, Melbourne. He was on a constant search for new beats and new scenes. As she started to get to know these people, she found them at turns attractive and repulsive. At

Georgetown she'd met a lot of well-off people, but she'd never spent much time with that crowd. A kind of force field, most likely self-imposed, kept her out. Now she had to pretend to be one of them. She spoke a lot of the same languages they spoke, a fact that had endeared her to them, but she was slowly and precariously learning the most challenging language of all, the one that could betray her completely—the language of the very rich.

"I doubt it. Hiro . . . that's the son's name . . . he was in town last week because of the Ghaffar family and some other friends. He's in his late twenties. Parties very hard. Very eccentric. The father's hard to track down. But give me more time."

"Okay. And Ghaffar?"

"I've connected with the family through the daughter. She says her mother"—Layla pointed to the photo of the matronly looking Noor Ghaffar, a pillar of Cairo's social elite and a prominent player in the high art and antiquities circles—"collects a lot of art and they travel to auctions all over the world. I think it's promising. But it's fresh. I'm still working it."

"The father?"

Layla bit her lip. "Trying my best to keep a safe distance from him. But I did bump into him at Farwadi's party. Of course you know he's high-ranking in the GID."

Anytime the General Intelligence Directorate came up, it sucked the air out of the room. It took an act of willful and collective denial and a ton of operational audacity to work undercover on the home field of one of the Middle East's most sophisticated intelligence agencies. *But here we are . . .* thought Layla, with perverse pride.

Pierce turned and stared at the board, clutching a green marker. "Okay . . . Okay . . ." She was talking to herself. Layla looked at the board as well, but it didn't reveal anything. She wanted to give Pierce something, *anything* to show that she was making progress.

"I met Bennett Rothkopf and his son, James Rothkopf. I think I might have an in through the son. He's part of the crowd that runs with Jehan Ghaffar, that's Noor and Gamal Ghaffar's daughter. But he's also part of his dad's business. I'm going to keep on that to find out more about the Rothkopf Gallery."

"Sounds promising," said Pierce unconvincingly, and Layla sighed with disappointment. That was all she had.

"Well, I'll let you know how it goes," she said.

"Thanks." Pierce nodded but she didn't turn around.

Great, thought Layla as she rose from the sofa. She knew there was a lot of work ahead of them, but she wondered if Pierce couldn't be just a *little* more supportive, a *little* more encouraging. Maybe she'd expected too much from Pierce, thought Layla. Or maybe she wasn't making progress as fast as she should. "I'll just . . . ah . . . let myself out." Layla sidled toward the door.

"All right," said Pierce, still not turning her gaze from the evidence board.

Layla glanced back at Pierce and for a moment she felt like Watson leaving Sherlock Holmes to a solitary session of deductive reasoning. She wondered if that's what it took to be as successful as Pierce, complete and all-consuming concentration.

She shook her head as she let herself out of the apartment. *How did I end up here?* she thought as she closed the door behind her.

FARWADI'S LAWYER, DAVID WASSERMAN, was an imposing, dark-haired man in an expensive suit. His office wasn't the mahogany-and-brown-leather man cave that Layla would have expected. It was comfortable, with soft gray upholstery and an overstuffed couch under a large window with the obligatory panoramic view of New York. Farwadi sat on the couch, looking so calm and collected that Layla suspected he'd popped a Xanax.

"My client would like to cooperate," Wasserman announced, facing the agents across his pale wood desk. "But wearing a concealed microphone is out of the question."

Pierce rose from her chair. "We've been through this . . ."

"Wait," said Wasserman, holding up a well-manicured hand and a wrist bearing a massive silver watch that must have cost as much as two years' worth of Layla's salary. "He would be willing to work with you to establish your own cover identity as an art dealer or collector, and introduce you to the people he knows."

Pierce gestured for Layla to join her on the far side of the room and huddled close.

"Pretend we're really considering it," she said quietly. "I don't want to shut him down right away."

"We're not considering it?" asked Layla.

"Can't. I worked in the embassy, remember? Someone might recognize me."

"Send me," said Layla, surprising herself with her own words.

"What?"

The lawyer and his client were now staring at them as Layla's mind raced, trying to comprehend why she had just volunteered for this insane, not to mention illegal, mission. In Cairo, of all places.

"I can do this. I can run him. I can be an asset. Just . . ."

"Shhh." The senior agent held her forefinger up to her lips and glanced across the room at Wasserman and Farwadi, who were conferring in low voices. Pierce squinted at her. "Listen. I don't know if you know what you're asking. Have you ever even been undercover before?"

"No. But . . ." she started, then hesitated. "I've transcribed audio from wiretaps, including for undercover operations." She regretted it as soon as she said it. She knew she sounded desperate.

Pierce thought about that for a few seconds. She didn't look impressed. "You grew up in Cairo. You're even more likely to get recognized than I am."

"I haven't set foot in Cairo since I was eighteen. I spent my childhood in a slum called Manshiyat Naser." As Layla spoke, it dawned on her that she had never told anyone this. "The locals call it Garbage City. Nobody who lived outside that place would know me. And no one who lived inside is going to pop up unexpectedly at a gallery opening." She knew that the anger in her voice was fueled by embarrassment. If Pierce reacted with disgust or, worse, pity, Layla thought she very well might sink through the floor and disappear.

Pierce crossed her arms and nodded. "All right," she said simply.

Layla exhaled, a long, pent-up breath. Pierce turned back to Wasserman. "How about this: Your client will work with Agent el-Deeb to establish her cover and introduce her to his friends."

Farwadi rose from the couch and approached Layla. "That . . . might work," he said as he examined her like a piece of art he might want to buy. "You remind me of my youngest niece."

"That's perfect," she said. "You can introduce me as your long-lost cousin who wants to start collecting art."

He considered this, then nodded.

"Good," said Wasserman, turning back to Pierce. "I believe we have a deal."

As they continued to discuss the details, Layla heard their voices through a kind of fog. She felt exhilarated, terrified, and triumphant all at the same time. For the first time in months, Layla felt completely alive.

She took the E train to Long Island City, then trudged another half mile to her apartment building. Her commute was a pain in the ass, but this was as close as she could get to the city without choking on the rent. And that was with two roommates.

Brianna and Sophie were there when she got home, eating pizza in the living/dining room, along with three other young women she didn't recognize, and didn't expect to see again. Her roomies seemed to go through friends like Kleenex. Layla had never been one of them. She'd answered their ad on a rental website when she transferred from Pittsburgh to New York two years ago. They were only a year or two younger than Layla, but utterly alien to her, working at jobs they didn't care about and blowing every cent they earned on clothes and clubs. If Brianna and Sophie had long-term plans for their lives, she would be surprised.

As she walked past the group, Sophie called out, "Oh, before I forget . . . the landlord told us that some of the pipes have been leaking again, so we should keep an eye out for water damage. We didn't see any out here, but I know you don't like anybody going in *your room*," she said, and two of the other women giggled at her emphasis on the words. "So we haven't looked in there."

"Thanks," Layla muttered, as she went into her bedroom. She noticed a distinctly musty smell that she attributed to a damp patch on the ceiling over her bed, which she soon discovered had dripped onto her pale blue duvet. She scooted the bed away from the leak as far as she could. In a ten foot by seven foot room, that wasn't very far. She emptied a plastic storage bin full of old coursework from her Bureau training and set it under the leak. She knew that most people would feel cramped in such a tiny bedroom, but after growing up in a three-room apartment with a family of five, having any amount of space to herself felt like a luxury. She put on pajamas, brushed her teeth, lay in bed, and listened to the water *drip-drip-drip* from the ceiling, thinking that in Cairo, on this extraordinary investigation, she might finally escape from a life she no longer wanted.

AS THE NEXT FEW weeks passed, Layla tried not to lose her mind, continuing with her mundane translation tasks as if her whole life wasn't about to change. Pierce left for Cairo early on. The day she'd flown out of New York she'd written simply "Adios, see you soon" in a text that Layla received while sitting in a mandatory three-hour briefing on changes to the Bureau's health benefits plan. Pierce had returned to her former job as legal attaché at the American Embassy in Cairo. The plan, as she'd explained before she left, was for her to take advantage of her position to establish operations in Cairo. She would set Layla up with a luxury condo and designer wardrobe suitable for a wealthy heiress. She'd also secure a safe house in a modest neighborhood near the embassy. As her departure approached, Layla felt a rising anxiety with each morning's arrival. In the end, though, she'd found it disturbingly easy to walk away from her life in New York. It had felt like it was time to go. What did she have to lose? She'd been on autopilot for nearly a year in the desk gig. She was tired of case files piled neck-high on her desk, waiting for the elusive approval of some

Associate Deputy Director who likely couldn't give a damn who signed them.

She dismantled her life in New York efficiently, quietly, discreetly. At work she filed away the mountain of paperwork, shredded documents, tied up loose ends. She spent late nights studying the materials Pierce had given her. Through Craigslist she sold the nice bicycle she had barely ever had time to ride.

She had her mail routed to the field office, dumped bags of her cast-off clothes at the Salvation Army, cleared what few dishes she had from the kitchen she shared with her roommates, whittled away at her life with the diligence and discipline of a performance artist committing an act of stoic self-eradication. The Layla she had been would be a cypher and a mystery to anyone who asked.

THE ROTHKOPF GALLERY WAS on the edge of Midan Tahrir, Cairo's bustling downtown district. Layla stopped at the curb and looked left and right. Opposite the building, a street vendor was cooking up something delicious. The scent of *ful* and *taameya*—two of her favorite foods growing up—made her mouth water.

She was intent on connecting with the Rothkopfs, on finding out as much as she could about their gallery and its operations. She planned to stop by the gallery and charm her way in. If Bennett was there she could find out more about him and it would be a win. If his cute son was there, it would be win-win.

She fished in her purse for some bills and headed toward the vendor. Bringing James and his father lunch from a street vendor might seem out of character for an heiress who had supposedly lived most of her life outside of Cairo. Then again, her partying with the rich had shown her that they had all kinds of quirks and tastes. So what if she could afford daily lunch at the Nile Ritz-Carlton but had a thing for street-vendor food?

Take-out bags of fava beans and falafel in hand, Layla dodged a moped that ripped down the street. The door to the gallery building led into a foyer, and a sign by a staircase and elevator read *Rothkopf*

Gallery of Ancient Art: Sales, Restoration, and Appraisals. The gallery occupied the second floor, above a dental practice. This was so different from the elegant facades she'd seen in the car with Pierce weeks ago as they drove through Manhattan. This gallery wasn't even open full time. The hours listed were only slightly more generous than those of its dentist neighbor: three days a week from ten a.m. to three p.m., or by appointment. She walked up the narrow staircase to the Rothkopf Gallery on the second floor. The sounds of Cairo—the bleating horns, motorcycles, and the muezzins' noon call to prayer—all of it slowly faded away, magnifying the clop of her sandal heels on the gleaming hardwood floors.

The main gallery space, a large room, was surprisingly dim, illuminated only by the sunlight coming in through a narrow window. "Hello?" Layla called out softly. Nobody responded. Maybe the sign on the door was wrong and they weren't open after all. She ventured farther into the room, taking in a wall of wooden funerary masks. Their dead eyes followed her. Layla shuddered.

She rotated slowly, taking in the gallery space, registering a door that led down a hallway to other rooms—the Celtic, Judaic, and contemporary galleries. Like the nearby Coriander Gallery, this modern space was probably once an ordinary office that had been repurposed. Its walls were gleaming white, just like any high-end gallery, and adorned with textiles, art, and limestone reliefs. Glass cases filled with relics formed a square in the middle of the room, and an old-fashioned wooden desk and chair occupied one corner. None of the cases were lit. She looked up and noted the location of several security cameras near the recessed lighting and in the corners of the gallery.

Someone stepped out of the hallway, seemingly out of the shadows, startling her. A tall, dark-skinned man with high, angled cheekbones glared down his nose at her. He wore black slacks, a black jacket, and a black baseball cap with the brim pulled down low. Her eyes flicked downward, out of habit. In his right pants pocket, she registered the bulge of a holstered pistol.

"Food is not allowed in the gallery," the man said, pointing at her bags. As he stepped closer, into the sunlight that leaked through a window, she let out a long breath. He was a security guard, not a robber. She'd seen him before, at the Coriander Gallery gala, standing at Bennett Rothkopf's side.

"I was looking for James. I'm a friend of his. I brought him some lunch."

"James is not here."

"Oh. When will he be back?"

"Soon."

Clearly he was a man of few words. Layla guessed that if she ever needed to talk to this guy at some point, it was going to be exhausting. "Great. Mind if I wait for him?"

"Be comfortable." The man gestured toward a stool.

She perched on the edge, feeling far from comfortable. He was polite, but his gaze was unsettling, as expressionless as the funerary masks on the wall above him.

"I have seen you before," he said. Layla tried to place his accent. Not British. Not Australian. "At a party, I think. At the Coriander. Yes?"

South African. That wasn't an accent she heard so often in Egypt. She wondered how he had come to be working with Bennett, in Cairo. But she had no time to answer his question or fire off any of her own. Rapid footsteps approached from down the hall, and then her person of interest, Bennett Rothkopf, appeared.

Though he looked a little more tired than when she'd met him before, he was dressed just as sharply, today sporting cream-colored linen pants and a blue short-sleeved button-up shirt. His steel-gray hair was slicked back with just enough product to keep it in place without looking too stiff. He seemed approachable, but in a carefully constructed way.

"Can I help you?" Bennett asked.

"Hi, Mr. Rothkopf. Layla Nawar," she reminded him. "We met at the fundraiser? A few days ago?"

"Yes! Layla! Of course! Good to see you!" Bennett hesitated a moment, as if unsure how to greet her. She extended her hand, American-style, and he shook it with enthusiasm. "Forgive my awkwardness," he said with a laugh. "It's just that I don't often shake hands with Egyptian women."

"It's no problem at all. I grew up mostly in San Francisco," Layla explained.

"Oh yes." His smile was warm. "James told me about you. He said you went to Brown and that you studied in Paris."

"Zurich," she corrected.

"Ah, that's right." He smiled, displaying white, even teeth. Expensive teeth.

Was that a test? she wondered. Maybe. She smiled back. Maybe not.

But the thought that James had mentioned her intrigued her. He was talking about her to his dad. Not that it mattered. This was work. She straightened her shoulders. "I was just in the area and thought I'd pop by to see the gallery." She held up the bag. "And to bring you guys some lunch."

"That smells delicious!" Bennett said. "Aren't you nice. We've been so busy today we might have forgotten to eat. Tell you what. I'll show you around the gallery while you wait for James. He had to run out to the FedEx office, but he should be back any moment."

Bennett gestured toward the security guard. "Have you met?"

"Not officially. We were just chatting."

Bennett clapped the other man's shoulder. "This is Mackalo Naidu. Mackey. He handles security for the gallery, and personal security for me when I'm on business in the region. Mackey's an old family friend."

She noticed the outline of the man's muscles beneath his shirt at the shoulders.

"Mackey, Layla is Nesim Farwadi's cousin," Bennett continued. "Newly arrived in Cairo and an aspiring collector, yes?"

"That's right," said Layla. "It's very nice to meet you, Mr. Naidu."

"A pleasure," said Mackey, though his smile was thin as they shook hands. "I have to go," he said, politely but decisively. "I must pick up some supplies."

He retreated down the hallway, leaving her alone with Bennett.

Bennett flipped some switches behind him, flooding the gallery space with light. The cases lit up, too. "We're conserving electricity," he explained. "It gets so hot in here, with the afternoon heat. The lights only make it warmer."

"It is warm," Layla agreed, glancing around and noting four oscillating fans in the gallery, none of which were turned on.

Bennett steered her from case to case, describing the different types of artifacts organized by era: Mesopotamian. Near Eastern. Greek. Roman. Etruscan. Byzantine. Coptic.

Coptic. That case called out to her. The flat images of saints painted on wood beckoned to her with their hands, their eyes, as if beseeching her to remember them. These were the saints who had given countless of her ancestors solace over centuries of persecution. She'd never felt religious, but her Coptic identity was strong. She lingered, letting her gaze rest on a shelf of them, but Bennett was walking on toward the rest of the Egyptian section, and she hurried after him.

"What a fantastic collection. It feels almost like a museum," Layla remarked. "I can hardly believe all these things are for sale!"

"Thank you. Our New York gallery is even bigger," Bennett said, smiling with uncensored pride. "We're not as well-established or extensive as your cousin's gallery, of course. As an Egyptian native, Nesim enjoys certain *advantages* in this business." He shrugged. "I'm just a guy from New York. But we hold our own. And while your cousin carries some contemporary art, we stick to the classic antiquities and attract a slightly different client base in that way."

"Who is your typical client?" asked Layla.

"Oh, we have a wide range," replied Bennett. "As you can see, our artifacts and prices vary. We have trinkets that sell for mere hundreds of dollars, often to tourists passing through Cairo. Then we have pieces of far greater value and rarity, for the more discerning collector. We work with individuals and with institutions, at any level. We also pursue special requests."

"So, if I wanted to find a specific item, you could get it for me?"

"Within reason, yes. I'm confident we can find almost anything. We have a vast network of connections, both here in Egypt and internationally." He looked at her closely. "Why do you ask? Are you . . . looking for something?"

"Maybe . . ." Layla stooped down to scrutinize a slate-blue ring with a *wedjat* eye.

Just at that moment, the gallery door swung open and James strode in. She watched him, wondering if her impression of him from the Arts Council fundraiser had been on target. His bright eyes, his athletic build, and the confidence of his gait as he walked across the room riveted her attention. She could investigate him all day—or night—long, she thought with a mischievous smile.

"Sorry I'm late." He said. He was distracted, juggling his motorcycle helmet while pulling the strap of his leather satchel over his head. "Those damned checkpoints. The embassy neighborhood was almost completely blocked off . . ." He stopped mid-sentence as his eyes landed on her.

She grinned. It was good to see him, not to mention to see how happy he was to see her.

"Layla dropped by," said Bennett, turning toward his son, "and was kind enough to bring us lunch."

"Wow. Thank you. That's so sweet of you. There's a kitchen just down the hall," said James. "I'll get some plates."

"I'll come with you."

She walked beside him. He was, she realized, one of those rare people whom she liked immediately. It didn't hurt that he was really good-looking. And, of course, he could be useful. As they walked down the hall, James hesitated. "Hey," he said, taking hold of her hand to bring her to a stop. "I was thinking about you."

"Oh?" Her fingers tingled where he held them.

"I wondered if you'd like to go dancing with me and some friends? We're headed out this Saturday. Some new place, right by the river." He seemed a little nervous and it was totally adorable. "Jehan will be there, I think. Hiro, too."

She smiled brightly at him. "I'd love to." She wanted to believe her excitement was purely due to the prospect of getting closer to three of the main families on her evidence board. But the idea of a night of fun in James's company had its own unprofessional appeal.

COULD A MAN SMELL *sweet*? Or was *fresh* a better description? Other words—like *delicious*—played in Layla's mind. The Arabic word *laziz* repeated over and over in her thoughts as she danced and indulged her desire to hold James.

They were at Infusion, a nightclub, with Jehan, a Jordanian girlfriend of hers named Huma, Huma's Canadian boyfriend Dylan, Hiro, Muhammad, the Goldman twins, and a few others.

Muhammad Pahlavi was the scion of an Egyptian family that owned and ran a multinational conglomerate. He was handsome, cool, and courtly, and he clearly adored Jehan, but it was hard to tell exactly how Jehan felt about him. It was hard to tell how Jehan felt about anything, for that matter. Jehan was clearly into men and women and was as indecisive and, to Layla's view, as flaky about her romantic relationships as she was about where she might travel next to soak up the sun. On the few occasions that Jehan had encroached on Layla's personal space—a lingering touch here, a gaze held too long there—Layla had used subtle body language to let her know she wasn't interested. But something else was going on between Jehan and Muhammad. When Layla watched them together, she thought she saw flashes of the familiarity and ease of real lovers.

To the initiated, Infusion was a local gay club that catered to gay and straight alike. It was one of the hottest clubs in the city and one of the hardest to get into. Exclusivity wasn't just a matter of keeping the right mix of hip in the club. Gay life in Cairo had once flourished, but over the past decade the city police had started a campaign of irregular, brutal raids aimed at clubs like Infusion. The idea of the police raiding the place made Layla nervous. The last thing she wanted was a conversation with Cairo police officers. But she'd have to risk it if she wanted a chance to get to know Hiro Tanaka and if she wanted to cultivate this thing with James, which could get her closer to Bennett and the Rothkopf Gallery operations.

It was the Goldman twins' birthday. Some of the group had flown into Cairo for the event. Some of them intended to drop in for just a few days before heading to St. Tropez to while away the spring weeks in the sun.

The music throbbed and Layla felt it in her veins. Almost as soon as she'd arrived, she and Jehan had done shots of whiskey with James, and now she was feeling it—the liquor, the music, and the movement of people all around her made her feel loose-limbed and free.

"You enjoying yourself?" said James.

Layla smiled and nodded. She felt relaxed for the first time in ages. Between the constant anxiety about getting found out and the exhausting charade of her fake persona, it felt good to let the music move her. She swayed against him.

Someone tapped her shoulder and she stifled a twinge of annoyance at having to turn her attention away from James. It was Jehan. She was dressed in a black blouse and a short, cream-colored skirt that showed off her very long and shapely legs. Layla approved, but she wondered how Jehan's very conservative father might feel.

"Can I have her?" Jehan asked James. "For just a minute?"

"So long as you bring her back," said James with a chivalrous smile.

Jehan looked worried as she pulled Layla to the less crowded edge of the dance floor.

"What is it?" said Layla.

"I wanted to ask you something. I was planning to go to St. Tropez. My birthday's coming up and I've been planning it for weeks. But my mom wants me to go to our place on Lake Geneva with her. It's gonna be full of old aunties and uncles. Anyway, I don't want to die of boredom and I don't want to be there alone with all of them. I'm hoping Muhammad can come but the jury's still out on that."

All the words came out in a rush and Layla wondered what the point was. Lake Geneva. St. Tropez. *Do people really live this way?* she thought.

"Anyway," continued Jehan, breathlessly. "I wondered if you would come?"

Layla set her hand on her chest. "You want *me* to go to Lake Geneva with you?"

"Yeah!" Jehan smiled. There was something vulnerable in her eyes.

"Mmm . . ." Layla thought fast. A trip to Lake Geneva meant she could home in on Noor Ghaffar. She wondered if the family kept art and artifacts there. In any case, it was an opportunity, and one she couldn't fumble.

"Yes," she said impulsively.

"Yay!" said Jehan, embracing her.

She smelled of sweat and lilac. Layla thought about the cost and wondered if Pierce would support it, but she couldn't hedge. If she had to say no, she figured she could renege later.

Hiro sidled up and set his hands on their shoulders. They danced *à trois* briefly, Jehan and Layla laughing as Hiro did his hip-hop thing, which looked like the mating dance of a slender and exotic bird. Then Hiro leaned toward her.

"I have something you might like," he whispered in Japanese.

"What is it?"

"You'll have to see," said Hiro, taking her hand.

"Where're you headed?" said Jehan.

"I don't know!" called Layla, laughing as Hiro pulled her from the dance floor. On the way, he took Huma's hand as well.

He led them to one of the many cozy dining nooks and VIP areas that surrounded the dance floor. Past a curtain of beads, he sat on a leather couch and pulled a baggie of pills from his pocket.

"C'mon, Hiro," said Layla in English. "That shit'll put me to sleep."

Hiro laughed. "Okay. Just keep us company."

"I'll have some," said Huma, sitting down beside him.

Layla sat in a chair opposite. She watched as Hiro held the bag up and described its contents to Huma.

"The green ones are totally synthetic, Swiss. They make you feel tweaked but they can also make you paranoid."

"Paranoid doesn't work for me," said Huma. "Last time I got paranoid I nearly jumped off the Brooklyn Bridge."

Hiro nodded. He turned the baggie slowly around. "Here. These. These red ones. Organic, from Indonesia. They're like a gentle ride into hyperfocus."

"Hyperfocus sounds tiring."

"Ah," said Hiro.

Layla's phone buzzed and she peered at the message that Rami had sent: *Thank you for the money, Layla. I'm good for this school session.* She stared at the words. So close and yet so far away . . .

An angry shout from the far end of the dance floor startled her. She turned back to Hiro and Huma. They didn't seem to have noticed. Hiro was looking for a third kind of pill to help put Huma into a custom-made altered state. These kids with their drugs and their games. If they were in New York she didn't know if she'd even be interested in busting them. It just seemed like such an expensive and tiresome waste of time. Her refusal to participate, though, made her feel like she stood out, which only heightened her anxiety. What if any one of them started to suspect her? Another shout interrupted her train of thought—a woman, or maybe two women, screamed. Layla glanced over and saw the dancers closest to the edge of the dance floor stop and strain to peer across to the far end of the room. It sounded like a fight had broken out.

But then the crowd on the floor split like the Red Sea parting and there, in the midst of all the young people, Layla spotted a clot of men, some in police uniforms, some in plain clothes, tearing through the crowd with black batons and their fists. The nightclub exploded into chaos as the policemen lashed out.

Huma glanced over her shoulder. "Holy shit," she shouted.

Layla bolted to her feet. The police must have come in through the main entrance. Those in the crowd with any presence of mind ran the opposite way, toward a narrow hallway in the back where she knew the restrooms were and, she suspected, the exit.

"Run!" she yelled.

Hiro fumbled with his little pharmacopoeia. The pills spun and rattled on the tabletop as he tried to get them back into the baggie.

"Leave the stash," called Layla. "You'll spend ten years in jail if they find that stuff on you."

Hiro's eyes grew wide but he did what Layla said and dropped the bag of pills to the floor. The dance floor was a riot of police officers by then, pulling and tugging at flailing partygoers who were trying their best to get away. Layla watched aghast as a policeman a few feet away slammed a baton against the thighs of a young man who crumpled to the ground in agony. She turned to see Hiro and Huma staring at her in a rising panic.

"What do we do?" said Huma.

The tide of clubgoers filled the narrow hall like a horizontal avalanche. Terror blurred the faces of girls in club clothes and bare feet and young men in dress shirts and jeans. Layla had heard of stampede disasters at concerts and soccer matches, but she'd never understood exactly how someone could get crushed to death in a crowd of people until now. If she lost her footing, she knew she'd be dead.

"Huma!" she heard Hiro call out. He reached back. Huma grabbed his hand and he pulled her into the fray. He had a huge advantage in height over the rest of the crowd. He dragged Huma through the hallway toward the back of the club.

"Wait! Huma!" shouted Layla. "Hiro, wait!"

She tried to push her way toward them but was batted back by a tide of larger bodies. Her eyes locked for a moment with Hiro's and she could tell that he had seen her. He blinked and turned away, pulling Huma in his wake and out of Layla's sight. *You have got to be kidding me*, she thought as she watched them disappear. The crowd suddenly swelled and she was crushed against the wall by a big man in a yellow tank top. She struggled to breathe.

The current of people ripped the man away and Layla took a huge gulp of air. She looked desperately around for James. Had he already gotten out? Had he left her like the others? Then she saw him. He was pushing his way through the crowd, away from the exit, his eyes fixed on her. She pressed forward, too, until they met in midstream. He wrapped his arms around her.

"Are you okay?" he asked.

"I'll be okay when we get out of here."

The current carried them down the hall. Finally, Layla could sense the pressure ease in front of her. They burst into the night air as if they'd been ejected by a catapult. The parking lot beside the club was full of people weeping, shouting, running. Cars careened out into the streets.

"My bike's over there," said James. He started toward the far edge of the lot. Layla stopped him.

"What about the others?"

James looked around. He squinted at something and pointed. "You mean them?" he said.

Hiro, Huma, and Jehan were climbing into a bright green Mercedes convertible.

"They're fine," said James. "Let's go."

She let him guide her by the hand to the side of the club. There, he handed her a helmet and she climbed onto his motorcycle behind him.

"Where do you live?" he asked.

"In Garden City, near the British Embassy."

Soon they were riding fast along the Nile Corniche. The lights of Cairo jeweled the sky. She held him tight, feeling the thud of her own heart against his back as he navigated through the late-night streets of Cairo. When they got to her apartment, she climbed off and handed him the helmet. She wanted nothing more than to ask him to come upstairs with her. But the stakes were too great. She was in Cairo to do a job, not for fun, not to fall for a cute guy who rescued her on the back of a motorbike. She could destroy the investigation and even lose her job if she took a wrong step. And what would Pierce do if she found out? She opened her mouth without a plan of what she was going to say, but before she could form a word his mouth was on hers. The adrenaline from the club still buzzed through her veins and suddenly her whole body was on fire as she kissed him back.

She thought for an instant of what Pierce had said about playacting. But this didn't feel like a lie or like work. It felt *real*. They broke off in the elevator under the unnerving gaze of a woman who boarded just after them. She held a small, shivering white poodle in her arms whose gaze was just as disapproving as its owner's. When they got off the elevator, Layla led James down the hall, barely breaking their kiss, even as they tumbled into the doorway.

The apartment was a luxurious, gleaming, ultramodern affair with cream-colored marble floors and crystalline floor-to-ceiling windows, making it seem as if the sprawling space was floating above the city. Pierce had leased it to further the illusion that Layla Nawar was a young and worldly woman of wealth and sophistication. The queen-sized bed, the walk-in closet, the marble-tiled bathroom with gold fixtures, all of it was intended to create an illusion.

James stopped at the sweeping view of the Nile from her bedroom window. River-cruise boats dotted the ancient black artery like spilled beads of gold. "Nice view," he said.

She watched him as he gazed out the window, then pulled him back toward the bed. She kissed his chest, his neck, his face.

His hands slid up her thighs, then grasped her hips with surprising strength as he flipped her over, so that he was on top of her. Soon he had unbuttoned her blouse and she held his head as he kissed her breasts through her bra. She turned her head to the side as he kissed a trail up her neck and caught sight of their reflection in the window. There she was, in bed with James, a person of interest in the active investigation in which she was an integral, undercover agent. *What the hell are you doing?* she thought. The whole thing was just . . . wrong.

The adrenaline and heat of the moment drained from her as reality set back in and the familiar anxiety returned.

"What's the matter?" he said, touching her cheek gently, his lips inches from hers.

"I'm just . . . It's just . . . a little fast."

He nodded and rolled off her. She was afraid that he might resent this, but he didn't turn cold. He kissed her gently on the cheek, rose from the bed, and left.

ON A RAINY WEDNESDAY night in Cairo, in the safe house, Pierce tapped at the photo of Kiyoshi Tanaka on the evidence board.

"We're not making progress here," said Pierce.

"I *am*," said Layla. "I'm just . . . trying to find my way in."

"What about Tanaka's collection in Tokyo? What about Los Angeles?"

"I'm still trying to find my way in," Layla repeated. "Tanaka travels all over the world." The vision of locking eyes with Hiro before he abandoned her in Infusion flashed through her thoughts. She barely knew him, really, any of them, but it hurt to have been left behind. That brief moment felt like a real betrayal. "One day he's here," she said. "The next day he's not."

Layla had to be conscious to keep any hint of impatience out of her voice. She knew Pierce was just being thorough. Her thoroughness was what made her so good. But Layla wasn't sure if Pierce also understood how thorough *she* was. She was trying her best to get access to Tanaka.

Layla stepped back and gazed at the photos under the label marked *Collectors* on the active board: Noor Ghaffar, Miriam Goldman, and a few others.

"Yo, Layla."

Layla turned and found Pierce tapping a pen against the tabletop, staring at her.

Pierce leaned back and sighed. "You're distracted."

"I'm just tired."

"Okay. So no luck with Tanaka and the son. Who next, then?"

Pierce's impatience put Layla on edge.

"I'm trying to decide between Ghaffar and Goldman," she said. She hoped she didn't sound like she was stalling, or defensive.

"Ghaffar's just a dilettante," Pierce said dismissively. "Plus, her husband's GID . . . It's too little for too much risk."

"Listen," Layla said, grabbing a marker from the table and pulling the cap off. "When I look at Goldman, I don't see a payoff." She drew an *X* beside Miriam Goldman's photo. "Criminal activity? Hell yes, but anything connected to the Muharib? I just don't see it. Plus, I don't have access to her, and her sons aren't involved in her business dealings."

"So?" Pierce's skeptical prompt nudged Layla from her reverie.

"Yeah . . . so . . . what're we looking for?" Layla stepped forward again and pointed to the cluster of collectors. "We're tracing the money, right? This is all about the money flowing from these people back through the dealers and the middlemen to the Muharib. Noor Ghaffar has the money, and she has the connections." She drew arrows from Ghaffar's picture to Farwadi, Rothkopf, Tanaka. "She might look harmless, but damned if she isn't connected." She turned. Pierce was squinting at the marks Layla had made on the board. Their eyes met and Pierce shrugged, but she didn't look convinced.

"Go for it," she said.

ALTHOUGH JEHAN GHAFFAR'S HEART was in a good place, she'd grown up with a solid sense that the laws of the world had been created not as rules that she must adhere to, but as guidelines intended for the many people who made her privileges and comforts possible.

Her casual disregard for the law was best illustrated by her carelessness when behind the wheel of a car. Layla pressed her hands against the back of the seat in front of her. Jehan was driving, Muhammad was riding shotgun, and Layla was in the backseat. Jehan careened through an intersection against the light.

"Jehan," said Muhammad. "Watch the lights!"

"I watch the lights!"

"Not just watch. You have to *do* things when you see the lights, like stop, or slow down."

For the second time that day, Layla thought she might be sick. They were in Lake Geneva and had spent the morning at the Grand Geneva Resort. But things had gotten hairy back there, on the slopes. Jehan had pressured her to go skiing that morning, but Layla had never skied before in her life. She'd feigned injury, claiming that a past knee sprain playing tennis at Georgetown made her wary of hurting herself.

"Georgetown? I thought you went to Brown?" Jehan had said.

"Ah, I meant, during a competition, between Brown and Georgetown."

So she'd spent most of the day alone in the lodge. They joined her for a good lunch, and now, with the skis on the roof, they were headed back down the steep road leading to the Ghaffar estate overlooking Lake Geneva. Layla had grown accustomed to the scenery that surrounded these very rich people, but she blinked at the snowcapped mountain peaks in the distance and the verdant slopes and chalets on the hilltops along the road.

When they reached the house, Layla reached up to help take the skis off the roof rack.

"What are you doing?" asked Jehan.

"Just . . . getting the skis."

"Stefan or Edvard will get them. They're on the household staff." Jehan turned and headed toward the house, and Muhammad followed.

Ah, how the other half live, thought Layla.

When they reached the house, Muhammad went to his room to get a fresh sweater and Layla followed Jehan to the solarium. That morning, before they'd left, a few of Noor Ghaffar's friends were just arriving, and by early afternoon, it looked as if there was a party in progress. A group of about ten people, mostly in their forties and fifties, sat eating sweets, drinking Turkish coffee, and laughing. A popular Egyptian soap opera, *And The Day Comes*, was playing on a large-screen TV, but the volume was on low. She guessed that the Ghaffars must have pretty amazing satellite reception up there in the rarified Alpine air. Noor Ghaffar greeted them with surprise.

"I thought you would be gone all day!"

"Layla is hurt—she couldn't ski today."

"Hurt?" Noor blinked at Layla. Her sharp eyes softened a touch.

"My knee," Layla said in Arabic.

"Ah," said Noor. "Go to the kitchen. Anna can give you some ice for that." She turned to Jehan. "Where is Muhammad?"

"He's getting his sweater."

"I want to speak to him now."

Jehan frowned. "Mother, what's wrong with you?"

"You know what's wrong."

"I'm not going to indulge you. You're angry, I can see it in your eyes."

"That young man—" said Noor. "That young man—"

One of the women seated on the floor, who seemed to be one of the few who was actually watching the TV, turned and said in Arabic, "I shouldn't have said anything. Now you're going to make me look bad and Jehan will be angry at me."

"What?" Jehan's voice quavered. "What are you gossiping about?"

When Muhammad entered the solarium, Noor and Jehan were yelling at each other.

"He'll ruin your reputation!" Noor hissed. "Do you know what I hear? Do you know what they're telling me? He's part of those protests at the university!"

"So what if he is? The whole country is falling apart and he has a stake in it just as much as anyone."

Noor glared at her daughter so intensely that Layla wondered if she would lash out physically.

"Do you know who else has a stake? Your father! Our family. Our family name . . . Can you imagine how your father will react when he finds out that that young man . . ." She couldn't seem to find the words. "Why can't you be with someone respectable, like Youssef?"

Jehan rolled her eyes dramatically. "Father's lackey? And what difference would it make to Father? He would barely notice. He couldn't even make it here for my birthday. And Muhammad hasn't hurt anyone. He has beliefs. Just because you think it will embarrass Daddy in front of his colleagues if he finds out Muhammad is an activist . . ."

"Jehan," said Muhammad calmly. "If my presence here is a problem . . ."

"It is a problem," said Noor. "You'll entangle my daughter in your political craziness. All these young people running around protesting like this . . ."

"They're protesting for a good reason," started Muhammad. "Egypt must recover its democratic principles. As a nation we—"

"Enough!" shouted Noor.

Layla doubted that Noor had expected mild-mannered Muhammad to challenge her, and at that moment she could see how his words inflamed Noor. She stood straight, eyes filled with rage. Layla was impressed, as always, by Muhammad's composure. Noor's friends murmured her name under their breaths, discreetly trying to convince her to calm down but without much impact.

"I need to use the—" Layla started, but she realized with relief that she didn't even need an alibi. No one cared as she slipped out of the sunlit room and down the hall that Muhammad had entered from.

She made her way upstairs, listening for any voices or footfalls. The house was grand and retro-modern. Noor had mentioned the day before that it had been built in the 1950s by some locally famous Swiss industrialist. It seemed that every view except those from the east and some of the north side, which overlooked the pool and part of the driveway, looked out on a pristine Alpine panorama. The mid-century modernism was accented by Noor's distinctly Middle Eastern touches. Gorgeous Persian rugs covered the floors. Beautiful art, paintings, and a few works of stone, tastefully presented, hung on walls or were featured on tables throughout the house. At the top of the central stairs hung a large section of an ancient frieze depicting the god Anubis weighing the soul of the scribe Ani. (Layla had spotted it the night before and, with a little research, had already determined that it was legit, purchased in 1992.)

She padded to an office room that she had also spotted the evening before. She listened again, but she was too far from the solarium to hear the angry voices she'd left behind. She gently pushed the office door open. There, on a table beside the desk, stood a stack of mail. She started to look through the items one by one, studying the address labels and the postage marks. She looked for evidence of items received over the past weeks from Egyptian galleries—Farwadi's or Bennett Rothkopf's—although she was skeptical that she would find anything of use. Why would anyone send mail to their vacation place in Switzerland and not their home in Egypt? Some of the return addresses were meaningless to her. One was from a gallery in the Netherlands, another was, tantalizingly, from Jordan. There were articles photocopied from academic journals in French, German, and English on ancient Egyptian artifacts, letters from the Cultural Heritage Organization, a batch of receipts from a company called Masterpiece Fine Arts Shipping, and so many gallery brochures—from New York, Tokyo, Melbourne, London, Delhi, and countless other locales—that Layla wondered yet again how far and wide these rich people traveled. The only way to know if any of it was of importance would be to take pictures and check on them later. She set the pile down, took out her iPhone, and started to take photos one by one. Halfway through the pile, she found a color printout of an artifact. It was difficult at first to tell what it was, but on closer inspection she saw that it was some kind of a flower, colored an ancient faded blue. A note, in Arabic script, was on a paper clipped to it: *A flower for your flower?* And the name below said simply *Amir*.

What does that mean? Layla wondered.

She must have lost track of time. She certainly wasn't paying close enough attention, because she found herself utterly surprised when she looked up to find Noor Ghaffar standing at the door, staring at her.

WHO DO YOU THINK YOU ARE?

· DIANA RENN ·

Layla dropped the stack of letters and met Noor Ghaffar's stony gaze. She opened her mouth to explain why she was taking pictures of this woman's mail but for once in her life, no words came. Not in any language.

Noor crossed the room in four strides, her gold chandelier earrings jangling. "Who do you think you are, inviting yourself into my private office?" She stood before Layla, hands on hips, glaring down at her from her heavily kohl-lined eyes.

Layla swallowed hard. What if it got back to Noor's husband that she had been poking around in Noor's office? Gamal Ghaffar could use his government connections to look into her. Her cover could be blown.

"I— I'm sorry." Layla sank to her knees and scooped up the envelopes that had scattered across the silk Persian rug.

Noor snatched the mail from Layla's hands and flung it on her desk. Then she turned on her kitten heel and strode over to the intercom panel, her manicured index finger extending toward the red security button.

Shit. Layla glanced through the window at the liquid pewter of Lake Geneva and the cold blue Alps beyond, as if a plausible excuse would materialize. When it didn't, she turned to a nearby ficus tree and dry-heaved into its decorative container, buying herself a few seconds more to think. Altitude sickness? No. They weren't high enough in Geneva.

Noor turned from the intercom and stared at Layla with an expression of horror. "If you're going to be ill, kindly avoid the rug. It's a priceless antique."

Ill. Drunk. Confused. Yes. That's how she'd play this out. That shouldn't be too hard. How many times had Layla woken in the night to steer her disoriented, partying roommates back into their correct rooms, or to the bathroom? Back home, that happened all the time. *Back home.* Wherever that was.

The room tilted. Her stomach lurched. And suddenly Layla wasn't acting anymore. *Osso buco*, Dover sole, *raclette*—the entire contents of a full day of lavish ski chalet meals and après-ski cocktails all emptied out into the ficus tree pot. The very real fear of blowing her cover had finally hit.

When she looked up, wiping her mouth, she saw Noor's face lined with concern, not unlike her own mother's face when Layla got sick as a little girl. She blinked away tears, remembering the steady presence of her mother's hand on her back.

"I was looking for the bathroom," Layla explained, deliberately slurring her words. "Think I had too much to drink. Took a wrong turn."

Noor shot an accusing glare at Layla's iPhone on the desk.

"I know it looks weird. I can explain."

"Please do." Noor pressed her burgundy-painted lips firmly together.

"I just love your taste in art. I wanted to see what galleries you support, and remember them so I can check them out myself." Layla turned on her phone and pulled up her photo gallery. "Once I realized I'd had too much to drink, I didn't trust myself to remember, so I took a picture of a brochure." She quickly deleted all the photos she'd taken except the last one, the return address of a gallery in the Netherlands. She showed that to Noor as proof.

"Well, my goodness, you could have just *asked* me that," said Noor. "I am *always* happy to talk about art." She gave an exasperated sigh, but then the hard lines in her face softened slightly, and the furrows between her thick eyebrows disappeared. "All right. I suppose I can overlook a certain degree of foolishness. That includes the drinking."

"Sorry about that," Layla whispered. She looked down at her lap.

"We have a modest supply of alcohol here, and I do not mind a glass of wine now and then, especially when we are away from Cairo," Noor continued. "But my husband does generally frown on drinking." Her eyes darted toward a framed photo of Gamal Ghaffar on her desk. "Use restraint, Layla. The circle we move in is rather small. You understand."

"Of course. *Thank you.*" Layla pressed her hands together, as if in prayer. "I'm really, really sorry, Mrs. Ghaffar. I made a huge lapse of judgment. This will never happen again."

Noor gave a graceful nod. "We're all human. And you've been a positive influence on Jehan thus far. Her father and I don't care much for the company she keeps in Cairo, but since meeting you she's even been talking of grad school a little. So I accept your apology." With a flick of her jewel-encrusted hand, she indicated that Layla should now stand.

Layla rose to her feet, unsteadily, leaning on the desk for support. She felt genuinely lightheaded now.

"I'm ordering you straight to your room to rest. I'll have seltzer water sent up to settle your stomach." Noor called the kitchen on the intercom, then took Layla's arm with a claw-like grip and escorted her out of the office.

LAYLA COLLAPSED ONTO THE bed and let out a long breath. Her hands, she noticed, were trembling, the reality of her near-miss with Noor finally hitting her. But as her breath steadied, the trembling stopped. She'd saved her cover. For now. She only hoped Gamal Ghaffar was too busy to care about his daughter's silly, drunken friend if Noor decided to mention the incident. The last thing she needed was to get on the radar of a GID officer.

She was itching to read through that folder of disorganized papers that she'd found in Noor's desk. When she'd leafed through the photocopies of articles, correspondence from the Cultural Heritage Organization, Masterpiece Fine Arts Shipping receipts, and gallery brochures, she'd noticed several appraisers' documents, all signed by one Dr. Hassan el-Sayed, an independent appraiser. She'd had to delete the photos she'd taken, but at least that one name had imprinted on her memory.

She reached for her iPhone and quickly Googled the appraiser. He had a modest website with some legit credentials. Scrolling through his affiliations list, she found a logo for the Egyptian Society of Appraisers.

Layla paused—she'd heard of the International Society of Appraisers. She hadn't heard of an Egyptian one. Another quick Google search confirmed her suspicion. There was no such organization.

Her heart beat faster. An appraiser with a fictitious affiliation made compelling evidence that Noor, knowingly or unknowingly, had purchased illegitimate relics. A dealer could have used that appraiser to legitimize stolen goods and included the document in the provenance file. She couldn't wait to pass on the name of this dubious-sounding expert to Pierce.

But she wouldn't be telling Pierce about her rookie mistakes this weekend. Layla rubbed her throbbing head. It had been stupid to take such a chance, snooping like that. She should have waited for an opportunity when people were out of the house or asleep.

Her biggest error? Losing herself. Imagining she was actually entitled to be here. Layla punched an embroidered pillow. She cringed, remembering how she'd lied to Jehan about a past knee injury so she could avoid skiing.

She couldn't be a skier. She was just a girl from Manshiyat Naser. A girl from a cinder block apartment, in a city built over a landfill. What a farce this all was.

Noor Ghaffar's words echoed in her ears. *Who do you think you are?*

Her suitcase buzzed across the room. She dove for it, hoping for a call or text from James. But the iPhone displayed no messages. She rummaged through cashmere sweaters and dug up the Motorola, the one tenuous link to her real life.

A text from Rami awaited her. She read his words in Egyptian Arabic. *Hey, big sister. I see on the news that a storm is coming to New York. Thinking of you.*

Layla smiled. Ever since he was a toddler, Rami had been fascinated by extreme cold, storms, hurricanes, tornadoes. She liked to think that was why he was studying engineering now, why the boy who drank in knowledge of wind currents and jet streams had become a young man who wanted to make wind turbines and work for Egypt's energy industry.

Layla typed: *Getting colder. Feels like snow.* She powered down the phone.

Outside the window, a fresh round of Geneva snow was beginning to fall. Not downy flakes, but granular ice pellets driving against the glass. Layla burrowed into the bed. She suddenly longed for the warmth of Cairo. Nobody here knew who she really was, and suddenly she didn't, either.

BACK IN HER GARDEN CITY apartment, Layla brewed some coffee and settled herself on the divan to read through a new file of articles Pierce had given her about black market antiquities. She needed to commit this information to memory. Still, she kept looking up to watch the boat traffic drift down the Nile.

Layla snapped the folder closed. Memorizing methods of disguising antique relics to look like tourist souvenirs was fascinating, but what she really needed to study right now was the weekend of social events she'd missed while in Geneva.

She reached for her work phone and pulled up CairoZoom, Jehan's favorite source of gossip about the Cairo socialite scene. She thumbed through pictures, looking for images of people she'd met and people she needed to meet. She knew which rock concerts Chloe and Huma had been to lately, which restaurants the Goldman brothers had frequented. The social information had nothing to do with antiquities, but understanding the habits of this set was vital to her interactions with them. What Pierce didn't know was that the language of affluence was the hardest language she'd ever had to learn.

She scanned photos of parties and glimpsed herself in some of them, smiling and chatting. *Passing.* Layla shivered. She barely recognized herself.

Someone had even snapped a photo at the recent Coriander party—a photo of her and James. They were standing close to each other, talking in a corner of the room. She enlarged the image. James was leaning toward her, smiling and listening intently. She was balancing a wine glass in one hand, tossing her hair over one shoulder, and talking with an expressive gesture. She let her gaze linger on it a moment longer, then thumbed through the rest of the recent updates.

One more photo made her pause. It was from a fashion show at the Nile Ritz-Carlton. Chloe, Huma, and Jehan were all in this photo, arms and long hair entwined as though they were posing as the Three Graces. Behind them was the entrance to the casino. And walking in was none other than Bennett Rothkopf. She could just make out Mackey behind him.

She tilted her head, looking at the photo from all angles. As Americans, they had every right to gamble in Egypt. There were numerous casinos in Cairo, most attached to posh hotels. But it seemed deeply out of character from what she knew of Bennett. He presented as conservative, even cautious in his business dealings, not a gambler. She needed to get to know Bennett better. Maybe he wasn't as straitlaced as he seemed.

Energized by this thought, Layla sprang into action. She put on a flowery long-sleeve blouse, skinny pants, and strappy sandals. She added an extra layer of lipstick and a quick spritz of perfume before heading out the door.

• • •

JEHAN CALLED JUST AS Layla stepped out of the apartment to look for a taxi. "Hey. I was just missing you. Why did you have to leave so soon? It's boring without you."

Layla stepped off the curb to hail a cab, then jumped back just in time to avoid a fleet of mopeds ripping down the street. "Isn't Muhammad still there?"

"He is, but things are tense after the fight with my mom." Jehan sighed. "We have to get out of here. We just got invited to Lake Como this Wednesday, but my mom doesn't want to let me go, at least not with Muhammad. Can you believe it? I am twenty-five years old! She won't shut up about setting me up with my dad's boring assistant."

"What's at Lake Como?" *Other than fresh air*, Layla thought, as she coughed in the exhaust fumes the mopeds left behind. "Isn't it the off-season?"

"Who cares? People are there! Hiro's there!"

Hiro. The last time Layla had seen him, he'd ditched her at the nightclub raid. Normally she wouldn't waste any more energy on an eccentric and self-centered party boy, but Hiro was the son of the elusive Kiyoshi Tanaka, a person of great interest on the evidence wall whom Layla had yet to meet. Layla gripped the phone more tightly with one hand and continued trying to hail a cab with the other. "I'd love to see Hiro. Why's he going to Italy?"

"He's got a deejaying gig at a music festival in Milan. He's staying at his dad's vacation villa."

Layla stopped looking for a taxi for a moment as the significance of Jehan's update suddenly hit her. "Wait, this thing's at the Tanaka villa? Is his dad going to be there?" Layla hoped she managed to filter the hopeful note out of her voice.

"No. Are you kidding? Why would we want to fly all the way there to hang out with someone's boring dad?" Jehan laughed.

Layla thought fast. Was she in enough with Jehan to invite herself along? It was an incredible opportunity, to gain access to one of Kiyoshi Tanaka's homes and art collections. She could learn more about his buying habits and see what kind of records he kept; surely he had a home office there like Noor Ghaffar did in Geneva. She did some quick math in her head, wondering what Pierce might say about two back-to-back trips to Europe. A jaunt to Lake Como from Cairo felt so extravagant. And yet, this was how Jehan and her friends lived. In perpetual motion.

"I wish I hadn't left you so soon," said Layla, as a cab pulled up to the curb. "I'm really regretting it. Hey, I know this sounds crazy, but what if I joined you guys there? You're mom thinks I'm a good influence, you know."

There was silence on the other end, and Layla squeezed her eyes shut, bracing herself for rejection.

"You would really do that for me?" Jehan asked. "Go as my chaperone?"

Layla snorted a laugh. "I'm not that much older than you," she said. "You make me sound like some old granny. But yes, you can tell your mom I'll keep you out of trouble."

After another long pause, Jehan squealed, so loudly that Layla had to move the phone off her ear. "You're the best!" Jehan shouted.

"Glad to be of service," she said in a wry tone.

"Call the Goldman twins," Jehan commanded her. "Marcus and Adrian are flying out to meet us, and they'll take their family jet. Plenty of room for you."

The family jet. Of course. Layla felt light-headed. "Great. I'll do that." At least the expense of booking a last-minute flight was solved.

For a moment, she let herself fantasize about asking James to join them. After she searched the Tanaka villa, they might even have time to enjoy the sights together. Take a boat ride on the lake.

The taxi driver looked at her strangely through the rearview mirror as she laughed out loud at herself. Lake Como was an *FBI mission*, not a romantic mini-break.

She shook her head and refocused on the mission at hand: getting Bennett to sell her some "unique" object and see what kind of stakes he was really playing for.

• • •

"LAYLA! WHAT A PLEASANT surprise!" Bennett greeted her at the gallery door. "James said you were in Geneva with Jehan and her mother." He looked casual today, wearing a blue blazer and khakis and a white shirt partially unbuttoned, yet he ushered her inside with almost courtly formality.

Stepping inside, Layla became aware of Mackey's presence at a small desk in a corner. He was reading an electronic tablet but peered over it to observe her. She gave him a friendly wave, which he did not return.

"I just got back," Layla explained. "I was passing by and thought I'd say hello to James, if he's around?"

"He's right in the middle of a restoration job but should be coming up for air soon. Can you wait?"

"Sure. I'd actually love to look around your gallery some more."

"Of course! Did anything catch your eye the other day?" Bennett put his hands behind his back and strolled alongside her as she walked the length of a glass display case.

"I'm open-minded," said Layla. She paused and bent down to inspect some *wedjat* eye necklaces.

"It's wonderful that someone so young is taking an interest in antiquities," said Bennett. "Aside from this scarab amulet craze, which is sure to blow over soon, it's hard to cultivate the younger buyers. They tend to perceive most of these things as old and dusty." He laughed, but wryly, and smoothed his wavy gray hair with a sigh. "I worry, though, seriously, about the longevity of the profession, if we can't get people your age interested."

"That's partly what I hope to do," said Layla. She moved on to the next case, choosing her words and calculating her next moves. Her heart was pounding. Pierce hadn't authorized her to make an illicit purchase today, but it seemed insane not to try when she had Bennett's undivided attention and only Mackey in the room.

"This Cypriot amphora might be an attractive piece for you," said Bennett, pointing at a striped vase. "And it's a safe investment. May I ask your price range?"

"It's flexible," said Layla.

He raised an eyebrow. "Flexible," he repeated.

"That's right." She took a deep breath. "I'm most interested in unique and rare Egyptian relics. I'd like to find something nobody else has."

She stole a glance at him. He scratched his head. He appeared to be deep in thought. "There is, I suppose, one thing I could show—"

The gallery door opened, and a young couple walked in.

"Excuse me," he whispered to Layla, and moved away to greet them. Layla bit back her frustration. She was sure he'd been about to suggest something interesting.

While Bennett tended to his customers, Layla took a turn around the gallery on her own, peering into cases, reading the descriptor tags. She watched and listened as Bennett accompanied the couple to a case of faience vessels.

The woman pointed to an elegant greenish-gold flask with a narrow neck. Bennett placed it in her hands gently, as if it were an infant. While the woman cradled it and inspected its surface, the man asked some questions in halting English. The couple conferred in hushed tones, and Layla's ears pricked. Bennett was speaking basic Arabic and English to them, but their native tongue was Turkish. She could sense growing frustration on each side with the halting communication.

Maybe she could make herself useful and score some points with Bennett, points that could help her get back to the topic of buying something special later.

"Pardon me," Layla said in basic Arabic, approaching Bennett and the customers. "I couldn't help overhearing. I speak some Turkish. Would you like me to translate?"

All three of them looked relieved, especially Bennett.

Her cautious Turkish soon picked up speed as she translated. *This is a New Year's flask from the Saite Dynasty, circa 540 BC. Its purpose was to hold sacred water from the Nile at the start of the new year festivities. The body is intact. The spout has been restored.* If only she could slip in and out of her identities as smoothly as she did languages.

At the husband's request, Bennett then produced a file explaining the complicated journey of the flask, which Layla also translated out loud. He had documentation for the object, going back well over a century. An archaeology professor had owned it for many years. It had been loaned out for a traveling exhibition in Europe. A museum in France had purchased it, then sold it to another museum in Germany, then Poland, then Turkey. It had been written up, along the way, in various scholarly articles. The vessel broke during an earthquake, was restored, and then sold at auction to a private collector in England. The collector had died, and the estate had sold it privately, which was how it came into Bennett Rothkopf's hands. Bennett's son had done further restoration work on the object, and while it still retained its luster and a rich history, the item was selling at a fraction of its value because of a small, nearly invisible crack. A very good deal, Bennett assured the couple, and Layla, translating his assurances, came to feel it was, too.

The couple set the flask aside and drifted over to the case of Coptic icons. These Layla knew a thing or two about; modern versions of the paintings on wood had decorated the church she'd attended growing up, and they'd had a few in her childhood home. The wife in particular seemed pleased to hear her explain the various iconographies.

The next thing she knew, the Turkish man was counting out clean, neat bills. All cash, in US dollars. Eight thousand for both the faience vessel and a Coptic icon of Mary. "The vessel is for us, but the icon is a gift for a dear friend," the woman explained in Turkish while her husband went over the paperwork. "She will be so pleased, and now I can explain to her the illuminating history you have told me. Thank you."

"My pleasure." Layla smiled. The success of the transaction had produced a rush of adrenaline. She'd been hungry for some kind of success, after several weeks of just poking around, asking questions, and snapping photos.

Bennett conferred with Mackey briefly, and arranged for him to drive the couple back to their hotel so that they would not have to walk the streets of Cairo carrying the expensive items. Mackey and the couple left.

The gallery quiet again, Bennett sank onto a nearby stool, rubbed his hands together, and gave Layla a long look. He pulled up another stool and gestured for her to sit opposite him, on the other side of a display case.

"Just how many languages do you know?"

"Oh, I don't know. A handful." She looked down at her feet. She wasn't acting as the heiress now. This question always made her self-conscious.

"No, really," he persisted. "How many?"

Layla squirmed. "It depends on what you mean by 'know.' I'm fluent, I guess, in English, Arabic, and French. I have a working knowledge of Turkish, and I can get by in a few others, I guess."

He whistled. "That's quite an accomplishment."

Basking in Bennett's admiration felt like sitting under a heat lamp.

"When you were talking to the Turkish couple before they made the purchases," he said, "were you talking to them about Coptic art?"

"I was," said Layla. "I guess that's why they sprung for the icon."

Bennett leaned forward. "How do you know so much about Coptic Art? It's a fairly specialized field."

Layla froze. Could he know anything about her Coptic upbringing? Her real past in Egypt? She'd spoken of that to no one. Still, she had to be careful. She thought fast. "I spent the past few days touring around Old Cairo," she explained. "The Coptic Museum really sparked my interest. So many unique objects. Actually, speaking of unique . . . before those clients came in, you were saying you might have something special I would like?" She met his eyes without blinking. "Price isn't an issue. I want to find something totally unique."

Bennett tilted his head to one side. "Your cousin Farwadi cannot help?"

"I'm not sure mixing business and family is a great idea," she replied. "He gives me good counsel, but purchasing something significant from him would be, well, awkward."

"I see," he said slowly, scratching the faint silver stubble on his chin.

Bennett rose to his feet and crossed the room to another display case on the opposite wall.

Layla got up and went to his side to see what he was grasping for in the case. Her anticipation rose as she waited for him to reveal what she hoped would be her "something special."

He stood and handed Layla a ten-inch bronze statuette of a cat wearing golden hoop earrings.

"This is nothing to sneeze at," said Bennett, almost defensively, as Layla studied it carefully. "It's twenty-five hundred years old and is valued at three thousand US dollars. It can be yours for two thousand."

"I—I'm not really a cat person," Layla admitted, turning the heavy item around in her hands. Despite its sleek body, this particular cat was very unappealing, with its wide glaring eyes and mouth that seemed to grimace. It reminded her of the feral cats that her sister Sanaa used to feed outside their childhood apartment.

"This is a solid investment," Bennett insisted. "It's aesthetically pleasing, has solid provenance, and a high resale value." He explained its history and how it had at one point been owned by the British archaeologist Howard Carter, who had discovered King Tut's tomb.

After looking over the paperwork, which seemed to tick off all the boxes for legitimate art—recognizable institutions and dealer names, no gaps in chronology—Layla decided she had to buy it to prove herself as an eager collector who could take his advice. She said she'd buy the cat and bring the money tomorrow.

"Take it today," said Bennett. "Bring me the money anytime this week. I know you're good for it."

Layla nodded. Turning down the item after all Bennett's efforts would not help build the relationship. Surely, Pierce would understand that when she saw the bill. Besides, Bennett had his guard up. He seemed to be steering her toward the most conservative purchase she could make. If he really had illicit items for sale, they wouldn't be displayed in his showroom, and she'd have to build some trust before he revealed them. As Bennett donned a stylish pair of reading glasses and wrote up a receipt for the sale, she suddenly had an idea.

"I'm so glad we had a chance to speak today," she said. "I've been looking for a mentor, and I think you're just the person I could learn from."

Bennett touched his hand to his chest. "Why thank you, Layla. That means a lot to me."

"Along those lines, I'd like to make an unusual offer. Or a request, I guess," she said. "I'd like to work here."

Bennett stopped writing the receipt and lowered his glasses to look down his nose. "I'm sorry?"

"I'd be happy to sit in on your appointments with international clients and translate like I did today. In exchange, maybe you could tell me more about the art in your collection, and the marketplace."

Bennett appeared thoughtful. He twirled his pen in his fingers.

"You do have a nice way with customers, and your linguistic background—not to mention your intimate knowledge of the type of clientele we deal with—would be helpful to me. It's just . . . I'm unfortunately not in a position at the moment to offer compensation—"

"I'd like to volunteer," Layla cut in. "I don't need the money. The compensation would be the knowledge I gain." She tried to look calm as she waited for his response. If she was a volunteer at the gallery, she'd see deliveries go in and out. She'd have access to paperwork, current clients, and all kinds of information. Not to mention access to James.

"Well? What do you think?" Layla prompted.

Slowly, Bennett grinned. "I think this is my lucky day." He extended his hand, and she shook it. "Welcome to the family. Let me give you the tour."

As Layla followed Bennett through the gallery, carrying the cold bronze cat in her hands, the warmth of his words spread through her. *Welcome to the family.* Of course he was just talking about the gallery. But it felt so personal.

She forced her mind back to the tour and committing the gallery layout to memory. The front of the suite held the main gallery with two smaller adjoining showrooms. One doorway off the main gallery led to a corridor of back rooms. The door at the very end had a sign saying *Storeroom.* Along the corridor, there were two office doors on one side and three on the other, as well as a restroom and a small office supplies closet with a photocopier.

The largest office, nearest the storeroom, was for Bennett. Just before it was a closed door that said *Studio,* with brown paper taped up over the window. As they reached it, Layla heard the tapping sound of a chisel on stone and a low *whoosh* of a ventilation system.

"I'd love to see what James is working on," she said, putting her hand on the doorknob. It didn't turn.

"Unfortunately, for insurance purposes, studio access is restricted," said Bennett. He steered her toward a door marked *IT* and opened it, revealing a gaunt, acne-scarred guy about her age hunched over a computer keyboard. "This is Hamadi Essam. He takes care of all our IT needs here in Cairo and manages our website. Hamadi, meet Layla Nawar. She'll be volunteering for us now and then as a translator in the coming weeks."

It could be handy to have a computer guy in her back pocket, should she need access to Bennett's electronic files. Layla gave Hamadi her friendliest smile. It was not returned. He wasn't cold, like Mackey, but gloomy and preoccupied. His eyes flicked briefly her way, then returned to the glow of his screen.

They walked past the door marked *Security*—Mackey's office, she guessed—and Bennett pushed open the next door. He showed her a room not much bigger than a broom closet. "Your quarters, should you need a place to keep your personal belongings or to catch your breath between clients on days when we're tightly scheduled." There was just enough room for a tiny desk, a computer, and small shelf of reference books and auction catalogs. "It's humble, I'm afraid, but much of the time you will spend in the gallery, interacting with customers."

Layla thanked him and set the bronze cat on the desk.

"Now, let's talk scheduling," said Bennett. "I'd love for you to come in the day after tomorrow. I have a German-speaking customer coming in, and your translation help would be invaluable."

"Sure, I can—" Layla stopped herself. "Oh, wait." Wednesday she'd be flying to Lake Como. "Actually, I'm sorry, the earliest I could start would be this Friday."

Bennett frowned.

"I'm *so* sorry." Layla sighed. The conundrum was real. She wanted to continue to impress Bennett with her skills, and to meet all his clients, but the chance to get to Tanaka's house was too good to pass up. "It's just, I already committed to going to Lake Como for a couple of days with some friends."

"Right." Bennett ran his fingers through his hair.

"But once I start this Friday, I'll be here whenever you need," Layla assured him. It would be easy enough to do. As an heiress, except for the occasional jaunt to Europe, she had nothing but time on her hands.

"Look, I'll be grateful for *any* time you can give us," said Bennett. He twisted his wrist and glanced at his Rolex. "Now, if you'll excuse me, I need to dial into a conference call with London." He shook her hand once more and said, "See you Friday," before hurrying back to his office.

Alone, Layla picked up the unwanted bronze cat. She turned it over in her hands. It really was ugly.

A noise by the door startled her. Turning around with the cat, she saw James in the doorway, smiling at her, his dazzling blue eyes crinkling around the corners. Involuntarily, she smiled back.

"Look at you," he said. "The cat's meow."

Layla leaned against the desk and held up the cat. "Like it?"

James laughed. "It's sort of hideous. I've never liked those things."

WHO DO YOU THINK YOU ARE?

Layla laughed, too. "I know, right? But your dad somehow convinced me this was the thing to buy."

"Well, he's right," James said. "They're highly collectable, and you'll have no trouble getting your money back out of it. Why are you hiding out in here?"

"It's my office," she said, gesturing expansively at the tiny room. "I'm going to be working here as a translator."

"Wait—seriously?"

Layla briefly explained what had happened.

"So now we're co-workers," James concluded.

"I'm just a volunteer," she corrected.

"Still. This means I can see you anytime. How good is that?" A sly grin spread across his face. He took a step into the office. Because the space was so tiny, they were suddenly just inches apart. So close Layla could smell his aftershave. A sandalwood scent. She breathed it in deeply. "It's very good," she said.

"And maybe, once in a while . . . I could do . . . this?" He leaned forward and kissed her on the cheek, then slid his lips over to her mouth.

"Maybe," she whispered. God, what was happening to her?

"Though it's probably against the rules," he murmured. "Consorting with a colleague." His tongue gently parted her lips.

Electricity ran through Layla's entire body as her tongue met his. She shivered. "I don't know. I didn't read the employee handbook," she whispered between kisses.

James drew her close. "Let's move this thing," he said in a low voice, taking the bronze cat out of her hands and setting it on the desk. He pushed the door closed, then returned to her, kissing her with more urgency.

Layla could hardly breathe. Partly from desire for James. Partly from fear. She'd vowed to slow it down and not to cross a line. She should pull away now. Keep things light and flirtatious only. But James's arms around her, after the chilly atmosphere of the Ghaffars' Swiss villa, felt incredibly good.

"So I guess you missed me?" she managed to say when she came up for air.

"Are you *kidding*?" His kisses traveled to her shoulder. "It was such a long week." His hand slid down her back.

Layla pulled away. This was heating up way too fast. "Really? I didn't hear much from you," she said.

"I know." James released her from his embrace, except for one hand, which he gently pressed between both of his. "I'm so sorry about that. We've been seriously swamped here. My dad has me working overtime trying to get this restoration job finished and shipped by a deadline." He glanced at a wall clock. "Speaking of. I'm on a timer. I have to apply another coat of resin."

"What are you working on in there?" Layla asked. She studied his face carefully. He had dark shadows under his eyes, as if he really had been burning the midnight oil.

"Restoring gilding on some statuettes," said James.

"I'd love to see," she said hopefully.

"I'll show you when it's all done. Right now the fumes are pretty vile."

"Okay." Layla pushed away from the desk and picked up the cat again. "I should go. I have some stuff to do, too. Like packing."

"You're leaving again?" His face fell. "You just got back."

"Hiro has a gig in Milan and is having some kind of house party at his dad's villa on Lake Como. I'm going on Wednesday as Jehan's 'chaperone' so her parents will let her go." She smirked. Then she heard herself ask, "Any chance you can come?"

He shook his head and laced his fingers through hers. His hands, she noticed, looked delicate, with long, tapered fingers, but they felt strong and roughened by hard work. She noticed flecks of gold on them, and a streak of black.

"I wish," he said. "Believe me, I could use a break right now, and Italy with you would be amazing." His eyes shone at the thought but quickly darkened again. "I have to work. You go have fun. And when I'm out from under this project next week, we'll go out somewhere. I promise."

"Okay," Layla said. But relief washed through her, even as he drew her close for one more kiss. She was definitely crossing the line. Getting out of town again was the smartest thing to do.

KIYOSHI TANAKA'S VACATION VILLA stood at the end of a long gravel drive, past iron gates and a guardhouse. Emerging from the private car Hiro had arranged, Layla drew in a sharp breath. Even in the weak, late winter sun, the estate dazzled. Manicured cypress and pine trees flanked a rolling lawn and a brick terrace. The mid-nineteenth-century mansion towered before her, its stucco the color of lemon gelato. Even the Goldman brothers, who had kept up an exhausting banter of frat boy humor in German the entire flight over, seemed momentarily awed by it as they followed her to the front door. The place was strangely quiet, as if it were under some kind of enchantment. The oblong pool was covered up, the marble fountain dry.

The door was flung open, breaking the spell. Hiro, sporting a new deep blue hair color, greeted them all with his lopsided grin. "Welcome to Villa Tanaka!" he said. "You're just the people I have been waiting for. Now our party can begin!" From somewhere deep inside the house, the bass of a techno beat pulsed.

Layla felt a flash of irritation at his effusive greeting and flinched as he kissed her on both cheeks. *Thanks for leaving me behind at Infusion, asshole*, she wanted to say. But she needed to be the perfect houseguest.

Hiro led them through the marble-floored foyer, past a silent welcoming committee of white marble statuary, and into the massive kitchen. There, Jehan and Muhammad were making alcohol-infused smoothies. Jehan, hands covered in lemon juice, ran to Layla with a little squeal and threw her arms around her, then around Marcus and Adrian. "You made it!" she said, thrusting drinks into their hands. "Here. Imbibe. Then come meet everyone."

Layla tasted the smoothie. The freshest lemons. The strongest alcohol. Her eyes watered, and her next sip was fake. This was a business trip, after all.

Hiro led them down a corridor. The pulsing beat intensified. The corridor led to a large sitting room overlooking the lake, with French doors leading out to a balcony. Tall windows with the shutters open let in the light and offered up a breathtaking view of Lake Como; it glittered silver, blue, and white, reflecting the shades of the mountains beyond. An ambitious early season ferry glided by.

The Ghaffars displayed their art in proper and traditional ways, all of it kept at arm's length, framed or under glass. But here, the Tanaka collection was surprisingly accessible, and interspersed with contemporary and ordinary objects. Ancient Italian statuary and busts occupied the room and seemed to mingle with the guests. A marble Italian bust sported headphones.

Layla's gaze shifted, taking in the disrespectful treatment of the Japanese collector's vacation villa. What looked like an antique candy dish was being used as an ashtray, with several still-smoldering butts in the center. What would the notoriously meticulous collector say if he walked in the door right now?

In one corner was an elaborate setup of beatbox equipment. Hiro took up a position behind it and started playing with the sub-bass settings and speeds, laying down a new track. The undulating sounds added to the surreal, Alice-down-the-rabbit-hole feeling.

Layla shook herself loose from Jehan and approached Hiro.

"Well? How do you like the place?" Hiro asked her in English.

"I love it!" she said. "I can see why you'd rather stay here than in Milan."

"Yes, here it is very peaceful," said Hiro, cranking up the volume switch on the beatbox. She could feel the bass throb in her veins. "I can actually hear myself think." He pointed meaningfully to his head.

Hiro was spacing out, falling into the music; she had to keep him on topic while she could. "It's almost like a museum," she said. "Your dad sure has a lot of art. All these marble busts and statues! Amazing."

Hiro shrugged. "These are everywhere in Italy. They are not so valuable."

"Did you put the valuable stuff away for the party? If I were you, I'd be really worried about theft and damage."

"Well, there are some things upstairs in glass cases, but they are locked and alarmed," Hiro said. "And the oldest, most valuable stuff is not here."

"Oh? Did he get rid of some things?" She hardly dared ask. Hiro was perpetually buzzed, stoned, or high, but too many questions might arouse even his curiosity.

"No, no," said Hiro. "They're in Crete. At our other vacation home."

Their *other* vacation home. Of course. She should have known there'd be more than one. "Why there?"

Hiro lost himself in a groove for a moment, swaying slightly, and she wasn't sure he'd heard. "My father has a different theme in each of his houses," Hiro explained. "The Crete villa is more rustic, so he likes to keep the older artifacts there. They fit in better."

"Makes sense," said Layla, still struggling to make sense of it all. Why buy all this art to take up space in homes you were rarely in? She thought of the one Coptic icon on wood that her mother used to display in their tiny apartment, how she would lovingly dust it with a rag once a week and pause in her cooking to admire it.

Hiro's eyes were glazing. Layla ventured just one more question, gauging his degree of intoxication. "You mentioned he has some pieces here in glass cases," she said. "I'd love to see them. I geek out over ancient art," she added with a laugh. "Because of my cousin's business, I guess. It's in the blood."

Hiro shrugged. "I do not judge people. Enjoy the art. The staircase is that direction." He pointed. "The cases are on the landing on the next floor up."

Before Jehan or anyone else could see her disappear, Layla darted out of the room and ran up the bridal staircase two steps at a time. Palladian windows along the landing offered more stunning views of the lake, but the antiquities, a collection of fifteen items, interested her more. They were in cases affixed to walnut stands, or in glass cases attached to the walls. Good. Maybe they'd stay safe from the revelers downstairs.

She took out her iPhone and quickly took pictures of each object. They were mostly earthenware or terra-cotta vessels and figurines. Nothing was labeled, but her two visits to the Rothkopf Gallery and all the reading she'd done for Pierce had given her some sense of what she was looking at. As the noise grew louder downstairs, she felt like an adult at a kids' party. The feeling reminded her of her senior year at Georgetown, when she already had her sights set on the FBI, and everyone else suddenly seemed so young.

"Layla? Where's Layla?" Jehan's voice echoed up from the ground floor.

Layla tiptoed away from the stairs and down the corridor. She located the master bedroom suite, sparsely furnished in a Mediterranean style. Drawers and closets revealed little. She opened the nightstand drawers, cringing at what she might find. A lonely man's porn collection? No. She breathed a sigh of relief. Only a copy of *Smithsonian* magazine, with a sticky note flagging an article. She turned to it and read the headline to see what had caught his interest. "The Amulet Men of Faiyum," by Dr. Katherine Danforth, Distinguished Professor of Egyptology, University College of London. She skimmed the first few paragraphs. The article was about amulets from the Faiyum region of Egypt, which were believed to have been worn by healers who called themselves "Magic Men." The article was lengthy and dense, so she just took some photos of the pages and resolved to read it later.

The thumping bass from the party kicked up a notch, calling her back to her central mission. She needed to find Tanaka's home office. She found it at the opposite end of the corridor: a relatively humble room closed in by heavy floor-to-ceiling shutters. She made a beeline for the desk and rifled through the drawers and file cabinets, searching for any documents that corresponded to the fifteen antiquities on the landing.

In the lower left desk drawer she found a file hand-labeled in kanji: *Lake Como Collection: Antiquities.* It almost seemed to be waiting for her, daring her to find it. Layla took photos of all the receipts and provenance documents in the file, glancing over each one. Most of the items upstairs had been purchased from Farwadi's galleries in Cairo and in New York; Tanaka seemed to be a loyal client of her "cousin." She made a note in her phone to ask Farwadi later about the extent of Tanaka's purchases.

Two vases had been purchased from Bennett Rothkopf. In both cases, the documentation looked solid. No appraisals from the dubious Dr. Hassan el-Sayed. Still, Pierce would be able to look more carefully at the paperwork, her practiced eye more capable of seeing gaps in the narrative.

Just as she snapped the last photo, a text buzzed in from James. *Get out while you're ahead.*

The words jolted her. She felt her blood drain away. Did he know something? She stared at the text a moment longer, frowning.

A second text appeared. *Sorry!!! Thought I was texting Dad. How's the villa?*

Layla sent a thumbs-up emoji but kept staring at the words of the misdirected text. *Get out while you're ahead.* What did that mean? What was Bennett up to?

IT WAS A RELIEF to report for "work" at the Rothkopf Gallery, to have some kind of schedule and shape to her day. After searching Tanaka's office, she'd gotten sucked in to the party at last, avoiding the drugs but drinking more than she would have liked, fending off advances from one of the Goldman brothers—she still couldn't tell them apart—and winding up with the world's worst hangover. She'd wanted to get more information from Jehan about her mother's collecting habits and her use of appraisers. But Jehan and Muhammad had decided to let the conflict in Geneva make them stronger, and they spent much of the time in a guest room with the door locked. Layla had then, fueled by wine, emailed the dubious Dr. Hassan el-Sayed through his website contact form.

Hello! My name is Layla Nawar, and I recently purchased a bronze cat statuette from the Rothkopf Galleries. I need it appraised for insurance purposes and would like to schedule a time to bring it in. Please let me know your availability.

Getting any information from Hiro about his dad had also proved impossible. Once his gig in Milan started, he left his guests to take over the villa, then sent in a cleaning crew to cover up any signs of the party.

Bennett had a full schedule, with back-to-back clients to take advantage of Layla's time. None of them were from the evidence wall, and the purchases were fairly pedestrian. Bennett sold a few decorative ivory boxes, a hair comb, a vase, and a bronze statuette. In each case, the provenance appeared watertight.

As she listened to Bennett tell his clients the stories behind the relics, she thought about her own spotty provenance, the holes in her own story that she was always discovering. Her business wasn't all that different. She had to sell people on her authenticity. She looked good on paper, until you looked too closely.

James was mostly locked up in his studio, as before. "I'm way behind schedule," he apologized. "There was a problem with the adhesive batch, and I had to start again." Still, he found ways to pop into the gallery on his short breaks.

Near the end of her shift, she went into the supply closet to use the photocopier. Bennett needed some receipts copied, and Layla was also copying provenance documents, which she planned to hand over to Pierce. She heard the door open behind her and moved quickly to block the documents in the out tray.

But it was just James. He shut the door and embraced her. "I think I heard you speaking four different languages out there today," he said.

"Nerdy?"

"God no. *Sexy.*"

"Really?" She laughed.

They kissed while the copier behind her churned out duplicitous documents, page after page.

• • •

BACK IN HER APARTMENT, her brain tired from all the translating she'd done, Layla allowed herself the simple luxury of a take-out meal and a generous glass of white wine. She sat on the divan, sipped her wine, and watched the feluccas with their crisp white sails scudding down the Nile. Then she shifted her gaze and saw the almost accusatory glare of the bronze cat Bennett had sold her.

She'd placed it in the center of a small floating shelf near the window. Or, at least, she was pretty sure that was where she'd put it. Now it was toward the end of the shelf and facing a different direction.

She set the wine down and rose to look more closely at the statuette. If there were cleaning people coming to the apartment, she could see how the cat might have been moved for dusting and not replaced exactly where it was. But Pierce hadn't ordered a cleaning service for her; that was too risky.

A chill ran through her. Had someone been in the apartment? What else was awry?

She ran to her bedroom and opened the bottom nightstand drawer. Breathing fast, she pulled out a box with an image of a sleep mask on it. It felt reassuringly heavy. Inside, beneath the lavender eye bag, the Glock 22 gleamed in the light. She breathed a long sigh of relief and replaced it.

Still, something unsettled her as she leaned against the nightstand and looked around the room. The scent in the air—was it the sandalwood room spray she'd bought? Or someone else's cologne? Now she couldn't be sure. She moved from room to room, looking for more objects out of place, footprints in the plush carpet, stray hairs in the bathroom. She found nothing. Paranoid, she decided. This undercover gig was getting to her.

Frowning, Layla moved the bronze cat back to the center of the shelf. Pierce had grudgingly doled out cash for the purchase before Layla left for Lake Como. "Next time, ask me before you splurge. This puts me in an awkward position with Monaghan." Layla had felt like a kid who'd run through her allowance. Pierce must have recognized that, because she'd added, in a kinder voice, "I do admire your balls in trying to buy something illicit from Bennett. Just hold off for now. We don't want to freak him out."

At least Pierce had been pleased with the outcome of the Lake Como trip, Layla reflected, stepping backward to check her new positioning of the cat. The two vases Tanaka had bought from Bennett were in the clear, but some of the items he'd bought from Farwadi had suspicious dates, so Pierce was digging deeper.

Layla suddenly remembered the article she'd found in Tanaka's nightstand and photographed on her phone. "The Amulet Men of Faiyum." In the daze of the party that had followed her snooping around, she'd almost forgotten about it. As the sun slowly set over the Nile, she read Dr. Katherine Danforth's article about a collection of amulets in a Faiyum museum, which were believed to have magical powers. It was interesting, but the pictures were small or cut off in the photos she'd taken so quickly, and part of the article text was blurred.

Or maybe it was the wine; she was on to her second generous glass.

She glanced up at the cat on the shelf. She could practically hear the hiss and yowl of the feral cats in her old neighborhood. She got up and moved the statuette to a closet shelf, down by the floor. She went back out to the living room couch and turned on the TV. She flipped through channels, filling the room with the conversations of strangers—Egyptian period dramas, game shows, *Seinfeld* reruns translated into Arabic—until she fell asleep.

ALL THE INGREDIENTS WERE there for a romantic lunch: a cozy sidewalk café table on the sun-splashed south side of Tahrir Square. Egyptian pop music pulsing from a speaker. Platters of rice and kebabs. Fizzy lemon drinks. James sitting opposite her on a rare hour-long lunch break.

The only thing marring the scene was James's mood, which was unusually downcast. Trying to lift his spirits, Layla commented on the antics of the cute child approaching them now with a tray of trinkets for sale.

"No, don't buy anything," said James, as she reached for her wallet. He made a shooing motion with his hand, which triggered a flare of rage in Layla. The child turned to go, but Layla beckoned her back and looked at the tray of wares.

"Scarab amulets are all the rage," she said, holding her new purchase out to James. "Haven't you heard?"

"You do know it's entirely fake."

"Of course. It's plastic. But in a dark nightclub, no one would be the wiser, right?" She slipped it around her neck.

"Let me see." James inspected it, turning it over and over in his practiced hand. "Not plastic. This one's a notch better. For a fake, you got a good deal."

"Not plastic?"

"It's bone." He tapped it. "Old bone. They feed this to turkeys. The gastric juices create an aging effect that can look pretty realistic."

James released the amulet and stirred the ice in his drink, staring into space.

"What's on your mind?" Layla asked. "Seems like it's been such a good week for business. Your dad seems happy. Why aren't you?"

James sighed. "Yeah, we had a lot of foot traffic and sales this week, but it doesn't cover what my dad needs right now to keep certain people happy."

Layla put a hand over his. She was genuinely worried about James. She'd never seen him look so distraught.

Get out while you're ahead. James's mis-sent text to his dad floated back to her. In what circumstances should a person quit something while they're ahead?

She shivered as the pieces came together in her mind.

Gambling. She thought of the CairoZoom image of Bennett at the casino. Bennett wasn't just looking for a quick win to solve a financial issue. He had a problem. She sat up straighter. "Your dad gambles, doesn't he."

James looked startled. "What? No."

"James, I saw his picture on CairoZoom." She pulled out her phone and showed him.

James blew out a long breath. "Great. Now the whole world knows."

"I don't think so," said Layla. "The picture's not focused on him, and people who read this don't care. But I do. What's up with your dad?"

James sighed. "His buying trips are mostly gambling trips. While you were in Geneva, he was in Monte Carlo. Pissing away money. And while you were in Lake Como? He was at the Omar Khayyam Casino. That place is open twenty-four hours, and I don't think he slept. Now he's off to the new casino in Dubai. And that's why I couldn't text you much while you were away on your trips," he added. "I was trying to run things here and also talk some sense into him."

"So that's what the text was about? The one you accidentally sent me?"

"Yeah. He said he was on a winning streak. I wanted him out before he lost it all."

"Did it work?"

The look on his face said it all.

"He's losing money faster than he can make it. It's funny, I repair things all day, but this is one thing I can't seem to fix." James slouched in his chair, one jeans-clad leg crossed over the other, his foot twitching. "Absolutely no one can know about this," he added. "Seriously. It would break him."

"No one will know," Layla promised.

James squeezed her hand. "If I can't always respond to texts or calls right away, now you'll know why," he said. "I know people say I'm this crazy workaholic—and I *do* work hard—but a lot of my work is covering for my dad. It's like a secret life."

"I get it." Layla squeezed his hand back and looked deep into his eyes. "I really do get it."

. . .

WHEN LAYLA LET HERSELF into the safe house, she found Pierce finishing up with a phone call in one of the safe house bedrooms—with Monaghan, Layla guessed, judging by the agitated quality in Pierce's voice. "That's fair market value," Pierce was insisting. "Not only that, the dealer *dropped* the price."

Layla cringed, hoping this wasn't about the bronze cat, yet certain it was.

Pierce poked her head around the bedroom door and signaled to Layla to have a seat in the living room. Then she shut the bedroom door and continued talking, though her words were now muffled.

Layla removed her hijab and went to the kitchen, looking for a cold beverage. Funny how the safe house was beginning to feel like her second home, even though it lacked all the luxuries of her Garden City penthouse. Especially today. All that was in the fridge was a bottle of diet soda and a packet of dried figs. She helped herself to some water in a dusty glass. As she drank the water, she looked out at the neighborhood of modest brick apartments encrusted with satellite dishes, and wondered if Pierce was too busy with her end of the investigation to go out and get groceries.

After using the bathroom, she wiped her hands on a towel with a hedgehog design on the border. She smiled. She'd also glimpsed a hedgehog coffee mug in the kitchen, and hedgehog socks outside the bedroom door. No doubt Pierce, if confronted, would hotly deny having any type of hedgehog collection. But the hedgehogs were hints of her inner life. Tempting as it was, Layla decided not to tease her.

The hedgehog hand towel was clean, but the rest of the bathroom was definitely overdue for a cleaning. Housekeeping services didn't come to a safe house, and Pierce's cleaning abilities seemed to be about on par with Layla's cooking. Layla opened the drawers beneath the sink, wondering if Pierce even had any cleaning products. She could leave out some bleach as a hint. All she found were four cardboard boxes from Amazon stored beneath the sink; the open one contained only cotton balls. Hearing Pierce exit the bedroom, she hurried to the living room to join her.

Still fired up from that phone call, Pierce was in full business mode, a clipboard and pen in hand, a focused expression on her face as she stood before the whiteboards. "I'll go first today. Okay. So. This Dr. el-Sayed you found in Noor Ghaffar's files? We've looked into him. You were right. A fraud."

Layla sat on the couch. "I knew it!"

"Yup. In fact, he appraised three of the fifteen relics you found at the Tanaka villa, only Farwadi never passed those documents on to Tanaka. He thought better of it."

"Farwadi knows Dr. el-Sayed?"

Pierce nodded. "According to Farwadi, this el-Sayed is—or was—a legitimate scholar, but he's a sell-out. His opinion can be bought. Apparently so many dealers have purchased it lately, he's gone dark for a while. I don't expect you'll get any response to your email query. But we should keep an eye out for his name and follow up on what Noor had him appraise." She scribbled something on a sticky note and slapped it onto Noor's picture on the whiteboard. Then she pointed at various photos, as if deep in thought, and stopped when her pen hit Bennett's. "What's new at the Rothkopf Gallery?"

Layla shared what she had learned about Bennett's gambling habit. Her words faltered when she saw Pierce was not taking notes.

"And this is useful information because . . . ?"

Layla threw up her hands in exasperation. "Isn't it obvious?" she said. "Depending on who he owes money to or what thugs he might have pissed off in the casino circuit, we have a motive for him to get involved in the illegal antiquities trade. I think he's in even deeper than we first thought."

Pierce tipped her head to one side, studying Layla. "Yes," she said. "Sure, a gambling habit might make him more vulnerable to us. But we aren't looking for Bennett Rothkopf's *motive*. We're looking for *middlemen* and *suppliers* so we can follow the money trail back to the Muharib."

Layla hadn't expected to be shot down so fast. "You think finding all this out was a waste of time?"

"I do." Pierce shrugged. "It's interesting trivia, but it's irrelevant. How often does he move his inventory among his various galleries? Who brings him new acquisitions? Have you witnessed any?"

Layla shook her head. "Not yet. But don't you think if we understand how badly he's in debt, or who he might owe money to, or who he has to keep happy, we can find some of his associates?"

Pierce waved Layla's comment aside. "What are the shipping companies Bennett uses to transport his goods to his clients?"

Layla looked down at her lap, embarrassed that she had no answers. So far she'd logged twenty hours in the gallery, hanging on Bennett's every word as he described the ins and outs of the business, but she now realized he'd talked in very abstract terms. He held his cards close to his chest, not revealing any names or companies, the very information she'd needed. And when she did work there, despite her best intentions of breaking free to snoop around, he'd kept her on a tight rein. Mackey was always present, too, always just around the corner, restricting any opportunities to snoop in the offices.

"If you're going to stay on at the Rothkopf Gallery, you've got to do more. Get access to the computer system. Work the IT guy you mentioned. Look for shipping labels and manifests. And look for loose papers. Off-book dealers often prefer old accounting methods. Easier to destroy."

Layla nodded. "I'm on it."

"Sounds like James is really opening up with you, by the way," said Pierce, tilting her head in the other direction. "That's nice. What do we know about him, anyway? Other than he's covering for Dad's little habit?"

Layla tried to brush aside the memory of James's lips on hers. "He does restoration work. He's in his studio a lot. He's not involved in the buying and selling."

"Keep the gentle pressure on him. He may reveal more about his dad in good time," Pierce advised. The harshness was gone from her voice now.

"I'll do that," Layla promised, though inwardly she squirmed. It was one thing to decide on her own, in the moment, to work on James for information. It felt entirely different to do so at Pierce's command.

A slight smile further softened the hard lines of Pierce's angular face. "By the way. I noticed he's pretty easy on the eyes. Try not to get distracted, will you?"

Layla scoffed, as if the very idea was ridiculous.

LAYLA TOOK THE STEPS to the Rothkopf Gallery slowly, rehearsing her plan.

She was arriving deliberately early. Bennett was at the consulate to see about his visa for Dubai. James was at the Ministry of Antiquities to get travel documents. Hamadi, the IT guy, was taking a rare day off to take his sick mother to the hospital. That left only one person standing in between her and Bennett's office. Mackey. She took a deep breath and rang the buzzer. There was no room for error if she was going to pull this off.

Mackey opened the gallery door and looked at her in surprise. Then he narrowed his eyes and scrutinized her closely. He loomed over her, his body seeming to take up the entire doorframe.

"Morning, Mackey!" she said in the most cheerful voice she could muster.

"We are not yet open. There is no client expected until ten," he said.

"Oh, I know. But Mr. Rothkopf said he got the proofs of the new multilingual brochure back from the printer," said Layla, grateful for this last-minute development James had mentioned when they'd talked on the phone last night. "I thought I'd come in a little early and review them."

Mackey hesitated.

"I know the printer wanted final approval today," she said. "Otherwise we'll miss this week's print run. It'd be great to get the brochures done so we could have them on hand for the fundraiser."

Mackey looked at her questioningly.

"You know, the Rothkopf Foundation event? Mr. Rothkopf and James told me about the Girls' Education Initiative. Even though it's for a cause and not the gallery, it can't hurt to have the brochures on hand."

"Come in, then." Mackey grudgingly let her enter. "I will get the proofs from his office."

"Oh, no worries. If they're on his desk, I'll just work there, since he's out." Layla moved toward the door that led to the corridor of offices.

"Forgive me," said Mackey, pushing past her. "It is better, I think, if you work in your own office." He strode down the hall and entered Bennett's office, returning a couple of seconds later with a file containing the printer proofs. He thrust them at her.

Layla staggered backward from the unexpected force of the file handoff. "Thanks," she said, smiling through clenched teeth. "I'll get right to it."

She went into her tiny office and stared at the proof pages, not reading a word. James's appointment wasn't long, and the Ministry of Antiquities was mere blocks away. She had less than an hour to get Mackey out and to leave herself ample time to search Bennett's office. Time for plan B. She allowed five minutes to pass, then returned to the main gallery and approached Mackey, who was polishing a glass display case with surprising gentleness.

"Hey, Mackey," said Layla, trying to sound concerned. "I just looked out the window and saw a couple of guys outside near the delivery door. It kind of looked like they were inspecting the lock."

Mackey looked out the back window. "I see no one."

"Maybe they're still in the area." She wrung her hands. "I'm worried they're casing the place." She went on to describe the two young guys in soccer jerseys who had followed her before.

"Our security camera by the back door should show them," said Mackey.

"Please, can't you look? I'm scared they might come back. What if they're armed?"

This idea seemed to rouse Mackey. He unlocked a desk drawer, took out a handgun, and left the gallery, his stride brisk and efficient.

Layla waited until his heavy footsteps receded down the stairs and she heard the main door to the building slam shut. Then she dashed down the hall to Bennett's office. The wild goose chase she'd just sent Mackey on wouldn't last long. She went to the computer.

A quick glance at the program files confirmed her suspicion that Bennett used state-of-the-art inventory management software, all of it password protected. She opened the desk drawers, one after another. She found heartburn medication, aspirin, sesame seed snacks, rubber stress balls, and a gag gift of a Zen garden in a box. Clues all pointing to acid reflux and stress, but not shady dealings. No paperwork was filed in the desk; he was probably smarter than that.

She turned her attention to a bookshelf behind the desk. It was lined with books on antiquities and catalogs for auction houses around the world, stacked in no particular order, sticky notes marking pages. She saw some blank letterhead and envelopes with the company name Global Relics, LLC, and an invitation to an upcoming event at the Egyptian Museum.

Behind one row of books, though, a corner of a page stuck out, as if it had slipped behind the books—or been hidden behind them. Layla pulled out the paper: a handwritten note on cream heavy laid paper, with a familiar blue monogram swirled across the top. She'd seen that stationary in Noor Ghaffar's office.

Dear Bennett,

Thank you for procuring the beautiful jade scarab amulet necklace. It made the perfect present for Jehan's birthday. I know it was no small feat, on such short notice, and as ever, I am grateful for the extra care you have shown me in locating such unique pieces. If ever I can return the favour, do let me know, I am at your service.

Very truly yours, Noor Ghaffar.

Each sentence of the letter came as a jolt.

Rothkopf had procured the amulet necklace on short notice. He had found Noor other "unique pieces," which was likely a euphemism for "illegal."

Calm down, Layla told herself, trying to steady her trembling hands. She closed her eyes for a moment and pictured the exquisite jade scarab necklace Jehan had worn at the Coriander Gallery party and again in Geneva. Then she photographed Noor's letter with her FBI phone and carefully replaced it.

She ran her hand behind all the books, fishing for more papers, finding nothing . . . until she reached the lowest shelf and found a small spiral-bound notebook. The first pages of the book were still blank. Then there was a section of ten pages filled out in pencil. Names and figures in columns. Layla's heart pounded with excitement as she flipped through the pages and read the entries.

Miriam Goldman. Judean miniature oil lamps. $450.00 ($45,000)
Marco de la Cruz. Valdivian stone abstract idols. $400.00 ($4,000)
Kiyoshi Tanaka. Roman mosaic: Aphrodite. $375.00 ($37,500)
Noor Ghaffar: Jade scarab amulet. $250.00 ($25,000)

The names went on and on. Many were known to her from Pierce's wall, or they were people she'd met through Farwadi. Following each name were items and double prices. She thought about the articles Pierce had given her, and the various ways shady dealers cooked their books. Bennett could be recording "official" prices for his records versus the actual amount of money that changed hands. If collectors appeared to have bought items of relatively low value, they would be less likely to face any questioning. *Is that an $18,000 Aramaean incantation bowl? Why no, it's a tchotchke. See? I paid only $400.00.*

After ten pages, the notes ended. The rest of the notebook was empty. Deliberately shutting off her emotions, as efficiently as a machine, Layla took out her work phone and took a picture of every page.

As she was finishing, she heard the main door to the gallery open and shut. Heavy footsteps thudded on the gallery floor, then down the corridor. Mackey was back, sooner than she had expected. And she was still in Bennett's office. There was no way to explain what she was doing there.

It was Geneva all over again. No. Geneva had prepared her for this. She'd survived that close call, and she could do better. She grabbed her phone from her tote bag and frantically texted Pierce. *CALL FRONT DESK ROTHKOPF GALLERY.* She needed a distraction, something to halt Mackey's inexorable progress toward Bennett's office.

"Layla?" she heard Mackey call, as he tapped on her own office door a few doors down. "Are you here?"

URGENT! NEED DISTRACTION!! CALL ROTHKOPF GALLERY NOW!!

The phone did not ring. Pierce didn't respond. "Shit, Pierce. Come on! Look at your texts!" Layla muttered. Even if Pierce was working at her cover job at the embassy, there was no excuse for ignoring this text.

"Layla?" Mackey was now checking James's studio and calling for her there. He was one door away from Bennett's office.

Swearing under her breath, Layla clutched her bag and the useless cell phone to her chest, rotating. She looked for a window to leap out, a fire escape, anything.

The gallery door opened again, the soft electronic buzz signaling a newcomer.

"Hello? Is anyone here?" a deep male voice called out. Layla detected a German accent.

Whoever it was, Layla wanted to run out there and wrap her arms around him for his incredible timing. Already she could hear

Mackey's footsteps as he hurried down the corridor, toward the main gallery.

She counted to three, then silently eased open the door to Bennett's office and turned to close it behind her. As she looked up, one hand still on the doorknob, she saw Mackey at the opposite end of the hall.

Their eyes locked.

STOLEN TREASURES

· DIANA RENN ·

Mackey's gaze traveled to Layla's tote bag, which she instinctively clutched to her body. It contained all three of her phones. On one phone were the incriminating photos of Bennett's double-accounting ledger and the thank-you note from Noor. Unlike her close call in Geneva, though, Layla had no time to hit the delete button. If Mackey demanded to see the contents of her bag—which as a security official he had every right to do—she'd have to comply. Game over.

But she wasn't Layla el-Deeb. She was Layla Nawar. And if she'd learned one thing about the super-rich, it was the profound sense of entitlement they conveyed. They walked like they owned every inch of the land, like they owned the very air. Her mind flashed to the elegant Turkish couple for whom she'd first translated at the gallery, and the respect they had commanded the moment they came through the door. She thought of Noor Ghaffar. Layla squared her shoulders, lifted her chin, affixed a serene smile to her face, and glided down the corridor toward Mackey.

Mackey rushed forward to meet her halfway. "Why were you in there?" he demanded—though in a harsh whisper so the man in the gallery would not hear.

"One of the proof pages was missing," Layla whispered back. When the lie came out automatically, a current of pleasure ran through her. She always said if you could think and dream in a language, you were truly fluent. Now, along similar lines, she knew if she could lie without planning, she could *be* Layla Nawar, not just act like her. "I thought it might have been left in there," she went on, when Mackey's eyes narrowed at her. "It wasn't. I'll call the printer. Anyway, sounds like we have a customer out in the gallery! Shall we go see who it is?" She strode past him down the corridor, using her smile to deflect the heat of his glare.

She reached the doorway to the gallery before Mackey caught up with her. He blocked her and gripped her arm. "No," he said in a low voice. "Your translation is not needed for this customer. You may return to your office."

"Really? Why? I thought I detected an accent." Layla stood on her toes to try to see over Mackey's shoulder and into the gallery. She was just able to glimpse a stocky man with a mustache and slicked-back hair, looking at a display case, tapping his foot impatiently. He wore a white linen suit and a dark expression. An angry red scar traversed his neck. He looked like a gangster right out of central casting, so much so that it was almost comical. Until she saw the holster of a pistol sticking out of his trouser pocket. Nothing funny about that. Layla was now alone in a building with two men packing heat. She ached for the Glock in her nightstand.

"Go. Go now," Mackey said, his jaw jutting toward her office door. "You are only in the way here."

"All right, all right." Layla slunk into her office, the feeling of owning the room now gone. But she left the door ajar as Mackey went out to the gallery to greet the customer. She tried to hear what the two men were talking about, but they were speaking too softly, or maybe her heart was pounding too loudly. Was this a buyer or a seller? He didn't look Egyptian, and his accent was German, but no matter; relic runners came in all stripes.

She crept down the hallway again and flattened herself against the wall just before the gallery door. Catching sight of her shadow on the opposite wall, potentially visible to the men in the gallery, she inched backward about two feet until it was gone. Now she couldn't see the men at all, but she caught the end of their conversation in English.

"Then it will be next Friday," said the man in the white suit. "Tell Mr. Rothkopf that is the very latest I can extend. You tell him. I expect full payment. No partial installments. No trinkets or curios this time. Cash only."

"Mr. Rothkopf is aware of your terms. We will meet with you a week from Friday. He will have the full payment ready," said Mackey.

Because he's going to Dubai to gamble? Because he's selling some more illegal items? Layla's mind reeled with possibilities. One thing she was sure of now was that the man in the suit was not peddling relics. He had the air of someone who had come to collect. Perhaps a loan shark. Whoever he was, Bennett was clearly up to his eyeballs in money problems.

The gallery door slammed shut, and Layla ran back to her office. She quickly emailed Pierce all the photos she'd taken in Bennett's office and deleted them from her phone. Remembering the lie she'd told Mackey about looking for a missing page, she took the last page from the brochure proofs, ripped it into little pieces, ran to the bathroom across the hall, and flushed them down the toilet.

Back at her desk, resisting the urge to text Pierce every invective she could think of—in every language she knew—she turned the phone over and tried to focus on the multilingual proofreading task she'd claimed to be working on. Her ears were alert for Mackey's footsteps, but the gallery was strangely quiet. She texted James. *Missing you. Hurry back!* Any second, Mackey could burst through her door to interrogate her.

When the door to the gallery opened again, though, it was not James, but Bennett, back from his visa errand at the embassy of the United Arab Emirates. She stood up and cracked her office door open again to listen. Bennett and Mackey conferred in low voices, too low to hear specific words. No doubt they were discussing the visitor Bennett had narrowly missed. But they could also be discussing another narrow miss: her unauthorized visit to Bennett's office.

She needed to win points. She raced through the rest of the proofreading, catching fifteen linguistic errors and finishing her pass through the document—minus the now-missing page—before Bennett knocked on her office door.

"May I have a word with you? In my office?"

"Of course." Dry-mouthed, she got up and followed him down the hall.

Closing the door behind them, Bennett sat down behind his desk. He gestured for her to have a seat opposite him. His face looked more lined than usual.

Layla handed him the stack of edited proof pages with a confident smile, but he took them wordlessly and set them aside. She put her hand to her throat. "I hope I'm not in some kind of trouble." Her gaze swept around the room. Had she put everything back exactly where she'd found it? The corner of Noor's thank-you letter looked just a bit askew in the bookshelf, poking out at the wrong angle—or was she imagining that?

"Trouble?" Bennett frowned. "Why would you be in trouble?"

"I feel a little like I'm in the principal's office," she said with a strangled laugh. "And you look a bit serious. Everything okay?"

He smiled apologetically. "Yes, I'm sorry. I don't mean to concern you. I have a lot on my mind, with my travel plans. I'm leaving tonight for Dubai. I have quite a few loose ends to tie up first. You know how it goes."

"I get it," Layla sympathized, relieved that he wasn't calling her out—yet—on having gone into his office alone. Now that she didn't seem to be in trouble, she wished she could find some way to ask who the suspicious "customer" was.

"There is something I would like to ask you about." Bennett paused and regarded her carefully, drumming his fingertips on the desk. "James and I are going back to New York next week."

Her heart sped up. "Permanently?" She was surprised at the force of this news, how the thought of James suddenly leaving—and even Bennett suddenly leaving—almost knocked the wind out of her.

"No, no," he corrected. "Just for a couple of days. I don't like to be away from the spring festivals here for too long. But there's an important auction I need to attend in Manhattan. And I thought you might like to come along. You'd learn a lot."

"Really?" New York. *With the Rothkopfs.* She still couldn't quite catch her breath. This development was even more unexpected. She was getting used to wrangling invitations to places, but here was an opportunity handed right to her.

"I'm eyeing a collection of Egyptian artifacts that Columbia University is de-acquisitioning." Bennett slid a catalog across the desk toward her and opened it to where a neon pink sticky note marked a page containing photos of sculpted clay figures. "If I can acquire them, I hope to sell them to some of my Egyptian clients. It's my way of helping to repatriate objects. Of bringing them home."

"That's wonderful," said Layla. Conflicting feelings surged in her, like waves in a riptide. He wanted to repatriate relics. Could such an ethical-sounding dealer be involved so deeply in the illegitimate side of this business?

The creases around Bennett's eyes deepened, and their twinkle returned. "Now, I know it's not as exciting as partying in Lake Como, but if you come, I think you'll get a different perspective on the business. It will be a good education for you."

"I'd love to come!" Layla exclaimed. "Thank you." She smiled as she pictured sharing New York with James—a walk in Central Park, or a stroll through the Strand basement, or dinner at her favorite Indian restaurant in the East Village. Of course, she'd have to pretend she didn't know the city like the back of her hand. But after what she'd just pulled off with Mackey, pretending no longer scared her that much.

"I see a lot of potential in you," Bennett continued in a serious tone. "You might consider crossing over to the other side."

Layla hesitated before responding. "Um . . . the other side . . . of what?" Maybe he was playing with her, a cat batting a mouse around.

"From collecting to dealing."

"Ah. Right."

"I know someone in your position might not need to earn a living, as such, but I think you'd find it stimulating work, even part-time. Who knows. Maybe I can retire and leave my business in good hands." He winked.

Layla wasn't sure if he was joking or not. "What about James?" she asked. "He seems like the logical person to take over someday."

"James is very talented. Don't get me wrong," said Bennett. "But his talents are different. He's got artistic skills like you wouldn't believe. He brings lost objects back to life. He has patience, and a steady hand. But he doesn't have a head for business. And he doesn't have something else I see in you."

"What's that?"

"Grit." Bennett thumped the table. "The number one quality you need to succeed in any business. I see it in you because I have it, too. And I bet I know how you got it." He leaned closer with an almost conspiratorial look. "You didn't grow up wealthy, did you."

Layla's breath caught in her throat. But she returned his gaze, projecting confidence. *Own the room.* "That's quite an assumption. What makes you say that?"

"I hope I didn't cause offense. I just recognize something in you, something—"

"Did *you* grow up without wealth, Bennett?" *Turn the tables. Focus on him.*

He smiled wryly. "Me? I grew up with next to nothing, in a two-bedroom walk-up on the Lower East Side."

"Wow. Sounds rough." Inwardly, Layla bristled. Compared to a one-bedroom walk-up on the fourth floor for five people, with a river of raw sewage outside her window, this was hardly a violin-worthy story. But maybe "rough life" was a relative term, and however Bennett had entered the world, it was far from where he sat now. They'd both wanted something more and pursued a better life.

"I was the youngest of five," he elaborated. "Which meant I had the last of everything. No new gifts for birthdays or holidays. And no extras. If I wanted a bike, I had to get a paper route and earn the money for it. If I wanted a college education, I had to work afternoons at my uncle's shop, and nights at a parking garage."

"What kind of shop did your uncle have?"

"An antiques shop. He was a dealer. Nothing too fancy, mostly dead people's belongings, but he started to make certain connections, and his inventory improved."

Layla picked up a Nefertiti paperweight on the edge of his desk and turned it around in her hands, wondering how he'd come by such a tacky object. *Treasures of Egypt*, a label stuck to the bottom insisted. "So why didn't you stay in his business?" Layla asked. "Why the switch from antiques to antiquities?"

"I know classics doesn't exactly seem like the most direct path to riches. But I knew a thing or two about business. I'd logged hundreds of hours in the shop. I knew how to sell old things and make them seem alive. Even *necessary*. I could tell someone why they needed a God-awful lamp with a fringed shade, and they'd go home with it. I lost some sales, but I recovered and improved. That's grit. Persevering when the world says, 'Why bother?'"

Layla smiled. That she could relate to.

Encouraged by his new captive audience, Bennett continued. "My uncle started going to estate sales, and then auctions for higher-end furniture and decorative goods. He took me along. I started to cross paths with buyers who were into antique coins. From there, I got on the trail of people who loved even older relics. I came to love those relics, too. Now, *they* have grit. Think of it. How can a piece of pottery stand up to the centuries? Or a page from a manu-script? Civilizations rise and fall, but these things endure."

"But don't you think James has a bit of grit?" Layla thought of how James worked double-duty, covering up for his dad.

Bennett shrugged. "James grew up with everything I never had. I wanted to give him that. But he doesn't have that killer instinct. You won't find anyone more loyal than James. That's an outstanding quality. But it's not enough to ensure that the Rothkopf legacy will live on. If you know what I mean."

"I understand." Layla leaned back in the leather chair and basked in that warm, heat-lamp feeling that positive attention from Bennett always seemed to create. Like James, he seemed to notice something deeper, something essential about her. Around both father and son, she felt a sense of acceptance, a feeling so powerful she hadn't known how much she craved it until now.

JAMES CAME BACK TO the gallery later than expected, just as Layla was leaving her shift for the day. To make it up to her, he sugge-sted a walk to get some tamarind juice from a vendor nearby.

"So. Guess who's hijacking your New York trip?" Layla said, as they made their way down the stairwell from the gallery.

James paused mid-step. "What New York trip?"

Layla turned around and stared at him. "Your dad said you guys are going to New York next week. For an auction?"

"Ah." James bit his lip.

"He asked me to come along so I can learn how auctions work. I'll pay my own way." She frowned. "God. Don't look so excited," she added, as a worried expression flickered across James's face.

"No, I'm excited!" he said, pulling her close "It's just a surprise. My dad tends to decide on these things last minute." He sighed. "I try to roll with it."

Layla thought of the scarred man in the suit. Was this sudden New York trip a backup plan if Bennett couldn't pay off his debt in time? A way to skip town? She needed to know how dangerous that guy was before she got on a plane with Bennett. Since James already knew his dad's gambling was a major problem, maybe he knew a little about the mysterious man.

She lowered her voice, then glanced up and down the stairs to make sure they were alone. "James. I have to tell you something. A man came to see your dad this morning. He had a German accent and a scar on his neck. I wasn't in the gallery, but I heard him say something to Mackey about getting paid on Friday and accepting only cash. I'm worried."

James rubbed his forehead. "Yeah. He's come around before. It's okay. My dad will either win back what he needs in Dubai or sell some stuff in New York. We've been down this road a couple of times before. The guy's mostly a lot of bluff and swagger."

"He looked like some kind of thug."

"My dad doesn't always borrow from banks," said James grimly. "Let's just leave it at that."

As they walked out into the street, the air was no cooler than the steamy stairwell. Layla wondered about the debt collector. She noticed the tension still in James's face, and his hunched shoulders. James knew about his dad's gambling and debts. But did he know about the probable involvement in illegal antiquities dealing? Maybe it was wishful thinking, but she suspected he had no clue about that. James had just spent the entire morning getting legitimate travel authorization for restored artifacts, making extra sure his shipments followed Egyptian law.

Layla felt a text buzz in on a phone in her tote bag. She glanced at it. Pierce.

Just got messages. Everything OK? Still need me to call front desk?

She started to type back, then stopped herself. Pierce could see what it felt like to get no response. Let her call the damned front desk number at the gallery if she wanted to. Let her wonder.

She dropped the phone back in the bag.

As they crossed the street, Layla noticed Mackey exit the gallery building and follow them. "Let's take the long way around," she said, steering James in the opposite direction, as a test.

Mackey, too, did an about-face and continued to follow them. By now he probably suspected that she'd made up the story about the possible burglars to get him out of the gallery, so that she could get into Bennett's office. All he had to do was review security tapes from the exterior cameras to know that no one had been skulking around the back door.

"What is with your creepy security guard?" Layla asked, glancing back, hoping James might send Mackey on his way.

James gave her a funny look. "Mackey? Why do you say he's creepy?"

"He's following us. Look."

"He's at a newsstand. Buying a paper and a pack of cigarettes. He always does at this time of day." He waved at Mackey, and Mackey waved back. "See?" said James.

Layla shook her head. "I don't know. I don't think he likes me, for some reason."

"Yeah, okay, he's not the smiliest guy," said James. "He hasn't had it easy. But he's all right."

They reached the tamarind juice vendor, and James ordered two juices, in halting Arabic, which Layla didn't bother to correct. She also didn't bother to answer the ringing phone in her tote bag, since it could only be Pierce.

"You want to get that?" James asked, looking at her bag.

"No," said Layla. "It's no one. Anyway, tell me more about Mackey."

"He's worked for my dad forever," James answered, while their juice was poured. "And now that you know he sometimes borrows money outside the traditional banking system, you can see how useful it is to have Mackey around."

"I guess so." Layla considered this.

"In fact," James went on, "given the unexpected visitor you saw this morning, that's probably why Mackey's hanging out here right now. Keeping an eye open."

They took their drinks and sipped them as they walked back toward the gallery, the security guard still following from across the street. "Your dad and Mackey just seem like the unlikeliest pair," she said. "But they're joined at the hip."

"Yeah, they're almost like brothers," James agreed.

"So why's he so loyal to your dad?" Layla asked between sips of her juice. "Did he give him a kidney or something?"

James laughed. "Just about. My parents both helped Mackey's family when we were living in South Africa in the nineties."

"How so?"

"I was just a little kid when we were living there, so I don't remember much," James admitted. "But Dad met Mom in college in the States. My mom was from South Africa, and they went to live there after they graduated. Dad got a Fulbright and in their spare time they went to rallies and political events to protest apartheid. My parents knew Mackey and his dad from their activist group and got to be friends. Then one night, Mackey's parents got arrested at a rally that turned violent. My mom had some government connections and lobbied hard to get them out, but Mackey's dad was murdered in prison."

"My God," said Layla, glancing at Mackey across the street.

"She did get Mackey's mom out. She died a few years later. Cancer. But he never forgot that my parents helped his parents. He joined the military for a while, and then he and my dad reconnected a few years back, when my dad started doing a lot of international travel. That's when Mackey came to work for him."

Layla nodded, taking this all in. "That's quite a story," she said. "I feel for him. I just wish he weren't so suspicious of me. I mean, who does he think I am?"

"I promise you, it's not personal," said James. "He's just on the lookout for gold diggers and con artists. Galleries can attract those types. And he's probably wondering what to make of you, since you're not an official employee. It's annoying. I get that. But think of it as a weird vetting process. It won't go on forever."

"And your dad *pays* him to do all this?"

"My dad pays him to provide security," said James, as Mackey lit up a cigarette and continued to watch them from across the street. "Mackey interprets that however he likes."

• • •

LAYLA BURST INTO THE safe house and slammed the door behind her.

Pierce was sitting at a computer, wearing headphones as she typed something. She immediately removed her headphones and stood up when she saw Layla. "There you are! I've been trying to reach you!"

"A bit late." Layla threw her tote bag on the kitchen table. "Where. The fuck. Were you? I sent you three urgent texts this morning. Thanks for having my back."

Lines appeared in Pierce's forehead. "Layla, I'm so sorry, I—"

"No. Listen to me. I sent Mackey out of the gallery to chase fictitious burglars. He came back early. I needed you to call the front desk phone and distract him to buy me some time to get out of Bennett's office. But you didn't reply. Crickets." She took a glass out of a cupboard, slammed the cupboard door, and filled the glass with bottled water from the fridge. She let the fridge door slam, too, so hard a hedgehog magnet fell off.

"He just about caught me in Bennett's office. I was saved at the last possible second by some Euro-gangster who showed up to collect money from Bennett."

"Thank God," Pierce breathed.

"Not really. The guy had a gun on him. Mackey had a gun, too, of course. It could have turned into a shootout at the O.K. Corral, and I, of course, carry no firearm, per regulations of the joint task force." She flung herself into a chair and scowled at Pierce.

Pierce looked genuinely remorseful. Her bony shoulders slumped. "My excuse will sound flimsy, but I want to explain. I haven't been sleeping well at all. I barely slept last night, so I slept late this morning. I had my earbuds in. I didn't hear the texts come in. I was kicking myself when I saw the messages I'd missed. I was so worried about you."

"Hmm," said Layla, but her anger was slightly dulled by the genuinely stricken look on Pierce's face.

"Do you want to hear about the gangster or not?" she asked, suddenly uncomfortable with the uncharacteristically vulnerable Pierce.

Pierce turned to the evidence board. "He's not up there," said Layla, relieved to be getting back to business. "Different racket. He said he wasn't interested in curios or trinkets, only cash payment. Mackey seemed to wrangle some kind of extended deadline to next Friday."

"And Bennett's office?" said Pierce. "What'd you find?" She pulled up thumbnails of Layla's images on her computer screen and clicked through them while Layla explained.

When Layla had finished by revealing her invitation to New York with the Rothkopfs, Pierce stood up and walked over to the evidence wall. She then moved Bennett Rothkopf's photo to the center of the board of suspects.

The center. Layla tensed. Seeing Bennett's picture moved there suddenly made it all real. For a moment, she deeply regretted having scrounged up this data and laid it at Pierce's feet, like a dog with a bone, waiting for a pat on the head. Bennett wasn't a bad person. He was a person with problems. And now she might destroy his life, and wreck James's life in the process.

Pierce turned to face her. "You did good, Layla. The note from Noor, combined with the authentication documents from Dr. el-Sayed, can help us to go after Rothkopf."

There it was. The pat on the head from Pierce. It wasn't quite as gratifying as she'd expected. Layla fought back her conflicting emotions and went into full-on professional mode. She enlarged the photo of the double-priced ledger and studied the figures. "So the numbers in parentheses might show the real price these people paid?"

"This looks to me like off-balance sheet accounting," Pierce confirmed. "I haven't seen something quite so old-school as a hand-written notebook ledger, but I have seen versions of this. Makes me wonder if he has others."

Layla zoomed in on the page documenting Noor Ghaffar's purchase of a scarab amulet. "I saw Jehan wearing that jade necklace," she said. "It's really striking. I can't tell if it's worth twenty-five thousand dollars. You think that's what Noor paid?"

"It's possible," said Pierce. "In all these sets of double figures, the high figure is probably the real one. The lower number is probably what he put on the receipt and any 'official' paperwork."

"Why would he do that?" Layla asked with a sinking sensation.

"I think he's devaluing certain items, passing them off as less expensive souvenirs in case any collectors want to move them out of Egypt and not have customs officials look too closely at them. Now we need to know who's supplying him with these items. We have to step up our investigation of him." Pierce paused to rummage through a file of papers. "I've confirmed Bennett's little gambling habit that you mentioned," she added, removing a document from the file. "ATM withdrawals and credit card transactions tell us Bennett's been at five casinos in the last eight weeks, including Monte Carlo and Omar Khayyam." She handed Layla the paper.

Layla skimmed the list of transactions before handing it back. "I thought you weren't interested in his gambling. You said motive was less important than actions."

Pierce ignored the dig. "Turns out, he owes a lot of money, to banks and probably to outside organizations, like the friendly loan collector you saw this morning. You're right, there's a strong motivation to engage in illicit sales, and probably a pretty robust client base for that side of the market, in the company he keeps."

Layla's heart pounded. She thought of Bennett sharing his life story. Bennett's excitement just this afternoon about the upcoming New York trip. And James. She'd betrayed James, too. All this was accelerating because she'd told Pierce that Bennett gambled, and she'd used James's trust in her to learn that very fact.

"Now, we can't rush in and nab him today." Pierce paced the small room, thinking out loud. "We have suspicions. A motive. A thank-you note. Some shady accounting records. No irrefutable evidence yet. We need to catch him in the act of selling stolen goods to a willing buyer if we want to build a prosecutable case. And that willing buyer is not you," she added, as if reading Layla's mind. "You already tried, remember? He got spooked and put you in your place. We can't compromise your role or raise any suspicions."

"Think he might cut a deal like Farwadi?" Layla tried hard not to sound hopeful.

"Oh, no. I think this one will play out quite differently. I think the last stop for our friend Mr. Rothkopf is going to be prison."

Layla's heart sank as she pictured the endgame. Agents surrounding Bennett's Chelsea gallery, guns drawn. Bennett and James backed up against a wall. But this was all part of the job. Any emotions she felt were her own fault for letting things get so personal.

"We'll set him up on the New York trip so we can arrest him on American soil," Pierce continued, efficient and emotionless, oblivious to Layla's discomfort. "Operation Old College Friend begins right now. Call Bennett. Tell him you have a friend in Manhattan who's eager to have you introduce him when you're in town."

Layla brought up Bennett's number on her phone, using all her willpower to numb herself to the task at hand. She'd crossed over from investigator to family friend, and had no one to blame but herself.

LAYLA GOT OUT OF a taxi at Tahrir Square and, out of habit, turned down the street that led to the Rothkopf Gallery, even though it was sunset. Catching her mistake, she pivoted on her black high heel and headed instead toward the Egyptian Museum—quickly, since she was late. She'd had to change into party clothes after her check-in with Pierce, and then stopped at a salon to have her hair done. She hadn't felt like dressing up that much. The last place she wanted to go was a gala event. To counter her reluctance, she tried to remind herself she was just playing a role, and in fact, being Layla Nawar felt easier than being Layla el-Deeb right now—the real Layla was still feeling pretty guilty for her role in the Rothkopfs' impending demise.

The sky was deepening to indigo. Spotlights illuminated the pink facade of the Egyptian Museum, the enormous sphinx, and the lake with floating lotus. Fumbling for her event ticket, Layla caught her reflection in a window and didn't even recognize herself at first. Smoothing her deep green cocktail dress, she felt the stares of men passing by. For an instant, she wished James were by her side. "Too much to get done before the New York trip," he'd explained earlier today when she asked if he was going. The thought of the trip now filled her with dread.

At least a huge party like this offered some diversion from her gloomy thoughts about Bennett's imminent arrest. She found the ticket Pierce had gotten for her and handed it to the security guard. As she did so, she caught the event name. *Stolen Treasures.* The name came as a jolt. What was this event for, anyway? All these fundraisers were beginning to blur together, especially as she'd been so focused on the Rothkopf Gallery this week.

She hurried over to an event poster and read the fine print. *Stolen Treasures* was a fundraiser to expand the exhibit of twenty-five restored relics that had been discovered after the 2011 Egyptian Museum looting. Ten more relics had since been found and needed to be restored. Layla wondered who might come to such an event . . . and who might rather avoid it?

Entering the central hall, she found the party already in full swing. Guests with drinks roamed the atrium space below the dome, taking in the enormous sarcophagi and the statues of pharaohs. Balancing plates with hors d'oeuvres, they strolled brazenly past the *No Food or Drink* signs and made their way into the galleries branching off the rotunda and upstairs, where they leaned on the railings and surveyed the scene below. An Egyptian jazz band played at the feet of a massive throned statue.

Layla began her own orbit around the enormous vaulted room, listening to whatever conversations she could while scanning for familiar faces. Compared to the other events she'd been to, a grayer crowd dominated this scene. Lots of dusty academics.

High-maintenance as Jehan could be, Layla found herself wishing she was there, so at least she'd have someone to help her look like she belonged. Layla would have to work this room all on her own. In her impossible shoes. What had Pierce been thinking when she bought this pair of spike heels as part of her "heiress" wardrobe? Couldn't an heiress wear sensible shoes? She leaned against a pillar and stepped out of them for a moment, flexing and curling her toes.

"Layla!" She heard her name called from a few yards away. Huma was waving at her, beckoning her over to a group of young people. Shoes in hand, hurrying over to Huma, she discovered mostly familiar faces. Chloe was among them, as well as the Goldman twins, whom she hadn't seen since Hiro's party.

Huma turned to Layla, eyes shining with anticipation. "So Marcus and Adrian were just telling us all about the crazy time you guys had at Lake Como. What's your story? Everyone seems to have a wild tale about Tanaka villa parties."

Layla smiled enigmatically, emulating the sphinx statue beside her. "What happens at Lake Como stays at Lake Como."

"Come on," Huma pleaded.

"Layla is a true lady of refinement," said Adrian. "She does not play our games."

She felt everyone's eyes on her. This was exactly what she feared. Standing out as separate, aloof. She needed to blend in. She struggled to remember the latest CairoZoom picture she'd seen Adrian in. She had to shift the spotlight off herself.

"I think she was pining for someone," said Marcus. "Someone who was, sadly, absent from the scene."

"Who?" demanded Chloe.

A sly smile spread across Adrian Goldman's face. "I think it's a certain workaholic American."

Huma grinned. "James? It's James! I knew it! Oh my God." She clutched Layla's arm. "Are you guys an item?"

"I— Uh— We—" Layla faltered. What was their relationship status? Secret agent and unwitting target?

"So does that mean he won't be taking that job offer in Sydney, in order to stay here with you?" Marcus Goldman asked.

Layla stared at him. This was new. "What job offer in Sydney?"

"At the Nicholson Museum conservation department. I think he just has a week to decide," said Marcus. "Personally, I'd hate to see him go."

Layla felt the kindling of anger somewhere within her. Was James planning to ever mention this job offer to her? Jesus. These Rothkopf men were all the same, playing their cards close to their chests. She wanted to ask Marcus more about the job, but then noticed, a few feet away, an elegant couple making their way into the atrium, walking slowly with a regal air. The silver-haired man was so tall he walked with a slight stoop. His wife wore a modest but stunning emerald pantsuit, and a dark hijab with stars that sparkled like the night sky. They looked familiar. As they turned and passed under a spotlight, Layla caught her breath. It was the Ghaffars. *Both* of them. They were trailed by the young Egyptian man she'd seen at the Coriander, the one Jehan clearly wanted to avoid—Youssef, whom Noor kept pushing on Jehan. The Ghaffars, noticing Youssef, turned and beamed at him. Youssef fell into step with the older couple, almost jogging to keep up with Gamal's long strides, as they all talked animatedly about something Layla could not hear. Then Youssef shook hands with Gamal and slipped into the crowds. Layla thought she detected a look of disappointment on his face. No doubt because Jehan was not at this event with her parents.

Layla had expected to see Noor here. But her husband? She hadn't seen him since Farwadi's party, and according to Jehan, he rarely went to gala events, preferring to keep a low profile because of his position in the GID.

Gamal's presence added a whole new layer of stress to the scene. Layla couldn't get Noor into a conversation about Dr. el-Sayed, the dodgy appraiser, with her government official husband standing next to her. In fact, Layla would have to spend much of her time avoiding Noor, in order to avoid Gamal, whose radar she did not want to be on at all. Layla glanced at her slender wristwatch. Was it too early to leave?

"So? Are you or aren't you?" Huma was asking her with a gentle nudge.

"What?"

"An item!"

"Oh. Right." Layla nodded vaguely, even though she wasn't sure what to call herself and James, especially in light of this job offer news. Taking her response for a yes, Huma and Chloe whooped and talked about all the clues they'd noticed.

Layla smiled and nodded, trying to keep up the appearance of tracking this inane conversation, all the while eyeing the Ghaffars. Noor quickly disappeared to talk to a circle of women friends. Layla's eyes tracked Gamal Ghaffar as he shook hands with two men and conversed briefly with them. One of the two men was short, blond, middle-aged. Something about his dress style and demeanor suggested an embassy type—British embassy, she guessed.

The other guy—who looked to be maybe in his mid-thirties— was someone she'd noticed at a previous party. He was tall, lanky, and olive-skinned, with a thick head of wavy dark brown hair, reaching almost to his shoulders. He wore stylish but slightly crooked tortoiseshell glasses, and a linen sports jacket over his dark blue jeans. He didn't look Egyptian, or American. His clothes were slightly rumpled, but not enough to peg him as an academic or archaeologist. They were classy, but not expensive enough for a jet-setter. In a cosmopolitan city where most people fit some category or other, he seemed completely unique. Maybe he was some kind of development worker. Except he lacked their cynical look.

"Hey, do you guys know who that is?" Layla asked, interrupting the romantic speculation and gesturing toward the man with her chin. "I've seen him before, but never met him."

They followed her gaze. "Oh, the Italian guy," said Adrian.

"Arturo. No, Alberto, I think. Alberto Rossi," his brother chimed in. "He's a journalist. Writing something about the art scene, I guess."

Huma sniffed and cast him a dismissive look. "He's a bore," she said. "He followed us around at a couple of parties asking a bunch of stupid questions."

Layla nodded without taking her eyes off the journalist and Gamal. She couldn't leave this party without meeting this Italian and finding out what he was interested in. Evidently she wasn't the only investigator in the room. Why was he talking to Jehan's dad?

A few minutes later, Gamal Ghaffar took his leave and pushed on through the crowds, into another room, followed by the guy she assumed was from the British embassy. The journalist, swirling the ice in his empty glass, made his way up to the bar.

The path clear, Layla saw her chance. "Hey, guys, if we're going to dish about my love life, I'm going to need a beverage," she announced. "Anyone want anything?"

"We're good. Hurry back," said Chloe.

"Details. We need details," said Huma.

Layla slipped her shoes back on and limped to the bar as fast as she could, positioning herself in line directly behind Alberto Rossi. Hating herself a little for her next move, she purposely turned her ankle, wobbled, and let the guy catch her arm as she stumbled forward.

"You should take care in those shoes," said Alberto, looking at her heels. "This floor is quite slippery." Though his accent was strongly Italian, his English was excellent.

That was good. Layla didn't want to speak Italian with him, knowing it would turn the spotlight on her. Lately, she was finding people always wanted to know how she knew so many languages. Looking like too much of a polyglot, beyond a reasonable worldly education befitting an heiress, could raise suspicions about her. "They are pretty ridiculous," she admitted. "Especially for an event of this size. Is the party taking over the whole building?"

"Oh, no, certain galleries are closed. The Tutankhamun Galleries, naturally. And the Mummy Room," said Alberto.

"No one's eating canapés among cadavers, huh?"

"I think not. Present company excepted." He gestured vaguely toward the people in their vicinity, who were all well into their seventies and eighties, two in wheelchairs and one with a walker.

Layla made a face at him. "That's not very nice." But she couldn't help smiling. After the tension of trying to fit in at this event, Alberto's unexpectedly snarky humor was refreshing.

They reached the bar, where Layla ordered a ginger ale and Alberto ordered a beer. "I think we've met before," she said. "I'm sorry, I've forgotten your name."

He squinted at her. "Alberto Rossi. But I don't think we've met. You must be mistaking me for someone else."

"I guess that's possible. I meet so many people. But you look really familiar. Are you famous or something?" In full Layla Nawar mode, she used a light, teasing voice and sidled closer. Noting the gleam of a gold wedding ring, she then took one step away. Maybe she'd have to find another approach.

Still, her words produced some effect. Alberto patted his hair self-consciously and puffed out his chest a little. "Maybe in my country, in Italy, I am somewhat known, but not famous. I'm afraid I am just a humble journalist."

"That's not humble. Journalists are important. You're a truth-seeker," said Layla, now choosing earnest and admiring from her palette of available tones. "We need you guys." Journalists, in her professional experience, were slippery. And potentially useful. "Well, it's nice to meet you. I'm Layla Nawar."

"Yes, I know," he said, shaking her hand.

She blinked, surprised. "You know who I am?"

He smiled. "Are you not the long-lost cousin of Nesim Farwadi?"

"How did you know that?"

"I am a not-so-humble journalist," he reminded her. "It is my business to know things. And I think you are just a little bit famous, at least in Cairo. I have heard some talk of you."

"Uh-oh. Nothing bad, I hope."

"Not at all. I hear that you are a budding collector. You are here in Cairo to shop, yes?"

"A little. Tonight, though, I'm here to support a cause," she said, gazing around the room. "It's wonderful to see such a turnout for this fundraiser."

Alberto grunted something unintelligible.

"You don't find it wonderful?" Layla asked.

"I find it disappointing."

"Really? Why?"

"Everyone in the art world in Cairo should be here for this cause. Key people are missing."

"Like who?" said Layla, instinctively wondering about Bennett Rothkopf.

Alberto shrugged. "Many people in the Ministry of Antiquities are absent. It suggests that this event, and this collection, are below their concern."

"But there are some government people here," Layla pointed out. "Didn't I see you talking to Mr. Ghaffar a few minutes ago? He's my friend Jehan's dad." She grabbed the glass of ginger ale that the bartender gave her and took a delicate sip.

"Yes, I had the pleasure of meeting Mr. Ghaffar for the first time this evening," said Alberto, plucking some lint off his jacket sleeve. "He is a strong supporter of repatriating lost Egyptian art. He has quietly financed many recovery efforts."

Ironic, thought Layla, *considering the evidence pointing to his wife's habit of purchasing illicit relics.* Either Gamal Ghaffar was totally clueless, or he looked the other way. Still, Bennett's double-accounting entry burned into her memory. Could a twenty-five thousand dollar purchase fall beneath Gamal's notice?

"There are people with deep pockets, art patrons, missing as well," Alberto went on. "And not enough young people to learn about this issue. It is all very well to support exciting contemporary artists at the hot new Cairo galleries, but not at the expense of the old. If people don't care about looted objects, they won't care about financing their return and repair, or paying for security to prevent future losses. It is a vicious cycle."

"I couldn't agree more," Layla chimed in.

Alberto raised his beer bottle. "Well, cheers to that, then," he said. "Let's hope those who are here drink copiously and give generously. Enjoy the evening." He turned to go. He had lost interest in her.

Layla frowned. As Layla el-Deeb, she wouldn't be shocked if she failed to hold some man's interest at a party, being neither the flirtatious nor chatty type. But she wasn't at all used to being brushed off in her role as Layla Nawar.

"I'd love to hear what you're writing about," said Layla, catching up with him.

"You're not truly interested," he said.

"I am."

"No. I know the party types who come here." Alberto shot a meaningful glance toward Huma, Chloe, and the Goldman brothers, then back at Layla, making the connection clear. He'd noticed her with them before. "They would rather collect superficial experiences than understand history. They visit the Pyramids, maybe buy some curios from a bazaar, visit the clubs, smoke a little *shisha*, and then leave without learning a thing."

"I'm not like them," Layla insisted.

Alberto took a long pull of his beer and raised an eyebrow at her.

"Look. I know all about this museum's looting," Layla said, grateful for the hours she'd spent poring over Pierce's files. "January 25, 2011. The revolution. Police vacated Tahrir Square, leaving this museum vulnerable. Thieves stripped the gift shop, then broke into the museum. Fifty-four relics were taken. The thieves then realized they could not sell the items anywhere because Interpol immediately registered them. So they kindly returned them to the museum." Layla made air quotes around "returned."

"Yes. That was good of them, wasn't it?" said Alberto, with a sarcastic edge to his voice. "Go on, then. Since you are an expert. What happened next?"

"They only returned twenty-five relics," Layla said. "As a token gesture. They damaged them, put them in bags, and threw them in garbage bins and on the museum roof, where employees found them. The rest are still missing, except for ten that have resurfaced and are awaiting repairs. Hence this fundraiser."

Alberto gave her a long look, his expression softening somewhat. "Forgive me. Perhaps I judged you too quickly."

"As a journalist, you should know better," she scolded with a smile. "Like I said. I'm interested in this stuff. I believe every relic has a story."

Alberto looked around the central hall. "I'm afraid you and I are in the minority. Most of the people here tonight, aside from museum staff and the scholars, don't truly care about lost national treasures. Most people here are just interested in philanthropy because it makes them look good. Antiquities all look the same to them, and the supply seems endless, so what is the loss of a few?"

A server came by and offered hors d'oeuvres. They both took a sampling of unidentifiable meat on a stick. Layla studied Alberto. "You're so cynical. It sounds like this isn't your scene. Why'd you come here tonight?" She popped the meat into her mouth and made a face. "I'm guessing it's not for the food."

"No." He hesitated. "I am here to pursue a lead for my story. I am writing about the Faiyum looting, and there is a scholar in attendance here tonight who may be able to provide some details."

Faiyum. That definitely rang a bell. Layla hadn't seen anything on Faiyum in Pierce's files. But she'd read of Faiyum in that article Tanaka had in his nightstand, "The Amulet Men of Faiyum." That article hadn't mentioned a looting, but the magazine issue was more than a year old. "I know Faiyum is a town not far from here," she said, "but I don't know about any looting."

"Then you should go do your research," said Alberto. "It was very nice chatting with you, but I am actually here this evening on business. I am sorry." He pushed past her and headed up the marble staircase to where the party spilled onto the second floor.

Layla took the stairs two at a time, feeling the pinch of her dress and the heels, and caught up with him near the top, where she blocked his path again. She couldn't let Alberto slip away. He was too good a catch. "I might be able to help you," she said.

"Not only am I Farwadi's cousin, I'm a volunteer translator at the Rothkopf Gallery. I see and hear a lot. If the Faiyum relics are circulating on the black market, I might hear something about it."

Alberto paused, considering this.

Encouraged, Layla continued. "You might even find you need a translator at some point in your work here. And I don't charge a fee. That should be music to the ears of a humble journalist," she added, looking down at his scuffed loafers.

Alberto took off his glasses, quickly cleaned them on his shirt-tail, and put them on again as if to see her better. "All right," he said. "You win. I will tell you about Faiyum. But quickly. And if anything in my story sounds relevant to something you know, I trust that you will tell me."

"You have a deal." Catching sight of the Ghaffars rounding the corner, Layla quickly turned and continued up the stairs. "Let's talk up here, where we can find some quiet," she suggested.

They walked up to an alcove with an arched window, away from the crowds, and sat on a bench beneath it. Palm fronds rustled outside in the breeze. Alberto looked around, then turned to her and spoke in a low voice. "Five months ago, a collection of relics was looted from a small museum in Faiyum. This crime made the news, but very quickly, the story died. Can you think why?"

"Nobody cares about that museum," Layla guessed. "It's small."

"Correct. Because no one thinks of Faiyum, the crime begins to feel like ancient history. The story gets buried under bigger stories. And nobody cares about amulets, either, because Egypt has so many. They are constantly surfacing at excavations and earthquakes."

Layla frowned. "That's not true," she said. "I mean, I agree, there are tons of amulets in Egypt, but I also know some of the socialites are collecting them to wear as unique pieces of jewelry. So at least some have to be valuable enough to be desirable." She thought of the article she'd read from Tanaka's nightstand, published before the looting. "I happen to know there's some scholarly interest in the amulets from Faiyum," she added. "They were believed to be mag-ical because they came from a group of magicians and healers."

Alberto smiled. "I am impressed," he said. "You know of the article by Dr. Katherine Danforth?"

"I've read it. It was interesting. Were those among the relics that were stolen?"

"They were, in addition to a marble frieze and a collection of six vases and statuettes," said Alberto. "I have reason to believe that someone commissioned Dr. Danforth to write that article in advance of a planned looting."

"You think it's a fake article?"

"No, Dr. Danforth is a legitimate and respected scholar," said Alberto. "But her article and several others about Faiyum artifacts were published around the same time. It is possible their efforts were financed by someone who wanted to give the items more value, anticipating they would surface on the black market at some point."

"And that's who you want to meet with at this party?" Layla asked. "Is Dr. Danforth here?"

"Not her. I have already communicated with her in London. I am here to speak with a different scholar, who wrote of a Faiyum frieze, also in advance of the looting," he said. "If the same person commissioned or financed the research of all of these scholars, that information would lead me closer to the organization responsible for the looting."

"And what organization do you think that is?" Layla whispered.

Alberto pressed his lips together and shook his head. "I have told you the lead I am pursuing, and I can say no more. I have to protect my sources."

Layla nodded and shifted uncomfortably on the bench. A new, dark theory was beginning to take shape in her mind. She didn't want to go there. But she had to. "Are there any pictures of these looted relics? I'd love to see what they look like. Especially the amulets."

"The museum posted photos online, in an effort to aid recovery," said Alberto. "Unfortunately, they are not yet registered with Interpol, for complicated bureaucratic reasons. So despite the photos, they are easily sold to gullible buyers with cash to spare. Ah." He looked past Layla. She turned and saw an elderly man with a cane making his way down the hall to another gallery. "The scholar I am seeking. I must speak with him now." He handed her his business card. "Take a look at the Faiyum Museum website. If you have seen or heard mention of any of the relics in question, let me know."

"Sure," said Layla, placing the card in her purse. Her mind was racing, the dark theory now growing and taking a monstrous shape.

"Or you can reliably find me at Zamalek Rooftop," he added, "in the Nile Zamalek Hotel, where I am staying. It is my favorite bar in Cairo." He then flashed her a smile—a warmer, more genuine smile this time—and hurried to catch up with the elderly man. The two of them turned a corner and disappeared into an adjacent gallery.

Remaining on the bench, Layla took her work phone out of her purse and quickly Googled "Faiyum looting." The first link she saw was in *Al-Ahram*, a major Egyptian newspaper. She skimmed it. The article was brief, and contained no accompanying photo, but the facts seemed right. Thieves raided the museum's storerooms and took twenty items, including a collection of ten amulets. The amulets had belonged to a very specific group of professional magicians, or "amulet men," and were said to bring great fortune upon the wearer.

Kiyoshi Tanaka had been interested in Dr. Danforth's article, enough to flag the page in the magazine. Did that mean he would be open to buying such a relic if it appeared on the black market?

Heart pounding, she went to the Faiyum Museum website. It was a humble site, full of broken links, but eventually she found what she was looking for: "The Stolen Treasures of Faiyum." She scrolled through several vases, statuettes, and decorative pots, until she came to the amulets. She scrolled through the thumbnails, taking in the beetle-shaped jewelry, the stunning greens and blues of the glazes, the intricate patterns, until she came to the last photo and nearly dropped the phone as her suspicion was confirmed.

She enlarged the photo and gazed at the jade beetle with the distinctive, intricate pattern of markings on its wings. She knew exactly where she'd seen that scarab amulet before. Hanging from Jehan's neck. It had been purchased by Noor Ghaffar.

From none other than Bennett Rothkopf. This was the unique item he had gone out of his way to procure for an astronomical sum.

THERE WAS NO TIME to go back to her apartment and change, or even to kick off the high heels from hell. She didn't have the blue hijab disguise she usually wore to the safe house, but she would have to take the risk and go there in her party attire. There was no time to lose, and Pierce, infuriatingly, was once again not answering the burner phone, or any phone. When a cab saw her and slowed, she immediately hailed it and sped toward the safe house neighborhood.

She had proof Bennett had purchased and sold a stolen item. A *recently* stolen item, so hot it was radioactive. Now they had to figure out from whom he had bought it, and if he'd sold similar items to anyone else. Just how deeply was Bennett into this deadly game? Was it all part of a desperate move to pay off his debts, or was he a man with no conscience?

And James. He thought so highly of his father, imagining his one flaw was the gambling addiction. He saw the gambling, and the related debt problem, almost as a disease, for which Bennett needed help. But dealing in illicit relics? That was no illness. That was criminal activity. James had no idea who his father really was.

Or did he?

That new thought chilled her. Maybe she was being naïve, willfully so, by not considering this idea sooner.

Furious as she was at Pierce for being AWOL again, she had to talk to her about all this. She had to tell her about Alberto. He could prove extremely useful to their investigation, as long as they played their cards carefully with him.

Plus, she liked him. She felt an uncanny sense of kinship with him, as if she had a colleague out there working toward the same goal. With Pierce's permission, Layla wanted to meet with Alberto and get him to look into Noor Ghaffar's purchases. She could tell him she'd heard a rumor of Noor purchasing a costly amulet from Bennett Rothkopf. She could get the evidence she needed without having to ask too many questions herself, and keep her careful distance from Gamal Ghaffar.

Layla had the taxi driver let her out at an intersection a few blocks from the apartment. After making the sure the taxi was out of sight, she ran to the safe house, as fast as she could. Hobbled by the ridiculous shoes, she slipped them off and ran barefoot. As she neared the safe house building, she slowed to a brisk walk, not wanting to attract attention. It was nearly ten p.m., but a warm night, with families strolling through the streets eating ice cream, and a group of boys playing soccer. As she passed each streetlight, she ducked her head, shielding her face from view. Most of the women wore hijabs and modest clothing here, and she could feel the stares. The call to prayer blaring from the nearby muezzin interrupted some of the street activity as people turned to face the mosque out of respect. Some men pulled out pocket prayer rugs and dropped to their knees. Layla took the opportunity to pick up speed toward the safe house.

A stray cat near the safe house building yowled and skittered out of her way. It seemed almost an eerie incarnation of the damned bronze cat she'd bought from Bennett Rothkopf, and she cursed it for making noise and drawing more attention.

Layla ran up three flights of stairs and down the open-air corridor to the entrance to Pierce's apartment. Seeing no light from under the door or around the shuttered windows, she guessed Pierce had gone to bed early, or maybe was working in the back bedroom. But if she was asleep, that would explain why she hadn't answered the phone again. Pierce's sleeping habits had seemed extremely erratic lately. She always looked either tired or wired.

Propelled by her pent-up energy, Layla wanted to burst into the apartment. But the last thing she needed was to piss off Pierce by startling her. Or, worse, make her think someone was breaking in. She could easily be greeted at gunpoint if she didn't watch herself; she knew Pierce slept with a pistol under her pillow.

She entered the dark apartment and softly closed the door behind her. "Pierce? It's me, Layla," she called out. "Are you here?"

The only answer was the call to prayer still audible outside, and the drip of the kitchen faucet, which hadn't been turned off all the way. Water was pinging off one of the hedgehog coffee cups in the sink. Layla turned it off, noting the remains of a half-eaten meal on a plate and couple of blood-spotted cotton balls. She guessed Pierce had had a minor kitchen injury. She continued down the hallway, toward Pierce's bedroom.

She knocked softly, then pushed open the door. Moonlight leaked in through the closed shutters and cast a striped pattern on the white sheets that made Layla think of prison bars. Prison, she thought guiltily, where Bennett would shortly end up, thanks to the information she was about to reveal to Pierce.

She backed out slowly. Maybe it wasn't too late to back out of the safe house and leave this whole Alberto chapter unreported.

She heard a scraping sound in the bathroom. The door was closed, but a ribbon of light leaked out from under the door.

Layla paused before the bathroom door. "Pierce?"

No answer. Only the low thrum of the bathroom fan within.

She waited a respectful minute, then jiggled the doorknob. It was locked. Then she heard an indistinct sound against the white noise of the fan. A moan.

Layla had never kicked down a door before. And if she was wrong this could be a huge violation of privacy. This was her boss, not some criminal suspect.

But alarms were going off in her head. Something wasn't right here.

She studied the door hinges to make sure it swung inward. She was relieved to find the door was made of cheap hollow-core material. Minimal force would be required.

Her high heels would be useless, though. She ran back to the bedroom closet and rummaged for Pierce's standard-issue, size nine, steel-toed boots. She laced them up tight. As she ran back to the bathroom door and hiked up her cocktail dress for more range of motion, a word from her conversation with Bennett popped into her head. *Grit.*

She backed up, took a deep breath, and placed a forceful kick directly at the weak point below the doorknob. The doorframe splintered. The door gave way.

Layla stumbled forward and staggered into the bathroom.

Pierce, wearing earbuds, sat on the tiled bathroom floor in a nest of bloodied cotton balls, gauze, and bandage wrappers. She was holding her right leg just behind the knee, as if she were nursing a wound, her pant leg rolled up high. Layla realized the earbuds and the bathroom fan had probably muted the sound of her entering the apartment.

"Pierce! Oh my God, are you hurt?" Layla asked. Then she drew in a sharp breath as the pieces came together.

Pierce, glassy-eyed, looked up at Layla. She quickly unrolled her pant leg, but not before Layla saw the piece of rubber tied above her knee, and the syringe in her hand.

FAMILY AND FRIENDS

• PATRICK LOHIER •

Pierce's eyes sharpened and her expression turned eerie and malignant. She pulled the earbuds out of her ears and they clattered to the tile floor.

"Get the fuck out," she growled.

"Pierce? My God . . . what the fuck are you doing?"

Layla's gaze darted from the syringe to Pierce's face. It would have been weird to stumble on *anyone* shooting up. But this was crazy. Pierce was an FBI agent and she was also one of the most revered and respected women in the Bureau. She was the kind of agent you heard about *before* you met her, the kind of agent people looked up to. And yet there she was, shooting up like a junkie in a safe house bathroom in Cairo.

Layla backed away from the door. Pierce rose from the floor with the slow deliberation of a drunk or convalescent and shut the bathroom door without taking her eyes off Layla. Layla turned and walked quickly out of the safe house, closing the door quietly behind her, as if it mattered. She rushed down the stairs and stopped at the sidewalk, then paced back and forth in a state of sheer, rising panic. She couldn't breathe.

Finally, she put her face in her hands and whispered, *What the fuck. What the fuck. What the fuck.* The investigation was completely and possibly irredeemably compromised.

She took three deep breaths before climbing back up the stairs to the safe house door.

She knocked, and knocked again. Pierce didn't answer. Layla kept at it for about five minutes before Pierce finally opened the door.

She looked unfazed by Layla's glare. "We'll talk at our next debrief," she said, matter-of-factly.

"No, I . . . Pierce, I . . ."

Pierce started to shut the door. "Good night, Layla."

Layla had always known Pierce as "Pierce," the legendary agent, the hero of the FBI's most dangerous operations. She had to dig into her memory to even remember her first name. "Ellen . . ."

Pierce's eyes darted to her. She clearly noticed the effort toward a greater intimacy but she wasn't having it. Layla's use of her name only angered her.

She started to close the door again. Layla clenched her jaw in exasperation and pushed it to hold it open.

"Don't piss me off," murmured Pierce. The venom in her voice shocked Layla. "This is completely out of line. Leave and we'll talk when we have our next . . ."

Layla leaned into the door with all her weight, and finally Pierce gave up and stood in the open doorway.

"Did you really just say 'out of line'?" said Layla. She'd found her own rage. A derisive chuckle escaped her as she stood panting in the doorway. She wanted to scream at Pierce. But part of her also wanted to ask if she needed help. "Out of line," she repeated again, dully. Waves of rage clashed against waves of confusion and doubt. She brought her hands up in a gesture of desperate supplication. "What . . . *the* . . . *fuck* . . . are you doing?" she said.

Pierce shook her head and stepped back from the door. Layla followed and closed the door behind them.

"What *the fuck* are you doing?" she asked again.

"Leave me alone," Pierce said. She went into the kitchen, poured herself a glass of water, and drank it thirstily before leaning against the counter. She looked pale, and Layla could hear her heavy breathing. "You shouldn't have come here. We can talk tomorrow."

"Tomorrow? Were you ever going to tell me you're an addict?" Layla frowned as she thought about that for a moment. She thought of the times in recent weeks and months when Pierce couldn't be reached. She thought of the time she'd been stuck in Bennett's office, when she'd heard Mackey approaching and Pierce hadn't answered the phone. Had Pierce been shooting up then? Had she been high? Had she endangered Layla's life?

Pierce poured more water and placed the glass on the table. She sat and motioned toward the opposite chair. "Sit down, please. Just . . . for a minute?"

Layla took a breath and leaned against the wall. "I'd prefer to stand."

Pierce looked like she was struggling to focus, to even sit up straight. She looked like she was going to be sick. "It's a long story," she said, almost in a whisper.

"Take as much time as you need," said Layla. She noticed that Pierce's fingers shook around the glass clutched between them. Was she nervous? Or was she high?

Pierce cupped her hand over her mouth and closed her eyes. She sat quietly like that for half a minute. Finally, she looked at Layla and blinked as if she'd woken from a deep sleep. "Just so you don't get the wrong idea, I'm not apologizing," she said. "This isn't really any of your business. But I'll tell you anyway."

"What are you talking about? It *is* my business. We're in the middle of an investigation. We're in a dangerous situation here. Do you understand the danger you're putting us in? Just tell me the fucking truth."

Pierce let go of the glass and set her hands on the table. She stared at the glass intently, as if she were trying to find herself by focusing on something, or as if the glass was the only thing that mattered. Layla had seen the same expression on Pierce's face when she studied precious relics.

"A few years back I was in narcotics. I was working in New York on a special task force. We found the core group coordinating the drug traffic around New York and northern New Jersey. I got close to them, undercover. It was all centered around a guy named Howard Butler, an Army vet." She frowned, sighed, grew silent for a moment as she stared at her glass. Finally, she looked up.

"One night, things got out of hand," Pierce continued. "He might've been high or maybe he was just paranoid, but he held a gun to my head and told me if I didn't shoot up he'd kill me."

"Jesus . . ." whispered Layla.

"It's not the first time that's ever happened to an agent."

Layla hesitated. She couldn't yet let go of the respect and admiration she felt for Pierce. The fact that her drug use started while she was working undercover was a complicating piece of the puzzle. She'd been doing her job . . . Layla wanted to sit down at the table across from Pierce but resisted. "You got hooked?"

"Not at first." Pierce shook her head. "It got me out of that jam. Howard and his crew trusted me after that. They let me further in." Pierce looked at Layla and her eyes narrowed. "I'm pretty sure my bosses at the Bureau knew what was happening."

Layla's eyes locked with Pierce's. "But they let you keep going . . ."

Pierce shrugged. "You've got an active investigation, making progress with a good likelihood of prosecutions. What would you do?"

"What happened to the case?"

"Busted them." Pierce smiled. "Howard and his four top crew members went in for fifty years each. They'll all die in jail."

"But then . . ."

"Me? Using? Well, I thought about it a lot after that. I had other cases—some were undercover. I was barely talking to my husband . . . my ex." She leaned forward, set her elbows on the table, and cradled her face in her hands. Layla could see the shadow of sadness in her eyes.

"I didn't know you . . . were married."

"Well," Pierce smiled bitterly. "That's kind of the point. Neither did I. I went under, totally undercover. The bitch of it is that I was an addict a long time before I put a needle in my arm. I couldn't get enough of undercover. One night I came home and my husband had cleared out with my son."

"I'm sorry," said Layla. "But how do you keep this up? With the drug tests?"

"It's not hard. Powdered urine. You can buy it online."

"And no one's ever noticed? No one knows?"

"Not till now." She sighed and clenched her eyes shut.

In the brief silence that followed, Layla stepped toward the table and sat in the chair across from Pierce. When Pierce opened her eyes, they were filled with an alarming fatigue.

"The strange thing is that keeping the secret might be just as addictive as the stuff itself."

She understood what Pierce meant. Keeping secrets *was* addictive.

Layla turned her gaze from Pierce to the glass that stood on the table between them. Pierce would lose her job if the Bureau found out she was using. But she had told Layla everything, and that mattered, didn't it? The fact that Pierce had gotten hooked while working cases should make some kind of difference. She'd sacrificed herself to put scumbags in jail. But Layla couldn't summon everything she needed to absolve Pierce, and she quickly gave up the effort. She couldn't shake her shock and disappointment at the knowledge that the agent she most admired was compromised so badly.

"I need time to think," she said.

"To think about what?"

Layla looked up. Pierce was eyeing her. There was a kind of plea in her eyes, but there was also impatience. She wanted this done and settled. She wanted Layla to commit to keep her secret. Layla felt her anger rise again.

"To think about what you being an addict means to this investigation." Layla stood and walked from the kitchen to the hallway. She wanted to get out of the place as quickly as she could.

"I'm not apologizing for any of this . . ."

"You already said that," said Layla, as she set her hand on the doorknob.

LAYLA SPENT THE NEXT day restlessly wandering around her apartment, flicking through daytime TV and ignoring her investigation files. Thoughts of Pierce churned through her mind. She hadn't even had a chance to find out how she got the stuff. Had she smuggled it in with her when she had come from New York? Did she have a dealer in Cairo? And how could they continue with the investigation? It all felt like some kind of cruel charade. What the fuck was she supposed to do with this awful knowledge?

She wished she had someone to talk with. She'd have to keep most of the details to herself, but perhaps with some white lies . . . She glanced at her watch. Nearly two p.m. It was her day off from the gallery, but maybe she could lure James out for lunch.

Relief washed over her when James answered the gallery buzzer. He held her tight and she felt safe in his arms, as if everything might be okay again, if she could just keep holding him. When she murmured hello he leaned down and kissed her. The waves of anger and confusion subsided to a quiet and peaceful stillness, centered on the softness of his lips. She almost resisted as he pulled away to ask her what had brought her to the gallery.

"I came to get you," she said.

He kissed her again. "What for?"

"I thought I'd take you out for lunch."

He smiled and she felt thrilled at the sight of it. But then his smile faltered and she winced. "I'm sorry, Layla. I can't. There's too much to do here." At the sight of her disappointment he added, "But stay and hang out for a few minutes. I missed you."

He put his arm over her shoulder and guided her across the gallery foyer.

She followed him to the storage rooms and conservation offices. The only other person there was Hamadi, working at a laptop in the IT office.

James stood behind him, peered over his shoulder, and pointed at the screen. "These two here. Put notes on those. They'll need climate control at the specifications I emailed you." He turned back to Layla and brushed her hair back from her face. "I'm sorry I can't leave for lunch. We'll have hell to pay if we don't get these shipments out of here today."

Layla looked down, trying to hide her sadness, but James took her hand and led her to the hall, where they could have privacy.

"What is it, Layla? What's wrong?"

She leaned in to him, close enough that she could feel his heartbeat. She clenched her eyes shut to better feel the warmth of him, his solidness and strength.

"What is it?" he whispered into her hair. "Tell me."

She looked up at him and did her best to put on a brave smile. "It's nothing. We'll talk later."

His brow furrowed with worry. "Are you sure?"

"Yes," she said. She kissed him one last time and headed up the hallway. "Don't work too hard."

She stepped out onto the street and felt her breath catch at her sudden isolation. She had no other genuine friend in Cairo. With spring had come rising heat and dust. Most of the expat crowd had fled to far-off places and cooler climes, to estates and vacation villas in the Mediterranean and the Caribbean. The city still hummed with life. Storefronts and signs glowed brightly along the crowded sidewalks. Every block presented bustling new vistas, brightly colored signs in Arabic competing with ads for Coke and McDonald's, Samsung and Apple. But she was alone. She turned this way and that for a moment, until, like a note carried through the air and dropped at her feet, she recalled the name of the bar Alberto had told her about, Zamalek Rooftop. *Why not*, she thought. If Alberto was there, the day would not feel entirely lost. Pierce might not be focused on their mission, but she still was. Layla hailed a cab and asked the driver to take her to the bar.

The place was packed with locals and a few expats. She quickly spotted Alberto sitting by himself. She tapped on his shoulder and he grinned when he looked up and saw her.

"Hey, Layla! Good to see you again so soon." He peered into her face and his smile turned to concern. "You look like you could use a drink."

"I definitely could." She slumped down in the chair next to him. "How are you?"

"I'm good." He smiled. "Have a drink with me," he said.

Layla felt at ease. Alberto seemed to have shed the wariness he'd worn like a shield the night she'd first met him.

A waitress came and she ordered orange juice and vodka on ice.

"Now, tell me, what happened?"

She hesitated.

"I got some really weird news. About a friend of mine back home. It turns out she's got a serious drug problem and no one knew."

Alberto pushed his tortoiseshell glasses up the bridge of his nose. His eyes sharpened with genuine concern. "I am so sorry to hear that. It's a very sad thing when people get involved with drugs."

"There's that, but there's also this thing about hiding it. How could she have hidden it for so long?"

"For how long? Do you know?"

"A couple years, I think."

"My goodness. She must be exhausted."

Layla frowned. She knew Alberto's observation was well intended, but it annoyed her. "What do you mean, exhausted? It was her choice."

"Well . . ." He nodded, shrugged. "Maybe, at one point, it was her choice. But if she's struggling with addiction now, then she might not feel like she has the strength to choose anymore."

He sighed and took a long drink, squinting at Layla as if assessing how much he could confide in her. Layla shifted awkwardly under his momentary scrutiny. He took another drink and spoke, finally.

"I went through something similar years ago. A friend of mine, another journalist, got addicted to heroin. He was covering Italian forces in Iraq, around the time when the Italian base at Nasiriyah was attacked by a suicide bomber. He wasn't hurt but he saw a lot of bad things. He came back a mess and it was a long time before he got help. Your friend needs your help now."

The waitress came back and set Layla's drink on the table. Alberto lifted a tumbler half full of what looked like whiskey in a toast.

"To your friend. May she win this struggle"—they tapped glasses—"with your patience and support."

Layla drank. Alberto's advice was generous and humane, but Layla wondered if she had that kind of generosity in her to share with Pierce. And would Pierce even accept her support if she offered it? She put her glass down and looked into Alberto's open and thoroughly kind face.

"Thank you. You are a very wise man."

"Hah! Not at all." He held up his hands, palms forward. "And you don't have to take my advice. I'm only someone who has perhaps seen a few more things than you."

"Maybe . . . How about you? Are you drinking away your troubles, too?"

He took another sip. "I have made no progress on my story. The scholar I spoke to last night was no use at all." He placed his elbow on the table and his chin on his fist with a defeated expression. "Also, to be honest, I really miss my family."

"Do you have kids?"

"Two little girls."

"Have you got any pictures?"

He grinned as he woke up his phone. He showed her a photo of a beautiful woman with long black hair and laughter in her eyes, her arms wrapped around two little girls. He swiped to show her a short video of the girls singing and dancing in the surf on a sun-drenched beach. Layla blinked. Would she ever have a life like that? A life filled with love and laughter? A family? Could she have that with James once he knew the truth about who she was?

"They're beautiful," said Layla. "You are a very lucky man."

"Thank you!" he said, laughing. "They keep me busy, always on my toes." The faces of his little girls disappeared as his phone began to buzz.

"Please excuse me, Layla," said Alberto, rising from his chair. "I must take this." He answered it and moved off toward the hall leading to the restrooms. He was still close enough that Layla could hear him if she concentrated. "Yes. Ah. How are you?" His eyes widened and he pulled his notebook and pen from his pocket. He set the notebook against the wall and started to scribble. "Mmm . . . hhhhmmmm. *Grazie, amico. Grazie.*" He sat back at the table, stifling an excited smile with another sip of whiskey.

"What is it?" she asked.

"Ah." He shook his head. "It was nothing."

"Oh, c'mon, Alberto. If you have good news you better share it. I could use some good news." She grinned. The investigation had been dealt a bad blow by Pierce's behavior, but Layla wasn't going to let the day go entirely to waste. She would get something useful out of Alberto.

That flash of appraisal crossed Alberto's eyes again. He glanced toward the other tables before leaning forward and speaking in a hushed voice.

"It was my contact at UNESCO. They have some involvement in policing the antiquities trade. My contact knows someone who uses satellite imagery to identify illegal excavations around historic sites and is willing to share some images. This could be a real break for me."

"That's great." Layla smiled. Her brief acquaintance with Alberto was already paying dividends. It didn't hurt that she liked him, too. She lifted her glass in another toast. "To the use of satellite imagery to identify illegal excavations around historic sites."

Alberto laughed, clinked his glass against Layla's, and drank. He pushed his glasses up again, which Layla had begun to note was a kind of cue or tell. He seemed to push up his glasses just before he said anything of real importance or substance.

"You know, this isn't just about theft," he said.

Layla squinted. "What do you mean?"

"I mean . . ." Here he glanced around again, as if gauging the distance between them and any ears that might be too close. He leaned even closer. "Terror groups in the region use the money from the sale of these stolen items to fund their activities. I am nearly certain I've traced money from these digs to several attacks orchestrated by the Muharib in Iraq over the past two years and, more recently, in Libya, Yemen, and Syria."

"Oh my God," said Layla, feigning shock. She was impressed by Alberto's resourcefulness and determination. But he was telling her things she already knew. She wondered if she'd overestimated his value. She tried another angle. "So this money is funding terrorism? Do you have names? Specific contacts?"

Alberto frowned. The questions clearly hit a nerve. "Nothing so clear as that, unfortunately," he said. "What I've observed, though, in the past year, is a correlation between the amount of illegal digging and the number of attacks." Alberto took a drink. "This money earned through selling Egyptian antiquities is clearly a significant resource for them. I have heard that as much as twenty-five percent of the Muharib's operational budget is raised through these activities. So you see, it's not just about ethics and the law, it's about international security."

"That's . . . that's crazy," said Layla, doing her best with a wide-eyed and open-mouthed expression to look like an astounded ingenue.

"It's really the core objective of my work, to find and prove this connection."

"So that's what the satellite images are for?"

"Exactly."

Layla nodded. She'd established that Alberto hadn't yet proven the connection, and that was valuable enough. He'd serve as another pair of eyes and ears on her own investigation—unwitting, of course, but with important satellite imagery to offer. It was slightly ridiculous that this journalist had access to resources she did not, but the illegal nature of the FBI investigation meant that reaching out to the NSA for access to satellite images was easier said than done. She sipped her drink and glanced around the bar, which was growing quieter as the lunch rush died down. When she turned back, she found Alberto gently swirling the ice at the bottom of his glass.

"So, when will you see them?" she asked.

"The images?" he said.

"No, your family!"

"Ah. Hopefully by next week, if I can find some answers here."

"And the images could lead to the answers?"

"That's right. I'll have locations I can check out."

Layla thought about that. If she could access any information that Alberto found that connected dig sites to the Muharib, she'd have a key piece of the puzzle tying Cairo's antiquities market to possible terror funding. She was feeling reckless after what she'd discovered about Pierce. Now she glimpsed a chance to make progress with Alberto's help. "In that case, I have to help you." She smiled. "I'll go with you."

Alberto squinted and shook his head. "Layla, this isn't a game. It's important that I don't compromise or endanger my sources. Why would you even want to go?"

She went with something straightforward. "I've been learning more about the antiquities market, how provenance is established, the connections between collectors and dealers and the opportunities for corruption." She leaned toward Alberto. "My cousin, my friends, they all think I'm just some dilettante here to spend money on antiques. But I care about these objects. These artifacts are part of my heritage and my history and I'm determined to see them protected." She smiled, hesitantly. "What I really want to do is set up a foundation to deal with this issue, but I need to see it for myself. For real. And besides, you may need a translator if you run into trouble." She smiled mischievously. "Let me help you."

He nodded. "Egypt certainly needs more voices speaking out against the abuses that are destroying the region's heritage." He sat back and crossed his arms. "Let me . . . think about it."

LAYLA AND JAMES WERE on a plane to meet Bennett in New York. Bennett had left before them. Over the few days following Layla's discovery of Pierce's drug habit, the two agents had established unspoken rules of engagement. Each evening, Layla sent a briefing on the day's progress via encrypted email. But the channels that had been more personal between them, more like the growing bond between a mentor and a mentee, had sealed shut. Neither of them spoke about or acknowledged what had happened, and Layla imagined that Pierce felt as wary about her as Layla felt about Pierce. She still couldn't fathom how Pierce could have built such a successful career in the Bureau while maintaining a drug habit. How much longer could she keep it up? The memory of her frantic pleas for Pierce's help when she'd been trapped in Bennett's office made her whole body tighten with rage. It seemed to Layla that it wasn't a matter of *if* Pierce would mess up, but when and how badly. She didn't intend to get killed because of Pierce's recklessness.

In any case, the two of them had cobbled together the blueprint for their sting focused on Bennett Rothkopf. They were going to introduce Bennett to a buyer and see if he might be persuaded to offer up illicit artifacts that could prove his involvement in the network of crooked dealers. The buyer would be an old school friend of Layla's, whom, of course, she had never actually met.

At some point, Layla fell asleep and dreamed that she walked into the Rothkopf gallery and found Pierce standing quite still inside the foyer. Pierce blinked and presented a syringe in her upheld palm. Layla startled awake with her head on James's shoulder.

"I'm sorry," she said, rubbing her eyes.

"It's okay." He smiled, kissing the top of her head.

They took a cab from JFK. The Rothkopf place was a West Village townhouse. The interior was like something out of a period novel, with the occasional startling piece of modern art thrown in. Old pieces appeared adjacent to new ones, and mixed in among the art and antiquities was a mesmerizing collection of bric-a-brac that told the family history. The walls were painted in bright, eclectic colors. Books lined almost every surface and were piled high in heaps in every corner. The place was beautiful, eccentric, full of character and personal history. Bennett had gone to see a lady friend the night before and had not yet returned home.

Layla watched James cook omelets in the bright kitchen, giggling as he lip-synched expertly to radio pop, including an extraordinary rendition of Katy Perry's "Roar," complete with choreography. He was casually expert and precise at the stove, and she felt comfortable in his home.

But as she watched James cook, she also felt a rising anxiety. Layla's sense of what family meant was deeply colored by her own painful story. But standing in the kitchen with James, surrounded by his family photos, she realized it was possible for family to feel like a blessing.

This stark fact struck her most as she spotted and picked up a photo of James as a boy, standing between Bennett and a beautiful woman. She froze when she realized its significance.

"Your mother," she said.

He looked toward her, saw the framed photo in her hand, and nodded.

"She's beautiful."

"She was," he said.

"What was she like?"

He glanced at her. "She was funny, sweet, smart, kind. All the stuff a kid wants in a mom." He forced a smile but he also changed the subject. "This is actually her family's old house. They were New York blue bloods, a family going back to the old Dutch settlers of Manhattan."

"Blue bloods?"

"That's right. One of her great-grandfathers started a little bank on Wall Street."

"A little bank!" said Layla, laughing.

"That's right."

"It did well, I'm guessing."

"It did. Anyway, the family was rich for a good long time."

"*Was* rich?"

"Well, those people back then didn't work. We have to work."

She nodded and thought about that. "The stuff you told me, about your dad's gambling, was that an issue between him and your mom?"

"I think so. But I'm not completely sure. They used to get into some god-awful fights. They traveled together, everywhere: the Far East, Latin America. They spent some time in Ghana and then later on in Jordan and Oman. They ended up falling in love with Cairo. They started the gallery there—or the cooperative, before they started the gallery."

"Where were you born?"

"Here in New York. By the time I came along, Cairo was already a big part of their lives. What I can piece together is that my mom was drawn to my dad's sense of adventure. She used to say that he had more energy than any man she'd ever met. And I think for her that sense of risk couldn't be separated from the risky things he did. Heading out to digs in the deserts of Tunisia or along the Gulf of Aqaba was no different than losing ten thousand dollars in one night in Macao."

"It was just who he was?"

"That's right. Or, at least, that's the story I've told myself, to explain everything. I'm not gonna get much out of my dad when it comes to those days."

"He doesn't want to talk about it . . . at all?"

"Not to me."

He slid an omelet onto a plate. "Let's eat."

They ate on the veranda. Layla was almost starting to feel like they were on a real vacation when her phone buzzed.

Meet u at Bleecker & Wooster

Place called Tercet's

3 o'clock tomorrow?

It was followed immediately by a photo of "Zach" accompanied by the text: *Me.*

She studied the photo closely, then deleted it. She paused and peered across the table to spy James's eyes straying across the headlines of the *New York Times*. She used the moment to take a quick selfie. The shutter release sound caught James's attention.

"Selfies for the Cairo crew?" he smiled.

"Just a little something for Jehan," said Layla, as she sent the photo of herself to Zach.

Layla scrolled through her phone contacts and found Bennett's New York cell number as James rose and started to clear away the plates.

"Hey," she said to James. "My friend Zach wants to meet your dad. He's interested in looking at some objects."

"Amazing," he said.

She was happy that he seemed distracted. Her hope was to isolate Bennett, to keep the sting focused on him. She composed a new text: *Bennett, Layla here. Great news! My friend Zach wants to talk to you about buying some pieces.*

She wondered if that would do it, if Bennett would fall easily into the trap they were setting for him. *He'd deserve it*, she thought. But it was starting to really pain her to consider how much this whole thing would hurt James. For a brief moment she tried to cast the impact on James as a kind of collateral damage, a necessary negative outnumbered by overwhelmingly significant positives. If all went as planned, by the end of the investigation they would prosecute the major players, choke off the Muharib's funding, and prevent future attacks. If they did that, then the pain James would suffer at his father's arrest would be a small price to pay for saving lives.

James kissed her on the head as he collected their plates and headed back to the kitchen. Her phone buzzed with a text from Bennett.

That's awesome, Layla! Happy to chat with Zach anytime.

She rose and joined James in the kitchen. He grinned as she hugged him, and she rested her head on his chest. She suspected that the best place to hide from him was in his arms.

THE NEXT DAY, SHE met Bennett outside the coffee shop where "Zach" had asked to meet.

"You weren't waiting long, were you?" she asked Bennett.

"Not at all. Let's get going."

Her pulse quickened as they entered the café. As soon as she entered, a young man at a booth waved to her and stood.

"Layla," he said, looking genuinely thrilled to see her.

"Zach." They hugged. Zach looked her up and down. "It's so good to see you. How long has it been?"

"I was just wondering that. About three years, I think."

"Jesus." Zach was a young white man of average height. He had sandy blond hair and a small patch of beard in the center of his chin. He extended a hand to Bennett.

"You must be Bennett. Layla's told me a lot about you."

"Nice to meet you, Zach," said Bennett.

They shook hands and Zach invited them to sit with him. The coffee shop was bright and not too full. Layla watched Zach's face for any cues or signals, but he navigated the improv with ease. This was all going to be improv, she realized. After a polite amount of small talk he leaned forward, intently. "Layla tells me you might be able to help me. What I'm looking for . . . What I'd like to find is something really special. I know there's this whole scarab craze going down now, but that's not what I'm talking about. I want something"—he waved his hands in the air in an effort to convey the indefinable—"unique."

Bennett smiled. "I might be able to help you out. We have a local and specialized team. We could get you some items that are quite rare."

Layla glimpsed the salesman in him, his innate charm and intelligence setting clients at ease. He leaned back and nodded.

Zach grinned again. "That's great." He turned to Layla. "It looks like I've come to the right place."

Layla smiled, although her thoughts were a riot of emotion. On the one hand, she felt like the simple little sting they'd set up was working perfectly. On the other hand, Bennett, at least at this early stage, seemed to have fallen into the trap so easily that it was heartbreaking.

"I'm glad I could bring you two together," she said with a weak smile.

"Zach, why don't you come by the gallery and I can show you some things. Let's aim for tomorrow."

Zach said he would see them then and took off. As soon as he was out the door, Bennett set his hand on Layla's shoulder and smiled warmly at her.

"Wow, Layla. You really are great for business." He sighed and grew thoughtful. "It also doesn't hurt that my son is head over heels for you."

"Thank you, Bennett." She tried to smile back at him but it felt false. She was going to destroy Bennett's business and break his son's heart.

LATER THAT NIGHT, JAMES and Layla walked hand in hand down a dark West Village street. She'd briefly considered asking him about the job offer he'd gotten in Australia—he still hadn't mentioned anything—but she didn't want to spoil the moment. Her mind turned to the months before she'd left for Cairo. She recalled the endless days and drudgery of desk work, the long commutes, the dreary apartment and drearier roommates. New York, a city she loved, had seemed colorless then, stripped of life. But ever since she'd met Pierce and gone to Cairo, and most especially since she'd met James, her life had become vibrant. Walking with James now, her life in New York, as FBI agent Layla el-Deeb, seemed like a long-ago dream. On Thompson Street, or maybe Sullivan, she spied the arched entrance to a garden apartment, a bench nestled under an ivy-covered arbor, all thinly lit by a gas-fueled flame. Emboldened by the wine they'd consumed at dinner, Layla quietly opened the gate.

"Where are you going?" whispered James.

She put her forefinger to her lips to signal silence. "You're coming with me," she answered, giggling and pulling him by the front of his shirt.

They tipsily lowered themselves to the bench, never once breaking contact. She took James's face in her hands and looked deeply into his eyes. Her joy at finding their secret garden melted away as his beautiful face reminded her again of what she was going to be forced to give up so very soon. She closed her eyes and sighed. She felt his lips as he gently kissed her closed eyelids, her nose, and then her lips. His hands disentangled from her hair and slid down her neck to her waist, wiping her mind of what was to come the next day.

LAYLA WAS RIDDLED WITH anxiety as she traveled alone to the gallery the next day, a rainy Thursday afternoon, to meet Bennett. Zach was due to arrive in a few hours. James had some errands to run and would meet her later.

Bennett was already there, stepping out of an open storage unit. Long drawers held some of the Rothkopf Gallery's most priceless stock, including relics from ancient Egypt, Syria, Iraq, Jordan, and Yemen. Bennett put on white cotton gloves and gave Layla a pair. He took a few items out and they sat together at a desk to examine them.

There was a bust wrapped in cloth in a plastic case. It was the head of a young woman the size of a fist, an ancient funerary mask. The lapis lazuli inlays had cracked but still stuck to the stone channels in which they had been glued millennia ago. The back of the head was broken, but the face was intact and startlingly vivid.

"It's beautiful."

He nodded. "Say hello to a princess." He seemed nervous. His hands moved fast as he worked and Layla couldn't detect whether or not they were shaking. She wondered if he was nervous because the object was so clearly priceless and daunting to handle, or because he was doing something wrong.

He unwrapped the other items. There was a bust of a man that looked similar to the one of the woman, but this one was larger and the tip of the nose was sheared off. He also unwrapped a broken chunk of a bas-relief frieze depicting four women seated in a row in what looked like noble finery.

"These are pretty special." He looked at the bas-relief with an expression of unfiltered and unself-conscious reverence. The way he handled them indicated to Layla an expert's ease and confidence mixed with true love of the work. He smiled timidly at Layla. She realized all of a sudden how important this was for Bennett. "Do you think Zach will like them?"

"Are you kidding? He's going to *love* these."

Bennett beamed and laughed out loud. "Excellent! Let me get some coffee started." He left her, and she studied the busts and the frieze without touching them.

"Coffee's going to take a few minutes," he called to her. "I'll pull the paperwork on these. Can you keep an ear out for the buzzer?"

"Yes."

She wondered if this was what it felt like, to be at the center of something, undercover, to see the crime unfold with your very own eyes. Her heart ached at the thought that *she* would be the one to bring Bennett Rothkopf to justice. She felt suddenly sick and clasped her hand to her mouth.

"You okay?" said Bennett.

Layla startled and turned. She pulled her hand away from her mouth. "I'm . . . fine."

Bennett shrugged. "Okay. You looked a little troubled for a second there." He held a few file folders, which he set down on the desk, and Layla couldn't keep her eyes off them.

"I'll be right back."

As soon as he went into the kitchen, she looked up at the security cameras that hung from the ceiling. *Are they my allies or my enemies?* she wondered. They were in the States now. Anything they captured could be introduced as evidence, but what if she were to look in the folders right now? Might Bennett see that? How often did he review the security footage, if at all? Did Mackey have access to them? But she quickly set all that aside. She was Bennett's employee, after all. Would it really be that weird for her to look in the folders? She decided to chance it. She opened the folder labeled *Bust of Princess - 19th Dynasty - Akhmim*. There were, in fact, some shipping records and copies of receipts, but she eyed them with suspicion. The dates were all fairly recent, within the past three years. These relics were ancient, but their provenance on paper was very new. In the file folder on the second bust, she found provenance documents similar to those that belonged to the funerary mask. She froze at the sound of Bennett in the far room and looked up. When she was satisfied that he wasn't coming back yet, her eyes fell on the case on the desk. She prized open the clasps. It was lined with protective black foam, and nestled in a concave form was a garish mask. She peered closer. It was a painted knockoff of a famous bust of Queen Nefertiti. It smelled of cheap rubber and it looked like the kind of thing someone might buy in a gift shop. She touched it and saw that it was made of plastic or rubber and it had a rip or seam at its jawline. She opened it. The inside was hollow. She glanced at the bust and saw that it would fit pretty well inside. The cheap-looking Nefertiti had likely been used to hide the priceless bust of the princess from inquisitive customs agents.

"Layla," called Bennett.

She quickly shut the case. "Yes?" she called out.

"Do you prefer cream? Or milk?"

"Cream, please," she said.

She waited. Her heart was racing. Finally, he returned.

"Bennett," she said, rising from her chair.

He looked at her and frowned. "There's that look again." He set the tray down and looked at her with real concern. "What's wrong, Layla?"

The buzzer rang and they both turned.

"That must be Zach," said Bennett. He looked at her again. "Are you okay, Layla?"

Her mind was a rush of thoughts, of competing lies she could cast out to buy them all some time. "These files here." She pointed to the stack in front of her. "Have you had a chance to really look at them? I mean, just to make sure everything looks okay?"

Bennett frowned again. "Yes, of course. Everything should be fine."

"I only bring it up because Zach's dad is a federal judge. I think he's retired now, but I know these types of purchases can get . . . contentious sometimes." She stuffed her fists into her pockets. "Just thought you should know."

Bennett stood staring at her. His expression was calm and thoughtful. She felt that he had understood exactly what she meant. She stepped around the desk and toward the door. "Listen, I'll go get the door."

"Okay," said Bennett.

She went to the front of the gallery and let Zach in.

"Hey, Layla." Zach smiled and hugged her.

"Hey, Zach."

She took him to the back office. When they entered the space, Zach stopped in his tracks. "This is amazing."

Layla glanced at the desk. The files Bennett had brought up earlier were no longer on the desk. The artifacts were gone, as was the case that held the ugly plastic bust.

"Bennett was . . . just here. But I'm sure he'll be back any minute now."

"No problem." Zach gazed up admiringly at the mass of artwork and personal photos on the walls. "This is so cool." He peered around at the items.

Layla's eyes scanned the desk again. Had Bennett understood exactly what she had meant? She glanced at the door to the kitchen. How long should she give him? Had he cleared out in his alarm? Just when she was starting to get nervous, Bennett came in with a stack of artifact cases.

"Hey, Zach," he beamed.

"Bennett," said Zach. "Your gallery is amazing!" He pointed to a photo set on a file cabinet. "Is this you as a kid? Where's this picture from? Is this Brazil?"

Bennett's eyes widened in surprise. "That's exactly right. That's in Natal, back in the eighties, right along the coast."

Zach, Layla concluded, was a very good agent.

"What are those?" asked Layla, pointing to the stack of boxes in Bennett's hands.

Bennett set them down and shrugged. "Just a few items I thought Zach might like."

Bennett presented three pieces: an alabaster jar, an alabaster canopic jar lid, and the small brown quartzite head of a man, its features rounded and worn. There was no bust of the woman, no bust of the man, nor the bas-relief frieze.

Zach studied the objects. Bennett told them about the pieces, what they represented, the characteristics that made them emblematic of a specific period of ancient Egyptian art, and the traits that made the pieces unique.

"Interesting . . . interesting," said Zach, nodding.

Layla's palms were sweating. She'd warned Bennett and he'd covered himself. That was bad enough. But now she might complicate things even further if Zach bought or committed to buying items that she knew were legitimate—especially if she didn't tip him to what was really going on. Thankfully, as Bennett rooted in a drawer for a magnification loupe Zach could use to see some of the finer details on the artifacts, Zach squinted at Layla, a signal that he was looking for guidance. She took the brief opportunity to shake her head back and forth: *No.*

Minutes later, when Zach learned that the quartzite head of a man cost twenty-five thousand dollars, he didn't blink. But Layla noticed that he wasn't as effusive about the artifacts as he'd been about the gallery space.

"Ah, listen, Bennett, don't you have anything more . . . unique? Something that really pops?"

"Pops?" said Bennett. Having observed him for many weeks now, Layla could tell he was on edge.

Zach set a forefinger on the edge of the alabaster jar. "I mean something rare, something that no one else has. You know what I mean?"

"These don't interest you?"

"Well, they're beautiful—really, really nice." Zach smiled nervously. "I don't want you to think I don't appreciate your showing me these," he said, gesturing toward the objects. "I'm just hoping for that thing that really knocks people's socks off. You know what I mean?"

Bennett glanced at Layla. She couldn't read the look in his eye. Zach was clearly fishing for something rare, and any of the objects she'd seen earlier would have fit the bill.

"Sure. I know exactly what you mean, Zach." Bennett smiled and nodded.

It looked to Layla as if he was trying to play this right, without being too obvious.

"Listen," he said. "Why don't you give me a few weeks. I'll look around, see if we might have something you might like. Meanwhile, is there anything more you want to know about these pieces?"

"I'm good," said Zach. He didn't even glance at the artifacts again. "I've gotta go, though. Headed up to Vermont tonight to meet up with some friends."

"Well, Zach, you know where to find me now."

Zach pumped Bennett's hand. "That I do. That I do. If you find that special something give me a call, okay?"

LAYLA FOUND HERSELF BACK in Cairo alone. Bennett had had some business in Montreal and James needed to detour through London to consult with a client. Feeling exhausted, she took a cab home from the airport. The radio was chattering. It was news of some kind of protest, something at a local university. When she got to the apartment building she waited for the elevator. A woman with a poodle and a woman with a cat in her arms came into the lobby. They too were talking about a student protest, but this time she caught the location: Ain Shams University. They were talking about a riot at her brother's university. As soon as Layla got to her apartment she sent a frantic text to Rami.

What's this about a protest? Are you ok?

She sat on the edge of the sofa, still, eyeing the phone as she waited. Thankfully, she didn't have to wait long.

I'm ok. Just a little bruised. How'd you find out? We heard the media was blocking the news.

He'd been hurt. She hesitated. How would she have discovered the news? She closed her eyes. She felt so alone. James was gone, she couldn't trust Pierce, and she had just derailed an FBI operation. She didn't even know who she was anymore. Her need for connection was overwhelming.

I've got strange news, Rami. I'm here. I'm in Cairo, for work.

She waited again for him to text back, pacing anxiously back and forth in front of the window looking over the city. Finally, he responded.

Can I see you?

Yes, she wrote.

She held the phone tight in her fist. She felt expectant and scared all at once. She wanted nothing more than to see her little brother for the first time in eleven years.

LAYLA WAS GLAD TO discover that the café Rami suggested was far away from the safe house. When she walked in, she scanned the crowd and her eyes stopped at the gaze of a young man who looked both similar and completely different from the nine-year-old boy in her memory. He smiled.

"Layla," he said.

They hugged. He was taller than she was, his hair cut short and clean. His face was so familiar it was like she was looking into a kind of gender-changing mirror. It felt good to hold him. She closed her eyes and squeezed him tight. She let go, and they sat and beamed wordlessly at each other for several seconds.

Rami wore a crisp white button-up dress shirt and jeans with brand-new-looking, green-striped white Adidas high tops. The boy with the big eyes and child's voice who'd sometimes snuggled beside her at night to escape from nightmares had grown into a handsome young man. She couldn't help but feel proud, although she knew she'd had nothing to do with it. Layla noticed two young women seated at a table nearby, casting furtive glances at him and whispering to each other. They could wait, she thought, as she touched his face possessively.

"You're okay," she whispered, relieved to see that he was all in one piece.

"Yeah. Yeah. Everything's okay. And everything's gonna be okay. I'm sorry you had to be here now, when this is happening. I'm sorry you got worried."

"Don't apologize." She paused. She wanted to know more but she was worried she might come across as too heavy-handed. "Rami . . . What were you doing at this protest?"

He smiled. "Fighting the good fight." She was struck again by his charisma.

She blinked. He could see that she didn't understand.

"It was a protest against all these government people on campus. The government's given the police the power to come on campus and harass us without warrants. They're constantly watching us, putting pressure on us, arresting us, harassing the faculty, keeping an eye on everything so they can control the campus. They're criminals. They're thieves stealing the future of our country. They're trying to stop the young people's support for Fareed Monsour. He wants the same Egypt as we do. A modern Egypt. It's our duty to support him."

If he hadn't been so passionate and so eloquent, if his words hadn't sounded so earnest and his insights so hard won, she might have wondered if he was parroting someone else. This was her brother. He wasn't taking the insults of the world sitting down. Layla smiled; she couldn't help herself.

He squinted, wary, as if he suspected she might be making fun of him, or humoring him. "It's not a funny situation," he murmured.

She set her hand on his. "I'm not laughing. I was just thinking that it sounds like they should be the ones afraid of you."

He nodded. Pride glimmered on his face. "Damn straight," he said with a grin.

They burst out laughing, loud enough that the people at the other tables turned to look at them.

"So who was at the protest?" asked Layla.

"Mostly students. It wasn't even that big a crowd."

"But your friends . . . from school." She was fishing for clues about his life, the context in which he lived.

"Yeah. A couple of my friends were there. My friend Abdel got hit in the head with a flying bottle. He got ten stitches right here." He pointed to the side of his head above his right ear. "Two hundred students at most. We were just walking, protesting peacefully, and those fucking thugs—"

He stopped. "Sorry about that."

She shrugged. "I'm just glad you're okay," she said, frowning with concern.

"It's all good. I got kicked but I'm fine." His eyes glowed with tenderness and Layla understood that her little brother was a man now. He was trying to reassure her and it had worked.

"Hey, sister . . ." He took her hand and held it between his two strong hands. There was something almost . . . paternal about it, although she could not remember their father touching her so gently. "I don't want to talk about me. There's really not much to say. You know it all. I'm here, in Cairo. Going to school—"

"Busting heads . . ."

He laughed. "It's home. It's the world we know. What about you, in the big wide world out there? What are you doing? What is your life like?"

She sat back. How could she tell him about her life without revealing the truth of her presence in Cairo? She had to tread carefully. "It's hard to describe. It's just . . . busy, *really* busy, *all* the time, and it's also *really* dull. I work in the comptroller's office for a division of the State Department. We're doing an audit at the embassy here. Just a couple weeks. It's not that interesting, but it's a job." She told him more. All the details were pieced together from plausible, perfect little lies that concealed her completely.

"Mama would be so proud," said Rami.

The mention of her mother made her stiffen. "Rami . . . you don't have to say that."

His eyes widened in mortification. "Hey, I didn't mean to upset you."

She wondered what her face looked like, that he should look so concerned. But she also felt a sudden burst of emotion: love and a sense of loss for the little boy who had somehow magically turned into the gentle man seated across the table from her. She had no patience or desire to talk about her mother, with whom she hadn't spoken in years, or her father, who had died years ago. She was surprised and embarrassed when she felt her eyes watering.

Rami leaned forward and peered closer into her eyes. "It's true," he whispered, as he squeezed her fist. "She'd be proud of you."

They sat in silence for a little while, almost in a mutual meditation. Layla wiped her eyes with a napkin.

"Listen," said Rami. "Don't get angry. I just . . ." He sat back, sighed, and rubbed his face with his palms.

"What is it, Rami?"

"I know it's been a long time, way too long, but I know . . . I know she'd love to see you."

The idea of it jolted her. She had no intention of seeing her mother. At some point, years before, she didn't know when exactly, her antipathy toward her mother had calcified into a hard protective shell of denial.

"Why? I didn't even come to Baba's funeral . . ." She felt tears prick her eyes again, despite herself.

"Layla, that's the past. You're here now. We can be like a real family again. Mama and Sanaa would love to see you. Come. Come with me and we can go see Sanaa, at least."

"I . . . I just don't see how. I'm leaving in a few days . . ." She shook her head. She had run out of excuses. What he offered sounded so . . . tempting. Could it really be so easy?

"I'll make it happen," said Rami. He leaned forward, intent. She could see how earnestly he was trying to sell the idea. "And I'll make it easy for you, for both of you. I'll be like Jimmy Carter when he got Sadat and Begin to shake hands." He brought his hands together in a mime of the former president bringing the two heads of state together in peace.

Layla burst out laughing. "You're crazy," she said.

He turned serious. "I'm not crazy, Layla. I'm just sad. And I've been sad for half my life. We haven't been a family, really, since I was a kid." He paused and peered at the steaming coffee and the bowl of ice cream on the table in front of him. "I don't want you to think I don't remember. I do. What Baba did, the things he said, trying to keep you from doing what you wanted to do . . ." He looked up at her again. "And I can understand that you're angry with Mama. She didn't defend you."

Layla nodded. She hung onto every word he said. The only other people who knew the truth of what had happened were their mother and Sanaa. Rami saying it out loud made her feel for the first time in eleven years that she really did have a family, a family that knew everything, the good and the bad, the way James must feel about his father. Now the tears flowed freely down her cheeks.

"But can't we forgive one another?" he continued. "Can't we learn to trust one another again? You and me and Mama and Sanaa are the only family we've got."

She took the napkin from the table, wiped her tears away, and nodded. "Okay," she said. "But you've got to help me get out if things get too . . ."

"Weird?"

She nodded.

He smiled. "Okay, I promise."

LAYLA WOKE FROM A nap as dusk fell and lay in bed gazing at the pinkish light above the city. Her stomach churned, and she sighed. Other than the glimmer of real joy she felt at having seen Rami, her thoughts were clouded by guilt and doubt. It paralyzed her. She'd done very little that day other than pad around the apartment dwelling on the mess she'd made of things. She'd tipped off Bennett about the sting. She'd made contact with her brother when she'd been expressly told not to. She'd fallen for James. She had almost no contact with Pierce—would they be making more progress if she hadn't found Pierce in the safe house bathroom? She knew she shouldn't feel guilty about it, but she did.

When evening came, she dressed in a black, high-waist, sleeveless jumpsuit and took a cab to a gallery opening at a place called Khamsin. Bennett had asked her to go. Bennett was still in Montreal, and James was still in London. So she went as a representative with some of the gallery's cards in her purse. Most of the crowd she'd gotten to know during the winter was out of town. The opening was a celebration of a longstanding collaboration between a notable Scotland-based dealer and local investors and art enthusiasts. Contemporary art hung on the walls of the gallery. Some of the themes depicted were overtly political. There was a series titled "Tahrir" that depicted the rise of the Arab Spring in Cairo in the form of transformative shapes: the circles, ovals, and other configurations that formed moments of human solidarity since the unrest had begun.

She was surprised, while scanning the trajectory of a tray full of delicious lamb skewers, to find one of her most elusive targets looking at her. Kiyoshi Tanaka stood only feet away, gazing over the shoulder of the man with whom he was talking. She smiled as seductively as she could and turned away.

His gaze telegraphed that he was the type of man who was used to getting what he wanted. She quickly decided to ignore him, hoping to lure him to her that way. She mingled and made small talk with other guests, but quickly concluded that none were on the evidence board or fit the profile of big-ticket collectors whose money would be funding the Muharib. Tanaka was the only target. She felt anxious to reel him in. Losing this opportunity would be disastrous. The investigation was in shambles. She had nothing left to lose, and so she presented herself as bait. She distanced herself from the rest of the guests and was standing alone, studying an 18th-century painting of the Nile, when Kiyoshi Tanaka strode up and stood beside her.

"It's a beautiful event, is it not?" His voice sounded like sandpaper, tough and decisive.

"It is," she said in Japanese.

His eyes lit up. "You speak Japanese."

She continued in Japanese. "I speak it okay. Not so well."

"You speak it well." He crossed his arms. His suit was sharp and he was tall and very intense. He had the face of an actor, expressive, almost mournful, but his eyes were charming. Layla got a strong sense of where Hiro got his charisma from. She also wondered if the father was the source of the son's wayward moral compass.

"Are you a buyer?" she asked. "Or are you involved in some other way? I would not take you for an artist."

"Ah, you might be surprised . . ." He smiled.

"So you're an artist?"

"No. You were correct. I'm a buyer, or I should say I'm a *potential* buyer. But I do not think that I will be buying anything this evening."

He was charming, coy, and very self-contained. Layla felt a bit out of her depth in a way she hadn't with Bennett or Noor. This man operated on a different level.

"What kinds of things do you buy?" she asked.

"I love ancient art and artifacts. I have a great collection at my home in Crete. My most valued Middle Eastern possessions are there."

"Crete?"

"Yes, in the western section, Chania."

"What an unusual place for a home," she said.

"You've been?" He sipped at his glass of red wine.

"No. I've always meant to go. My friends tell me it's charming. I've always been captivated by the myth of the Minotaur."

"Ah," he said, shaking his head gently. "The myth originates from a different part of the island. The Palace of Knossos, where the labyrinth is supposed to have been, is in Heraklion, not Chania."

"That's fascinating," she said.

He smiled. "In any case, a beautiful young woman might want to think twice before going anywhere near the labyrinth."

They both laughed. "But seriously," he continued, "it is a beautiful place, like a work of art in and of itself."

"And what kinds of things do you keep there?" She was wary of being too obvious, but she was also anxious not to lose this opportunity. The questions seemed appropriate, in the context of the event. She needed to find out what she could before he vanished again.

Tanaka smiled. "Some of the rarest and most beautiful ancient artifacts known to man." He said it with conviction and naked pride. His eyes betrayed a desire to seduce her with his power and wealth.

"Oh my goodness, that's fascinating." She smiled. She realized that although she could mention Hiro, it might be best to play this out in a different way. Tanaka gazed at her as if he hoped to make her part of his collection. It was intimidating, but if it gave her an opportunity to find out more about his collection, she would use whatever tools were at her disposal.

Tanaka took a long drink of his champagne. "You shouldn't have to wait too long to see Crete, or to see my collection. You can come with me. It would be my honor to have you as a guest."

She smiled demurely and set her palm for a seductive second against his chest. "You're too kind," she said. His moss-green tie felt like the softest silk. "I might take you up on that sometime."

He raised an eyebrow and took another sip from his drink. "I was going to go to Paris tonight, to see a friend, but that can wait. My private jet is at the airport. I could show you my collection in Crete and ensure that you get back to Cairo . . . or wherever you want to go next . . . safely."

Layla's mind raced. Tanaka's motives had been obvious from first sight. She'd played the bait and he was biting the hook. Now he was offering her an exclusive tour of his art collection. This was her chance. With the trip to Lake Como, she'd blown a good percentage of her travel budget and had come up empty-handed. Then Pierce had proven to be compromised. In New York, in an impulsive moment, Layla herself had compromised the mission—no, she thought with a gut-wrenching stab of guilt, she'd *sabotaged* the mission. And she'd done it not to advance the investigation, but to further compromise it because of her feelings for the son of one of the prime suspects. She couldn't claim the moral high ground over Pierce. She had done her own damage to their cause.

But here was an opportunity to set things right and get the investigation back on its feet. She took a sip from her glass to buy herself another second. She might not get a chance like this again. And it was easy. All she had to do was pretend to be a little flighty, a little tipsy, a little more . . . bubbly than she actually was. She gazed up at him and stepped close enough that he might feel her warm breath. She reached for his tie, stroked the edge of the silk. "How can I travel with you to Crete if I don't even know your name?"

He smiled. "Ah," he said.

TANAKA'S DRIVER TOOK THEM to the airport. Almost as soon as they climbed into the back of the big black Mercedes, Tanaka set his hand on her bare knee.

"*Mister* Tanaka," Layla said with a smile, as she firmly but gently removed his hand and set it on his own knee. "A man of your . . . position. I assume there's a *Mrs.* Tanaka somewhere?"

That seemed to break his steely self-confidence, but only for a second. He chuckled but he said nothing. The driver drove fast and efficiently to the airport. The plush black seats smelled of fresh leather. Tanaka described some of the objects she would see: a stela, a pharaoh's flail and crook, a bust of Amenhotep III.

The driver turned into a service driveway at the airport, drove past dimly lit terminals, along lanes meant for airport vehicles. He stopped at the edge of a quiet stretch of tarmac, quiet so late in the evening. There, gleaming cream-colored with a swoosh of crimson, sat a sleek-looking Gulfstream jet. Tanaka, in his courtly fashion, waved her up the stairs before him. She didn't have words to describe the luxuriously appointed jet. A young Japanese man greeted them, and when they were seated comfortably, he served them flutes of champagne. The engines roared to life, the jet hummed.

Tanaka reached across with his glass upheld to raise a toast. "To *adventure*," he said, rather intensely.

Layla raised an eyebrow, smiled, and clinked her glass against his. "To *Crete*."

TIES THAT BIND

• LISA KLINK •

Tanaka's villa was a sprawling, two-story mansion with white stucco walls, a red tiled roof, and, of course, gorgeous views of the Mediterranean. No matter how many of these luxurious vacation homes Layla visited, she never failed to be awed.

They were greeted by a middle-aged Asian woman with high cheekbones and a strong, square chin. "This is Seung," said Tanaka. "She looks after me."

Seung nodded politely, as if it wasn't at all unusual for her employer to show up with a lady friend at three in the morning. "May I take your things?" she asked in perfect Japanese. Layla handed the woman her Michael Kors clutch and watched her disappear down a long hallway.

Tanaka led her to a large, open living room. It was sparsely furnished, with a dark brown leather couch and two matching chairs flanking a wrought-iron coffee table. Plain white walls provided a clean background for several display cases containing ancient Middle Eastern ceramics and figurines. A life-sized marble statue of an athlete poised to throw a discus stood by the wall of windows overlooking the Mediterranean. Layla walked over to the windows and gazed out at the spectacular view. "Beautiful," she murmured.

"Yes, it is," said Tanaka, from too close beside her. Before she could move away, he had wrapped his arms around her and planted his mouth on hers, kissing her so ferociously it almost hurt.

With some effort, Layla extracted herself from his embrace. She began to protest but he cut her off with another kiss. This was hardly the first time in her life that a man had come on too strong. Under normal circumstances, she would shove her suitor away, tell him loudly and clearly to keep his hands off and, if necessary, use her FBI combat training to kick his ass. But the situation was different with Tanaka. He was a major player in the international art scene, and potentially her investigation. She couldn't afford to antagonize him. Which sure as hell didn't mean that she was going to give in and sleep with the guy, but she had to be careful not to hurt his pride with a blunt rejection.

Layla broke off the kiss, then gave him a shy smile. "I was raised very conservative, and those lessons have really stuck with me."

"I'd be happy to help you liberate yourself."

She was running out of tactful ways to put him off. It was time to use her backup plan. "A drink might help me relax. Why don't I get us something?" she suggested.

"Don't trouble yourself. Seung can bring anything you like," said Tanaka. Layla realized that she wasn't thinking like a rich person. Someone who had been raised with servants would simply expect to be served. She needed a reason to lift a finger for herself.

"My father used to make a wonderful cocktail. He called it a Crimson Sunrise." She hoped desperately that this wasn't the name of a real drink that Tanaka might know. "It's difficult to explain his method. I'd rather make it for you myself." She bowed her head slightly as she said this, playing the subservient woman who wanted to please him.

"All right. I can show you to . . ." He began to lead her out of the room, but Layla stopped him with a quick kiss on the cheek.

"I saw the bar near the dining room as we came in. You just relax. I'll be right back." She scampered off before he could object any further. First, she went back to the front hall and followed the path she'd seen Seung take. This led her to a coat closet, where she found her purse. She opened it and fished out a small white pill containing a five-milligram dose of Ambien. Pierce had advised her to always keep a sleeping pill in her bag, in case of just such a situation. A small dose of Ambien, combined with alcohol, would effectively put Tanaka to sleep for a couple of hours and give her time to do a quick search of the house.

She went to the fully stocked wet bar she'd spotted just off the dining room, mentally thanking the annoying instructor at Quantico who liked to make his students close their eyes at random intervals and describe every detail of the room they were in as a test of their situational awareness.

All she had to do now was invent a Crimson Sunrise. The flavor would have to be strong enough to cover the bitter taste of the Ambien. She crushed the tablet with the bottom of a glass and dissolved it in rum, then added club soda, cranberry juice, orange juice, and a squeeze of lime. Layla took a small sip to make sure it was palatable enough and, more importantly, hid the taste of the drug. Then she fixed herself a similar drink, with less rum and no surprise ingredients, and rejoined Tanaka among his treasures.

She gave him the spiked cocktail, waiting as he took a sip. He pronounced it "very good," but didn't drink any more. Layla took a belt of hers, hoping he'd follow suit. No luck.

He edged closer, clearly wanting to pick up where they'd left off, so she moved away to examine the statue of the athlete. "I think this might be my favorite piece in your collection. He looks so . . . alive."

Tanaka smiled. "I found this in a tiny little marketplace in Ankara. The seller wanted ten liras for it. Can you believe that? He had no idea what they had. A less honorable man could have taken advantage of their ignorance. I paid him a hundred thousand and still considered it a bargain."

He was obviously telling the story to boast about his own generosity, but if it was true, she had to give him credit. "That was very noble of you," said Layla. Then she felt his hand on her lower back, creeping south. She stepped aside and turned to him. "We're so lucky, aren't we? To be in a position to change the lives of those less fortunate, and less knowledgeable, than ourselves." She raised her glass. "To helping the less fortunate."

"To helping the less fortunate." He touched his glass to hers and took a drink.

She moved away from Tanaka and approached another display case, containing a small jade figurine of a lion that was missing part of its mane. "Where did you get this one?"

"The Tap Seac Gallery in Macao. Have you ever been there?" he asked, moving closer.

"Macao? No." Layla walked around the display case, examining the lion from different angles. "My cousin Nesim says it's difficult to do business there. Too many export restrictions."

"It's certainly complicated. You have to know the right people."

She faced him, a wide-eyed novice ready to be impressed. "The right people?"

He smiled and took another drink. *Good.* Then he closed in again, running a hand down her bare arm. "You don't really want to hear about all that stuff."

Layla looked at him intensely, trying to sound provocative. "I find it fascinating."

As he told her about his close personal relationship with the Director General of the Macao Customs Service, he finished off his Crimson Sunrise and began to sway, putting out a hand to steady himself.

"Are you all right?" she asked innocently.

"Yes," he assured her. "Your father's cocktail packs quite a punch." He made his way to the distressed leather sofa and sat down.

Layla sat beside him. "Can I get you some water?"

He tried to pat her hand but missed, landing on his own knee instead. "I'll be all right. I just need to . . ." He leaned his head back on the soft upholstery and closed his eyes.

She waited until his breathing grew deep and even, then prodded his shoulder and asked, "Kiyoshi?" He was out.

Layla got up, slipping off her heels so she could move more quietly. Tanaka wouldn't hear her, but the housekeeper might. She crept down the hall, peeking into a couple of guest bedrooms, a library, and a private screening room. The place looked like a model home, scrupulously neat, with the furniture staged just so. She would be willing to bet that Tanaka had never set foot in half of these rooms.

His office, at least, looked like he actually used it, with pictures of smiling people in scenic locations on the desk and a paperweight shaped vaguely like a duck. She wondered if young Hiro had made it. Layla locked the door, then returned to the desk. She turned on the computer. It was, of course, password protected. She tried a few of the obvious passwords with no luck. She looked through the neat pile of papers sitting beside it on the desk but found no sales receipts, shipping invoices, or incriminating thank-you notes.

Increasingly frustrated, she tried the desk drawers, but they were locked. She was tempted to break the lock on the file drawer. She really wanted to bring some useful evidence back to Pierce, to ease her guilt for derailing the sting operation in New York. But the next time Tanaka went to open that particular drawer, he would see what she'd done. So she left it alone.

She looked through the trash can and bookshelves, and behind the picture frames. Nothing. He certainly seemed to make more of an effort to keep everything in this office safely tucked away than he did in his Lake Como office. Maybe this was where he kept the information worth hiding.

She went upstairs to the master suite, a suitably decadent lair with an elevated four-poster bed draped in red silk, a fireplace, and elaborate crystal chandelier. She searched the massive walk-in closet, checking the pockets of his jackets and pants for any forgotten bits of paper or business cards from clients or other dealers. She wasn't surprised to see that every piece of clothing bore a designer label and at least half of them still had the tags attached, purchased but never worn. She kept an eye on the time as she searched. Tanaka would probably be out for at least another hour, but she didn't want to push her luck.

She ducked into the bathroom. It was, of course, enormous, the walls and floor covered in black-and-white tile. On the wall over the Jacuzzi tub, she saw a piece of weathered marble, about the size of a skateboard, carved with dancing human figures. It definitely looked familiar. On her phone, she quickly checked the pictures of the items looted from the museum in Faiyum. There was the same chunk of marble, broken off from a frieze in the Temple of Aphrodite. Tanaka had it hanging in his bathroom, presumably so he could admire it while enjoying the massage jets in his tub. He must know where it had originally come from, she thought; he was too meticulous not to. She couldn't help wondering how a man who seemed genuinely proud of himself for not screwing over the poor local dealers who'd sold him the statue downstairs could justify buying stolen property. What kind of story did he invent to convince himself that he wasn't really hurting anyone?

Layla took several pictures with her phone to show Pierce. The thought stirred up fresh anxiety about the state of their professional, and personal, relationship since Layla had discovered Pierce's addiction. She shoved those worries aside and focused on this incredible find. She wished she could tell Alberto about it.

Layla returned to the living room to check on Tanaka, still passed out on the couch. His breathing remained steady.

"Is he drunk?" asked a stern, Korean-accented female voice.

Layla spun around to see Seung, the housekeeper, glowering at her from the doorway. "I'm afraid so," she replied in Japanese, not bothering to pretend that she was just learning, as she'd done for Tanaka's benefit.

Seung snorted in disapproval, apparently unsurprised, then walked back out of the room. Layla decided to follow. She'd picked up a trace of resentment when she and Tanaka had first come in. If Seung wasn't happy, Layla might be able to use that to get her talking. Nobody knew the secrets of a household better than the staff that worked there, always in the background, watching and listening, trusted not to tell.

She followed Seung into the kitchen, an aggressively modern space, all gleaming metal and stark white. She moved toward the refrigerator to get herself some water, then reminded herself to act more like a spoiled brat. Layla perched on a stool by the raised marble counter and asked, "Get me a glass of water, would you?"

She watched Seung move confidently around the spotless kitchen, pouring ice water into a crystal glass. The entire room was meticulously clean. This woman clearly took pride in her work. Layla gazed around in apparent amazement as Seung brought her the water. "I don't know how you do it."

"Do what?"

"Keep this place so perfect. My housekeeper could certainly learn a thing or two." She'd overheard this at one of Farwadi's parties and had been tempted to smack the smug socialite who'd said it. But Seung seemed to appreciate the compliment, nodding and barely concealing a proud smile. "Maybe I'll just steal you for myself," she ventured. The other woman gave her a brief, hopeful look, making Layla regret that she had no real job to offer. "Do you care for all of Kiyoshi's houses this well?"

She learned that Seung oversaw the domestic staff in Tanaka's main residence just outside Tokyo and no less than four vacation homes, traveling between them as necessary, hiring seasonal help and managing the household budgets. "Wonderful!" said Layla. "My current housekeeper had no head for figures. That's why I'm letting her go. What kind of system do you use?"

"QuickBooks." She sounded eager to show off her skills.

"How do you classify the expenses? May I see?"

Seung nodded and went to retrieve her laptop. She sat beside Layla at the kitchen counter and opened the program. "This is the money Mr. Tanaka deposits into the household account," she explained, indicating a column on the spreadsheet. She took her potential new employer through her system of classifying expenses, encouraged by Layla's constant stream of praise for her cleverness.

The most interesting element was the collection of receipts that Seung had scanned into the computer. Layla saw at least one or two every month for deliveries from a company called Masterpiece Fine Arts Shipping. She'd seen that name before, in Noor Ghaffar's office. She pointed to the most recent receipt on the screen. "Is this the only shipping company Mr. Tanaka uses for his art purchases?"

"The only one I know about," said Seung.

"I've begun collecting art myself," Layla explained. "And I'd like to find a reliable carrier. Masterpiece has never lost or damaged any of his pieces?"

"No."

"Even that marble frieze in the upstairs bathroom? Ancient stone can be surprisingly fragile."

Seung nodded, getting back to the subject of her responsibilities. "Yes. I open the boxes and check the condition of every piece before the deliveryman leaves. Mr. Tanaka insists."

"Great. Let me get their information and I'll be sure to give them a call." Layla used her phone to take a picture of the receipt. This was a valuable discovery. Masterpiece was one of the links on the chain Pierce had sketched out, connecting at least one stolen item from the Faiyum collection to its final buyer. Layla would be very interested to find out how many of the other collectors on the suspect board were clients of Masterpiece Fine Arts Shipping.

"There you are!" said a familiar, slurred voice. She turned to see Tanaka staggering into the kitchen, awake but still groggy. He tried to sling an arm around her shoulders, but she slipped away, her mind racing to come up with a way to get out of here without blowing her cover. He reached for her again. "I'm sorry I drank so much . . ."

Layla slapped him. Hard. Tanaka stumbled back against the counter as she declared, "If you think that excuses your appalling behavior, you're very much mistaken."

"My . . . ?" He struggled to remember what he'd done. "If I was too forward . . ."

"Is that what you call it? I've never been so offended in my life." She tossed her head, as she'd seen one of Jehan's overindulged friends do when she didn't get her way. "Bennett Rothkopf speaks of you so highly. He said you were a gentleman. That's the only reason I agreed to come here tonight, alone. He'll be very disappointed to hear the truth."

Tanaka looked horrified by the prospect. He bowed to her. "My behavior was terribly disrespectful. Please accept my most sincere apologies. I would be very grateful if you didn't say anything to Mr. Rothkopf."

"Well . . ." She pretended to consider it, leaving him in suspense for another agonizing moment. Layla felt almost sorry for the guy, but she had to shame him into silence.

He gently took her hand. "Please, Miss Nawar. My private jet is at your disposal, to take you home or anywhere else you'd like to go. And we can leave this regrettable evening behind us."

Finally, she nodded. "All right. I won't discuss this with Bennett. Or anyone else."

"Thank you." He bowed again, touching his forehead to her hand before releasing it. She noticed Seung watching all of this with just the hint of a smile. She could tell that Layla was playing her boss, and seemed to find it satisfying. Layla hoped the housekeeper wouldn't be too disappointed when no new job offer arrived.

Tanaka summoned his chauffeur, who drove Layla to the airstrip. The jet was fueled up and ready to go. As she settled into the flight, Layla felt pleased with herself for the neat bit of psychological jujitsu she'd pulled on Tanaka but, at the same time, a little unsettled by how naturally it had come to her.

She reviewed the pictures she'd taken of the marble relic, which had made the whole trip worthwhile. It really was too bad that she couldn't share this discovery with Alberto. She wouldn't have recognized the piece as stolen if he hadn't drawn her attention to the looting in Faiyum. She thought about inviting him to the Rothkopf Foundation fundraiser for the Girls' Education Initiative that she was due to attend that night, but didn't expect anyone more important than Rothkopf himself to be there. Then she remembered another event coming up next week. The Egyptian Minister of Culture was holding a reception for visiting members of the UNESCO World Heritage Centre. Farwadi had gotten Layla on the guest list. He could do the same for Alberto. She sent Farwadi an email with her request.

She saw that she'd missed several incoming text messages from Pierce. The first had been sent near midnight, asking, *How was the party?* Then another one two hours later: *Check in pls.* And an hour after that: *Where the fuck are you?*

Meet 8 a.m. in safe house, Layla texted back.

She had also gotten a text from Rami that read, "Badru wants to meet you," attached to a picture of a chubby, dark-eyed baby. Rami had been sending her a steady stream of pictures of eight-month-old Badru, her sister Sanaa's first child. Layla had trouble imagining little Sanaa, fixed in her memory as an annoying seven-year-old pest, as a wife and mother. Their own mother must be thrilled, thought Layla. At least one of her daughters had embraced the life she'd wanted for them both.

She knew that Rami had dreamed of reuniting his divided family ever since she'd left. He had stayed in touch with Layla, against his parents' wishes. Then he'd convinced her to meet for coffee, against her better judgment. Now he was using Badru as enticement for her to visit Sanaa, who still lived half a mile from the apartment where they grew up in Manshiyat Naser. Next, he would probably want her to sit down for a nice family dinner with Mama. But their mother had made her feelings very clear on the day Layla had walked out eleven years ago, "If you leave now, you leave forever. You will no longer be part of this family."

"Good," she had shouted back. With a last, regretful look at her little brother and sister, Layla had stormed out of the apartment, slamming the door behind her. She had made her decision. She would never go back there again.

Layla looked at the picture of Badru. With his wide, solemn eyes, he looked just like Sanaa had as a baby. To her surprise, she really did want to meet her nephew, and to see the woman her sister had become. Pretending to be someone else, ironically enough, was making her want to explore who she really was.

But it was out of the question. She'd already taken too much of a risk and disobeyed Pierce's direct order by getting together with Rami. Layla knew that the streets of Cairo were crawling with informants. Pierce had already recruited a few to tip her off to illegal art transactions and to watch the Rothkopf Gallery at night. "Security consultant" Mackey undoubtedly had some of his own. Of course, Layla had learned how to avoid surveillance at Quantico. And, as she'd told Pierce, she wouldn't run into anyone who knew her "heiress" persona in Manshiyat Naser . . .

She shook her head, firmly dismissing the idea. She couldn't afford to take unnecessary chances. This investigation was too important, and Layla had too much to prove.

From the Cairo airport, she took a cab directly to the safe house. She walked in to find Pierce on the phone, in mid-argument. "What the hell do you expect? It's only been a couple of months . . ." She stopped, cut off by the male voice Layla could hear faintly as he shouted through the phone. "You want to come out here and run this?" Pierce demanded. "Yeah, didn't think so." She hung up.

"Was that Monaghan?" asked Layla.

The other woman didn't bother to answer. "I've been trying to reach you. Where have you been?"

"Kiyoshi Tanaka's villa in Crete." Layla imitated his entitled attitude: "Why not go right now? My private jet is standing by."

Pierce wasn't amused. "So you flew off with a total stranger. Kinda risky, don't you think?"

"That's what these people do. To them it's like sharing a cab. And I didn't know if I'd ever get near Tanaka again."

"You should have sent me a message to let me know what you were doing," Pierce insisted.

Layla had gotten similar criticisms from other colleagues at the Bureau. After a lifetime of going it alone, she still hadn't fully adjusted to being a team player. But Pierce wasn't exactly the perfect team captain, either. "Just look at what I found," Layla said, as she opened the picture of the marble in Tanaka's bathroom on her phone. "He has a piece of marble that was stolen from a museum in Faiyum last year, by none other than the Muharib."

Pierce took the phone and studied the picture intently. "This is good," she had to admit. "I'll get a warrant for Tanaka's finances, start following the money trail back to his supplier."

"One step ahead of you," said Layla. "He uses a company called Masterpiece Fine Arts Shipping."

"He told you that?"

"Not exactly." She smiled. "While he was showing me his collection, Mr. Tanaka tried to get me into bed. So I followed your advice and slipped him some Ambien." She dropped her head to one side and let out a fake snore. "Worked like a charm."

The senior agent chuckled and Layla's chest warmed with pride. Her old need to impress her mentor was still strong, even after everything that had passed between them.

"While he was snoozing, I got a look at the housekeeper's record of deliveries." She brought up the image of the receipt. "Masterpiece handles all of his international art purchases. And at least some of Noor Ghaffar's." Layla went to the suspect board and pointed to the woman's picture. One of the words jotted on the board next to it was "Masterpiece."

Pierce broke into a grin. "I knew that company was dirty! They route all of their shipments through their main warehouse in Singapore, I suspect to hide the real point of origin. I just haven't been able to prove that any of them are illegal. But if we have evidence that they handled a stolen relic from Faiyum, I can get a warrant to tear apart that warehouse."

"Count me in."

The other woman hesitated, her smile fading. "Let's see how the timing works out," she said. "I don't want you to get stuck explaining too many mysterious trips out of town to the Rothkopfs."

Layla nodded reluctantly. It made sense. But that didn't mean she was happy about being excluded. Especially when she couldn't help wondering if Pierce was deliberately keeping her at a distance, if Layla's very presence reminded her of the secret she was so desperate to hide.

She took a cab back to her apartment. There seemed to be an increased military presence on the streets, and she wondered if it was in response to any particular threat, or just another show of government force. She took a hot shower and changed into comfortable clothes, then settled on the couch with a stack of reports she'd borrowed from Pierce, determined to educate herself about international shipping laws and how companies like Masterpiece Fine Arts got around them. Three hours later, she woke up feeling dazed, cranky, and too old for the party-all-night lifestyle of the socialite set.

As she re-energized herself with a run around the Gezira Sporting Club, her phone buzzed with an incoming text message. It was from Alberto: *Got the party invite from your cousin. Thx.*

She texted back a smiley face emoji. *My pleasure.*

No response appeared for a long moment. Then: *Got a lead on a dig.* Layla grinned. His archaeologist friend must have come through with satellite images. *Still interested?*

Hell yes, she was interested. She knew that Alberto had reservations about bringing her along, so she kept her response business-like: *Yes. When?*

Meet in front of Zamalek, 20:00, he replied.

See you there, she answered.

Layla arrived at the Zamalek Rooftop a few minutes before eight p.m., feeling wide awake and ready for adventure in her gray T-shirt, khaki pants, and boots. At a few minutes past, Alberto pulled up in a battered black Jeep. "You're here," he said, with some surprise. "I wasn't sure if you were really serious about this."

"Now you know," she told him. He pushed open the passenger side door and she climbed in.

He drove west, skillfully navigating the narrow, winding streets. "The site's about an hour away. There's a satellite photo in the glove compartment."

Layla dug out the photo, turning on the overhead light to examine it. She saw a heavily magnified image taken by a thermal camera, looking down on a mostly dark, cold area. Alberto pointed to several blooms of warm red and yellow, clustered in one spot.

"You got this from your friend . . ."

"Who works with UNESCO, yes. Teresa is a professor of Egyptology at the Università di Bologna, but she prefers the term 'space archaeologist.'" He laughed. "She gets satellite images from the military and uses them to look for sites where ancient ruins might be buried. Something about the terrain and erosion—I don't really understand it. But the thermal imagery also shows the heat signatures of people." He pointed to the red blobs on the image. "In this case, at least three."

Layla studied the image. "How do we know they're working on an illegal dig? Couldn't they just be a group of Bedouins around a campfire?"

"Could be. This trip might turn out to be nothing more than a pleasant midnight drive through the desert."

"But you don't think so."

He shook his head. "If they were in the middle of nowhere, maybe. But this group is suspiciously close to an authorized excavation by a French team near Saqqâra. Illegal digs have a tendency to pop up around legitimate sites. Where there's one ancient ruin, there must be more, right?"

"I assume your friend also shares these images with the local police."

Alberto snorted a laugh. "She does. But they don't have the manpower to chase down every report of an illegal dig. And half of the cops are probably getting paid off by the same people who hire the diggers."

"And work for the Muharib," she concluded.

"Right."

They drove past the Dahshur pyramids and turned onto a small road, then onto an even smaller, unpaved trail. There were no visible lights and no signs of human habitation, just miles of rocks and blowing sand in every direction. Alberto kept track of their position on a GPS app as they approached the coordinates of the dig. He stopped the car near an outcropping of dark, volcanic rock when they were still a quarter mile away. "I don't want to get too close with the Jeep," he explained. "We should walk from here."

"Glad I ditched my heels, then," joked Layla.

But the journalist wasn't laughing. "I shouldn't have brought you into this."

"I'm kidding. I won't slow you down, I promise."

"That's not it." He faced her, his eyes dark and serious. "The men who work at these sites are dangerous, and they do not like to be spied on. If they see us, they'll start shooting." He grabbed his backpack from the backseat and pulled out a Beretta M9. It was an accurate weapon, but Layla had always found the grip a little too bulky. "Are you sure you want to come with me?" he asked.

She wished she could reassure him that she was a trained federal agent, not a pampered heiress he had to protect. But she had to stay in character. "I've spent my whole life being sheltered from reality, from the consequences of my actions. I don't want to live like that anymore. I want to see the truth."

After a long moment, he nodded. "Just stay close and follow my lead," he instructed. He put the gun into the front pocket of his tan jacket and slung the pack over his shoulder.

They walked into the desert, climbing up and over the shifting dunes. Layla felt her heart pounding in anticipation. This was the kind of mission she had trained for at Quantico, not sitting behind a desk, translating reports about other agents' adventures in the field. Other than the sound of their feet digging into the sand, it was utterly quiet. Alberto shone his flashlight just ahead of them, with his hand over it to dim the beam. When they spotted the lights of the dig, he turned it off. As the two of them approached, they could hear the sharp impact of metal hitting stone.

Alberto waved for Layla to stay put as he crested a dune and peered cautiously over the top. He pulled a pair of binoculars from his pack and looked through them, pushing his tortoiseshell glasses back on his forehead. His jaw tightened at what he saw. Layla crept up beside him. They were still several hundred feet away from the dig, and she couldn't see much in the bright glare from the flood lamps surrounding the site, powered by a humming generator. Alberto finally handed her the binoculars.

She saw four bearded men wearing long, loose caftans working at the site, digging up and disassembling the ruins of a small building. Two of the walls were still standing, one about ten feet long, the other one at least twenty. They were made of what looked like limestone brick and plastered smooth on the inside, painted with ancient symbols and hieroglyphs, just visible beneath a thick layer of dust. The other two walls had collapsed long ago. One of the men shone a flashlight through the narrow gaps in the pile of rubble, as if looking for something buried inside.

Another man was in the process of tearing down one of the remaining walls. He stood inside the structure, using a sledge-hammer to smash the ancient limestone into pieces. Layla winced as he hit the wall, casually destroying a piece of her heritage that had survived for thousands of years. "This is barbaric," she whispered to Alberto.

He nodded grimly. "It's happening all over the Middle East. Hell, all over the world. I can't even think about how much history we're losing every day."

A third member of the work crew was sorting through the broken chunks of limestone, looking for decorative pieces to sell. *Like the engraved marble on display in Tanaka's bathroom*, thought Layla, feeling sick. When he found something suitable, he handed it up to the man standing by the edge of the pit, who appeared to be supervising the dig.

The man turned the chunk of stone over in his hands, examining it, pleased. He looked a little older, and considerably cleaner, than the others. His nose had obviously been broken at least once, and not set properly, so that it bent slightly to the left. Layla noted the holstered gun on his belt.

"That's Khalid Yasin," Alberto said quietly. "He runs several of these crews."

"Runs them for who? The Muharib?"

He nodded. "And they've been keeping him awfully busy lately, digging up more relics to sell. They're raising money for something special."

Layla thought about the huge cache of weapons that Monaghan had found in the shipping container. "That can't be good."

"No. It can't."

Then the man with the flashlight called out in Arabic, "I see it!" This prompted Yasin to shout to someone outside the bright floodlit circle. A dark-haired little boy, no more than seven years old, stepped forward in response. He was painfully thin, in baggy clothes so filthy it was impossible to tell their original color. The sight of him made Layla go cold. He looked just like the kids she'd grown up with, the *zabbaleen* of Manshiyat Naser. Under all that dirt, he could have been Rami.

He scrambled down a ladder into the pit and joined the man with the flashlight, who gave him instructions Layla couldn't hear, pointing to one of the gaps in the rubble, barely a foot wide. The boy began to wriggle through, his skinny frame just small enough to fit between the broken chunks of limestone. The unstable pile shifted and Layla gasped, afraid it would collapse on the boy. It didn't. For now. The kid kept inching forward, his feet disappearing into the small mountain of rubble as the man shone the light in through another gap.

Finally, a barely audible voice shouted, "I have it."

"Bring it out," the man told him. But apparently, the boy was taking too long to crawl backward through the tight space, so the guy reached in, grabbed his ankle, and dragged him. This movement disturbed the delicate structure of the rock pile. It shifted again, collapsing some of the gaps and creating others. The boy's head emerged seconds before it would have been crushed.

"Jesus," muttered Alberto. Layla exhaled the breath she didn't realize she'd been holding. "He was lucky. Twenty-six kids just like him died in illegal digs last year alone. They're disposable to these assholes," he said, his voice growing nearly too loud. She shushed him and he quieted down, speaking just as intensely. "They go to the poorest neighborhoods to recruit these skinny, starving little boys, and sometimes girls. The kids know perfectly well how dangerous it is. They know they're risking their lives for a few piastres. But they need the money. Not for a new toys or designer clothes, but to keep their families from starving."

"I know that!" she snapped. *Better than you think*, she wanted to add. She could hardly blame Alberto for being condescending to the person he thought she was. She doubted that Jehan or Hiro, or even James, had ever considered the question of what they would do to survive. Or to help their families survive. Layla knew what she would have done when she was a child, if someone had offered her the equivalent of a pantry full of food in exchange for the chance of being buried alive. She would have taken it, as would Rami or Sanaa. It was pure luck that no one had ever asked.

Alberto quietly took a camera out of his backpack. He lay flat against the dune and stretched out his arms, pushing the lens as far as he could toward the dig. He took a dozen pictures, then crawled forward a few inches, moving even closer than he had with the binoculars. Layla touched his shoulder and whispered, "Be careful."

"I will," he assured her but, emboldened by his success, he edged just a little closer, angling the camera to see around the side of the generator. The bright floodlights glinted off the lens, catching Yasin's attention. He turned toward Layla and Alberto as they quickly ducked out of sight. They weren't quick enough. "*Hunak!*" he called to the other men. *Over there.*

Alberto pulled the Beretta from his pocket, but as soon as he looked over the top of the dune, Yasin drew his own gun and fired. The journalist dropped back. "*Cazzo!*" he yelled. "*Siamo inculcati.*" *Fuck! We're fucked.*

Layla knew she had to act fast, before the men climbed out of the excavation pit and surrounded her and Alberto. Of course, doing anything other than screaming uselessly might blow her cover as a sheltered heiress, but that seemed preferable to being captured or killed by terrorists. She grabbed Alberto's gun, expertly twisting it out of his grip.

"What are you doing?" he demanded.

"Get back to the Jeep. I'll be right behind you." She felt completely calm, detached from her own fear. Agent el-Deeb could handle this.

"What? I can't . . ."

There was no time to argue. Layla quickly edged along the side of the dune, moving a few feet to the left. Yasin's attention should still be focused on where he'd seen Alberto. She popped up, quickly took aim at Yasin, and fired, catching him by surprise. As she ducked back down, she heard a shout of pain. Layla grinned to herself. She'd hit him. She had no idea how badly, but she wasn't going to stick around to find out. The other men in the pit would have taken cover from the unseen shooter, which offered her a few seconds' head start.

She turned to Alberto, who was staring at her in utter shock. "Come on!"

She grabbed his hand and they ran, away from the bright flood-lights and into the dark, open desert. As their eyes adjusted to the dim moonlight, they were able to retrace the footsteps they'd left on the way in. They heard the voices of the men coming behind them, followed by the sharp crack of gunshots. Alberto ducked instinctively, but the men were too far away to hit moving targets in the dark. The surge of adrenaline made Layla feel invincible as she sprinted for the Jeep. Alberto had the keys in his hand as he got in and started the car. Layla quickly jumped into the passenger seat and he sped off.

She looked out the back window as they careened down the unpaved road, nearly swerving out of control on the turns. "It's okay," she said finally. "There's no one behind us."

He let up fractionally on the gas, shaking his head as he sputtered, "What was that? How did you . . . ?"

She was tempted to tell him the truth. But despite the intense experience they had just shared, she hardly knew the man. And he was, after all, a reporter. "My father taught me how to shoot," she said simply.

"At terrorists?" he demanded.

"At empty bottles, actually." She shrugged.

Alberto glanced at her, his expression unreadable. She resisted the urge to embellish the lie with too much detail. He said nothing and looked back at the road. They drove for most of the next hour in silence.

"You can drop me back at the Zamalek Rooftop," she said.

"No, I'll take you home. It's late." Just a few minutes after 11:00, actually. The party was just getting started in clubs all over Cairo. But with everything that had happened in the past few hours, thought Layla, it felt a whole lot later than that.

As they pulled up in front of her building, she faced Alberto. "Thank you for bringing me along. I needed to see that."

"I should be thanking you, for saving my *culo*."

She laughed, and the tension between them eased. She offered her hand to shake, but Alberto took it and briefly touched it to his lips. "You're not at all what I expected, Miss Nawar." He looked at her like a puzzle he was determined to solve. One that she hoped he would leave in the box.

"I'll take that as a compliment." She got out of the car. "I'll see you at the Minister of Culture's reception next week."

"I'll be the one in the rented tux," he told her, and drove off in his very sandy Jeep.

Layla walked into her penthouse suite, finally able to drop all pretense. The adrenaline that had been keeping her numb to the reality of what had just happened drained away and she thought about the little boy at the dig. Her eyes stung with tears. She forced them back. In her family, to her father in particular, crying had been a sign of weakness, and it was hard to let go of that judgment, even now. She wished James could be with her. Not that she could tell him where she'd been or what she'd seen, but she always felt better just having him close. Of course, caring too much about someone was a weakness, too. She knew that he was off somewhere, schmoozing a potential client, but she'd see him tomorrow night, at the Rothkopf Foundation fundraiser.

Layla tried to sleep, but thoughts of the dig, plus the long nap she'd taken that afternoon, kept her awake for most of the night. She got out of bed just after seven thirty, to find a new text from Rami. It was an invitation to join him at Sanaa's apartment for lunch, accompanied by another adorable picture of Badru. Sanaa, he promised, would be delighted to see her. She thought of the little boy again. The little boy who could have been Rami. Layla told him she'd go. Rami responded with a string of happy emojis and the words *Meet you at el-Sayeda Zeinab Station at 12:30.*

She spent the morning reviewing her notes from the investigation, adding what she'd learned about Tanaka and what she'd seen at the dig. She composed several text messages to Rami, telling him that she couldn't come with him to visit Sanaa, but sent none of them. The truth was, she wanted to go. But she knew she had to be very careful. If anyone connected with Pierce, or Rothkopf, for that matter, saw her with Rami, she could be in real trouble. By eleven thirty, Layla was dressed in black pants, a white blouse, and a red-and-black print cardigan, accessorized with a black hijab. She went downstairs and got in a cab, asking the driver to take her to the Giza Zoo, which was on the other side of the Nile, in the opposite direction from Manshiyat Naser. At the zoo, she went into the ladies' room and took off her sweater, leaving the simple white blouse and black pants. Then she pulled a pale blue hijab out of her purse and traded the black one for it. She finished the outfit with a large pair of sunglasses.

Then she went back out to hail another cab. This one took her back across the river, followed her directions on a circuitous route through the city, and finally dropped her off a block from the el-Sayeda Zeinab station at 12:31 p.m.

Rami was already there, waiting for her. When he saw his sister, he looked confused. "What's with the hijab?"

She'd forgotten to take it off, she realized, and quickly did so now, trying to come up with an explanation. "It's . . . not important. Never mind."

Still haunted by the boy at the dig, she pulled her little brother into a fierce hug. "Are you all right?" he asked.

Get your shit together, Agent el-Deeb, she told herself. She took a deep breath and smiled. "A little nervous, maybe."

"Don't be." He started walking down the sidewalk, and she fell into step beside him. "Sanaa and I have been talking about this. Sure, she wasn't too happy when you left home. And left us behind."

"I had no way to bring you with me . . ." she began, but Rami held up a hand to stop her.

"I know that," he said. "So does Sanaa. I think having a baby has really changed her perspective on life."

She had to laugh. "Her perspective on life? She's eighteen!"

He grinned, and it made him look like the little boy she remembered. They crossed the street, heading into their old neighborhood. Manshiyat Naser wasn't so bad on the outskirts, where it bordered "respectable" Cairo. The streets were narrow and the apartments were small, but there were no piles of trash rotting on the sidewalk. Living conditions got worse as they approached the Mokattam Hills, which bordered Manshiyat Naser to the east. Garbage City, with its eternal stench, sprawled along the base of the cliffs. That's where Layla had grown up and, as far as she knew, where her mother, Halima, still lived.

Sanaa had moved a few blocks farther away from the hills, to the relative comfort of a three-hundred-square-foot apartment with electricity and, most of the time, running water.

Rami led the way into a redbrick apartment building, up two flights of stairs and down the hall to their sister's door. Layla braced herself as he knocked. The young woman who answered was about her height but a little heavier, with curves where Layla wished she had them. Her dark, straight hair was pulled back into a ponytail, and her eyes were rimmed in black. Layla felt no spark of recognition. Sanaa might as well have been a stranger.

Sanaa hugged Rami, then turned to the sister she hadn't seen or spoken to in eleven years. She hesitated for a moment, then hugged Layla, too. "Welcome to my home."

"Thank you for having me." The exchange was a little stiff, but friendly enough. Sanaa ushered them inside. The tiny apartment was scrupulously clean and carefully organized, with every inch of space put to good use. The sofa folded out into a bed, and the kitchen table lay flat against the wall when not in use. Layla couldn't helping thinking that, in Manhattan, this would be considered a trendy "micro-apartment," renting for a thousand dollars a month.

Sanaa went over to the wooden crib tucked in a corner and scooped up her baby, cooing to him as she turned him to face his aunt and uncle. "This is Badru."

"Oh, he's beautiful!" said Layla. The kid had been cute in pictures, but in person, his bright, curious gaze and bubbly smile made him just about irresistible. She held out her arms, and Sanaa handed her Badru.

Layla was dubious about having children of her own, but she was delighted by her nephew, making silly noises as he wrapped her finger in his tiny fist. She saw Sanaa and Rami exchange a distinctly conspiratorial look. They weren't plotting to get her settled down, too, were they? If either one of them mentioned a nice guy they knew who happened to be single, Layla was out of here.

Sanaa put Badru on a blanket on the floor, keeping an eye on him as she served lunch. It was quite a feast, starting with flatbread and hummus, followed by a whole roast chicken, baked vegetables in a spicy tomato sauce, and cabbage leaves stuffed with rice. Layla couldn't help wondering how much of the family's weekly food budget had gone into this one meal, intended to demonstrate that they could afford it. Of course, Layla couldn't ask about money. She knew that her sister wouldn't take money from her. Maybe if she called it a college fund for Badru . . .

"I'm sorry my husband couldn't join us," Sanaa told them, clearly more proud than ashamed of the fact. "He works at the recycling plant."

"Tarek's a great guy. You'll like him," said Rami, automatically assuming that they would meet.

Layla tried to steer the conversation away from herself as they talked and ate. She dismissed her fictional job in the comptroller's office as too boring, while asking more questions about Sanaa's family and Rami's engineering studies. She caught her brother glancing at the clock behind her. The second time he did it, she asked, "Are we keeping you from a hot date?"

"What? No," he said, a little too defensively, in Layla's opinion.

"So it's not until later, then?" she teased.

"I . . . there isn't . . ." He looked so flustered that both his sisters had to laugh.

Rami was saved by a knock at the door. He and Sanaa exchanged another significant look. "What's going on?" asked Layla.

"Nothing," Sanaa said, as she went to answer it. Now she sounded defensive.

Layla stood up, looming ominously over her brother. "Rami . . ."

Before he could answer, Sanaa opened the door. Halima bustled in, handing her a small bag of lemons. "I got these from the nice woman upstairs . . ." Then she saw Layla and froze.

Her mother had gotten old. That was the first thing that occurred to Layla as her initial shock began to clear. Halima was only in her early fifties, but her hair had gone mostly gray, and her constant frown lines had settled into wrinkles, which deepened as she stared at her eldest child. "What are you doing here?"

Layla glared at Sanaa and Rami. "Getting ambushed."

Rami approached her, holding up his hands in a gesture of peace. "I know you're angry, and I'm sorry for tricking you." He turned to his mother. "Both of you. But Layla won't be in Cairo long enough to convince you to talk to each other."

"Talk?" She scoffed. "I have nothing to say."

She started for the door, but Rami caught her arm to stop her. "Please, Mama. Don't you think it's time for you to forgive each other?"

Halima jerked her arm away. "And what do you think I've done that needs forgiving?"

"I just meant that . . ."

"Are you suggesting it was my fault that your sister abandoned her family?" she demanded, fixing him with a withering stare. "That I somehow drove her away? Is that what you think?"

Before she could stop herself, Layla stepped between them, as she'd done so many times in their childhood, coming to her brother's defense. "Stop it. I don't like being manipulated, either, but he was just trying to help." She shot him a look. "In his own completely misguided way."

"You have no right to lecture me about my own children," Halima said coldly. "Not after you turned your back on them. On all of us."

"I went to college!" Layla shouted, warning herself not to get dragged into the same old argument but unable to help it. "Some parents might even have been proud of their daughter for earning a full scholarship."

"Your family needed you here."

"To do what? Earn a little extra money?" She thought about the boy at the dig site again, then pushed the image away. "The family was doing fine. Baba was getting steady work . . ."

"Don't you dare talk about your father," cried Halima. "You didn't even have the decency to be at his funeral."

"You're the one who told me never to come back!"

Eleven years of pent-up anger and resentment came pouring out. As the two women shouted, Badru started to cry. Sanaa quickly picked him up, stroking his back as she spoke earnestly to her mother. "Please stop, this isn't how family should behave."

Halima jerked her chin at Layla. "She doesn't know the meaning of the word. I've never seen such a selfish child."

"Selfish?"

"You thought only about what you wanted. No one else."

Layla flinched, stung by the accusation. "We tried so hard to teach you respect, so you could grow up to be a good person, a good Christian. But you decided long ago that your ignorant family was holding you back. Perhaps it was for the best that you left. And that you'll be leaving again soon."

"No. That's not . . ." she started to say, but her mother was already walking out the door, closing it firmly behind her.

For a long moment, Badru's crying was the only sound. Rami went to Layla, reaching out to lay a hand on her shoulder. "I'm so sorry. It wasn't supposed to be like that."

"I trusted you," she said, shaking off his hand.

Ignoring his and Sanaa's pleas to stay, she kissed Badru on the forehead, then turned and left. She walked the three miles back to Garden City at a furious march, trying to put everything about Manshiyat Naser, her childhood, and her whole damn family behind her. How could she have been stupid enough to get suckered in by Rami's happy delusions? Hadn't she learned at Quantico to never, *ever* let her guard down? She knew better. At least, she would from now on.

She arrived home with a tension headache and the sour burn of acid in her gut. Layla changed into her favorite sweats and plopped down in front of her fifty-inch plasma screen to watch something mindless. Then she remembered the fundraiser she was supposed to go to with James. *Shit.* The thought of smiling and chatting with a bunch of self-satisfied society types all night made her stomach start churning again. Maybe, just maybe, she didn't have to. There would be no one related to her investigation at the event, other than the Rothkopfs. All she had to do was call James and tell him she couldn't go. He'd want to know why, of course, which she could hardly explain. She would just have to say she was sick.

She had never been so happy to reach voicemail. "I'm so sorry to do this to you, but I can't make it to the fundraiser tonight. I ate some bad *kofta* from that guy on Noubar Street and I've been sick all afternoon. I really am sorry. Call me later and tell me how it went."

She felt relieved to be off the hook but terrible about once again lying to James. This was a relatively innocuous lie, the kind that normal couples sometimes told each other, but somehow, that didn't make it any better.

She had dozed off in front of the TV when the doorbell startled her awake. She was just getting up to answer it when she heard James calling through the door, "Layla? Are you all right?"

Shit. She should have known that James would be thoughtful enough to come check on her, and that the doorman, having seen him with her so often, would welcome him into the building and send him right up.

She opened the door to find James all dressed up for the evening in a dark gray suit and maroon tie, looking at her and her ratty sweatpants with concern. "How are you feeling?"

The sight of him triggered a rush of happiness so strong it scared her. "I've been better," she said, honestly enough.

He came in and wrapped his arms around her. Then he stepped back, holding up a plastic bottle filled with a thick, milky liquid. "This will help. My father got it from a doctor in Johannesburg when he had food poisoning."

She peered at the faded label. It was written in Afrikaans, which she couldn't read. "What is it?"

"I'm not sure what it's called in English. All I know is that I've never seen Dad as sick as he was that night. He took two table-spoons of this, and half an hour later, he was as good as new."

She put a hand to her stomach as if feeling a wave of nausea. "I don't know. I think I just need to rest."

James set the bottle on the kitchen counter. "Well, it's here if you want it. Can I get you anything else? Maybe some tea?"

"It's sweet of you to check on me, but you don't have to stay. I know you've been looking forward to this fundraiser, and I really am sorry I can't be there." She felt terrible about bailing on him. Maybe her mother had been right to call her "selfish."

"You can't help it if you're sick," he assured her, making her feel even worse. He led her over to the couch and sat with her, pulling her close. "I don't want you to worry about anything right now. Just close your eyes and relax." As he began stroking her hair, she did allow herself to relax, shutting out her job, her fake identity, Pierce, Rothkopf, the Muharib, everything but this moment, feeling safe and warm in his arms.

"I wish we could stay like this," he said softly, voicing her thoughts. "Just you and me."

"Mmmm," she murmured in agreement.

She had reached a state of utter contentment when James said, "There's something else I wanted to give you." Her eyes popped open as she felt him reaching into his pocket. *It's too soon for a ring*, she thought desperately. *Please don't be a ring*.

She sat up to find him holding a black velvet jewelry box, too big for a ring. James opened the box to reveal a simple string of pearls. "These belonged to my mother. Seemed appropriate for tonight."

Layla was touched and terrified at the same time. His mother's necklace felt like an even more intimate gift than an engagement ring. "But if I'm not going . . ."

"I still want you to have them." He held out the box. She took it.

"They're beautiful. Thank you." She looked up to see him gazing at her with pure, unmistakable love. As he opened his mouth to say it, she bolted off the couch, went to the kitchen counter, and picked up the bottle of medicine. "Two tablespoons, right?"

"Right."

She tracked down a tablespoon in the gourmet kitchen she never used and gulped down a dose of the chalky, bitter stuff. Layla thought there was a decent chance it would actually make her sick. Which would be exactly what she deserved. James, however, deserved better. So she declared herself cured in time to join him at the fundraiser. She changed into a royal blue, full-skirted dress and stood in front of the full-length mirror in her bedroom, shaking off Layla el-Deeb's complicated angst and embracing the carefree simplicity of her alter ego. James came in and stood behind her, admiring her reflection. "How did I get so lucky?" he asked, carefully kissing her cheek so he didn't smudge her makeup. Then he held up the string of pearls. "May I?"

She nodded, and he gently draped them around her neck. He looked up, meeting her eyes in the mirror, and declared the result "perfect."

THEY ARRIVED AT THE Semiramis Intercontinental Hotel an hour late. As soon as they walked into the Cleopatra Ballroom, Bennett came striding up to his son, irritated. "I was starting to get concerned . . ." Then he saw the necklace Layla was wearing and stopped. For a moment, she was afraid he'd object, and she'd be stuck in the middle of another family blowout. But his expression softened and he said, "Those suit you."

The fundraiser was an elegant affair, with understated navy blue and gold decor that didn't try to compete with the spectacular, panoramic view of the city. Pictures of the girls who had benefited from the Girls' Education Initiative sat on every table. There was no denying that Rothkopf did a lot of good with his ill-gotten gains. Which only made Layla's job more complicated, she thought, taking a sip of champagne as she circulated through the crowd. *Why can't the "bad guys" be pure evil and the "good guys" paragons of virtue?*

Rothkopf had flown in several of the scholarship recipients, now grown women, to mingle with donors and inspire them to be even more generous. Layla listened to them describe the challenges they'd faced as intelligent girls trapped by poverty and restrictive cultures. It was all very familiar, right up to the part where a bunch of rich white people had shown up to rescue them, she thought, with a surprising burst of resentment. Nobody had rescued her. And nobody was rescuing that little boy she'd seen out in the desert, risking his life to feed his family.

Her gaze fell on Mackey, standing unobtrusively by the stage, wearing a perfectly tailored suit and his usual scowl. I know just how you feel, buddy, she thought, for the first time in their brief acquaintance.

"Are you all right?" asked James, startling her.

"Fine," she assured him, giving his arm a squeeze, forcing Layla Nawar back to the surface. "That stuff you brought me was amazing."

"Good."

Everyone took their seats for dinner and speeches. The meal was an expertly prepared salmon fillet with asparagus, with individual chocolate soufflés for dessert. Layla couldn't help thinking that Sanaa's roast chicken had been more satisfying.

Bennett Rothkopf, sitting across from her at the round, eight-person table, quickly downed three glasses of Scotch, with a fourth ready and waiting. She wondered if he was feeling the pressure of his stagnant business and growing debt, despite the outward show of extravagance. James certainly was, and he wasn't even the one responsible for the whole mess.

The executive director of the Girls' Education Initiative finished her speech, then introduced Rothkopf. He took the stage to loud, enthusiastic applause. He held up a hand to quiet his guests. "Thank you. Thank you, that's very kind." The slight unsteadiness of his voice was the only hint that he was buzzed. If there was one skill Rothkopf had unquestionably mastered, it was putting on a good front. "As much as I appreciate your support. I'm not the one who deserves it. The woman who does is, tragically, no longer with us: my beloved wife, Alice." He paused for another, more subdued round of applause. "I wish all of you could have known her. She was an inspiration to everyone. Myself included. This event, supporting an organization that was so close to her heart, is my attempt to keep that inspiration alive." His voice caught, this time from emotion. Layla saw James struggling not to get choked up as well. She took his hand and squeezed it. She'd felt nothing like this kind of grief when her father died. It had been more like a relief. Which only now struck her as its own kind of sad.

"Of course, the greatest gift she left to me is our son, James." More applause as he gestured grandly toward James. "I probably don't say this enough," Bennett told him, "but I see more of her in you every day. Her kindness. Her warmth." Now the four Scotches were catching up with him, making him well up with easy tears.

To Layla's surprise, James went up onto the stage and hugged his father, drawing a collective *awwww* from the guests. Rothkopf returned to the microphone. "I'm a very lucky man, with a wonderful family. And I'm not only talking about this kid . . ." He gave James a playful punch on the arm, prompting a few laughs. "I'm talking about honorary family: friends, colleagues, community. You know who you are." He nodded to several of the guests. Then his gaze fell on Layla. "There are some people who feel like family the moment you meet them."

If Layla could have ducked under the tablecloth and disappeared, she would have done it in a heartbeat. But Rothkopf was already pointing her out and telling the audience, "Layla Nawar has not only proven herself invaluable to my business, but priceless to my boy." More laughs.

Now James was beckoning her on stage. "Come on up here, Layla."

It seemed useless to refuse, so she decided to get it over with. She plastered on a smile and walked up three short steps to join the Rothkopf men on stage. Cameras and phones appeared in the hands of every guest, snapping pictures as Bennett, always recognizing a good photo op, put his arms around James and Layla, with the Girls' Education Initiative banner behind them. "This is my hope for the future, right here," he announced.

Layla found her smile becoming more genuine as she stood there with her "honorary family," savoring the feeling of acceptance, of belonging, that she'd been chasing all her life. But it was all based on a lie. "I'm going to get some air," she told James.

He immediately looked worried. "Are you okay?"

"I'm fine. Stay with your dad. This is your night." She slipped out from under Bennett's arm and kissed James on the cheek, then made her escape to the balcony.

The night was cold, but it was worth getting some goose bumps to have the outdoor space to herself. She took several deep breaths, focusing on the sensation of the air moving in and out of her lungs and reminding herself that this long, awful day was almost over. She heard the balcony door open behind her and turned, thinking it might be James. She was surprised, not very happily, to see Mackey.

"You may have fooled the Rothkopfs," he said, as he walked toward her with slow, deliberate steps. "And you may have fooled everyone in that room. But you haven't fooled me."

A brief burst of panic flared in her chest, but she kept her expression neutral. "Am I supposed to know what that means?"

He closed the distance between them in two strides. "Don't fuck with me."

"Wouldn't dream of it," she managed, trying to sound braver than she felt. She evaluated her chances of slipping past him and back into the ballroom. They weren't good.

"I looked into you, when you started sniffing around the Rothkopfs," he informed her.

She had to trust that Pierce had been thorough in setting up her false identity. *If Mackey found anything wrong*, she told herself, *he would have gone straight to Bennett. He wouldn't be hinting around, trying to make me reveal something.* "Good for you," she said.

A brief tightening of his jaw told her that wasn't the answer he was hoping for. "I don't know who you really are, or what you want with the Rothkopfs, but I'm not buying your sweet little heiress routine." Layla said nothing, resisting the urge to offer a useless denial, refusing to let him pressure her into making a mistake. She'd already given him enough reason to be suspicious by poking around Bennett's office.

Mackey leaned in close enough for her to feel the heat radiating from his body. His voice remained calm and implacable. "James likes you. And Bennett likes you. So I'm giving you one chance to walk away. Make your excuses and get out of their lives. If you don't, I will find out what you're doing and there will be consequences. Do you understand?"

He stood perfectly still, staring down at her, and she had no doubt he could wait all night for an answer. "Yes," she said finally.

"Good."

With that, he stepped back and returned to the ballroom. The cold struck Layla all at once and she shivered violently. She hurried inside, looking around for James, and saw him talking with one of the graduates of the initiative. He was listening, paying close attention to every word the young woman said instead of just waiting for his chance to talk. James may have grown up as a privileged only child, but he was the least self-centered person Layla had ever met. And she loved him for it. Both Laylas did. The realization felt even more dangerous than Mackey's threats. She had to get out of here, away from both of them. Right now.

As James finished his conversation, she went up to him and said, "My stomach is acting up again. I'm going to head home."

He looked at her, concerned. "Let me take you."

"That's sweet, but I want you to stay. I know how important this fundraiser is to both of you." Before he could protest, as she knew he would, Layla kissed his cheek and said, "I'll call you in the morning, okay?" She fled, out of the ballroom and down the hall to the bank of elevators, jabbing the call button repeatedly.

"Layla!" James had come after her, of course. She should have just left without telling him. How "perfect" would he think she was then? "What's wrong?" he asked.

"My stomach . . ."

He looked at her. "What's really wrong?"

She had to do it, had to push him away, before the situation spun even further out of control. "It's too much."

"What is?"

"All this 'honorary family' stuff. Playing house in New York. Giving me your mother's necklace. Calling me on stage to pose for a goddamned family portrait."

He stood there, stunned by the sudden onslaught. "I'm sorry. I didn't mean to make you uncomfortable. I thought . . ."

Layla felt a tightness in her chest, and it only made her push harder. "You thought that any girl would jump at the chance to be a Rothkopf."

"You know that's not true." Now James was getting angry, too.

Good, she thought. *Tell me to go to hell.* "Better use your name to snag an heiress before Daddy blows the family fortune."

"I don't just want an heiress, I want you," he shouted. "I love you!"

His words drove the air out of her like a blow to the gut. James lowered his voice and went on, "I know that scares the hell out of you. It scares me, too. Because I've never been so afraid of losing anything, or anyone, in my life."

She stared at him, speechless. She knew that he would lose her, and she would lose him, on the day he found out the truth. Or, if it was up to Mackey, a lot sooner than that. The fact that their time together was limited made it only more urgent to tell him, before another moment passed . . . "I love you, too," she said.

He kissed her, and she let the feeling sweep everything else away. She held him close, not daring to let go.

His driver took them to her building and they stumbled in the door of her condo, tugging desperately at each other's clothes. Layla drew him into the bedroom, unbuttoning his pants along the way. As they fell onto the bed, still kissing, he stopped just long enough to ask, "Are you sure?" She'd been the one to put on the brakes when they started getting physical before. Now she was flooring the gas pedal.

"Yes," she said. She pulled him on top of her and gladly lost herself in the pure, physical bliss.

TRAILS OF EVIDENCE

• DIANA RENN •

Layla stirred in bed and slipped out of a dream. Distant thunder rumbled. Her eyelids fluttered open. She turned to look at James, who was still sleeping soundly.

A peek outside the curtain at a cloudless dawn sky made her decide she'd only dreamed of thunder. She rolled over again to look at James asleep next to her. This was no dream. Her face warmed at the rush of memories from last night. Their entangled limbs, the blurry view of the Nile outside her window as they made love—the second time—on the divan.

Her gaze traveled to the trail of clothing strewn across the floor: her heels, his jacket, her full-skirted dress, his pants. Her bra had been flung halfway across the room, to the small desk by the window. Since she'd packed her own utilitarian underwear back in New York, never dreaming she would be hooking up with anyone in Cairo, she'd been glad to fling it aside before James could see it.

Now she caught sight of something else beneath the bra: the accordion file with documents from Pierce. Her ongoing homework assignment of updates on black market antiquities dealings. That was not for James's eyes, either.

Gently, she moved his arm aside, slid out of bed, and grabbed the accordion file. She stuffed some stray documents back into it, tiptoed to the kitchen, and shoved it deep inside a drawer of never-used cooking supplies. It would be safe there. Whipping up a big tagine dish was not high on her to-do list.

She paused by her purse, remembering that the flip phone concealed in an interior pocket had insistently buzzed at her late last night. Pierce's texts had been vague, typo-ridden, middle-of-the-night messages about checking in. Layla didn't know how seriously to take them; they had the tone of someone texting under the influence. Layla stretched and yawned, then slid back into the warm sheets. Pierce could wait. She was hitting the pause button on life. Her only plan was to linger in bed with James as long as possible, and let the rest of the world carry on. Here in her apartment, on a Sunday morning, she felt insulated from Pierce, from the whole operation, and even from Mackey, though his ominous warning to stay away from the Rothkopfs still reverberated deep within her.

She rested her head against the smooth skin just beneath James's shoulder. He murmured something indistinct, smiled, and held her close. She pressed her body against his. Her feet couldn't reach his toes. She lay there blissfully watching the sunrise leak in through the window and climb, across sheets, up his legs and torso and finally to his face, turning his skin to gold.

James opened his eyes. He reached out to stroke her cheek. "Hey, you," he whispered.

"Hey, you," she whispered back.

"Some night."

"I know. That was—" She faltered.

He sighed contentedly, gazing at her. "I love how it never feels like work, being with you. Everything feels so easy."

A chill ran through Layla. James *was* work, technically. A part of her work. And a huge distraction from it.

"You suddenly look thoughtful," he said.

"Mmm." She pulled him close for a kiss. "No thinking. Just being. Okay?"

The call to prayer from the mosque outside jolted them both out of the moment. James groaned and put the pillow over his head until it passed. When it was over, he reached for her again, only to pull away once more when a riot of sirens raced through the streets below.

They both laughed. "Okay, I give in. This must be God's way of telling me to go and take a shower," said James.

Reluctantly, Layla let him go, allowing her fingertips to slide off him slowly, as if afraid to lose contact. When he disappeared into the bathroom, she slipped on a robe and started a pot of coffee. Fleetingly, she pictured them in an apartment in New York doing exactly this. He'd go out to get the Sunday paper and walk the dog. A Yorkie. She'd make some coffee and—

She shook her head, tried to snap out of it. She was getting way, way ahead of herself. Was she even the kind of person to have a home, a Sunday paper, a *Yorkie*? Were such things possible for someone like her? She'd always chosen the harder path, the unconventional path. The dangerous path. It left little room for normal.

Mackey's words came back to her. *I'm giving you one chance to walk away.*

His eyes had blazed when he uttered those words. And yet, now that some hours had passed, in the light of day, the words didn't seem so charged. She'd thrown caution to the wind her whole life, and it had served her well enough. She wasn't going to stay away from James, or Bennett, for that matter, just because some hired thug decided he didn't like her. Mackey worked for Bennett, Bennett liked her, and Mackey was just going to have to get used to her being part of the family.

A new message buzzed in on the flip phone, interrupting her thoughts. Unable to ignore the urgency any longer, Layla reluctantly picked it up to check the message.

Get over to the house. Bring your key. NOW.

She sank onto the divan, suddenly nauseous. Suddenly last night's messages, combined with an urgent summons to the safe house, made Layla think Pierce was planning something big. Like the raid. She'd said she had grounds to stage one when the receipt turned up for Tanaka's marble relief shipped by Masterpiece Fine Arts. Had Pierce found her moment? Panic rose in her throat, tasting of bile. She was screwing up. Big time. Again.

By the time James emerged from the shower, deliciously tousled with a towel around his waist, she was already dressed and putting on shoes.

"What's going on?" he asked.

"It's Nesim. There's been a family emergency. I have to go right away." She fought to steady her nerves and her voice.

His eyes grew wide. "What kind of emergency? I thought my dad said the Farwadis had left Cairo for a while to travel. Are they back in town?"

Layla winced at her mistake. The Cairo art scene was so claustrophobic, she should have known word would spread quickly about the Farwadis' departure.

"Actually it's about his wife's sister-in-law," she said quickly, hoping the vague relation would stop any further questions. "It's a personal health issue for her. I can't say much more."

James leaned against the doorway of the bathroom, observing her with a concerned expression as she yanked on a lightweight cardigan and scraped her hair back into a messy ponytail. Then he scooped up his own clothes from the floor. "Are you going to the hospital? Or their house? I can wait somewhere nearby for you."

"It's okay. That's so nice, really. But my family insists on total privacy. I'm sorry." She grabbed her apartment key from the hallway table.

James yanked on his boxers and trousers. When his back was turned, she opened a drawer, grabbed her blue hijab—her usual disguise when going to the safe house—and stuffed it in her tote bag.

"Layla. Slow down." James hastily buttoned his shirt, his fingers fumbling. "Let me at least go with you in a taxi. I don't have to stay."

"No! I can't show up with you this early," she protested. "If they see you, my family will ask all kinds of questions . . ."

"Oh. Okay. Got it." James backed away, a look of disappointment on his face. He folded his arms across his chest.

"It's not personal," Layla added quickly, trying to smooth everything over. She didn't like his grim expression, his lips tightly pressed together. "Plus, my neighbors . . . it's just better if we don't walk out at the same time. I think they're already suspicious."

"Fine. Go do your thing, Layla. Like I said, I get it." He shoved his feet into his shoes. "I'll lock the door behind me. How much lead time do you need to avoid the nosy neighbors?"

"Two minutes. That will get me down the elevator." Much as she didn't love the idea of leaving James alone in the apartment, Layla also didn't like the scrutinizing look of the lady with the poodle who always seemed to be showing up at the elevators at the same time she did. Besides, it was only two minutes, and she'd hidden Pierce's file. And as James didn't seem the type to ransack her drawers, she'd have to assume the Glock was safe in her nightstand.

"No problem. Go do what you need to do." He leaned toward her and brushed her cheek with his lips.

"Okay. Thanks. I— I'm sorry." Feeling the flip phone buzz again in her bag, Layla gave him one last look before rushing out the door.

IN THE BACKSEAT OF the taxi, she tried to reach Pierce to let her know she was on her way to the safe house. No pickup. She leaned forward and urged the taxi driver to hurry.

Exasperated, he gestured toward the traffic as they approached the neighborhood of Coptic Cairo.

Layla glared at the infuriating traffic jam. The driver was doing his best to weave among the cars, buses, and *tuk-tuk*s, even going up on one of the crumbling sidewalks for a moment to pass a donkey cart, but it felt like traveling in slow motion.

She rolled down the window to let a weak breeze stir the soupy air, though it was hardly fresh. There was something in the air, an acrid, almost metallic taste masking the usual scents of cooking meat and spices from market stalls. This new and unfamiliar odor even masked the smell of garbage that the wind so often carried over from the slums.

The taxi wound its way deeper into the limestone labyrinth of Old Cairo, past the clusters of ancient churches with their soaring towers and crosses, past the Ben Ezra Synagogue, past the Coptic Museum and the Fortress of Babylon, where she knew a side alley would take her to her old neighborhood. She turned her face away from the alley, and from thoughts of home. Instead, she scrolled through Pierce's texts again. A raid would explain the urgency of her most recent message. What if Pierce was leaving imminently? What if Layla had missed her chance to go while lying in bed with James?

She leaned forward to urge the driver to speed up again, but suddenly her head slammed against the backseat as the taxi screeched to a halt.

"What was that about?" Layla demanded in Arabic, rubbing her head.

"Police blockade up ahead. I must detour." The driver turned right, away from the direction of the safe house, just as police, sirens blaring and lights blazing, raced by, causing a group of black-robed nuns on the sidewalk to startle and scatter like pigeons.

"Why here?" said Layla with an exasperated gesture. "There's absolutely no good reason for a blockade here."

"You mean you do not know?"

Layla met the driver's eyes in the rearview mirror and registered the sadness there. She stiffened. "Know what? Did something happen?"

He turned left, another detour. Police cars and barriers blocked nearly every street, turning the already ancient neighborhood into even more of a labyrinth than it already was.

"The church," he said. "It was bombed at daybreak this morning. A suicide bomber."

No. She gripped the seatback in front of her so hard her knuckles blanched. That thunder she'd heard and assumed she'd dreamed—that must have been the blast.

"Was . . . was it the Muharib?"

"They have not yet claimed responsibility, but they are suspected. I'm no lover of the Copts, personally, but what kind of criminal kills women and innocent children?" The driver scowled. "He went straight to the women's section and then blew himself up. They say the body count is at twenty and expected to be more, not to mention the injuries . . ."

Layla's stomach lurched. She rummaged in her bag and thrust a handful of piastres at him. "I'll be faster on foot. Thank you."

"Miss. Miss!" he protested as she exited the cab. "It is not safe to walk. The area is not secure. I will turn off the meter and take you where you need to go. Please, come back. Be safe."

She ran off, shoving her way through the throngs of pedestrians, street vendors, children, and a herd of bleating goats. She turned her ankle, slipping between the cobblestones, but ignored the twinge of pain and pressed on. The tension in the air was palpable, as was the smell of smoke. The metallic taste was even stronger now. She knew she needed to report to the safe house. But she had to see the blast site—she had to make sure her family was okay. Her mother and sister always went to Abu Serga on Sunday morning. She broke into a run, pushing through the crowd.

About a block away from the site, she realized she was heading toward the Church of Saint Barbara, not Abu Serga. Her family would not have been there. Still, she pressed on, as if drawn by a magnetic power. She'd come this far. She had to see for herself. And, though the thought sickened her, it was possible she knew victims. People from their neighborhood, or old friends from school. She took the edge of her hijab and covered the lower half of her face with it, partly to filter the dust and the smell, but mostly to avoid recognition. She couldn't linger long here; she was supposed to be undercover.

Some people who had evidently been near the site were walking the other way, coated with fine gray powder. Everyone's face looked hardened, like masks, except for the fear in their eyes. Nuns and priests, their faces drawn and haggard, helped some of the injured, or stood in the shards of glass and prayed.

Layla pushed through as close as she could. She saw covered-up bodies strewn on the blood-soaked ground, some of them small bodies. Children. Not twenty feet from where she stood, just past a yellow line of police tape, she saw somebody's detached arm, palm turned upward, as if in a futile gesture for help.

Sickened, she turned away as a police officer shouted for civilians to clear the area. She joined the crush of people moving away, the ashen-faced throngs. As she reversed her original course, cutting through a side street, her pace quickened, and her hands balled into fists. A strangled sound, a cry, caught in her throat. She choked it back down and continued to the safe house, on foot.

LAYLA FELT HER DREAD mount as she took the stairs to Pierce's apartment two at a time. She let herself into the safe house and found it eerily quiet, the air stagnant and already heating up from the scorching sun outside. "Hello?" she called.

No answer. She switched on two oscillating fans in the living room to create a cross breeze, then quickly checked the bedroom, kitchen, and bathrooms, half expecting Pierce to be passed out or even dead. She sent Pierce a simple text: *I'm here.*

Pierce's reply zipped in. *Turn on the computer.*

She did. The screen showed the corner of a brown, bunker-type building with almost no windows. The light on the building looked like afternoon sun, not morning glare. Clearly this location was nowhere near Cairo. She felt a sinking sensation. Pierce had gotten her raid, and Layla wasn't part of the action.

The screen pixelated, then shifted to a close-up of Pierce looking into the camera on her phone. An airplane could be heard taking off in the distance. Pierce's mouth moved, but between the poor audio quality and the airplane, Layla couldn't make out a word. She wanted to reach over and shake the monitor. To shake Pierce. Instead, she put on a pair of headphones, hoping for better audio quality.

"Where are you?" Layla asked when the airplane had passed.

The audio was only marginally improved by the headphones, but the word was clear when Pierce spoke. "Singapore."

Layla's heart sank. So Pierce had really gone there without her.

"Sounds like you're still at the airport. Where's the warehouse?" Layla asked.

"Right behind me." Pierce turned and gestured at a massive concrete building. "Masterpiece rents a storage vault in this freeport."

Layla nodded. She knew a little about freeports: warehouses for the wealthy, conveniently located near runways for private planes. Sheltered from VAT taxes, customs duties, and—except for now— government officials. Popular with art collectors. A headache for insurers, but collectors could sleep easy, knowing their precious Modiglianis or whatever were safe and out of government reach. "What's our objective?" Layla asked.

"You're late, so I don't have time to brief you on all the details. You look like hell, by the way." Pierce squinted at the screen. "Where were you." Her last question came out more like an accusation.

Unwinding her hijab, Layla glimpsed her own reflection in the computer screen. She didn't recognize herself. Her skin had a residue of powdery ash from the air of Old Cairo, making her dark eyes appear even darker. Rivulets of sweat from her walk through the oppressive heat streaked down her cheeks. She rubbed her face with her sleeve before facing the computer screen again to explain. "There was a bombing this morning. At a church. Looks like the work of the Muharib."

"Yes, I know all about the bombing. Were you anywhere near it? You all right?"

"No, not when it went off, but after I was in a cab that—" Her words faltered. She pictured the bodies, the children, the puddles of blood. The detached arm with the outstretched hand.

"Then put it behind you," Pierce snapped. "We're focusing on this now."

Feeling the sting of Pierce's rebuke, Layla winced. "We don't have jurisdiction in Singapore. Who's with you?"

"Our Singapore FBI legate. Agent Housman. We're embedding with Singapore authorities to search the unit. They like him because he's an experienced bomb detector."

Layla sat up straighter. "You think there are explosives in that unit?"

"I'm looking for relics. But we had to make it sound more urgent to get the Singapore police force on board, and to let us embed." Pierce glanced over at the warehouse. "Good thing you finally saw fit to show up," she added. "If Tremblay's flight hadn't been delayed, you would have missed the whole show."

"Who?" Layla struggled to keep up with Pierce's amped-up, rapid-fire speech on top of the bad audio feed.

"Richard Tremblay, the CEO of Masterpiece," Pierce snapped. "Jesus. I thought you did your research. We're going to confront him at the site and find out how much he knows about what some of his clients are storing there."

"Great." Layla slumped in the chair in front of the monitor and sighed.

"Your enthusiasm is overwhelming."

"Why didn't you bring me?" Layla demanded. "I'm the one who found the receipt from Masterpiece at Kiyoshi Tanaka's. I'm the one who saw those receipts from Masterpiece in Noor Ghaffar's office."

"Don't throw a tantrum. Look, I decided I can't bring you out of cover for this operation," said Pierce. "It's too risky. And I need you to stay on the Rothkopfs."

Layla started to tell her about Mackey's warning, but a male voice in the background interrupted her.

"Stand by." An American voice. Probably Agent Housman. "Tremblay's jet is on the tarmac, taxiing toward the unit."

"What am I supposed to do from here?" Layla asked in exasperation.

"See that notepad by the monitor? And the pen?"

"Yeah."

"Listen. Take notes."

Every cell in Layla's body railed against this whole situation. She was basically a secretary now.

"I'll be cutting out briefly while we pass through security," Pierce went on, "but I'll bring you back on an interior security camera once we're in the vault and you'll be livestreaming the footage. You can talk directly to me—I've got a separate earpiece so I can hear you—or text my burner."

"Before you go, let me just see the building," Layla pleaded. She wanted to get the bigger picture, and a sense of the players.

Pierce held up the camera and panned slowly, three hundred sixty degrees, capturing the windowless freeport building first, then the airfield. Layla leaned closer to the screen, squinting to make out the four tiny figures walking down the tarmac. A blond man in a suit with three Asian men flanking him, presumably some Singapore cops. Layla tried to console herself that this would be a sedate affair, as raids went. No flashbangs, no guns drawn. Still, she belonged there. Pierce had totally blindsided her with this maneuver. *Take notes?* Fuck that.

She reached out to the screen and touched it, as if it would magically transport her.

The screen went dark.

Layla waited for five endless minutes before the interior security camera view came on, showing a grainy picture, dimly lit, of the Masterpiece storage vault. She heard scuffling, murmurs with every other word cutting out, and then Pierce announcing the search warrant.

"But my clients!" Tremblay protested. "I can't just surrender their belongings!"

There were more scuffling sounds, more background voices murmuring indistinctly, and then Pierce stepped into the camera frame to speak directly to Layla.

"Housman's working on Tremblay right now," Pierce said in a low voice. "But check this out." She reached toward the camera and adjusted the angle, altering Layla's view. First Layla saw two men seated opposite each other at a small table. One must be Agent Housman, she concluded, and the other had to be Tremblay—a slight, blond man with an agitated expression, wiping sweat off his brow with a handkerchief. Then, beyond them, Layla saw the vault was crammed full of crates arranged in numbered floor-to-ceiling shelves, all around the room. A large storage berth labeled *Unit Twenty*, in a far corner of the room, contained unpackaged items too, just sitting out in the open, on shelves and on the floor. Marble statuary. Stone busts. Terra-cotta figures and urns. Bizarrely, it looked as if a branch of a museum had a traveling exhibit there. If these goods were stolen, this was an incredible haul.

"No bar codes on any of these items," Pierce said quietly. "So they're not inventoried. I'm willing to bet not one item is legit. Wait!" Pierce suddenly cried out as a police officer shoved a box of vases with his foot, then picked up the box and walked away with it. "Hey! Careful!"

As Pierce followed the officer, Layla turned up the volume on her audio feed. She could hear two other officers speaking in English. She texted Pierce: *Singapore police plan to seize all items from Storage Unit 20 immediately.*

"Tell them we're following protocol, Housman." Layla heard Pierce's commanding voice just seconds later. "Don't let a single box leave that storage unit. I want everything photographed before it's seized."

"Christ, Pierce. This is no time for art appreciation," said Agent Housman. "And the Singapore police are technically in charge of this operation. They want all this junk out of the way to do a clean sweep and look for explosives and weapons."

"All this 'junk' needs to be documented," Pierce insisted. "Relics have a way of falling into police custody and going missing again. And any one of these objects can point us toward terrorists. This isn't just about preserving history. It's about preserving evidence."

"All right, Pierce. You made your point." Housman got up to talk to the nearest police officer and gave the request. After some indistinct mumblings in the background, while a terrified Tremblay looked on, Layla heard Housman say, "Bingo." Then he stepped back into the camera frame.

He approached Pierce with a deadly serious look on his face. He was holding what looked like a black brick, almost a foot long and a couple of inches high. "I just found this on the floor. Looks like it might have gotten kicked beneath one of those shelves in unit twenty."

Pierce took the brick. She looked at it closely, reading the label. "C-4," she said. "Holy shit. Point of origin? The lot number's been scratched off the packaging."

"Not sure. I don't recognize this packaging. It has some features of US military-grade demolition blocks, but I don't think it's ours. Plastic explosives are turning up everywhere these days." Housman smirked. "Funny how things work out," he added in a low voice, yet still just audible enough for Layla to hear. "We come in pretending to check for explosives to get us in the door, and look what we find. I wonder what else might be in store for us here. I've got an explosives detector on me, so we'll get busy with that, and we'll want to run a K-9 explosives sweep, too."

Pierce nodded. "Game changer," she said. "You get the place ready, and I'll handle Tremblay."

Layla watched as Pierce turned to sit down opposite Tremblay, placing her burner phone on the table, as well as the wrapped brick of C-4.

"Mr. Tremblay," Pierce said, pushing the brick toward him. "Are you familiar with this substance?"

He looked at it, then shook his head.

"It's called composite 4. It's a type of plastic explosive that's commonly used in the manufacture of improvised explosive devices. It was found in unit twenty, right by the area with the sign that says 'transport to loading dock.'"

Tremblay stared at Pierce, open-mouthed. He reached out to touch the brick, then drew his hand back as if it might explode on contact.

"You can touch it," said Pierce. "It won't hurt you in this form. But if detonated? It really packs a punch. A little goes a long way. Just a small box of C-4 could take out a truck and a bunch of people. A crate full of it—like the shipping crates you keep over in that corner—could take out a whole building."

"My God," Tremblay whispered.

Behind the table, Layla could see a couple of the Singapore cops carefully opening lids of crates, no doubt looking for more bricks.

"Anything get shipped out of here recently?" Pierce asked.

"I don't know. I— I'd have to check . . ."

"Do that," Pierce said. "It's rare that someone would just keep one brick around. I'm guessing this is something that got left behind from a bigger shipment. I need to know about every crate that's been shipped out of here."

Tremblay stammered, "I couldn't possibly . . . I oversee many aspects of my business, but the day-to-day operations are not something I personally handle—"

Pierce cut him off. "You have records. Every shipping company keeps careful records." She narrowed her eyes at him. "You do keep careful records."

Tremblay looked down at his hands in his lap.

"Mr. Tremblay." Pierce sighed. "The manager of the Singapore Freeport will arrive at any moment. This is your opportunity to speak without his presence, and without our questioning other personnel within your company. We'll protect you if you share what you know, and you'll have a shot at saving your business. It's a matter of international security. I implore you to cooperate."

Tremblay swallowed hard and nodded. "I believe there was one recent shipment to the US . . ."

Layla watched as Tremblay fumbled with reading glasses and a tablet. Pierce tapped the brick of C-4 on the table. It was amazing how Pierce could create such tension with such a tiny action. "There has been no movement of crates out of this unit for the past six months, until five days ago," Tremblay said, scrolling down a page on the tablet. His voice shook. "Two crates were shipped to Fortress Self Storage, Washington, DC. It's at 567 Hamilton Street NE."

"Let me see that." Pierce took the tablet from him and read through the shipping record herself.

Once Tremblay had taken some deep breaths, Pierce began her interrogation again. "When and from where did the owner of unit twenty open this account?" she demanded.

"There's no specific individual in charge," said Tremblay. "It's owned by a company called Global Relics, LLC."

Layla, observing from afar, frowned and wrote that name down on a pad of paper. It sounded vaguely familiar, though she wasn't sure why.

"We'll look into them," said Pierce. "Do your records indicate who was expecting the shipment headed to DC, and where those crates might be now?

Sweat beaded on Tremblay's forehead. "No such information," he said, scrolling frantically through the documents. "There are spaces where such information could be entered, but it appears to be . . . incomplete. In this case."

"You're telling me there's no way we can track the transport of objects on the jets and vans you contract with?" Pierce sounded incredulous.

"Some, yes. For some," Tremblay admitted. "But for security purposes—for the discretion of our clients—certain clients, that is—no, we do not publicize our ground service shuttles, our store-house inventories, or our flights on private cargo jets. Whoever was managing this account apparently left such details out to avoid any scrutiny."

"Certain clients?" Pierce sneered. "Do you mean clients at a certain price point get to delete the details of their shipping transactions?"

Tremblay hesitated, then nodded. "We offer a white-glove level of service to certain clientele."

"So your extreme discretion can be purchased."

Tremblay did not respond.

"And perhaps your extreme ignorance as well," Pierce went on, crossing her arms in front of her chest.

Again, Tremblay remained quiet.

"Mr. Tremblay," said Pierce. "Global Relics, LLC, or whoever is operating this berth in their name, is likely housing stolen relics in it. None of these items in storage unit twenty have inventory tags like those in your other units. It's probable they're using Masterpiece

Fine Arts to ship illegally acquired antiquities, too. Now we have evidence of explosive material being stored here and quite possibly moved around through your company's transport services. It's not looking good."

While Pierce continued to probe, Layla, her radar up for bullshit, turned to a laptop on the table and quickly ran a search for Fortress Self-Storage, with the address she'd heard and scrawled down on the notepad. There was no such place. She zoomed in on Google Earth and checked the surrounding area. A laundromat and a check-cashing service called Kwik Check occupied that specific street address. There was no storage facility in sight. She texted Pierce right away. *He's lying or clueless. No Fortress Self-Storage there or anywhere.*

Pierce read the message, then pivoted quickly.

"As it happens, Fortress Self-Storage doesn't actually exist," she said to Tremblay. "It's vital that we get in touch with whoever requested this shipment. I need names and contact information for the Global Relics representative who set up this account."

Tremblay twisted his watch around on his wrist. "Look. I never met any representative of Global Relics personally," he said. "But I do recall speaking to someone on the phone, about two years ago, who made the initial inquiry into this unit. I'm sorry I don't recall his name, nor do I see it in the records."

"Where's he from?" Pierce demanded.

"Somewhere in the Middle East."

"Might it be Cairo?"

"It might." He hesitated, then faltered under her gaze. "It is. Yes, come to think of it, he was from Cairo. It's coming back to me."

"Now we're getting somewhere," Pierce grumbled. "And yet, even though this individual inquired about an account and then opened one, his name appears on none of the Global Relics paperwork?"

"I'm afraid not. Only the company name."

"For fuck's sake," muttered Pierce.

Layla chewed on the pen cap. Frustrating as the lack of information was, this was all starting to make terrible sense. She sketched out a mini flowchart on the notepad, putting a box around each significant fact she recalled. Alberto had told her that the guy at the illegal dig site, Khalid Yasin, was being kept busy organizing more and more digs. Pierce and Housman had just found a storage unit full of illegal relics, and a brick of a powerful explosive favored by terrorists. If that brick had fallen out of one of those recently shipped crates, more explosives were almost certainly well on their way to the States. To the nation's capital. No individual claimed to be in charge of unit twenty or its contents and shipping activities, while Masterpiece looked the other way.

Layla shifted over to the laptop and ran a quick internet search on Global Relics, LLC.

No such company came up. Likely a shell company was operating this unit, laundering antiquities and smuggling munitions, with the true owner's identity deeply buried under a chain of false names and documents.

Undeterred by the bust the Department of Justice had made in New York, the Muharib was still, apparently, planning something. Something big.

BACK IN HER GARDEN CITY apartment building later that afternoon, Layla rode the elevator and wrestled with the lock to her door, opening the protective iron gate and then the main door as best she could with trembling hands. She was the closest she'd ever felt to being a total wreck. The bombing, the raid, and the way Pierce had treated her had her boiling over. Her hands shook as she poured a glass of water. She still had a film of ash on her skin from her foray into Coptic Cairo that morning, and she couldn't wait to wash it off, right after she washed the bad taste of the day out of her mouth. That acrid, metallic flavor hadn't left her.

As she gulped a glass of water, her eyes drifted to the kitchen table. There was that damned bronze cat. A sticky note next to its foot read, in James's sloping handwriting: *Meow. Don't you love me? I don't want to be hidden away! Affectionately, The Hideous Cat.*

Behind the bronze cat was something covered with a kitchen towel. She peeled back the fabric. Freshly baked banana bread, still warm to the touch. She frowned. James had said he'd stay two minutes to let her get past the neighbors' prying eyes without him, and then lock up the apartment. Clearly he'd overstayed and made himself comfortable in her kitchen. That had not been the agreement.

But then she caught a whiff of the bread. She inhaled deeply. And she smiled. Banana bread was one of the first foods she'd eaten when she came to Georgetown, and she'd marveled at it then. No one ate anything like that in Egypt. And yet James—evidently remembering her confession that she loved banana bread—had managed to make this from the ingredients in her kitchen and the bananas she'd splurged on at the market last week. Not only that, he'd tidied up her kitchen and put all the dishes away. The thoughtful gestures touched her.

Cradling the banana bread in her arms, she glanced instinctively at the kitchen drawer where she'd put the FBI files about black market antiquities. Hopefully, James hadn't gone poking around too deeply for cooking supplies. Its presence would be one more tricky thing to explain. As would the Glock. She dashed to the bedroom and opened the nightstand drawer to check for it. There it was, safely tucked away in the box with the lavender eye pillow.

Layla shut the drawer and sighed. The day that had begun so luxuriously in James's arms had turned dark and strange very fast.

A text buzzed in. *Damn.* Could she never have even one moment to catch her breath? She fumbled in her tote bag.

It was Alberto.

Can you meet me at Zamalek Rooftop at 3 tomorrow? I have information about Dahshur.

Dahshur. That was the town near the illegal dig site Alberto had taken her to. What kind of information might he have discovered since their nocturnal trip there? She immediately thought of Khalid

Yasin. The man she'd shot and wounded before she and Alberto had fled. Could he have figured out that she and Alberto were there, observing the dig? She gripped the phone. Could Khalid Yasin somehow know that Layla had fired those bullets?

No. She steadied her breath, focusing on reasonable, rational thoughts. Alberto would have wanted to see her immediately if that were the case. He wouldn't have made her wait an entire day to find out she was in some kind of danger. So what else could this "information" be? She was due to meet Pierce at the safe house early tomorrow afternoon. How good would it be to deliver some vital nugget of information from Alberto, some missing link in their chain of clues?

I'll see you then, she typed. *But can you give me a hint? Or any chance of meeting up earlier to talk? I'm in suspense here!*

After a pause, Alberto texted back: *Sorry, no time. Can't meet earlier. I'm in Dahshur now, for research. Back in Cairo tomorrow. See you at 3.*

PIERCE HAD AN EDGY, almost hyper energy about her at the safe house when Layla showed up the next day. "Red-eye flight," she explained, sensing her colleague's suspicious gaze. "I haven't slept all night. But I have *lots* to report. Have a seat." She gestured to the couch, and Layla sat down obediently. Whatever the reason for Pierce's unpredictable vibe today, she didn't like it.

"The big news," she said, "is that although Housman and his team didn't find any more C-4 bricks, they detected traces of other chemicals that match those used at the church bombing the other day. Not a lot, but a residue that might have leaked. Housman thinks the Muharib are using a new chemical compound for the IEDs that can be smuggled across borders in smaller quantities, and that tends to avoid detection of most traditional scanners."

"Oh my God," said Layla. "Any leads on Global Relics or their representative for that storage unit?"

"Not yet. I have a team continuing to comb through the books at Masterpiece, but their record keeping is suspiciously lax."

"Clearly, Global Relics is a shell company," said Layla. "I'm guessing Tremblay knew that full well when he signed them on and didn't ask too many questions."

"Agreed," said Pierce. "I'd put money on Global Relics being a front for the Muharib, but I aim to find the specific person who's authorizing shipments in and out of that unit."

"We need to work fast," said Layla. "Those two crates left the storage unit less than a week ago. They could arrive in DC any day."

"Exactly," said Pierce. "I'm making some inquiries. I'm on it." She gave Layla a look as if to add: *And you are not.* "Monaghan's covering things on the DC end," she elaborated. "He and some DC agents will watch the laundromat and the Kwik Check on Hamilton Street to await that delivery. And he's already had an agent talk to the owners of those businesses. They claim to know nothing about a shipment of art or antiquities on the way."

"Well, someone's got to show up to intercept that delivery," said Layla.

"I know. I trust Monaghan knows what he's doing." Pierce shrugged. "I also fingerprinted unit twenty before I left, so hopefully that will reveal something if we get a match. And I've got someone obtaining access to the Cairo Police Department fingerprint database. It might be too much to hope for, that our terrorist representative is actually in that database, but I have to try."

Listening to the list of things Pierce was coordinating without her, Layla glared at the woman. "So what am I supposed to do right now?"

"Keep gathering evidence on our dealers and collectors, as you have been," said Pierce. "Every detail will help to build a prosecutable case when the time comes. The more dirt we have on everyone involved, the better." She sat on a swivel chair and spun around to face her laptop. She typed rapidly while continuing to talk to Layla. "Why don't you call your friend Jehan. Wrangle an invitation to their Cairo house."

"I thought we were done with Noor Ghaffar. Her name's in the double ledger. She bought a scarab amulet from Bennett, probably knowing it was the real deal, since he most likely gave her a receipt for a lower value than she paid."

"I agree, but we're speculating here," Pierce reminded her, still typing furiously. "We could use more proof. She might have more documents or objects connected to Bennett, or to Masterpiece. I need to tighten the net around that whole business," she added, almost under her breath.

Layla bristled at the implication that Pierce was taking control. She'd also hoped that Alberto could be the one to look into Noor's purchases, so that she wouldn't have to get too close to Gamal Ghaffar. But Pierce gave her a look that seemed to demand immediate action. Layla pulled out her phone and texted Jehan. *Hey there! Just realized I still have a sweater I borrowed from you. I can bring it over. Would love to catch up!* The disconnect between her chirpy text and the seriousness of the situation struck her as she pocketed her phone.

She had no doubt the Muharib was still planning an attack on the United States. On the country that had given her all the opportunity that would have been denied her had she remained in Cairo. She'd taken the church bombing personally, but this hit even closer to home.

"I really think I should do more," Layla said, pacing the living room. "The person behind Global Relics and unit twenty in the Singapore Freeport is the missing link. The connection between the Muharib leaders and the smugglers who feed the relics to the dealers. You really want me stuck in Jehan's parents' house looking through desk files again? Aren't we past all that now?"

Pierce stopped typing. She paused for a long time before she turned back around in the swivel chair and faced Layla. "Listen to me," she said, in the most serious tone Layla had ever heard her use. "We're going to make a major move any day now, as the evidence surfaces. I have no time or tolerance for mistakes. I need your head in the game."

Layla gave her a curious look. "Right. I know. I'll be ready. For anything."

"Really?" Pierce fixed her cool gaze on Layla. "You'll be ready. Even if it's at midnight? Or five in the morning?"

Layla blinked, wondering what Pierce was getting at. "Of course."

"Even if you're in bed with James Rothkopf."

Layla froze.

Pierce smiled, not in a friendly way. "How long did you think you could get away with that? Without my knowing?"

"I— I—" Pierce could be as intimidating as hell, and now Layla was caught in her headlights.

"I know all about it," Pierce said. "Nighttime adventures. Intimate lunches."

Did she know? Or was she bluffing, getting Layla to confirm a suspicion?

"I have an informant in your building," Pierce went on. "She saw you going in with James last night. She's also seen the two of you there before."

The woman with the poodle, who was always hanging out by the elevator. *Shit*.

Layla's mind then flashed to those two guys in the soccer jerseys who had followed her to the safe house shortly after she arrived in Cairo. Were they on Pierce's payroll, too?

"We were working on something related to the Rothkopf fundraiser," said Layla.

"Don't lie to me," Pierce snapped. "You know sleeping with a person of interest is against FBI rules." She narrowed her eyes. "I can report you for this, you know. I can get you sanctioned. Even fired."

Layla felt a surge of fear. No, not fear. Rage. She would not be threatened by Pierce like this. She'd worked too hard and come too far. She chose her next words carefully. "Actually," she said, fighting to keep her voice steady and calm, "I know things, too. About you. In case you forgot."

Pierce raised an eyebrow. "All right. You do. I'll grant you that. But don't think that gives you leverage." She pointed a long finger at Layla, almost accusingly. "You haven't put in your time yet. I have. And I have friends higher up the agency ladder. Don't you forget that for a moment."

Layla feigned indifference, but rage continued to churn inside her. She *hated* this side of Pierce. This wasn't the person she'd come to Cairo with. This wasn't the mentor she'd thought would guide her into a high-profile career. She should just walk away right now. With James, hand in hand, into some New York sunset. Put this crazy life behind her and start anew.

Then she pictured that boy clawing through the dig rubble near Dahshur, scavenging for relics, watched by armed men. The boy was a victim of this whole chain of crime, too. If she walked away from all this now, she'd never forgive herself.

"We're clear," she said to Pierce. "I screwed up. I'm sorry. I'll end it."

LAYLA HAD THE TAXI let her out two blocks from the Nile Zamalek Hotel, then ran all the way there to meet Alberto. In the elevator heading up to the bar, she removed her hijab and shook out her hair, heart thudding in her chest. She couldn't wait to find out what was so important that Alberto had wanted to see her in person before the Minister of Culture's reception next week.

The corner table they'd sat at before was open. Alberto wasn't there yet. She claimed the table and ordered a cheese and tomato plate for two and a cold beer. As an afterthought, she ordered a whiskey for Alberto, since that's what he'd been drinking the last time they met there. She tried, for five minutes, to pretend she was normal, even a tourist. Though tourists were few and far between now, with the summer heat lingering. Ten minutes passed. No Alberto. She ate the food, sipped her beer, and tried to follow the conversation of a group of Americans behind her. Their complaints about the scorching heat and the hustlers all over Giza soon turned to yesterday morning's church bombing.

"Well, I, for one, won't come back to Egypt again," one woman declared, turning up the speed on her handheld electric fan. "I've been to Giza, I can check it off the bucket list, and now I'm done. I don't feel safe here at all."

Her friends murmured agreement, and one woman said she was actively in the process of changing her flight and returning to DC a week early.

"Targeting churches." The woman with the handheld fan clucked her tongue. "What next? Shopping centers?"

"Hotels?" Her husband chimed in. "Tourist bars?"

They fell silent.

Layla had never felt so divided. Lately, she had a new appreciation for the country of her birth, seeing it from angles she'd never experienced before. The Muharib in no way represented Egypt. This is what she wished these American tourists would comprehend. Egypt was far too complex a tapestry.

She loved her adopted country, too. Fiercely. She loved it so much that she had made it her life's work to protect it. The FBI for her wasn't just professional. It was deeply personal.

So this meeting with Alberto—whose untouched whiskey she was now sipping, whose portion of cheese and tomatoes she was devouring, was vital for the investigation and her role in it. She pictured herself triumphantly presenting a street address, a phone number, to Pierce. Redeeming herself.

Where was Alberto, anyway? She checked her watch. Forty-five minutes had passed. She'd sent him two texts since arriving, and he hadn't replied. Hopefully, he was just tied up with some new lead. That was the nice thing about Alberto. If he was going to stand her up or be silent, she trusted it was for some good reason.

Her phone buzzed in her bag. Her personal phone, the Motorola. Alberto couldn't possibly be calling that number. Nor could James.

She didn't recognize the number on the display, but the city code was Cairo.

"*Allo?*" she said cautiously.

In response, she heard wailing. She instinctively moved the phone away from her ear. The Americans behind her, noticing, looked at her curiously.

"Sanaa?" Layla guessed, when the wailing had subsided into breathy sobs. That was her sister's cry, which she remembered well from childhood. Sanaa had cried so frequently as a child, and comforting her had been Layla's job for some reason; she was the one person who could calm her sister down back then. She wasn't sure if she could do so now. "What's wrong?" she asked in Arabic, when Sanaa's breathing sounded slightly calmer. "Is it Badru?"

"Badru is fine, *alhamdullah*," Sanaa replied. "But I have been calling the American Embassy for an hour to reach you. They did not know your name. They did not know who I was talking about. Finally, I found this number and your name on it, in a scrap of paper in Rami's jacket. I need your help. The jailers will not let me speak with him!"

"Jailers?" Layla's heart thudded. "What's going on? Is Rami in *jail*?"

Even though she was speaking in Arabic, her tone must have conveyed her frantic state. The American tourists were now listening and watching intently, sharing knowing looks, as if Layla's reactions just confirmed their deepest convictions: Egypt was a wild and dangerous place.

Sanaa began to wail again. Stepping away from the tables so the Americans couldn't hear, Layla leaned over the railing where the breeze could mask her words. "Just give me the facts, and I'll figure out what to do."

"There is a professor at Rami's university who has been speaking out against the heavy government presence on campus in support of Fareed Monsour," Sanaa explained between shuddery breaths. "He was fired yesterday. So the student leaders—including Rami— organized a march to protest this firing. Police came with weapons and tear gas. Fights broke out. Rami was injured. He was taken into custody before he could get medical help and—"

Layla cut her off. "He's injured? Is it bad?"

"I only know some of the details. Maybe a broken arm. Also a head injury. Some bleeding from the head. A friend of Rami's escaped and called me to let me know all of this. Please, Layla. You have to help him. You have to get him out of there! You work for the US Embassy as a secretary, yes? You must be able to do something for him."

"Of course," said Layla, not bothering to correct her sister's erroneous memory of the position Layla supposedly held. She worked in the comptroller's office for the State Department, according to the lie she'd spun for her family. But what point was there in correcting a misperception with an outright lie? "I'll do everything I can. Tell me which jail he's in."

TRAFFIC WAS IMPOSSIBLE, WITH the blockades still set up all around Coptic Cairo, and the train was equally congested, so Layla rode a *tuk-tuk* back to her penthouse. The driver could weave through the congestion and scuttle down back alleys. Despite the bumpy ride, she managed to tap out one more message to Alberto: *Family issue, had to run. Sorry we didn't connect today. Text me when you can, let's reschedule.*

In her apartment, she ripped off her casual outfit and replaced it with a conservative, expensive cream pantsuit, slick patent leather wedge shoes, a Coach handbag, and a rose silk hijab. Not exactly practical prison attire, but she needed to radiate wealth. She ducked into the bathroom and tossed a bottle of ibuprofen capsules into the purse, in case Rami needed painkillers. She lifted the mattress and took several bundles of cash—emergency spending money from Pierce—from her hiding place. She grabbed James's banana bread, wrapped it in newspaper, and tossed that in her bag, too; it might have been hours since Rami had last eaten. Then she sped out of the apartment, ignoring the curious stare of the poodle lady, who was approaching the elevator bank. As soon as she got in a taxi, an emoji-sprinkled text from Jehan came in. *Layla! I've been missing you. Yes, come over any time! My dad's got me practically on house arrest lately since there's been stuff about clubs and drugs in the news. Save me from death by boredom!! We can use the pool!*

Layla was so preoccupied with thoughts of Rami, and Sanaa's wails still echoing in her mind, she couldn't think of a word in response.

HER EXPENSIVE OUTFIT DID nothing to advance Layla in the long queue as she waited to speak with the sergeant at Cairo's central city prison. The lobby was filled with families and friends inquiring about whereabouts and conditions of loved ones, many of whom had been swept up in the arrests. By the time she got to the front, the sun was already hanging low in the sky.

She looked imploringly at the sergeant. "I am looking for Rami el-Deeb, my brother," she said in Arabic, in the most upper-crust accent she could articulate. "He was taken in today. I must see him."

"Regular visiting hours have ended," said the sergeant in a clipped voice.

"Then I request a special visit."

"There are no special visits for families of political prisoners," said the sergeant.

Layla opened the Coach bag—setting it in plain view on the counter—and tilted it toward him, displaying the thick stack of cash. "I was hoping an exception might be made."

The sergeant snorted. "There are no exceptions for political dissidents. Your brother chose to drag our city into mayhem." The sergeant pushed the bag back. "Take care with your money," he said. "There are plenty of people around here who will want to take your cash. I, however, am not one of them."

Layla glowered as she snapped the bag shut. Of all the bad luck. She had to get the one honest man in Cairo's entire prison system.

"Next," said the sergeant, looking past her to the family in line behind her.

Layla stood her ground. "I need to see your superior."

The sergeant raised an eyebrow.

"I demand to see your superior," she repeated, loudly, as she caught sight of a newspaper reporter clutching a camera nearby.

"All right. There's no need to make a scene," said the sergeant, waving the curious reporter away. "You may see him. But I assure you, you will get nowhere."

The Master Sergeant, it turned out, was not available, but the Lieutenant General was. At the sight of Layla, he came hurrying over and ushered her into an office. Layla explained the situation, all the while tipping the handbag toward him so he could clearly see the bundled Egyptian pounds.

"I apologize for the behavior of my subordinate officer," said the Lieutenant General. "He was not aware of recent updates to the policies. Nor was he sensitive to the distress you are clearly experiencing. Certainly exceptions can be made."

"Thank you," said Layla. "I appreciate your consideration."

"I will take you personally to a private visiting room," said the Lieutenant General. "Though you will need to leave your pocketbook behind, for security purposes."

"Oh—the whole bag? Really?" Layla thought of her phones and the bread and the painkillers she was smuggling in for Rami.

"Or just any valuables you may be concerned about."

That's what she'd hoped for. Just the cash. Layla reached into her bag and handed him the entire stack of bills. He pocketed them and rose to his feet. "This way," he said, gesturing to a side door.

THE VISITING ROOM WAS little more than a cubicle with two white plastic chairs and a dust-encrusted fan that only stirred up the soupy air and made it even more oppressive.

Nearly another hour passed. Layla had no cell reception behind these cinder block walls, no way to contact anyone in the outside world or receive their messages. Alberto could be looking for her, James could be trying to reach her, and Pierce could be summoning her. Layla would have no way of knowing.

At last the door opened and Rami stumbled in. The officer escorting him barked, "Five minutes only," and slammed the door behind him.

"Rami!" Layla cried, rising to help him move toward a chair and sink into it. He could barely walk. He clutched his ribs with his left arm. His right arm, clearly broken, dangled at his side. As she settled him in the chair, she noticed the blood still seeping from the back of his scalp. She took a tissue pack from her handbag and began blotting at it.

"There's a little food in my purse," she said, handing him the entire bag. "No cash. The Lieutenant General took it. I was hoping to leave you some extra for bribes. But I do have fresh banana bread and bottled water. And ibuprofen."

"Layla. Can you help me?" he asked, wincing as he adjusted his position in the chair. His voice was hoarse, almost inaudible.

"Shh. Don't talk. Yes, I will help you." She unscrewed the cap of the bottle and fed him four painkillers, cradling his head as he sipped the water.

"I mean help me get out of here," Rami rasped. "I have to get out."

Layla placed both hands on his shoulders and looked him in the eye. "I will help you get out. You need to be in a hospital. You know that, don't you?"

His eyes fluttered. He moaned softly.

"I am going to get you out of here. I promise."

Rami nodded. "Thank you," he whispered.

The officer who had brought him came back into the room and told them their time was up.

"My brother needs to be transferred to a hospital," said Layla. "Immediately."

The officer shrugged, and Layla watched helplessly as he grabbed Rami roughly by the arms—including the broken arm—and shoved him back toward the cells.

She exited through the door she had entered and strode to the Lieutenant General's office, even as three officers called for her to stop.

The Lieutenant General noticed her through his window and beckoned her in, only he didn't look nearly as willing to help this time, nor did he offer her a seat. He ran his hands through his thinning hair and sighed while she described Rami's medical condition.

"He must be transferred to a hospital. Immediately. I can pay any necessary fees," she concluded.

"I am sorry," he said, "it is not possible. But don't worry, all the new prisoners will receive full medical exams tomorrow, when they are transferred to Tora."

Layla's blood went cold. Tora Maximum Security Prison—dubbed "the Scorpion" by the inmates abused there—was the bottomless pit where dissidents and political prisoners were locked up without legal recourse. And left to die.

LAYLA RANG THE SAFE HOUSE buzzer repeatedly, cursing herself for leaving her apartment without the safe house key. No one came to the door. It was only nine at night; could Pierce be in bed so soon? Or was she comatose on the floor? Strung out? Layla could see a ribbon of light through the crack beneath the door and on one side of the blackout shades that were always drawn.

Footsteps approached from the stairwell. Layla spun around in full defense mode. She ached for her gun.

It was Pierce, carrying two plastic bags from a convenience store down the street. She almost dropped them, startled, when she saw Layla standing at her door.

"Jesus, you scared me!" Pierce hissed. "What are you doing here? Wait. Tell me inside." She opened the door and ushered Layla in first.

Layla appraised the bags. Had Pierce been out meeting a dealer?

Pierce shot her a look, as if reading her mind, and dipped her hand into a bag. She tossed Layla a pack of McVitie's chocolate-covered biscuits. "Where did you go in that get-up? You look like an Egyptian Hillary Clinton."

"I was in negotiating mode," said Layla. "I have a huge problem."

Pierce had been opening a bottle of soda. She set it down. "Something tells me I might need a stiffer drink." She turned to the small makeshift bar at the other end of the safe house living room and poured straight gin into a tumbler.

Without divulging the extent to which she'd been in touch with her family, Layla told her what had happened to Rami and the condition he was in—according to a "family friend" who'd seen him in the prison. "He'll be transferred to the Scorpion tomorrow," she finished, struggling to steady her voice. "He could die there. I need your help getting him out. You're keeping up a day job at the embassy. You're there every day. You could talk to the right people. I'll pay with my own money if they need bribes to deal with the authorities."

Pierce sighed. "Layla. I appreciate your struggle here," she said, not unkindly. "But Rami is an Egyptian citizen. You know the US can't interfere. If he were American, it would be a different story. But I'm afraid the embassy won't be sympathetic, even if they share the protestors' convictions about the current regime. They can't get involved with this. The political situation is too unstable."

"Even if Rami's my immediate family and I'm a citizen?"

"You know the answer to that. I'm afraid you're just grasping at straws here."

"But can't we—"

"Not only that, if you get personally involved with your family," said Pierce, suddenly stern, "you risk blowing your cover, as well as our agency's part in the operation here." Pierce gave her a steely look. "Sometimes family comes second. This is one of those times."

Layla glared at Pierce. "So my brother should, what, just rot in prison?"

"Layla. That's not what I'm saying."

"It is what you're saying. You just care about proving something to Monaghan, don't you." Layla could no longer hold back her words. "You're all about your work. Nothing else. It's all business to you, all the time, isn't it. No wonder your own family wants nothing to do with you."

Pierce's hands balled into fists. Layla registered the hurt expression on her face. But the words had been hurled, the damage done.

If Pierce really did have an emotional Achilles' heel, Layla had just hit the target. She turned and bolted out of the safe house, slamming the door behind her.

THE NEXT MORNING, AFTER a sleepless night, Layla burst into the Rothkopf Gallery an hour earlier than she usually showed up.

She dreaded facing Mackey, but she had more important things on her mind than defending her right to visit the Rothkopfs. She was relieved when James came to the door and Mackey was nowhere to be seen. But after a quick kiss, her relief gave way to impatience. "Is your dad here yet?"

"He's in his office. But why—"

"I need to talk to him right away." Layla pushed past James and ran down the hall, ignoring his stunned expression.

In his office, Bennett gestured for Layla to sit in an empty chair across from his desk and closed the door behind her. "What's happening, Layla?" he asked, his forehead furrowing with concern.

She took a deep breath. *One last lie. Then I'm done with lies.*

"I don't know if I've ever mentioned Nathifa el-Deeb?" At the last moment, she gave a false first name for her mother, to distance herself from her real identity.

"You have not." He leaned forward with interest.

"She's a nanny and housekeeper for my family. She's served our family for more than thirty years. Traveled with us all over the world. Well, her only child—Rami—made a really foolish mistake. He was marching with the student protesters who were arrested yesterday."

"Good for him!" said Bennett. "We need to keep the pressure on the regime. Fareed Monsour is Egypt's only hope."

"Rami was seriously injured," Layla continued. "I went to see him in the city prison last night, and he was barely conscious. He desperately needs to be transferred to a hospital. Before he gets taken to the Scorpion."

Bennett sighed. "I feel for him," he said. "I really do. But what could I possibly do?"

"You must know someone of influence," she insisted. "I mean, isn't that how you helped Mackey's parents?"

Bennett hesitated. "That was different. That was more . . . complicated."

"It's all complicated," said Layla. "But does that mean we just stop trying? And you hardly seem the type of man who shies away from complicated."

Bennett nodded. "You're right," he said. "We have to try. If you say you know this boy, and this family is important to you."

"I do. And they are. Very important to me."

Bennett drummed his fingertips on the desk as he thought for a moment. "I do know some people who have connections to the Interior Ministry. Gamal Ghaffar owes me a favor. A pretty big one. This might be a good time to cash that in." He reached for a notepad beneath the Queen Nefertiti paperweight. "What did you say the boy's name was?"

"It's Rami. Rami el-Deeb. And thank you." She beamed at Bennett as she stood up, even as her mind reeled with the name he had mentioned. Jehan's dad. Noor's husband. Gamal Ghaffar owed Bennett a favor. Noor was right. The world these people operated in was very, very small.

Leaving Bennett's office, she bumped into Mackey. Meeting his stern gaze felt like running into a brick wall. His body, too, blocked her way.

"I know what you're going to say," Layla said in a low voice. "You told me to stay away, and I'm here. But unless I hear that from Bennett himself, I'm going to keep seeing the Rothkopfs as much as I want."

"That's not what I was going to say," said Mackey, softer than she'd ever heard him speak before. "I just heard your story, about the housekeeper's son."

"You were eavesdropping?" Layla smirked. "I should have known."

"The walls are thin. Wait." He held up a hand as she tried to push past him. "I'm touched by your loyalty to the people who have served your family. If that's really what's going on," he added in a sardonic tone, almost under his breath.

"There's a nice boy in prison who shouldn't be there at all. I am trying to get him out. That's what's going on, Mackey."

"I hope he gets his medical transfer. I hope he recovers swiftly. Bennett Rothkopf is a good man. You can have confidence in him."

"Thank you. I hope you're right." She sidestepped him, grateful to escape his presence. She didn't know what to make of his sudden kindness. Maybe she'd passed some sort of test. But she didn't want to think about Mackey now. All her thoughts were with Rami.

SHE SPENT THE NEXT two hours in line at the prison to petition to see her brother. As she neared the registrar's window, her phone buzzed. A text from James. She held the phone to her chest for a moment, eyes closed, as if holding him close, then opened them.

Dad told me what happened. He says to tell you your housekeeper's son is being moved at this moment to As-Salam International Hospital. You can find him there.

Layla squeezed the phone and closed her eyes, as if in prayer. *Thank you*, she whispered—to Bennett, to God, to Gamal Ghaffar . . . she wasn't sure to whom—for performing what could only be described as a miracle, or at least a magician's feat: getting something done quickly in Cairo.

A second text came in a moment later. *Everything okay? I'm worried about you.*

Don't worry, she wanted to tell him. *It will only make everything harder.*

But now was not the time. Instead, she texted, *Tell your dad a big thank you. I'm so grateful he could help my brother.* And in a moment of weakness, she added a heart.

She stared at the impulsively sent text in horror for a moment, then texted again: *Whoops. Damn autocorrect! I mean, the boy who is LIKE my brother.*

Ha, he texted back, followed by a double heart.

Another slipup, another fast save. Her double life was spinning out of control, and there seemed to be no end in sight.

WHILE A DOCTOR EXAMINED Rami, Layla paced outside in the corridor, chewing a fingernail off. She'd made a deal with the devil. Now she was obligated to Bennett for Rami's continued care. The guilt she felt over working to imprison the man who had just freed her brother was overwhelming. But there was no other choice she could have made, at least not one that she could live with. Bennett might be trying to treat Layla like family, but Rami actually *was* her family.

A doctor came out to report on Rami's injuries. "He has a broken arm, two cracked ribs, and a bad concussion," he said when Layla jumped out of her seat to get the news. "It is a very good thing you got him transferred to the hospital when you did. He badly needed fluids."

"Will he be okay?"

"He will. With time."

"Thank you, doctor," said Layla, resisting the powerful urge to embrace him. "Thank you. Can I go in and see him now?"

"Yes, but only for a moment. Your friend needs his rest."

Layla tiptoed into the darkened room and kissed her brother's cheek. Half dozing, he reached for her hand. She stroked it, remembering, for a moment, the feel of his much-younger hand in hers. His hand at age two, tiny fingers curling around hers. His hand at five, placed trustingly in hers as they crossed a busy street. His hand at ten, uncurling to show her a treasure he'd found in the trash outside: a shiny hair comb with a butterfly pattern, a gift for her, even though their father had expressly forbidden them to touch the garbage.

That's what she now remembered most about Rami as a boy. He was always trying to get a smile out of her. Layla stepped into the corridor and called Sanaa on the Motorola. "He's safe," she said. "He's in the hospital. He'll still need to stand trial, and there's a chance he could serve time, but I'm going to help get him a good lawyer, too. He's safe now, though."

"*Hamdullah*," breathed Sanaa, praising God. "I am grateful to you, Layla. You saved his life. I will tell Mama now, and let's hope she can stop crying, at least long enough to visit him. It must be nice having a job where you have connections that can help you."

Was it her imagination, or did Sanaa, the consummate house-wife, sound just the tiniest bit envious of her?

"Yes. It's nice," Layla admitted, thinking not of Pierce and the FBI now, but of Bennett and James. Then a wave of sadness washed over her as she realized what she must do next. Leave James. It was the only way to protect both him and the investigation. The path ahead was suddenly clear, but this clarity did nothing to lift her spirits.

With the call to Sanaa now behind her, Layla felt like she could breathe fully for the first time since the nightmare of Rami's arrest began. Suddenly ravenous—she'd missed both breakfast and lunch—she headed for the vending machines in the hospital lounge. After purchasing a package of cookies, she noticed visitors and staff gathering around a TV, talking excitedly. She sidled closer to see what had everyone so transfixed.

A news bulletin from the BBC blared the horrific news: "An Italian journalist has been found dead outside of Cairo, apparently at the hands of the Muharib."

No. It couldn't be. But how many Italian journalists were there in Cairo?

Fearing the worst, Layla leaned forward, then dropped her snack and stared as an enlarged picture came up on the screen: a man in a blazer and white shirt, with longish hair and slightly crooked tortoiseshell glasses. It was Alberto Rossi.

DEADLY OASIS

• DIANA RENN •

Layla burst out of the hospital, her eyes stinging with tears, her breath coming in short, sharp gasps. A few people looked at her with sympathy as she hurried down the long hospital driveway.

Her tears baffled her. After all, she'd hardly known Alberto. They'd met only a handful of times. But as the words and images from the news report returned to her, she felt stabbed by the unmistakable sharp pangs of grief.

She ducked under the shade and protective cover of a palm tree at the end of the driveway. She covered her face with her hands, as if doing so could shut out the images from the news. But the pictures flashed incessantly in her mind. Alberto's body had been discovered on the side of a road in Dahshur, a black bag tied over his head, his wrists and ankles bound. He'd been shot in the back. This was how the Muharib typically left their victims. He'd probably been there since yesterday, which was why he'd failed to appear at the Zamalek Rooftop to meet her.

Clearly, Alberto had returned to Dahshur to dig deeper. But maybe he'd dug too deep and put himself in danger. Maybe she'd even encouraged him on that path by asking too many questions. Had her actions at the dig site put a target on his back? A wave of guilt subsumed her grief. She'd saved his life the night at the dig site, but she hadn't been able to save him this time.

She took several deep breaths to steady herself, then rejoined the pedestrians on the street, walking in no particular direction, ignoring the curious stares. What had Alberto been seeking in Dahshur when he texted her the other day? What knowledge did he have for her that now she'd never know? She cringed with guilt at this new line of thought; nothing mattered now that he was dead. And yet, the thoughts took root in her mind. Had he gone the extra mile to pass her information and gotten killed as a result?

Dazed, replaying every conversation she'd had with Alberto in her mind, Layla wandered for blocks with no destination. She ducked into a shopping mall and rode escalators up and down. She left the mall and plunged deeper into the city, through crowded marketplaces with produce spilling out of bins, then deeper still into dark neighborhoods with laundry hanging out the windows and gaunt dogs roaming the streets.

Eventually, she found herself numbly descending the stairs to a Metro station, even though it was nearing rush hour and the crowds below were swelling. The safe house hardly felt safe right now; she never knew these days what kind of mood or condition she'd find Pierce in. She'd go back to her apartment, take a warm shower, try to pull herself together. She stood on the hot, crowded platform, letting herself get jostled and bumped. She welcomed the pain of an elbow in her ribs, a boot on her toe. She wanted to be just another face in the crowd, where no one would look twice at her. In the Metro station, filled with preoccupied commuters and systems of order—timetables, signs, announcements—she found a few moments of peace.

The scream of the approaching train on the tracks interrupted her thoughts. She let herself get carried along by the river of people into the train car. Just as the doors closed, she realized she'd boarded a women-only car. An elderly woman, seeing her tear-streaked face, stood up and insisted that Layla take her seat. She looked into Layla's eyes for a moment and gave Layla's hand a squeeze with her own soft, wrinkled fingers.

Layla sank into the seat, guilty for taking it yet grateful for this moment of kindness from a stranger, of genuine human connection. In that moment, it didn't matter who Layla was. She was simply a person in need of some comfort.

She buried her face in her hands, took some deep breaths, and tried to pull herself together. When she looked up at the next stop, the older woman was gone, and the sign on the platform was visible. *Opera.* Just as the doors began to close, Layla jumped to her feet and hurried off the train. This stop was right near the Zamalek Hotel.

A human connection. That was what she'd felt with Alberto, a shared sense of purpose. Yes, she'd barely known him. But they were the same in many ways. Their paths had come together, briefly, on their pursuit of the truth. And so she found herself at the Zamalek Rooftop, occupying the corner table they'd shared before. She ordered a vodka and orange juice and, as an afterthought, a straight shot of whiskey, for Alberto. He'd drunk whiskey the evening they'd met there and discussed Pierce's drug problem. "Expecting someone?" the server asked her when he set the whiskey down by the empty seat.

Layla roused from her stupor a little, suddenly embarrassed at how her thoughts had taken over. "What? Oh. No. They're both for me." As if to prove it, and because the server kept watching her curiously, she grabbed Alberto's whiskey and downed it, feeling the burn in her chest. The server raised an eyebrow and glided away.

Layla started in on her vodka and juice.

The worried Americans from the day before were now replaced with some locals, smoking *shisha*. The fruit-scented tobacco from the neighboring tables drifted her way, and she closed her eyes and breathed it in, wishing Alberto would just appear again when she opened them, like a genie out of a bottle.

Someone had been on to him. Maybe he'd spoken to the wrong person. She wished she could go to Dahshur and trace his footsteps there. But Pierce would never authorize such a massive sidetrack of the investigation. Journalists were targeted by terrorist groups with some regularity. Pierce would not be interested.

As she finished her drink, Layla had an idea. Alberto had stayed in this very hotel. Maybe his belongings were still here. He must have taken his laptop and phone to Dahshur, and surely his assassins had destroyed those by now. But he might have left something else in the room. A notepad, or a name scrawled on paper in a pants pocket. Some clue about what he knew, who his sources were, and why he'd been killed.

Layla took the rickety elevator down to the hotel's small, darkly furnished lobby. A bored-looking man in a gray suit was sitting at the computer at the front desk, stifling a yawn as he stared at the screen. A small oscillating fan whirred beside him; the air-conditioning seemed ineffective. Layla approached him and noticed that he quickly clicked out of a computer card game. Summer in Cairo meant fewer tourists. He rose to his feet with a nervous glance toward his screen, his cheeks flushing slightly.

"Pardon me," she said. "I'm here to meet my friend, Alberto Rossi. He's expecting me. But I forgot his room number."

"I am not permitted to give out the room numbers of guests, but I can call him for you. One moment." The receptionist, who evidently had not tuned in to the news of the day yet, turned to the computer, looking for his name. For a moment, Layla held her breath, letting herself hope that she would knock on the door and find him there. Maybe the body had been misidentified. Maybe he was still alive.

"Ah," the receptionist said at last. "It appears that he checked out this morning."

Layla stared at him. "What?" she said, hoping her voice conveyed innocence.

The receptionist frowned at the screen. "I have a note here about his room. It seems his wife requested his belongings be mailed to her. My manager packed up the clothes and a courier picked up the box at noon. Housekeeping should be in the room now."

Layla felt the ground fall away from her. The thought of Alberto's life being packed up and scrubbed away so quickly was chilling. She was too late.

Still, she could not suppress the urge to at least visit Alberto's room, even if it was empty. "I believe he had something of mine. May I go up and talk to housekeeping in case they find it?"

The receptionist looked hesitant, then nodded. "Yes, I suppose that would be all right since he is no longer there. He was staying in Room 435."

"Thank you!" Layla called over her shoulder, as she rushed to the elevator.

She got off on the fourth floor and ran down the hall to room 435, which had a housekeeping cart parked in front of it. She offered the two maids a few piastres, asking if she could have a few minutes alone in her friend's room. "I will never see him again," she explained, her voice choked with emotion she did not need to feign.

The maids nodded sympathetically, pocketed the money in their smocks, and drifted down the hall to give her a few minutes alone.

Layla shut the door behind herself and looked around. It was an extremely modest room, furnished with one double bed, a nightstand, a desk, and an old TV affixed to the wall next to the air-conditioning unit. A rumpled, faded Oriental rug adorned the cold tile floor. Layla walked over to the window and pulled back the long red drapes. The window and balcony offered a view of the traffic-choked street outside rather than of the Nile—no wonder he frequented the rooftop bar. She sat down on the bed for a minute and watched the warm air from the open window rustle the curtains. Car horns blared outside. She couldn't feel Alberto's presence here. This was just an empty room.

Mechanically, she got up and opened the closet, which was empty. He couldn't have kept many clothes there, considering how small it was. As she was closing the door, a scrap of paper on the floor caught her eye. She knelt down to pick it up and turned it over. It was a family photo. Alberto and his wife and two girls were standing against a backdrop of mountains, maybe a family vacation. He stood with one arm protectively around his wife, a fit-looking woman with long dark hair and an earnest smile. His two girls stood on either side of their parents, like happy bookends. One girl grinned impishly and held out a bouquet of wildflowers. The other girl gazed at her father with an adoring smile.

Layla stared at the photo a moment longer. It seemed like such an exotic image. Not because it was taken against a dramatic mountain backdrop, but because it represented the kind of life she would probably never have. A close, loving family that took vacations together. A spouse and children. Normalcy. It all seemed so impossible. She slid the photo into her tote bag. It felt wrong to leave it behind.

On the way to the door, she passed the small writing desk. She opened the three drawers. Maybe he'd left some work behind. All were empty except for a pencil with the hotel logo. On top of the desk was an unused ashtray, the room telephone, and a notepad, also with the hotel logo.

Layla picked up the notepad and looked at it closely. Despite all the fancy surveillance tactics she'd learned in the FBI, sometimes the low-tech clues, like Bennett's double-entry ledger, gave up the most information. She tore the top sheet from the pad and held it up to the window, rotating it until the light confirmed her suspicions. She grabbed the pencil out of the top desk drawer and rubbed lightly over the indentations on the page. *Yes.* She grinned, suddenly feeling like a kid revealing invisible ink. The previous sheet of the notepad had indeed been written on. The pressure of the pen had left the imprint of the words, which the light pencil rubbing revealed. She soon saw that it was a string of numbers, followed by a name.

Khalid Yasin.

Layla dropped the paper, startled, then scrambled to look again. There was no mistaking the name. That was the man she'd shot and wounded at the illegal dig site, the man Alberto said organized the local digs for the Muharib. She didn't think Yasin had seen them. But if he *had* seen Alberto, and known who he was, he could have summoned Alberto to Dahshur to find out how much he'd seen at the dig site that night, maybe with the tantalizing promise of providing more information.

Layla took her iPhone out of her tote bag and dialed. Only after the phone started ringing did it occur to her that she had no plan, nor was she authorized by Pierce to make this call. But she couldn't ignore the notepad. It felt almost like a message from Alberto directly to her. This could have been the lead that brought him back to Dahshur.

The ringing gave way to voicemail. An automatic message, but the name was clearly stated.

"My name is Layla Nawar," said Layla, speaking in English. "I got your number from a friend who said you might have some unique pieces to sell. Please call me back."

LAYLA'S PHONE RANG THAT evening while she was in her apartment, but it wasn't Yasin. Reluctantly, remembering the ugly words she'd hurled at Pierce when she wouldn't help Rami, Layla picked up after the fifth ring.

"You see the news today?" Pierce asked without even saying hello.

"I did. They got Alberto Rossi."

"You doing okay?"

"Do you really care?" Layla replied without thinking.

"Of course I care. Are you doing okay?" she repeated, more insistently.

"Sure," Layla said in a flat tone. "Life goes on. The investigation goes on. These things happen."

"Look," said Pierce. "We've all lost people along the way. It's not easy. But you're right, we move on. Shit like this is the exact reason we do what we do."

Layla could hardly bear to hear Pierce's voice. She didn't believe for a second that Pierce cared—not about Rami, and certainly not about Alberto.

"I visited Alberto's hotel room," Layla confessed, switching to business mode. "It was cleared out already, but I found a lead. I've got Khalid Yasin's phone number." She hesitated a moment and then added, "I called him."

Pierce spluttered as if she'd been taking a sip of something right at that moment. "You did what?" she asked, raising her voice.

"I left him a message," said Layla, unperturbed by Pierce's reaction to this news. A strange sense of calm had come over her. "I said I got his number from a friend—I didn't say who—and that I was interested in buying directly from him."

Pierce whistled under her breath. "You should have cleared that with me first. Give me the phone number."

Layla read her the numbers from the imprint on the paper she'd torn off from the hotel notepad.

"You took a big risk calling Yasin," Pierce went on, with a note of admiration creeping into her voice. "Let me know if he calls. If we can get him to admit to selling looted relics to Rothkopf, we're tightening the noose. Maybe he even knows something about Global Relics and who's in charge there. We could float the name by him, see how he reacts."

"Are you trying to get me killed? I'm not bringing that up directly with this character."

"All right, calm down. I see your point," said Pierce. "In the meantime, maybe the name Global Relics rings a bell for Nesim Farwadi. Maybe even Bennett Rothkopf knows something. I'll talk to Farwadi myself, but I want you to get back over to the Rothkopf Gallery tomorrow to see if you can find any connections."

Layla said nothing. The thought of getting more incriminating evidence about Bennett's activities, after he'd saved her brother's life, made her feel sick. And the thought that Bennett might have anything at all to do with Global Relics or with putting explosive materials in that warehouse seemed outrageous.

"Layla?" Pierce prompted.

"Yeah?"

"Speaking of Rothkopf. You broke things off with the son?"

"Of course," said Layla after a slight hesitation.

"Good," said Pierce shortly. "Glad to hear it. Because things are going to heat up around here, and this is no time for distractions. Don't forget what we talked about."

After hanging up the phone, Layla switched on the news. Pundits were discussing Fareed Monsour and his Open Society party's role in the rising conflicts at universities all over the country. Layla felt a flicker of pride at her brother's dedication to the cause, but the pride was tinged with sadness. The story of Alberto's death was already old news.

She couldn't let his work die, too. She'd force herself to go to the gallery tomorrow and end things with James, partly to finish this investigation with a clear head, and partly—no, largely—to protect him.

Or was she trying to protect herself now, building walls around her heart? Maybe this is what had happened to Pierce over time. Maybe, in this job, it was the only way to survive.

"MR. ROTHKOPF IS OUT this morning," Mackey informed her when she appeared at the gallery bright and early the next morning. "We were not expecting you today." He wasn't as hostile to her as he'd been before, but he remained guarded, watching her face closely, obviously trying to read her.

"Oh! My mistake." Layla shrugged and smiled sheepishly. "I must have written down the schedule wrong. I thought he had a client he wanted me to translate for. In that case, I'll just say hi to James and be on my way."

"James is working."

"Don't worry. I won't take up too much of his precious time." Layla pushed past Mackey and strode down the corridor, trying to shut off emotions and mentally program her next move. *Break up with James.*

She paused at the door to her closet-sized office and put her hand on the wood. She recalled stolen kisses with James in there, his hot breath against her neck when he ducked in on his breaks.

All that was soon to be in the past. She turned away abruptly and noticed an open door, to Hamadi Essam's office, with a key ring sticking out of the doorknob. She peered inside. He wasn't in there, but his computer was glowing; he'd probably just stepped away and forgotten his keys in the door. She'd heard his mother was in poor health and he had a lot on his mind.

But a ring of keys sticking out of a door lock was just too good to pass up. She'd seen Hamadi with these; she recognized the key chain with the flag of Egypt on it. She had no idea how she'd use them with all the security cameras, but maybe some opportunity would arise. She knew Hamadi had keys to every office so he could get in and troubleshoot IT issues. Every office—including Bennett's.

A toilet flushed in the restroom. Quickly, she brushed against the door as if she were looking for Hamadi in there, pulled the key ring out of the lock, and slid the keys into her pants pocket. She hoped this theft wouldn't get him into trouble; she didn't have anything against Hamadi. She vowed to get copies made as soon as possible and then return the keys to him.

Walking briskly, she continued on to James's studio and turned the knob. As usual, it was locked. "Freaking Fort Knox around here," she muttered. She almost wanted to use one of Hamadi's keys, but of course they had to stay hidden. And she needed to get out of the hallway before Hamadi saw her. She rapped loudly on James's studio door.

James's face registered surprise and then happiness when he saw her, even though he stood blocking the doorway and didn't let her in.

"Fumes," he apologized.

"I don't mind fumes. We should talk," said Layla. She stepped forward, and he backed up to let her in. She closed the door behind herself. He was right about the fumes—the smell was reminiscent of paint thinner, but nothing she couldn't handle.

When she saw James's desk, she stopped short. Although it was cluttered with artifacts, pottery shards, papers, and hand tools, the desk itself was identical to Bennett's. Layla remembered rifling through Bennett's desk drawers and then his bookshelf, and suddenly recalled where she had seen the name Global Relics Limited before.

Bennett had some sheets of letterhead from that company on the bookshelf. She'd dismissed it as unremarkable at the time. It was blank.

But the company didn't exist; they'd determined that. Could *Bennett* be running this shell company? Was he in the know about the explosive materials? If so, Pierce's hunch about the degree of his involvement could be right.

Her heart pounded with this new thought. But it made no sense. Bennett was American. He was dealing in illicit relics out of selfish reasons, to keep his head above water financially, to pay off lenders. That was bad, but not terrorism. Still, if he had any knowledge of Global Relics, and the explosives in storage unit twenty, she needed to know.

"Everything all right?" James asked, his forehead furrowing with concern.

"It's—it's the fumes," Layla said. "I think they are getting to me a little, actually. Maybe we could open a window or something?"

Except for one high up near the ceiling, all the windows were covered with brown paper. "Sunlight can affect pigmentation in some of my materials," James apologized, following her gaze. "But I can adjust the fan." He cranked the fan to high and turned back to her.

"What do you want to talk about?" he asked. "In person, on your day off? Should I be worried?" He pulled a face of mock concern, mischief twinkling in his eyes.

"No, I just—" Layla faltered. *Break it off*, a voice inside her head urged her on. *You have keys to the gallery. You don't need him now.*

"Something's on your mind," he guessed. "You have that look you get when you're preoccupied."

He knew her too well.

She nodded.

"You can tell me anything, you know." He looked intensely at her.

Layla nodded again. No words came. She wanted to be known. She could never be known.

He stepped forward. His arms closed around her. He did not kiss her, just held her in a long embrace, which she eventually returned, leaning her cheek against that soft, safe spot on his collarbone.

As she did, she found herself facing his computer screen, which had been angled away from the door. It was open to a page on the International Council of Museums website. She knew that site; Pierce's files contained numerous printouts from it. Like Interpol, the ICOM posted photographs of stolen antiquities, designed to help curators, dealers, and auction houses identify them. The photo displayed on the screen showed an ancient Egyptian terra-cotta jar with a blue pattern of flowers and grapes, similar to the terra-cotta sitting on a small pedestal in the center of James's desk.

Layla's eyes widened. The jar sitting on James's desk wasn't just a near match to the one displayed on the website. It was the same jar. The pattern was identical, except for where James was cleaning the pattern along the rim of the jar.

Wait. Not cleaning it.

Covering it.

"So what's on your mind?" James murmured.

She felt sick, and not from the fumes. All this time, she'd wanted to cordon James off from this investigation. She'd worried how he might react if they took his father down, never dreaming Bennett would be implicated to this degree. But James was in it, too. He was in it all the way.

James pulled away from her. His face hardened as he followed her gaze.

Layla took a step toward the desk, then another. "These artifacts. They were stolen."

"No," said James. "Why do you—"

"They were stolen!"

"They weren't!" He grabbed a paint rag and tossed it over the jar in a futile attempt to disguise it. She snatched the rag away and glared at him. "I understand exactly what you're doing. Now I know why you never let me in here."

James watched her with a stricken expression as she paced the room, looking over the shelves filled with artifacts, the bins of materials. "Is everything in here stolen?" she asked, as she grabbed a funeral mask from a drying rack and shook it at him.

"No."

She made a move as if to hurl the mask to the floor. Which she suddenly felt like doing.

James lunged for the mask in her hands. They grappled with it for a moment, and then he managed to wrest it from her.

"Layla, it's complicated." James stood with the mask clutched tightly in both hands, breathing heavily, as Layla circled the room again, taking in the damning evidence everywhere.

"Complicated." Layla stalked to another part of the room and looked at a table of projects. She felt a sensation like acid traveling through her veins when she saw an open box of cheap plaster vases with three open spaces. It was no doubt awaiting the three vases on the drying rack. Beside the box was a stack of papers, documents certifying the vases as imitations only. Layla turned to face James. "They'll all get re-restored on the receiving end, right?"

"Listen." James made a pleading gesture. "We're not criminals. What we're doing here is *good* for the relics."

Layla rolled her eyes.

"Hear me out," said James. "We're saving these artifacts by getting them into the hands of private collectors who will care for them. There are more artifacts in Egypt and elsewhere in the Middle East than these countries can handle. They get junked in museum storerooms, where they're going to get stolen or forgotten. Our buyers have the resources to store and display them properly. They appreciate them."

"Wow."

James blinked. "What?"

Layla paced angrily back and forth. "That is so patronizing—so freaking colonial. Who are you to decide to remove artifacts from their rightful homes? Egypt is perfectly capable of taking care of its own relics and curating its own history, thank you very much."

"Why are you defending Egypt? You've barely lived here," James shot back, following her as she paced. "You blow in out of nowhere and act like you know everything about it. But you don't."

Layla stopped pacing. "I know enough," she said in a quiet voice. "I know that slum children are hired to dig these things up and sometimes they get killed doing it. When you sell illicit relics, you're keeping that system of oppression alive. Even if you have good intentions."

"That's ridiculous," said James. "Where did you hear that?"

"It's a known practice," said Layla.

"No, really, I'd like to know," said James. He flung himself into a chair, crossed one leg over the opposite knee, and put his hands behind his head. "Enlighten me. What's your source?"

Layla froze. "What do you mean?"

"Why are you so interested in the illicit antiquities business?" He tipped his head and regarded her carefully.

Anger surged in Layla. She didn't like his tone, the suspicion behind his voice. She and James never played power games like this.

"When I made banana bread in your apartment, and I was looking for a loaf pan, I found a file in your kitchen drawer," James went on, unclasping his hands and placing them on the arms of the chair. "It was full of articles about black market antiquities. Interesting reading. You're so angry with us for selling, but it seems a lot like you're looking to buy."

Suddenly, he seemed to see not just into her but through her. Could he suspect she was an undercover agent?

She lifted her chin. *Be Layla Nawar.* "That file is part of my due diligence as a collector. I have to be able to spot fakes, so I don't get swindled." *Time to change the subject.* She took a deep breath. "Do you work with a company called Global Relics?"

"No. Never heard of them. Who are they?"

She held James's gaze for a long moment. He didn't look away. Conflicting emotions roiled within her. James had presented himself as an upstanding, ethical person, all the while knowingly using his talents for an illegal business. But she wasn't living an honest life, either—her secrets from James ran deep. She felt the sharp stab of Hamadi's keys in her pants pocket, reminding her of her own deceptions.

James looked down at his hands, his fingers tenting together. When he looked up at her again, his eyes were glistening with emotion. He looked like the James she knew again, as if the mask he'd put on—shrewd businessman, a younger Bennett Rothkopf—had slipped and fallen. He was hurt. They were hurting each other.

"I should have been up front with you." James's voice cracked a little. "I lied about my work, and I'm sorry about that. But you have to understand, this side of the business is just a small part of my job. Ninety-five percent of my work is totally by the book and comes with watertight provenance documents."

Layla regarded him coolly.

"Do you believe me?"

What would Layla Nawar say? Would it be the same as Layla el-Deeb's response? "I guess," she said after a pause, still unsure which of her identities was speaking. "And yes, you should have told me. How long have you been doing this?"

"About two years." James scratched the back of his neck. "My dad wanted me to come to Cairo to learn more about Middle Eastern artifact restoration, and then he started giving me these special assignments. I didn't want to do it at first, but the more I heard him explain it, and the more I heard collectors talk, the more I realized we were providing a kind of service, and saving the relics, in our way."

Layla picked up a small vase from a shelf and traced its rim. A crack ran down one side. She stroked it with her finger, then wistfully put the vase back on the shelf. "I remember the night I first met you," she said, "and you showed me that exhibit at the Coriander. You talked about kintsukuroi, about the beauty of that style of repair. You said it honored the past of the object. I loved listening to you talk that way."

James looked stricken. "I wasn't misrepresenting myself," he said. "That really is what I believe. But I can't just do what I want. Not yet."

Layla bit back the words that immediately came to mind. *Neither can I.*

"But you could be doing so much more than this," she said, gesturing around the office. "You could be making a name for yourself. You're extraordinarily talented. You could have your pick of legitimate jobs."

"There aren't that many."

"There's Sydney. The Nicholson Museum."

James opened his mouth.

"You think I didn't know about that?"

"Who told you?"

"Marcus Goldman. I've known for weeks. When were you going to tell me you might be moving to the other side of the world?"

"There was no point," he said, shaking his head morosely. "I can't take that job."

"Why not?" Layla flicked her wrist in an impatient gesture. "Take the job. It's your ticket out of this mess." *And possibly your ticket away from an FBI dragnet*, she thought. He'd be implicated if they arrested Bennett. Unless she covered for him. Could she do that, in light of all the evidence in his studio?

He shook his head fiercely. "My father doesn't want me to leave his business. Not right now, anyway. And I won't go against my father."

Layla's hands balled into fists. "Are you kidding me?" she burst out. "You don't have to prop up his shady business and his gambling habit."

"My dad's all about family. If I go that far away, he thinks we'll fall out of touch."

Layla felt a sneer spread across her face. "Really? You bought that? Isn't it really that he'd drown in his gambling debts if you weren't around to help him shore up his finances with all these illegal activities?"

"You don't know anything about it!" James retorted, getting up from the swivel chair so fast it rolled and crashed into a fan. "I've already lost one parent. I'm not going to lose another. He's all I have." He paused. "Unless . . . unless I have you, too."

Layla fought to quiet her breath, to steady her heart. She was being handed, on a platter, the opportunity she needed to end things with James. She thought of the stolen gallery keys in her pocket. There was nothing else she needed from James Rothkopf. Professionally speaking.

She hesitated, then shook her head firmly. "No," she whispered, her voice husky. "I can't do this anymore."

James looked taken aback. Layla, too, flinched at the sound of her own voice. She'd actually said the words.

"So that's it?" James asked quietly. "There's no way past this?"

Layla gave him one last, long look, shook her head again, and walked out.

THE FRESHEST AIR IN Cairo could be found on the Nile Corniche or, better yet, on the Nile itself. Layla purchased a single ticket for a one-hour felucca ride to try to clear her head.

She collapsed on the damp cushions at the back of the boat and watched the captain pole away from the docks. Out in the center of the Nile, as boats of all types passed on either side, he raised the red sail, and they glided along. The captain, a slight man in a voluminous brown robe and a white turban, offered to point out some of the sights, but Layla smiled politely and shook her head. She tipped her head back and let the breeze ruffle her hair, the sun bathe her face. The honking horns and the street music on the riverbanks receded into the distance.

Happy couples on other feluccas and motorboats passed by, snuggled together on the cushions, laughing and pointing at the sights, and Layla's serenity drained away. She felt truly adrift and alone—she'd lost Pierce as a mentor, Alberto as a colleague, James as a lover.

She took out the keys she'd swiped from Hamadi. She couldn't go back to the gallery now. Not with James there, not with all the ugly words they'd hurled at each other still hanging in the air. If she searched the gallery after hours, she could look around for anything related to Global Relics. Except there was the problem of the security cameras. She still didn't know how she was going to handle that detail. Maybe she'd been too impulsive in swiping the keys. It was probably only a matter of time before Hamadi realized they were missing, remembered he'd left them in the door, and learned that Layla had been in the gallery. She'd have to make up some story about noticing them there and taking them for safekeeping; she'd intended to give them back all along, of course.

Meanwhile, she was stuck. Pierce was talking to Farwadi and handling the investigation of the shipment to DC with Housman and Monaghan to aid her. Explosive materials were likely heading to DC at this very moment, and there was nothing Layla could do to stop them unless she discovered something about Global Relics to help connect the dots and find out who was moving those explosives through the Singapore Freeport.

She flung the keys into her tote bag and rummaged for her sunglasses. Her hand brushed a piece of paper—the photo of Alberto's family. As she gazed at those smiling faces, she thought of Mrs. Rossi receiving her dead husband's belongings in a small FedEx box in the coming days. So little to show for the work he'd done, the man he'd been.

Layla sat up straight. Maybe not so little after all. Mrs. Rossi might have access to something that didn't even need to be shipped to her: his email account. If Layla couldn't pursue the Global Relics angle right now, she could at least try to figure out what had happened to Alberto, and what he might have wanted to tell her.

She took out her phone. Within minutes she was speaking to a person at Alberto's paper who was willing to give her the name of

Alberto's wife. Giulia Rossi. The colleague refused to give her Giulia's phone number, however, and in her undercover role, there was no way to demand it.

Now that she had the idea of contacting Giulia, though, she couldn't let go of it. She scrolled through the online white pages directory for Rome. There were about fifteen people named Alberto Rossi listed. One, however, was listed in the Prati district. She recalled Alberto once talking about his neighborhood. She dialed the number.

Somewhere in Italy, a phone rang.

After four rings, a woman answered in a shaky voice. "*Pronto?*"

"*Parla Giulia Rossi?*"

There was a pause, then a wary "*Sì.*"

Layla introduced herself as a colleague and friend of Alberto's. "I am calling to express my condolences," she said. "I didn't know your husband well, but our professional paths crossed in Cairo, and I admired his work."

"Thank you," said Giulia. She sounded exhausted. "It is very kind of you to call. Today is a difficult day for us. Alberto's body is traveling back to Rome, and I am making the burial arrangements."

Layla swallowed back the lump in her throat. "I'm so sorry."

"What did you say your name was?"

"Layla. Layla Nawar."

"Ah, Alberto mentioned you."

Layla was so surprised to hear this, the phone almost slipped from her hand. She couldn't picture herself the subject of conversation between Alberto and his wife. "He did?"

"He said he was working with a detective in Cairo," said Giulia. "That is you?"

Layla clutched the phone with both hands, one finger hovering over the end call button. When had Alberto first had an inkling that she wasn't who she appeared to be? Was it that night at the dig site? She remembered his intense gaze when he dropped her off after their excursion. The questions he'd asked about how she'd learned to shoot a gun, and his silence after her breezy response. She should have known better than to think she could swap out the heiress act for GI Jane and not raise his suspicions. Now Giulia Rossi was on to her, too.

"I— I'm just a private detective," Layla stammered, still caught off guard by this revelation. "I work for myself. If you could keep this conversation just between us, I'd appreciate it."

"Do not worry, your secret is safe," Giulia assured her. "Alberto said you were both interested in the lost relics of Faiyum."

"That's right. We were pursuing some similar lines of investigation. Giulia, do you know what he was doing in Dahshur before— right before—"

"I do not know. I was hoping you might be able to tell me." Her voice sped up and took on a breathy quality. "Please, any information you have about his work, I would appreciate."

"I don't know much, either," Layla admitted with a sinking heart. She felt terrible for Giulia, whose grief was so much greater than her own. She wished she could offer some words of reassurance.

The wind whipped up, and the felucca captain looked at Layla questioningly. She gestured for him to steer back toward the shore. Any hope of enjoying an hour of escape was shot. "Maybe we can help each other," she said to Giulia. "I'm trying to find some answers. Do you have access to his email account?"

"I do. He gave me all his passwords before he left for Cairo." She paused. "In case anything should happen to him," she added in a softer voice.

"I need you to look through his emails and see if there is anything about the Faiyum relics or Dahshur. Did he ever mention the name Khalid Yasin?" Layla spelled Khalid's name for her.

"Never. Who is he?" Giula's voice grew urgent.

"I don't know," said Layla. "It's just a name that came up in conversation once." She guessed Giulia hadn't been told about the illegal dig site they'd visited together, or their run-in with Yasin. "It's just . . . someone he was interested in. I'd be curious if they were in contact."

"I will check and let you know." Giulia took a long, shuddery breath, then added, "Layla, I have to explain to my children what my husband was doing in Cairo, why he died there." Giulia's voice had been relatively steady throughout the call, but now it wavered and she was sniffling audibly. Layla could tell she was struggling to keep it together. "I need to tell them something."

As the felucca glided closer to the boat dock, Layla observed a father and his children, a boy and a girl, eating ice cream on the riverbank. He tousled the hair of his son and chucked his daughter under the chin. She felt her eyes well up with tears for Giulia and her children. "Tell them their father was working to make the world a safer place."

ON THE WAY HOME from her aborted cruise, Layla got a text from Pierce to stop by the safe house for a check-in. Layla let herself in with the key and went straight to the living room. She didn't bother getting a glass of water or a snack, or even taking off her hijab. She didn't plan to stay long at all. That would probably be fine with Pierce, who didn't even say hello when she walked in.

"Farwadi's never heard of Global Relics," said Pierce, without looking up from her computer screen.

"I'm fine, thanks. How are you?" said Layla, perching on the edge of the couch. She surveyed the floor with disgust. It was strewn with energy bar wrappers, empty soda bottles, and sandwich bags. Pierce was clearly burning the midnight oil. Layla hoped the junk food was a substitute for the drugs.

"No time for chitchat," Pierce muttered. She finished typing something, then turned in her chair to face Layla, drumming her fingertips on the arms of the chair. "I talked to Farwadi. He's never heard of Global Relics. It simply doesn't exist. It's got to be a shell company for the Muharib that exists solely to operate that storage unit and move relics and weapons."

Layla opened her mouth to tell her about the Global Relics letterhead in Bennett's office, then stopped short. She believed James when he said he'd never heard of the company. Maybe she'd been wrong about the letterhead being blank. Maybe whoever was behind Global Relics was corresponding with Bennett to create the illusion of a legitimate paper trail, a connection to a supposedly legitimate dealer, in case they were questioned by the Singapore Freeport or anyone else. She wanted to go immediately to the gallery and ransack the place for anything further connected to Global Relics.

"Meanwhile," said Pierce, "I just got off a call with Housman in Singapore. He said that unit twenty used third-party video surveillance on a hidden camera, and that their agency received it. Look." She hit a button on her screen and ran the footage. Layla leaned forward to see.

A date on the top corner of the screen read June 24. Four men, their faces obscured with black scarves, hoodies, and caps, entered the storage unit with two big crates on dollies. "These are the 'couriers' who met the delivery on the tarmac and escorted the crates to the loading dock and up the elevator to the Masterpiece Fine Arts vault," said Pierce. "Now let's fast-forward three days." She hit another button and the date on the screen changed to June 27. Again, four men appeared in the unit with crates and dollies. They opened the crates they had deposited before and transferred the contents, some cans and a large number of foot-long dark bricks, to the new crates.

"That's the C-4," Pierce said, pointing at the bricks.

"And the cans?" asked Layla with a sinking sensation.

"Housman says they hold chemicals," said Pierce. "You can just make out an ammonium nitrate label there. The other cans I'm not sure about, but I'm pretty sure they're not filled with vegetables and soup. Now, watch these guys closely. All the bricks and cans are going into the new crates. One guy dropped a brick—he's clumsy, working fast. You can see one at the edge of the shelving unit. That's the one we found on the raid."

"These guys are working fast. Transferring ammo and explosives into crates. Moving them on out. There they go, toward the elevator. That'll take them to the loading dock, back to the tarmac, and out to a jet."

"Shit. What was the date of the shipment Richard Tremblay said was headed to DC?" Layla asked. Her heart pounded as it dawned on her what she was looking at.

"June twenty-seventh. The same as the date on this footage." Pierce indicated the date on the screen.

Layla nodded, feeling numb.

"Monaghan's mobilized a larger team now to surround the expected delivery site. They're already in position," Pierce assured her.

Layla let out a long breath. "Well, we're sure about what's in that delivery now. But what if it doesn't go to the address listed on the manifest?"

"Monaghan's got all the storage facilities in DC on high alert," Pierce said. "He's on it. There's nothing more you and I can do now except keep rooting around for names, for the people behind Global Relics."

Layla thought she detected a trace of disappointment in Pierce's voice as she clicked out of the footage. She probably hated having Monaghan take things over as much as Layla hated having Pierce do the same to her. It was frustrating to get this far and not to see things through.

"So what do I do now?" asked Layla.

Pierce shrugged. "Take Jehan up on her invitation and hang by the pool. If you go on a weekday, Gamal will be at the office. You can try one more time to look through Noor's office for any more correspondence with Rothkopf. Help tighten the noose and find dirt on him so we can pick him up when he returns to the States."

Layla nodded numbly.

"Besides," Pierce said, "some sunlight and a pool day might do you some good. You look like you could use it."

AS THE CHAUFFEUR JEHAN sent for Layla left Cairo and drove through the arid landscape, Layla stared out the window, grateful for the increasing miles between her and James. Although a day with Jehan and her mother squabbling didn't exactly sound like paradise, this was maybe the closest she could get. If not paradise, then Dreamland, a gated community in 6th of October, a city twenty miles outside of Cairo.

As the arid landscape gave way to a golf course, palm trees, and impossibly green lawns, Layla sat up straighter. She gazed out at the pastel-colored villas and shops with a growing sense of distaste. It felt so far from the Cairo she knew—the protests, the church bombing, Alberto's death. Dreamland's insulation from all these problems made her want to scream. She quelled her anger with a few deep breaths as they pulled into the Ghaffars' driveway.

The Ghaffars lived in a pale pink villa iced with white trim and ringed with palm trees, with a view of the looming Giza pyramids just behind it. A lush green lawn unrolled before the estate, with a burbling fountain in the middle. *Wasted water*, Layla couldn't help thinking bitterly.

She got out of the car and waved at Jehan, who was already running down the lawn to greet her, wearing a swimsuit and a long, modest cover-up tunic. She'd pulled her hair up high on her head in a bun. Layla returned her eager hug.

"Did you bring your swimsuit?" Jehan asked.

Layla forced a smile and patted her tote bag. "Can't wait. This heat is unbearable. My air-conditioning can't keep up with it."

"I told you, *nobody* stays in Cairo all summer," said Jehan as if Layla were an endearing simpleton.

They do if they live in a regular neighborhood, Layla thought. *They do if they're stuck in a prison. Or a hospital.*

"You'll have to get out soon," Jehan warned, as she led her toward the front steps. "What are your plans? Are you going to join the Farwadis?"

"I'm still working stuff out," Layla said carefully.

Jehan showed her around the palatial house, pausing to greet Noor, who was giving instructions to the kitchen staff. Noor greeted her warmly, with a kiss on each cheek. But her face looked drawn with tension. There were dark circles under her eyes.

In the back of the house, a crescent-shaped pool glistened turquoise in the sun. "Where can I change into my suit?" Layla asked, glancing back at the villa and wondering which window belonged to a home office.

"Pool house," replied Jehan, pointing to a small outbuilding by the water.

Layla quickly changed and rejoined Jehan, who was floating on an inflatable raft in the water, drifting aimlessly, using the barest flicks of her wrists to keep the raft from bumping the sides of the pool. Jehan shoved an extra raft toward Layla, who clambered onto it and paddled after Jehan.

The energy at the villa was noticeably different from Geneva, where both Noor and Jehan had been in constant motion, meeting with decorators, planning ski excursions, or entertaining friends. Maybe it was the heat, or Layla's own mood shading the scene, but the more she watched the uncharacteristically quiet Jehan, the more she was convinced that something was definitely off at the Ghaffar household.

"So what have you been doing out here the past few weeks?" Layla asked. "You've been missing parties. That's not like you."

Jehan sighed. "I know. My dad wants to keep me away from all that for now."

Layla watched her face carefully. "Or away from Muhammad?" she guessed.

"Partly that. We're pretty much broken up, thanks to my dad." Jehan frowned and kicked at the water. "He doesn't like Muhammad's allegiance to Fareed Monsour. That doesn't make us look good while he's trying to get a promotion. He says we have to be extra careful of the company we keep. And how we look in public. He wants the whole family together right now." Jehan sighed. "It's his warped version of family time. He works from home sometimes so he looks like he's available for us, but all he does is bring his work stress right into the house. He's locked in his home office, but the stress is radioactive. It's driving my mom crazy. And me."

Layla nodded, taking all of this in. Then, with a new worry, she glanced again at the pale pink villa. "Your dad's not home right now, is he?" she asked. If Gamal Ghaffar was home, there was no chance of her going into Noor's office.

"Oh, he's here, working from home today. Busy, as usual. He's been on the phone all morning."

Layla felt a sinking sensation but wasn't about to give up on making progress. "What's so stressful for him?" she asked, yawning as if to suggest she could care less about the answer. "He's home with you guys. He should be relaxed."

Jehan shrugged. "My dad is . . . how should I put it . . . ambitious. He wants to be head of the GID. There's a rumor that the president is changing some appointments soon. So he's bending over backward to please everyone, and making sure I don't do anything stupid to embarrass him." She laughed wryly. "I'll just be glad when it's all over. Then we can stop walking on eggshells, and I can get my life back. Apparently, my dad's on to something that he's sure is going to get him a lot of acclaim, if he can just prove it. Now, can we please stop talking politics? We're in a pool. I hereby declare all political conversation banned from pools." Jehan playfully flicked some water at Layla. "I want to hear all about you and James. Huma said you guys are an item. I can't believe you haven't told me a thing!"

Layla flinched at the cold water, and the mention of James. He was the last person she wanted to talk about.

She turned her raft so Jehan couldn't see her face and startled at the sight of Noor standing a few feet from the pool, silhouetted against the fierce sun. Layla shielded her eyes.

"We have a visitor," she said. "Jehan, come out and put your cover-up on."

Jehan cast Layla a stricken look.

"Who's here?" asked Layla, but Jehan didn't respond. Instead, she spun stubbornly around on her air mattress, almost like a child, with her back to her mother.

"Jehan!" Noor sighed in exasperation. She grabbed Jehan's and Layla's cover-ups from a lounge chair and held them out. "It's

Youssef. He's here for the afternoon meeting with your father, but it's an opportunity to say hello. What will he think if you do not take the time to speak with him?"

"That I'm not remotely interested," drawled Jehan.

Noor's eyes blazed. Her long earrings trembled. "Now. Cover up!"

Jehan gave Layla a sad look before jumping off her raft and swimming to the ladder. "Sorry," she said. "I guess you get to meet the Bore. I promise I'll keep this short. I'm working on making him allergic to me."

Noor sighed heavily. She turned and furiously brushed some dropped leaves off an extra lounge chair while Jehan and Layla got out of the pool.

Grateful for the distraction from the James update, and vaguely curious about this unwanted suitor, Layla followed Jehan to the lounge chairs. She toweled off and donned her cover-up, too.

"Best behavior," Noor muttered to Jehan through clenched teeth. Then she flounced back inside the house to fetch Youssef.

"This is so embarrassing," Jehan said, buttoning up her tunic so fiercely that a button popped off. "My parents just cannot get it through their heads that I'm not into him. I don't want some boring guy with a stupid government desk job. He has zero personality, zero interests or passions outside of work, zero social life. We have absolutely nothing to talk about."

When Noor returned, she led a tall man with wavy black hair and a thick mustache to the poolside. Layla immediately recognized him as the man she'd seen trailing after Gamal at a couple of events, most recently the Egyptian Museum fundraiser, where she'd met Alberto. Up close, he looked to be around thirty, not bad-looking but not remarkable, either. He had a few acne scars on his face and a faint sheen of sweat from the heat, since he was wearing a dark suit and his shirt was buttoned all the way up.

"Something to drink, Youssef?" Noor asked in Arabic, after introducing Layla. She gestured toward an outdoor bar with pitchers of ice water and lemonade.

"A lemonade would be nice. Thank you," he replied. He glanced at a gold wristwatch. A nice watch, Layla noted, for a guy in a middle management job. "I can't stay long. Your husband doesn't appreciate lateness."

"Well, you'll need refreshment before you get started. It's a hot day." Noor handed him a glass, beaming.

"Thank you." He sat awkwardly on the edge of a lounge chair— bolt upright, as if refusing to—or unable to—lounge. He drank without looking up while Noor, Jehan, and Layla all watched him. Layla saw that he'd set his briefcase too close to the pool, and a puddle of water crept toward it.

Jehan stifled a yawn.

Noor gave her daughter a sharp look, then walked toward the kitchen door. "I'll leave you kids alone to chat," she called over her shoulder. "Always nice to see you, Youssef."

"The pleasure is mine, Mrs. Ghaffar."

Youssef drained his glass, then set it down on a table and looked shyly at Jehan, who was deliberately ignoring him, waving a long strand of grass at a curious cat that had come through the hedge.

Youssef looked helplessly at Layla, who shrugged.

"Is this your first visit to the Ghaffars' house?" Youssef asked Layla in Arabic.

"It is," she said. "It's a beautiful place."

"Yes, it is," he echoed. "A beautiful place."

Layla managed a polite smile. Jehan smirked, as if to say, *See what I mean?*

"Are you from Cairo originally?" Youssef asked her.

Layla decided to sidestep this question, considering his proximity to Gamal Ghaffar. The less she volunteered about herself, the better. "I'm living there now. But I've lived all over the place. Do you mind if we speak English?" she asked, switching over. "It's more comfortable for me," she added. She'd been speaking mostly English in her heiress role, and she didn't want Youssef to listen too closely to her Arabic accent and make any assumptions about her background. "What about you? Are you from Cairo?"

"I am a native Cairene, yes," said Youssef, puffing out his chest with obvious pride. "Originally from Garden City."

"Nice." She felt his eyes linger on her, and averted her own gaze to watch Jehan and the cat. She did not volunteer that she lived in Garden City now.

But as he glanced at Jehan and obviously failed to attract her interest or attention, he turned his attention back to Layla.

"Jehan tells me you lived in America?"

"For a bit. Also London, Zurich . . ." She made a vague gesture. "I'm kind of a citizen of the world." She laughed.

"The Western world," Youssef observed.

"I guess you could say that."

Youssef rattled his ice cubes in his glass, then reached in to pick one up and crunched it, all the while keeping his gaze on her, as if she were as much an unexpected curiosity and amusement as the cat. "Do you plan to stay here long?" he asked.

"We'll see where the wind takes me," said Layla, plucking imaginary lint off her cover-up. "For now, I like it. Though it's heating up. I didn't realize how hot the summers are."

"I am glad to hear Cairo mostly agrees with you," said Youssef. He smiled shyly. "And Egypt. America has many problems right now."

"So does Egypt," Layla couldn't resist pointing out, thinking of Rami in the hospital and the bodies that had littered the ground by the church after the Muharib's most recent attack.

"Yes, there are problems here, too," Youssef agreed.

"No political talk. It's been banned in the pool area," Jehan snapped.

All three of them watched the cat in silence for a moment longer.

A window two stories above them opened. Gamal Ghaffar leaned out.

Jehan waved. "Isn't it time for your meeting?" she called in Arabic. "Maybe Youssef should be moving along?"

Gamal's face was hard to read two stories up, but Layla was pretty sure she detected a grimace. "Yes, we are beginning soon, if

Youssef would like to come up now," he replied. "Who is with you?" He shaded his eyes from the sun, squinting down at them. Layla could feel his curious stare.

"My friend Layla," said Jehan.

"Ah." Gamal gave her a courteous wave. "Hello."

Layla waved back, then put on a wide-brimmed sun hat to shield her face from his view. She heard Gamal shut the window.

Youssef wiped his hands, which were damp from the condensation on the lemonade glass, and stood up. He plucked his briefcase from the puddle. "Well. I should attend my meeting. It was nice to meet you, Layla."

Layla nodded vaguely. "Nice to meet you, too."

The moment Youssef retreated into the house, Jehan exploded into laughter.

"What?"

"I just solved my problem." Jehan grinned. "I'm going to pawn Youssef off on you. I think he's a little bit smitten!"

"Don't you dare pawn him off on me," Layla said, playfully swatting Jehan.

"I know, I know. I'm just kidding," Jehan said, laughing. "I like you too much to inflict him on you. Besides, you have James."

"Right. I have James." Layla tore off her cover-up and dove into the water to avoid the topic once again.

When she reemerged she said, "Can't you talk to your mom? Make her understand she can't set you up like this?"

Jehan, now sitting on the edge of the pool, kicked her feet lazily in the water. "It just creates more conflict. I'm trying to ride it out. It'll end soon, and then I'll be free of house arrest."

"How soon?" Layla clambered up onto her raft.

"Just as soon as my dad catches up with the FBI."

Layla slipped off the raft. "What?"

Jehan laughed. "I know, it totally sounds like something out of a movie. But he's convinced the FBI is running some kind of secret operation in Cairo. He thinks they have a safe house. Some informant told him." She kicked her feet and propelled her raft a few feet away into the shaded side of the pool beneath a grove of palms.

Layla stared at her. She fought to keep her grip on the float—and reality—as she heaved herself back onto the raft and paddled after Jehan. "He told you all this?"

"I found it out on my own," said Jehan with a hint of pride. "I eavesdrop sometimes when he's on the phone. The only way I can endure my house arrest is to know what the end game is. I'm hoping I'll start getting my regular life, and my boyfriend, back tomorrow."

"Why tomorrow?"

"Because once my dad gets his promotion, he won't be so concerned about what I'm wearing or who I'm seeing anymore. I'll be free."

"But why tomorrow?" Layla persisted. "What's he planning to do?"

"It might even be tonight." Jehan flicked some water at the cat, who had come to the water's edge to find her. It turned tail and bolted. "They're planning to bust the safe house. That's what the meeting's about."

LAYLA APOLOGIZED TO JEHAN for the twentieth time as the driver pulled up.

"I totally get it," Jehan said. "When you have a fight with your guy, it's the worst feeling in the world. If you think you were wrong, you have to go back and talk it out in person. It's the only way."

Layla gave her a quick hug. "Thank you for understanding," she said.

Jehan instructed the driver to go as fast as possible back to Cairo. "Good luck!" she called, as the car pulled away.

Layla waved until the car rounded the corner, then immediately tried texting Pierce again on the burner. No response. Once again, in a grim repeat of the scenario in Bennett's office, Layla couldn't count on Pierce at a critical time. Fine. If she was going to risk compromising the whole operation, let her. Layla wasn't going to let all their hard work be for nothing. Not after Alberto.

She was about to drop the burner back in her bag when a text from Pierce buzzed in.

I'm on it. Striking the set. Get here as soon as you can.

Layla frowned at the phone. So she was there after all. That brought her some reassurance, but fresh worries. Was Pierce in good enough shape, mentally or physically, to pack up the safe house?

Once they were back in the city, Layla leaned forward and asked the driver to let her off at a different address, a few blocks away from the safe house. When the car was safely around the corner, she ran.

Pierce had clearly gotten right to work. Files and papers were neatly stacked next to surveillance equipment on the kitchen counter, a stack of boxes on the floor.

"You didn't waste any time," Layla said.

Pierce raised an eyebrow. "What'd you think I was doing?"

Layla met her gaze. "I don't know. You didn't answer right away."

"I was tied up in a meeting at the embassy about security protocol for Fareed Monsour's upcoming visit. I couldn't pick up without attracting attention. Here. Box these." She handed Layla some file folders. "And tell me what else you found out at Jehan's house."

"Nothing much. I couldn't ask Jehan any more questions without looking too interested. And as soon as I found out her dad was on to this place—and I have no idea how he is—I was out of there." She held up a map of Egypt with known dig sites circled in red. "Where are we going to hide all this stuff, anyway?"

"Your place," said Pierce. "Take it over there in a taxi. Stash it deep in your closet. Any idea when Gamal's guys might show up?"

"All Jehan said was that it might be tonight." Layla flipped up one of the shutter slats to look outside. The sunset had deepened to a burnt orange. She noticed three dark cars parked outside, a little ways down the street. SUVs with tinted windows; nicer cars than belonged in this neighborhood. She quickly closed the shutter.

They worked in silence for a while, packaging everything that could potentially signal an FBI operation.

Just as Layla was reaching for the last files to place in a box, there was a knock at the door. Layla and Pierce looked at each other.

Another knock came, more insistent. "Shit," said Layla.

Pierce grabbed a banker's box full of files and dashed to the bedroom. "Keep moving. Take everything in here," she said in a low and urgent voice. "Go. Fast. Take it out the bedroom window to the fire escape. Then hide."

"What will you do?" Layla asked, following with two more file boxes. Normally, she was cool-headed in adrenaline-pumping situations; a strange calm would settle over her. But not now. This was as real as it got. Getting busted for an illegal op in a foreign country was no joke.

"I'll try to buy you time. Whatever you do, don't let them see you. If Gamal Ghaffar shows up himself and sees you, it's over."

Layla opened the window and set the three boxes on the fire escape, marveling at how she had managed to spring into action so quickly and stay completely calm. Whatever problems she had on the personal front, Pierce was impressive when shit hit the fan.

Pierce ran out of the bedroom and came back with two more boxes containing laptops, extra phones, and surveillance equipment. Layla dashed back to the kitchen for the two heavy shopping bags full of operation reports, forensics information from Muharib bomb sites, and records of financial transactions from some of the main suspects.

The knock at the door was now an insistent banging. A gruff command, in Arabic, to open up the door. "We know you are in there," said the unmistakable voice of Gamal Ghaffar. Layla pictured him dragging her and Pierce off to prison. This could cause a fucking international incident. They could languish in Tora indefinitely while politicians fought over their fate.

Layla whirled around and noticed the one thing they'd forgotten. The most obvious thing. Her stomach lurched.

"The evidence board!" Layla pointed. Her hands had gone cold.

"Shit. Help me lift it," said Pierce.

Layla took up one end and helped Pierce lay the board down on the coffee table. Pierce draped a tablecloth over it and tossed an empty pizza box on top of that. Then she gave Layla a little shove toward the bedroom. "Get out of here!" she commanded in a whisper. Then she went to answer the door.

"Coming!" she heard Pierce call, in English. She heard the lock open, and the dead bolt. "There's no need to make such a racket," said Pierce. "I was in the bathroom. What can I help you with?"

Sweat rolled down Layla's forehead and stung her eyes as she heaved the remaining three boxes and two shopping bags out the bedroom window, while Pierce talked and tried to stall the men, explaining how long she had lived there and what she was doing in Cairo. Layla set the remaining boxes on the iron fire escape as quietly as she could and pushed them to the right, away from immediate view out the window.

"We need to search the premises. It has come to our attention that this apartment may be used to run some kind of operation for the American government," she heard Gamal say.

"Well, I'm an employee at the American embassy, and this is my home," Pierce said, sounding confused—on purpose, of course.

"Mind if we have a look around?" asked Gamal.

"I do mind. I want to see your paperwork. This is an invasion of privacy. We don't do things like this in my country."

Layla marveled at the confidence in Pierce's voice.

"With all due respect, madam, we are not in your country, fortunately for us all." said Gamal. "But you may see our paperwork. Youssef, do you have the documents?"

Layla felt dizzy. She peeked through the crack in the bedroom door and saw Pierce and the four men gathered around the evidence board tabletop, leafing through documents. If the tablecloth slipped, they were done for. Youssef was opening his briefcase—the same one she'd seen at the poolside just three hours before.

Layla got the shopping bags out onto the fire escape and took a moment to survey her work, hanging her head out the window. Five boxes and two shoppings bags, all heavy and nearly bursting with files, papers, and electronic equipment, all heaped together on the fire escape three flights off the ground. Fortunately, the neighbors all had crap illegally parked on their portions of the fire escape, from plotted plants to broken plastic furniture to a rusting bike, so it didn't look so out of place. If anything, the safe house apartment might have stood out by virtue of its exterior neatness. Still, the boxes and bags felt too close to the window for comfort. It would be good to move them farther down.

She heard footsteps approaching the door. Pierce could stall them no more. Layla pushed the window panel up to give herself more room to get out. The window slipped in its casement. And stuck. "Come on!" she muttered, as she pushed and then pulled on the window. She jiggled it and pushed up again. No movement. She felt around the interior frame, looking for latches or broken parts that might have caught. Nothing.

"How many bedrooms here?" she heard Youssef asking Pierce just outside the door.

Shit, shit shit. She knelt down and poked her head out the stuck window. She could maybe just fit, but it would be a squeeze. And there was no time.

Cursing under her breath, she quickly closed the window, taking care not to slam it, and closed the shutters. Then she ducked into the narrow closet and crouched on the floor, just as the bedroom door opened.

FAULT LINES

• PATRICK LOHIER AND DIANA RENN •

Crouching on the closet floor, her arms wrapped tight around her knees, Layla gulped down her breaths to stay quiet. Egyptian government officials were on to them. They suspected an authorized operation. They'd somehow figured out where the safe house was. It was only a matter of time until they found her now, like a doomed game of hide-and-seek. She cursed the stuck window that had prevented her from escaping the safe house.

The door to Pierce's bedroom opened and heavy footsteps approached. Layla licked her lips, then dared herself to peer through the slats in the closet door. She could see four men enter the room, including Gamal. And the man now opening Pierce's nightstand drawers—Youssef. If only Jehan could see him now. He was hardly boring. He held Layla and Pierce's fate in his hands.

Layla trembled as she watched Gamal circle the room slowly, his feet heavy on the tiled floor. He paused as he came toward the closet door. His hand reached for the knob. Layla's heart thudded so loudly she was sure Gamal could hear it. She could see, through the slats, the crease of his black trousers. The shine of his shoes. She felt her muscles tense, as if preparing for action. But she couldn't take out all four of these guys, not without a weapon. Pierce's guns were in a box on the fire escape.

Pierce strode into the room. "I'm calling my supervisor," she announced, causing Gamal to turn away from Layla's closet. "He can confirm my role at the embassy."

Layla's heart leaped with gratitude. Pierce wasn't giving up yet.

"That will not be necessary," said Gamal, his gaze still sweeping the room while Youssef and the two other men looked under the bed.

"I want you to talk to my supervisor," Pierce insisted, punching numbers on her cell. "I haven't done anything wrong. I'm a legate at the embassy."

"We cannot be too careful," said Gamal. "There has been concern for some time about American interference in Egyptian matters." He reached into the nightstand lamp and removed the bulb, then inspected the light socket carefully. The other men were also picking up objects and scrutinizing them.

"There are no bugs here," Pierce insisted. Then she paused and went on: "But maybe I've been infiltrated. Is it possible someone could be using my apartment when I'm at work or away on business trips?"

"Anything is possible," said Gamal, his gaze sweeping the room.

"In that case, would you mind looking in the living room for wiretaps?" Pierce asked, as casually as if she were asking a friend to come and check for spiders. "Now that I think of it, I did see something unusual about the ceiling fan. You'd probably know better than I would. I have to confess, wiretapping devices are a little above my pay grade." She laughed, almost flirtatiously, and managed to draw all four men back to the living room.

Layla marveled at Pierce's calm under pressure. But as soon as the bedroom door closed behind Youssef, she didn't waste any time. She bolted out of the closet. There was no getting out that window, and no breaking it without causing a scene. Her only hope was to get out through the bathroom window, which also looked out on the fire escape. She slowly opened the bedroom door and confirmed that all four men were with Pierce in the living room. They were already taking the ceiling fan apart. She dashed to the bathroom and softly closed the door behind her. Then she opened the small window above the tub. This one opened all the way, and she could just squeeze through it and onto the fire escape, pulling her tote bag out after her.

With only her tote bag and the box with Pierce's two guns, Layla hurried down the three flights of the fire escape and ran to the park around the corner. A police car sped down the street, siren blaring, just as a cat popped out from behind a garbage can, making the lid clatter. Layla's skin prickled. She sat on a bench and took a deep breath. The siren's wail faded as the cars sped away from her. The police were not coming for her. She had escaped. But she had to get the rest of the incriminating evidence off the safe house's fire escape, and fast.

Layla watched a group of teenagers play soccer on a poorly lit field and a young mother soothe a crying baby in a stroller. A breeze touched her face, so welcome after the stifling stillness of that closet, and she relished the sensation of air moving in and out of her chest. Never had she felt so relieved to stumble across such a boring scene. To breathe the fresh early evening air. She approached the teenagers and offered them money to quietly retrieve the bags and boxes from the fire escape. "I'm leaving my husband," she explained, pulling a thick wad of cash from her purse. "I'll give you half now. He cannot know. You must be very, very quiet."

The teenagers were gone a long time. She cursed herself. They might have gotten caught. A neighbor could have called the police, who could be sifting through the boxes and bags at this very moment. Or maybe they'd just taken her money and run. Frankly, she wouldn't blame them. She was a stranger. What did they care if she was leaving her husband and needed some help? The money didn't matter, but the bags did. If Gamal and Youssef spotted the items on the fire escape it would justify all their suspicions. Pierce had been so cool and calm. Now, Layla felt like she'd fumbled everything.

But this was Egypt. In Egypt, people went out of their way to show compassion, to offer help. She thought of the taxi driver who'd wanted to drive her away from the bombing for free. The old woman on the Metro car offering her seat.

She heard shouts behind her. "Miss! Miss!"

She turned to see the teenage soccer players walking toward her, carrying the boxes and bags from the fire escape. They passed under a streetlight and were lit up with an almost otherworldly glow. "Where do you want these things?" one of them said.

"I need a taxi," answered Layla. "Can you help load everything in?"

LAYLA LEFT HER APARTMENT the next morning in jeans, a hoodie, and sneakers, heading to get some breakfast from the bakery down the street; she hadn't shopped in days. She felt almost normal, as if she were leaving her old New York apartment to grab breakfast on the go. But things were far from normal, and new concerns weighed on her mind as she walked the three blocks to the bakery. Her Garden City apartment was filled with evidence of an illegal FBI operation. Pierce had told her Ghaffar and his team had left after searching the rest of the apartment, but she felt sure they weren't done with them yet. And Layla had woken to an email from Giulia Rossi, forwarding an exchange between Alberto and Dr. Katherine Danforth that had taken place a week before he died.

Outside the bakery, she found a seat at an outdoor table and ate her roll and coffee. She scrolled through her phone and reviewed the exchange. Reading Alberto's words made her shiver. She could imagine him sitting at that tiny desk in the Zamalek Hotel, writing this email late at night.

Dear Dr. Danforth,

I am a journalist from Italy pursuing a story about some relics that were looted from the Faiyum Museum in Egypt. I read your fascinating article about the Amulet Men of Faiyum. I am contacting you because I have noticed a number of articles were published about Faiyum relics within a span of less than one year. For artifacts in such a small museum, this strikes me as an unusual occurrence. I am therefore writing to inquire who might have suggested you write on this topic. Were you approached by any one individual or organization? Thank you for your time and assistance in this matter.

Kind regards,
Alberto Rossi

Dr. Danforth replied:

Dear Mr. Rossi,

Thank you for your note, and for your kind words about my article on the Amulet Men of Faiyum. This may shock you, but I typically come up with my own ideas. The Faiyum amulets were of particular interest to me, dating back to my undergraduate thesis work. That said, I did receive a grant to continue my research for this article. The grant came from the Egyptian Ministry of Antiquities. I do not recall applying for this particular grant, and was surprised when it arrived. Then again, my research assistant and my department here often put in applications for me, so I assume that is what happened. I was certainly grateful for the small sum and the words of encouragement. I hope this information helps you in your own research endeavor.

Very truly yours,
Dr. Katherine Danforth

Alberto's email response was sent mere minutes after hers:

> Dear Dr. Danforth,
>
> I hope I did not cause offense. English is not my native language, so perhaps I misrepresented my thoughts. It so happens that some scholars I have interviewed were approached by two organizations and encouraged to pursue certain lines of research about Faiyum relics. In all cases, these individuals were given grants by either the Egyptian Ministry of Antiquities or an organization called Global Relics Limited. The former denies authorizing any such requests or grants. The latter organization cannot be found, so perhaps has since been dissolved. In any case, I would be grateful if you could provide me the name of any specific individuals you might have communicated with regarding an interest in Faiyum relics.
>
> Thank you again for your time and assistance.
>
> Best regards,
> Alberto Rossi

According to Giulia Rossi, Dr. Katherine Danforth did not respond. The exchange was dated one week before Alberto's death.

Layla couldn't take her eyes off two words in Alberto's last email: Global Relics. The shell company.

She reread the entire exchange while she finished her breakfast. She rolled this information over in her mind as she walked back home with her paper cup of coffee. It made sense for someone in the Muharib to generate interest in the Faiyum items, knowing they would soon be released on the black market. It also made sense that they would use a shell company name. But how did the Ministry of Antiquities come into this? Especially when they denied any involvement?

Layla strongly suspected this was the information Alberto had planned to share with her. The information that got him killed.

As the muezzin sounded the mid-morning call to prayer, she stood stock-still, absorbing every note, overcome by the memory of Alberto, his intensity and kindness, as well as a profound sadness at the loss his wife and children must be suffering. The muezzin's voice seemed to pull her into a kind of reverential fugue, as she involuntarily rocked to its rhythm. Then she opened her eyes and realized it was the ground that was shifting beneath her, and that power lines were swaying crazily around her. Shrieks and shouts filled the air as people all around her ran for shelter, including a group of men who had been kneeling on prayer rugs. She knew this feeling, these sounds, from her childhood. An earthquake. A chunk of metal fell off a sign and landed just a foot away from her.

The high-rise buildings across the street visibly swayed. Traffic lights danced on their lines. Time took on that surreal quality of slowing down, even though she knew the earthquake wouldn't last more than a minute. She stumbled her way around a corner and down Saad Zaghloul Street, where she saw a few people running past the open gate of a building that looked like a giant villa. She recognized it as Beit el-Umma, House of the Nation. She followed. About a dozen people huddled there, gazing wide-eyed toward the street.

Layla felt transported back to the earthquakes of her childhood. How their apartment building would rock and sway and creak. She remembered, with a jolt, the quake that had taken out their first apartment building while she and her family were at church. She could hear, in the screams around her, her mother wailing, her siblings sobbing; she recalled her father dropping to his knees. Everything had been buried and lost. She'd thought they had nothing, and suddenly they'd had even less. She had picked through the rubble later and found just three of her beloved books, tattered and ripped and coated in a fine red dust.

When the tremor passed, Layla ventured cautiously into the street. Thankfully, there didn't appear to be too much damage.

Dislodged bricks from buildings littered the street. A fresh, gaping crack in the sidewalk, like a wound, had appeared.

Her iPhone rang. She dug through her bag for it, heart pounding. She hoped it wasn't Khalid Yasin calling her back. She wasn't ready for him.

It was James. She wasn't ready for him, either, but she answered the call.

"Hey," he said. His voice felt so close in her ear.

She cleared her throat. "Hey."

"I wanted to check you're okay. If you're safe."

"I'm okay," she said. "Are you okay?"

"The electricity's out in the whole neighborhood, and the gallery got hit pretty hard. We're all fine, though. Kind of rattled, but fine."

"Do you guys need help?" Layla asked. "I can come."

James cleared his throat. "Um," he said. "I don't know. I appreciate the offer, but . . . maybe it's better not."

"Okay." Layla closed her eyes.

"I just wanted to see if you're okay," James repeated.

"I am. Thanks for checking."

"Of course. Stay safe."

"You, too."

Sirens wailed as she listened to James hang up the call.

Layla returned to her apartment, which didn't appear to have suffered any significant damage. In her penthouse, she put back a few items that had fallen from shelves, including the bronze cat statuette, and then settled in to watch the earthquake aftermath on the news.

The area around Tahrir Square was one of the hardest hit. Several power lines had been downed, and the whole district remained without electricity. The map on TV showed the afflicted zone, which included the street the Rothkopf Gallery was on. She winced, picturing Bennett and James, Mackey and Hamadi, sweeping up the broken shards of valuable relics. Then she looked at the set of keys on her nightstand. She picked them up and turned them over in her hand, working up an idea.

THAT EVENING, LAYLA APPROACHED the Rothkopf Gallery at sunset. Walking close to the buildings, in the shadows, she entered the building, climbed the stairs, and used one of the keys to open the main gallery door. No power meant no security cameras, inside or out. She hesitated, letting a wave of guilt wash over her. The Rothkopfs were good people at heart—Bennett had saved her brother. She could never overlook that fact. But she had to find out why Bennett had paper from Global Relics in his office, and what else he might have that pointed to the shell company—or to Khalid Yasin. Did Yasin, as a dig organizer, also sell relics directly to dealers like Bennett? She was looking for proof, yet prayed that she would find none.

Inside the dark gallery, she turned on a small flashlight and surveyed the damage. There were cracks in the walls, and in two of the glass cases. Small shards of glass crunched under her feet.

She headed down the hall. First stop: Bennett's office.

She went to the bookshelf where she'd first seen the Global Relics letterhead and rifled through various papers until she found it. Two sheets of paper and an envelope. Blank.

"Damn it," she said aloud in a whisper.

She looked through the loose papers more carefully, and a note with a paper clip attached to it fell to the floor. Layla picked it up. In the distance, outside, a siren wailed. She thought she heard a door click downstairs and froze. If Bennett or anyone were to walk in now, there'd be no charming her way out of this situation.

But no footsteps came. She looked at the slip of paper in the light. And then she saw the writing—a faint scrawl, in pencil.

> Mr. Rothkopf. Kindly do me the favour of giving your opinions on the artifacts I showed to you the other day. I have enclosed paper and a return envelope for your response. I am appreciative.

The note was unsigned.

Layla felt the jolt of an idea, like an earthquake aftershock—could someone from Global Relics be trying to implicate Bennett? Was this a setup? By getting Bennett to write something on the letterhead, it might be taken to mean that he was some kind of Global Relics associate. Or maybe she just hoped it was a setup . . .

She quickly used her phone to snap photos of the note and the letterhead. She couldn't wait to share this with Pierce. She also felt more than a little relieved. The fact that Bennett had been sitting on this request felt promising. Maybe he'd drawn a line in the sand and decided not to consort with this group. She finished up, replaced the note and the letterhead in the places she'd found them, and slipped out of the office.

The hallway was silent. She passed the kitchen and heard the refrigerator humming. The sound of her own footfalls kept her on edge. She passed James's office door and willed herself not to go in there. She'd seen more than she wanted to see in that room.

One more stop. The storage room. The second room she'd never been able to access in all the hours she'd logged in the gallery.

She fumbled with the keys. The first two did not work. She breathed a silent thanks as the third one turned in the lock. The door hinge creaked loudly. Layla startled and looked behind herself. But she was alone.

She slipped inside, letting her flashlight travel across the walls, which were lined with tall shelves and boxes. More shelves in the middle of the room twisted into a labyrinth. She headed inward, suspecting that anything worth hiding—say, Faiyum relics—would be at the center, in the least accessible part of the room.

She knelt and pulled out a box on the bottom shelf of the interior shelving units. The contents of the box rattled and clinked. She held her breath as she removed the lid. Inside were some small terra-cotta boxes, traces of dirt clinging to them. She sniffed. Had they been taken from a dusty storage facility? Or recently looted from a dig site?

She moved on to the next box, but a sudden sound and a sliver of light made her freeze and extinguish her own light. Footsteps crossed the room. She heard the sound of a box being pulled from a shelf near the door.

Layla held her breath and peered through a two-inch gap between boxes. She could see a man with his back to her, holding a flashlight and rummaging through a box. Much like she was.

His stooped posture was familiar. When he turned his head to one side, his flashlight caught half of his face. It was Hamadi Essam.

What was the IT guy doing in here? Especially since she had his keys? He must have had a spare set.

As she watched, he slipped something into his pocket, then slid the box back onto the shelf.

Layla felt a flash of outrage on Bennett's behalf. How could Hamadi steal from him? Even as she had this thought, she registered its perverse logic. Bennett was stealing from all of Egypt. Another sound caught her attention. Someone else was entering the room, quietly.

Mackey. Layla stifled a small cry as Mackey took a gun from his pocket. He stole into the room, gun drawn and pointed at Hamadi, who was still busy rifling through more boxes.

It took all her willpower not to call out to Hamadi. Her agent's training wouldn't let her be a passive spectator to a crime in progress, though. And yet, once again she found herself unarmed. She'd headed out to the gallery thinking of herself as Layla Nawar, who of course would not be carrying a handgun. She instinctively rose to her feet and looked around the shelves for possible weapons. Spotting a tall alabaster candlestick, she clutched it in two hands like a baseball bat.

Mackey silently closed the distance between himself and Hamadi.

Layla sucked in her breath. Still hidden behind the shelf, she raised the candlestick. She could hurl it or drop it, and create a distraction.

Except a candlestick was no match for a gun. She watched, helpless, as Mackey brought the barrel of his gun right up to the back of Hamadi's head.

"What are you doing?" he asked in a low voice. With his other hand, he raised his flashlight higher. Menacing shadows danced across his face. Yet he showed no emotion. His expression was as unmoving as a mask.

Hamadi slowly raised his hands but did not turn around. His arms looked long and vulnerable and perfectly straight like stalks, but his fingers trembled. He made a soft whimpering sound. "Please. Don't shoot me," he said.

"You are not authorized to be here," Mackey said in a dangerous whisper.

"I can explain." Hamadi sounded tearful. "I— I was just— I came back to finish cleaning things from the earthquake, and—"

"Empty your pockets," Mackey interrupted.

Hamadi complied, making a fearful, sniveling sound.

"Turn around," Mackey commanded. "Show me."

Hamadi did so, slowly, and then shook visibly when he saw the gun now pointing directly at his face. "It is only some coins," he protested. "Only small coins."

"Those small coins are worth thousands of dollars," said Mackey, still eerily calm.

Hamadi shuddered. "Please," he said in a low voice. "My mother is ill. The sale will pay for months of treatment."

Layla felt for him. She knew the story was true. He frequently left the office early to care for his mother. Surely, Mackey would understand. Bennett and Elizabeth Rothkopf had helped Mackey's mother when she was ill, after all.

"There is no stealing from Mr. Rothkopf. There are no second chances," hissed Mackey.

Layla's heart sank. He sounded deadly serious, entirely unmoved by Hamadi's open weeping. She nearly dropped the candlestick. Her palms, she noticed, were so sweaty that it was slipping through her hands. She gently placed it back on the shelf, which immediately creaked.

Mackey spun his flashlight all around the room. Layla shrank as far back into the shadows as she could.

"Please," Hamadi said, recapturing Mackey's attention. "If you kill me, my mother has no one. No one." He held his palms together in a beseeching gesture. "She's my only family. I would do anything for my family."

"As would I," said Mackey. "Nothing is more important than family." He paused, looked up to the ceiling—as if in search of divine guidance—then looked back at Hamadi. "Bennett Rothkopf is my family," he added.

A shot rang out. Layla stifled a scream.

For a few seconds she was completely disoriented. The ringing in her ears blocked all other sound; the darkness seemed to engulf her. She tried to push herself deeper into the shadows, but she had no idea which way was which, and she felt sure she would stumble out into Mackey's murderous path. As she crouched on the floor with her head in her hands, the world slowly righted itself. She focused on a pool of light in the darkness. The flashlight Hamadi had dropped illuminated his body, and the pool of blood seeping out from under him.

Layla felt frozen in the shadows, her eyes locked on Hamadi's lifeless face. A thick thread of blood trailed down from a hole in his temple. She waited, barely breathing. After a few seconds that felt like a lifetime she heard footfalls again, and Mackey reentered the storage room. He spread a dark blue tarp over Hamadi and then proceeded to roll up the body. When he had completely wrapped Hamadi, he knelt and started to clean up with a towel. Layla could taste the metallic tang of blood on the air.

When he was done, Mackey stood stock-still and stared at the rolled-up tarp. He was so near she could hear his quickened breath slow to something more watchful, more predatory. She struggled to control her own breathing, but her body betrayed her. Her throat tightened, dried, and turned crystalline and jagged as if she had swallowed a mouthful of crushed glass.

Finally, Mackey stood, took one end of the tarp, and dragged it out of the room. Layla waited and listened for any further sounds. When she didn't hear anything, she bolted. She peered out the doorway and up and down the hall. No one was there. She stepped quickly down the hall, halting suddenly at what she thought was the sound of a door slamming. She picked up her pace. She reached the front door, pried it open slowly, stepped outside, and stood in the shadows for a few seconds in disbelief that she had made it out unnoticed.

Layla rushed down the street, head bowed, thinking that if Mackey peered out of the gallery entrance she might camouflage herself among the other pedestrians. But then she gave up any pretense and, a block away, broke into a sprint.

Mackey had murdered Hamadi. He had executed him in the most cold-blooded way over a few stolen coins. She recalled how close he had come to catching her inside Bennett's office weeks ago. She'd been in even greater danger than she had realized.

She panicked when she realized she was on her way to the safe house that no longer existed. Where was she supposed to go? She texted Pierce and a minute later received a map link to the new location. It wasn't too far away, still adjacent to Garden City, just a little bit farther south. She ran to the address, wound her way through the night streets, past the rows of street food vendors with their umbrellas all lined up along the curb, dashed across intersections heavy with traffic and sidewalks full of pedestrians who she could hardly believe were oblivious to the violence she had just witnessed. The extraordinary rush of relief she felt when Pierce opened the door was like a drug. She dashed past her into a small apartment that looked like an impoverished version of the safe house. Pierce closed the door and followed Layla into the apartment. Her face creased into concern at the sight of her.

"Hey. What's wrong?"

Layla's jaw trembled helplessly and tears cascaded down her cheeks.

"Jesus, what happened?" said Pierce with alarm. She held Layla by the shoulders and gently eased her back onto the sofa. "Just take your time," she said, as she drew a folding chair across the room and sat facing Layla.

Layla still felt like shards of broken glass were in her throat. The words she tried to form were just shuddering gasps.

"Let me get you some water," said Pierce, walking into the kitchen.

She brought back a glass and Layla drank it thirstily. Almost as soon as she'd drained the glass she felt like she was going to throw up, but at least she could talk again. "It's Mackey," she said. "The Rothkopfs' guy. He—He killed Hamadi."

"Hamadi . . . ? I thought you said he's just a low-level employee?"

"He's their IT guy," whispered Layla. "Or, he . . . was . . ." she corrected herself. She closed her eyes.

Pierce looked at her coolly. Her calm felt bizarre, but it was also kind of reassuring.

"How do you know this?" Pierce asked.

"I saw it . . ." Layla pressed back against the sofa and stared at the ceiling. The tears came again, but silently. Had she really seen it? It felt like a nightmare. She had to repeat it to believe it. "I saw Mackey shoot Hamadi in the head."

"Jesus," said Pierce again. She sighed deeply and sat back. She gazed at Layla evenly, but with something like pity in her eyes. Finally, she rose and took Layla's empty glass to the cupboard. She poured a shot of whiskey into it and handed it back to Layla. "Drink this," she said softly. "I think you need something a little stronger than water."

Layla drank the whiskey. She wasn't that fond of hard liquor, but she appreciated its burn just then. It reminded her that she was alive and had something precious to lose.

"What can we do?" she asked.

Pierce frowned and shrugged. "Do about what?"

Layla sat up straight. "About Mackey . . . Hamadi . . . This—This is murder."

Pierce leaned against the wall with her arms crossed. "Layla, there's nothing we *can* do. We're out of our jurisdiction. And as far as witnesses, there aren't any. You were never there. Do you understand? You're an undercover asset on foreign territory. You have to stay undercover."

Layla rose in disbelief. She reached for the nearest chair to steady herself from the sudden head rush. She'd seen the shooting, Hamadi's body on the ground. Her knees felt weak. It had *happened*. Mackey had murdered Hamadi despite Hamadi's pleas for mercy.

"But . . ."

Pierce set her hand gently on Layla's shoulder. "Layla, focus. The shipment is headed to DC as we speak. We have to stay on track. We'll continue as is, and—"

"As is?" Layla cut in.

"Yes!" barked Pierce. The sound of it was like a slap. Pierce's face had twisted to a mask of impatience.

"We continue *as is*," said Pierce. "We confirm the arrival of that shipment in DC, and most important we figure out who sent it. *That* is why we're here. It's the *only* reason we're here."

Layla looked at Pierce. Everything she had said made perfect sense and it also sounded insane. "But . . ." she started again.

"But what, Layla? You tell me. How is this supposed to go? Do we call the police and explain that you stumbled on a murder during an illegal FBI investigation? How exactly does that play out?"

Layla knew there was no feasible way for them to alert the police about Hamadi's murder. They were there to do a job, to save lives at risk in the United States. Despite all that, it felt awful to agree. "I understand," she whispered.

Pierce's expression softened. "Good, because we're under enough pressure as it is." She sighed and crossed her arms. "I tried to call you earlier but I couldn't get through during the earthquake. One of Ghaffar's guys went through the fucking garbage can in the bathroom."

Layla frowned. For a moment she wondered if they had found some evidence of Pierce's drug habit. "What did they find?" she asked.

"It's my own fault. I usually shred everything, but there were a bunch of photos from the evidence board we didn't need anymore. Mostly nameless faces, but it was enough to rouse their suspicions. Ghaffar filed a formal complaint with the ambassador. I've been called into a meeting tomorrow at the embassy. I'll be going in my cover as a legate, but this puts everything under extremely close scrutiny.

"You need to lie low for the next few days while we explain that this was just a big misunderstanding. It's gonna be tough. His whole team is coming over and they want answers." She sighed. "Not to mention Fareed Monsour, the one that all these students are cheering for, is going to be at the embassy tomorrow, too. If he's going to be the next president of Egypt we need to make friends now, and not look like a bunch of reckless idiots running illegal missions in this country."

"Jesus," said Layla.

"That's right. This stuff at the embassy is a mess. We basically have to pretend we don't exist." Pierce sighed and her expression softened. "What do you want to do?"

Layla looked around. Pierce had talked her down but her heart was still hammering in her chest. She was inside and she was safe, but now what? How could she go home? What if Mackey had followed her? What if he'd spotted her leaving and was now waiting at her apartment? She tried to take a calming breath but her chest felt tight.

"Can I stay here? Just for the night?"

Pierce looked like she might deny her for a second, then she nodded. "Okay. You can stay on the couch."

Layla thanked her, then tucked her feet up, getting comfortable.

"You want another drink?" Pierce asked when she came back from the bedroom with a sheet for Layla to use.

"Sure."

Pierce poured two drinks this time. When Layla reached up for the glass she saw that her own hand was still shaking.

"Have you ever seen anything like that?" Layla said. "Someone kill someone?"

"A couple of times." Pierce eyed her. "Listen, Layla. You'll be all right. You're safe now."

Layla knew that Pierce didn't intend it, but the word *now* was the issue. What about in an hour? Would she be safe? What about the next day?

Pierce sat in the chair. "People will never fail to surprise you, especially in this line of work." She leaned back and gazed at nothing in particular. "Layla . . ." she started. She held her glass in both hands and rotated it slowly. "That night you found me in the safe house, in the bathroom . . ."

Layla sat up and rubbed her face, wondering if she really had fallen asleep and might be dreaming. They had not spoken explicitly about that night since it happened.

"Leaving you hanging out to dry that night was one of the worst things I've ever done. I was out of it. And I put you in danger . . . I'm really sorry I did that."

Layla sighed. Pierce's words meant more to her than she had expected. She shut her eyes to absorb the moment, opened them, and looked at Pierce.

"Thank you," she said.

A flash of annoyance crossed Pierce's face. "Please don't say that," she said. "Don't thank me for something I should've apologized for a long time ago."

Layla nodded. They sat in silence for a while longer before Pierce rose.

"I'm gonna get some sleep. Tomorrow will be a trial." She squeezed Layla's shoulder and left.

LAYLA DREAMED THAT SHE was in a dark room, trying to feel her way around by touch, when she came into a lit clearing, a space into which she could see but from which, apparently, she could not be seen. She knew this because only feet away, in a cone of light, Mackey stood over Hamadi's dead body. She retreated into the darkness again but she could hear footsteps following her, as if her pursuer could track her by scent.

She woke covered in sweat and sat up in the darkness. Pierce was nowhere to be found, but she'd left a note on the counter: *Lie low*. Layla could get used to that idea, after everything that had happened the day before. She felt like she could hide in the tiny, grim apartment forever.

She made herself coffee and toast, all the while thinking of the route she might take to get back to her apartment—was someone watching Pierce's new place?—when she heard a phone ring. She turned, glanced around the room, and followed the sound down the hall until she found the phone buzzing on the floor beside the door. It must have fallen from Pierce's pocket as she'd left that morning. Layla answered, hoping it would be Pierce calling her own number in hopes of retrieving it.

"Hello?"

"Pierce?"

The voice was gruff, familiar. "Agent Monaghan?" she said.

"That's right. El-Deeb? Is that you?"

"Yes, it's me."

"Where's Pierce?"

Layla hesitated, not sure how much to say. "She's on her way to the embassy. She has a meeting with—"

"—Ghaffar. I know. She sent me the briefing on it. What are you doing?"

"Pierce asked me to lie low, until this thing blows over."

"So you're not together, I gather?"

"No, she dropped her phone."

"She dropped her phone," muttered Monaghan. "That's just great. Listen, I'm calling because the shipment has arrived in DC." He sounded impatient, intense. "We have it."

Layla felt a jolt of anxiety "What's in it?"

"Nothing."

"Nothing?" Layla responded lamely.

"Just two boxes of antiquities. No weapons. No explosives. This is a bust." It sounded like an accusation.

Layla wondered how Pierce would react if she were the one taking the call.

"What's the location like? Is anyone there to receive the shipment?"

"There's one guy. He was sitting in a ride-share car idling nearby. Says he was supposed to confirm delivery of the shipment but that's it. He wasn't instructed to take it or touch it, just set his eyes on the manifest and make a call to tell whoever is on the other end that the package arrived."

"That's weird."

"I agree."

The idea that they might actually be in agreement almost caught her off guard.

"So what are you going to do about it?" he barked.

Ah, thought Layla, sighing. The moment had been fleeting. "Did you trace the number the guy's supposed to call?"

"It's untraceable. Whoever gave it to him likely bought it off the web and tied it to a burner. We got nothing on this one," said Monaghan. "Big waste of time, and you can tell Pierce I said that." He hung up.

Layla closed her eyes and set down the phone. No ammunition, no explosives—what could it all mean? Waiting for the delivery to DC had been a bad assumption and, from Monaghan's perspective, a debacle. Monaghan wouldn't let them forget that anytime soon. But maybe there was something to it? The raid couldn't have been for nothing. Something was off.

She found Pierce's extra laptop, logged in as herself, and looked back through her operational report on the Singapore raid. *Tremblay*, she thought, as she read. The CEO of Masterpiece Fine Arts. She searched for his number and checked the time. It was early afternoon in Singapore.

A man answered. "Hello?"

"Is this Mr. Richard Tremblay?"

"Yes, it is. Who is this?"

"My name is Agent Layla el-Deeb, of the FBI. I'm following up on the investigation into the storage unit we searched in Singapore."

"I— I've spoken to my lawyer following that fiasco." His voice was tremulous, rattled. "You can talk to my lawyer. Actually, no. What am I saying?" He laughed, a nasty little chuckle. "Who are you? I don't even know who you are. You could be anyone. I'm going to hang up now, Agent whoever-the-fuck-you—"

"Please!" Layla cut in. "It's an emergency. I am who I say I am but I just need a piece of information from you." There was silence on the line. Even though Tremblay was an unknown, Layla was desperate enough to take a chance and reveal a key piece of operational intelligence. She might not get a second chance, or even another second. She spoke into the silence.

"We—my colleague and I—think that someone is trying to send explosives to the US from storage units that have been used to smuggle stolen art. We're trying to stop that. I'm hoping you can tell me about any other deliveries that left that unit."

The silence hung.

"Mr. Tremblay," she continued. "We're just trying to save lives. This is urgent. Can you give me the information I need?"

After a while Tremblay spoke. "Those files are at my office. I'd need to call you back."

"Mr. Tremblay, thank you. I appreciate your help."

LAYLA WALKED THE ROUTE back to her own apartment with extreme caution. It was still possible Mackey had seen her fleeing the gallery the previous night. She couldn't be too careful. Halfway down the last block, Layla's phone rang. She pulled it out of her pocket hoping it was Tremblay, but frowned at the unfamiliar number on her screen.

"Hello? Is this Layla Nawar?" said a man when she picked up.

"It is."

"This is Khalid Yasin."

Layla's mouth went dry. "Hello, Mr. Yasin."

"Please, call me Khalid." He had a strong Egyptian accent. His voice was quiet, businesslike. "I received your message regarding some items that you are looking to purchase?"

"Yes. Yes, that's right."

Khalid gave Layla the address for a place called the Hanover Club and asked her to meet him there at eleven thirty that morning.

Her mind raced. Her last memory was of putting a bead on his legs with Alberto's gun and seeing him stumble. She'd hit him for sure. It would be a stretch to assume he knew that, but it would be stupid to assume he didn't. She and Alberto had barely made it out alive. Maybe someone had spotted her or followed them. And then, of course, Alberto was dead. Who'd killed him? Could it have been Khalid or one of his people?

"Mr. Yasin, I don't know if I can meet so soon. Could we meet tomorrow?"

"Ah. That would not be possible. I must go to Minya tonight and I will be away for a few days. Perhaps we can meet at another—"

The best thing would be for Pierce to be with her, even if she stayed out of sight. At the very least, she wanted Pierce to know where she was, but when her eye settled on Pierce's phone she realized that that wasn't going to happen soon enough.

"No. No. I can meet with you this morning," said Layla. She was desperate not to lose this lead.

For now, she decided that when she met with Khalid she would keep a close eye out for any indication that he might know she was the one who had shot him.

After hanging up, Layla called Pierce's phone and watched it rattle on the kitchen counter. She left a voicemail on the off chance that Pierce would check her messages. She said that she would be meeting Khalid Yasin at the Hanover Club and left the address and the time of the meeting. Then she skulked back to her apartment. Every now and again she surveyed the block behind her, but she spotted no one following. Inside the apartment building she found nothing untoward. And when she got to her apartment, nothing looked out of place. She retrieved her gun from the nightstand. She wasn't about to meet Khalid unarmed.

Layla took a cab to the Hanover Club in the Imbaba neighborhood, on the other side of the river. She knew the area by reputation—it was a poor place. Not as poor as Manshiyat Naser, but it was not among the prosperous areas of the city, either. Imbaba was historically the marketplace for camels, which had been brought from all across the deserts from as far as the Sudan and Somalia. That role as a central marketplace had given it one fateful leg up in the sweepstakes of neighborhood legacies.

In the midst of a warren of dusty streets, the cab stopped under a bright white sign. The Hanover Club was some kind of colonial holdover. A brass plaque stated that it had first opened its doors in 1893. Layla entered hesitantly and took in the black-and-white-checked tiles of the entry corridor and the walls lined with framed prints depicting the Nile and the Suez Canal, the Great Pyramids, the Sphinx, desert caravans, and more. Layla peered about skeptically; she suspected that the place hadn't changed much since it had opened more than a century before.

Farther in, she saw dozens of men seated on benches at long wooden tables with coffees, some with *shisha* pipes, engaged in conversation. A long bar stretched down one side of the room. Behind it, lined on shelves across a mirror as high as the ceiling, were bottles of every kind of spirit and liquor you could imagine. But now was clearly the coffee hour. The rich smell of freshly brewed coffee wafted through the room. A few women were there, too, sitting at two long tables nestled behind a tall screen of dark stained wood.

Layla eyed each table but didn't see Khalid and now wondered if she would remember his face well enough to recognize him. So she sat down near the wall delineating the women's area, but at the border with the male side. She sat facing the entrance, keeping a

. 292 .

close eye in case Khalid, or anyone else, for that matter, might be intent on ambushing her. A few minutes later a man entered and approached with a wary smile. As soon as she saw his nose, which had clearly been broken at some point, she knew it was him.

"Miss Nawar?"

"Mr. Yasin."

She extended her hand. Her intention was the original, historic purpose of a handshake, to show that she didn't have a weapon, although her gun was in the pocket of her jacket. All she could offer him was the cold, nervous sweat on her palm. He hesitated, smiled, and shook her hand with a gentle grip.

He was very thin, with a friendly face made somehow friendlier by his crooked nose. He had on khaki pants, a white button-up shirt, a well-used and frayed dark blue blazer, and black shoes scuffed to gray at the toes. He was tall, and had to lean over to shake her hand.

"It is a pleasure to meet you," he said, grinning broadly. The palm of his hand was dry and crisp and cool. "Please let me get us some refreshments."

As he walked to the bar she noticed a telltale limp. She frowned and wiped the sweat from her palm as she studied him closely. He gestured to the attendant and stood idle for a moment as he waited. She turned away quickly when he glanced in her direction. He returned empty-handed.

"They will bring us some coffee," he said.

She was surprised by how normal it felt, to sit in a colonial-era club and wait for coffee with a man she knew she'd shot. More surprising was Khalid's courtliness. Here was a man who could very well be the critical nexus between the world of the art collectors and dealers she'd been getting to know and the Muharib itself. He seemed like the most average of men.

"I hope I can be helpful to you, Miss Nawar," he said with a salesman's smile.

Layla hesitated. Rattled by the events of the night before, she had to quickly recall the details of her cover. The gestures and attitudes of an heiress felt like an ill-fitting coat. "I'd like to buy some things, some . . . rare things. And I had heard that you might be able to help me."

"Are you a collector? Or do you plan perhaps to open a gallery?"

"No . . . I mean, not yet. For now my purpose is quite simple. I want to make sure the pieces you dig up don't fall into the wrong hands. If I can't stop you, I can buy from you." It was a bold move, and adrenaline thrummed through her veins.

Khalid looked at her. He didn't seem obviously taken aback, but his smile was fairly rigid. He sighed, as if genuinely disappointed in her low opinion of his business.

"Miss Nawar, I do a service to the objects that we find, liberating them out of the dust and into the hands of people who will care for them."

Layla thought of James making a similar argument but quickly pushed the thought away. She needed to focus. She didn't want to scare him off, but she did want to unsettle him a bit, to nudge him into an uncomfortable place that might trip him up or provoke him into giving information he might otherwise keep close to the vest.

She smiled. "You make it sound so noble."

He frowned, but it was a just a flash, and he recovered quickly. She'd clearly rattled him. "My business is good," he continued. "I deal fairly with everyone. I work with top galleries and collectors."

"Have you dealt with the Rothkopf Gallery?"

"Perhaps." He looked pleased with himself.

She sat back, stunned. A cold hand gripped her heart. She'd gotten something from him and now she wished she had never sought it out. But she steeled herself. She had to find out more. "In what way?" she asked.

"I have had dealings with Mr. Rothkopf over the years. I tell you this only because you doubt the value of my work—I can assure you that some notable people in the business rely on me. You may judge us, but our work gives men jobs that let them feed their families." He spoke with what Layla realized was a permanent and courteous smile, but there was an edge to his voice.

The waiter came with their coffee. Layla and Khalid smiled blandly at each other as the young man set small plates and coffee cups with floral designs before them and poured the thick Turkish coffee into their cups from a copper *cezve*. He set two glasses of water before them and after they confirmed that they needed nothing more, he left.

Khalid looked at her with a smile but there was a challenge in his eyes. "You know, many of the items we recover were buried to honor the wealthy and powerful. They ensure that the dead have safe passage and comfort in the afterlife. But do you know whose hands buried them in the desert to begin with?"

She knew where he was going with this, "Men and boys like the ones you employ."

"That's correct, men and boys. *Poor* men and boys. They have always been in Egypt and that is what they will always do, bury the rich, and when they are not looking, dig them back up." He smiled and she couldn't help but smile, too.

"You make it sound so simple."

He shook his head. "Don't you know that death is simple, Miss Nawar? I do not know where they go, the dead, but they have no use for the knickknacks left behind. But the living man, he has a wife, children, mouths to feed. He is alive and his children are alive." He paused. Perhaps he thought that he had said too much.

Layla thought of the boy she'd seen that night she'd driven out to the dig with Alberto. She recalled how he'd been pulled from the ruins within only a hairbreadth of being crushed.

"I hear you use boys, young children, on your digs. Are they safe?"

"Always," said Khalid with a wave of his hand. "I was a boy like these boys who wait across the street from my house each morning and beg me for work. A long time ago, I worked for a man much like me, who organized digs as far north as Alexandria, by the sea. By seven, eight years of age I was going up to Alexandria in the back of a truck or in boats to dig and come back with money in my pockets. Before me, there was another boy, and another. There have always been Egyptian boys digging. We dug for the Persians, the Greeks, for Napoleon's officers when the French came. And we did plenty of digging for the British." Khalid made a show of looking about the room. "Half of the treasures of Egypt are exhibited in the British Museum," he said, grinning. "New empires treasure the relics of ancient empires. The statues and urns in the sand are a bounty from our ancestors. These objects are the blessing of the history of Egypt, the gift of ancient kings and queens to the common people who carried the stones for their tombs and pyramids."

His logic was poetic, but still . . . "Who protects Egypt's heritage and its history from people who would sell it to foreigners vase by vase until there is nothing left?"

"You are talking about the future, Miss Nawar. And that is the great difference between people such as yourself and the rest of us."

"How's that?" she asked.

Khalid raised his coffee. "The kings and queens, the powerful, the rich—they have the luxury of thinking of their future and their afterlives. The countless poor have no such luxury." He sipped from his cup and Layla sipped from hers. She set her coffee down and crossed her arms. Her ill-fitting cover now felt like a straightjacket. Only she knew how much alike she and the countless poor that Khalid described really were.

"Miss Nawar . . ." said Khalid.

"Please. Call me Layla. I insist. But my question . . ."

He shook his head. "In answer to your question, it sounds like *you* are intent on protecting Egypt's heritage. We will all be in good hands, and I applaud you."

His face brightened for a moment and Layla wondered then if his smile was essentially sarcastic.

"Meanwhile," he continued. "I understood that you wanted to talk with me about business, not history."

He'd parried and subdued her. Now she decided to go at him from a different direction. "Can you tell me something?" she asked. "How do your clients, people like Noor Ghaffar, take receipt of the things that they buy?"

Khalid squinted as if he were appraising her. "Take receipt . . ." he repeated.

"How do you deliver the items they buy? Through regular shipping companies? Or do you have something more . . . discreet arranged?"

Khalid sighed deeply and sat quietly a moment, staring directly into Layla's eyes, and then he spoke. "How did you meet Mr. Rothkopf?"

Layla hesitated. She'd expected evasion, or at least a more subtle offense. "I met him at a party months ago, a fundraiser, soon after I arrived in Cairo."

Khalid nodded. "Did Mrs. Ghaffar introduce you?"

"No, actually. Jehan, Mrs. Ghaffar's daughter, introduced us."

He blinked and glanced into his coffee. "How did you meet Mrs. Ghaffar and her daughter?"

Layla eyed him closely. What was Khalid getting at? He was clearly pushing and poking at the edges of her cover. What might he do if he discovered she wasn't who she said she was? Would he risk attacking her in the Hanover? Or might he wait until she left the place? Might associates of his be outside the club ready to help him take her out? Finally, she answered, "I met them through Nesim Farwadi."

His eyes darted up. Her heart stopped.

"You know Mr. Farwadi?" he asked.

"Nesim? Yes, he's my cousin."

"Are you related to his mother?"

"My mother is his aunt," she said tersely. Her impatience was a defensive mask. Her palms were slick with sweat as she now found herself completely on edge. "His father's sister."

"I have worked with Mr. Farwadi for many, many years. He has told me much about his family. He never spoke of you. What is your mother's name?"

Layla swallowed. She had completely blanked on the name of Farwadi's aunt. Was Yasin armed? Should she simply stand and leave? She blinked. *Fatima? Fatma?* "Fatima," she said finally.

Khalid nodded slowly and frowned, as if he'd come to a deeper understanding. It was the first time she'd seen his face without the smile. "And she lived in the United States?" he asked.

Layla was flustered. "Yes. She lived for a period in the US and she also lived in the UK." She knew she was stating a mash-up of half-forgotten cover details. But she felt cornered. She noticed that his coffee was almost down to the dregs. If she blew her cover, he might lash out, and if Khalid were to suddenly leave, she would lose the chance to learn whatever he might know about Alberto. She decided to attack again, to turn the subject to anything else, even if it was risky, or dangerous.

"'Did you hear," she said, turning her coffee cup with both hands on the wooden tabletop, "on the news recently, about the murder of an Italian journalist who was investigating the Muharib's connection to illegal digs? Just terrible."

Khalid's eyes widened. He picked up his coffee but it shook in his grip. "I do not recall hearing about the journalist." He took a sip that must certainly have included some of the dregs. "Layla . . . Miss Nawar . . . I don't know anything about that world." He looked at his watch. "I'm so sorry. I must go. I have another client to meet. If you do wish to make a purchase, let me know."

"I will," she said.

She watched him thread past the tables to the long hallway, and caught his last wary glance back at her before he vanished into the afternoon. She leaned back and found that she was breathing hard. Her hands shook in her lap. They hadn't stopped shaking since the night before.

BACK IN HER APARTMENT, lying on the bed and staring at the ceiling, Layla felt dread in the pit of her stomach at the thought that Khalid might have figured her all out. Why had he asked her those questions? The reason was obvious: he suspected she was not who she said she was. And why was that? Because she'd tripped up somehow, revealed a crack in her cover that he had probed and tested until she'd panicked. She closed her eyes and worked to push the thought of Khalid out of her mind, searching for something, anything, to help her escape the idea that both Mackey and Khalid were now on to her. Finally, she was surprised to find that what filled the void of her fear were thoughts of James. His words still echoed in her thoughts and her own words to him made her wince. And then his call after the earthquake to check if she was okay . . . She was just about to pick up her phone to call him when it rang. It was Tremblay.

"Agent el-Deeb," he said, "I spoke with my lawyer. He advised me to be helpful." Layla let out a silent sigh of relief. "I hope that this will be taken into consideration in the course of your investigation." There was a pause, and then Tremblay continued, "I've got the information you asked me for. Only one shipment left Singapore around the same time as the DC shipment, and it was headed back to Cairo."

"Cairo?" Layla's mind raced.

"That's right." He gave her the address of a storage facility in the city. It was on el-Shaikh Rihan Street.

Layla sidled toward the evidence board that she had reconstructed, which was now propped against her bedroom wall. There was a map of Cairo taped on one side. She peered at it and saw that the storage facility was just east of Tahrir Square, which meant that it was also just blocks away from a number of foreign embassies, including the US embassy, all clustered together just east of the Nile.

She felt a surge of panic but didn't let it infiltrate her voice.

"Mr. Tremblay, you've been extremely helpful."

"I appreciate your saying so. I want no trouble with the police, and I want to co—"

She hung up. Her eyes were riveted to the location on el-Shaikh Rihan Street. She cursed Pierce for losing her phone and muttered to herself as she grabbed her gun from the nightstand.

Layla reached the storage facility within ten minutes by cab. El-Shaikh Rihan Street ran perpendicular to Garden City, and the facility was only half a block away from the eastern edge of that wealthy diplomatic hub. The building looked like a bit of a dive, really just an abandoned warehouse. But it was still open—the hours were printed beside the buzzer. She pressed it.

Eventually, a man in a security uniform came out, looking irritated at the interruption as he opened the door. He was chewing something. He had clearly been eating his lunch. Layla pushed past him. There was no time for niceties. She found herself in a cinder block–walled foyer painted a dreary, antiseptic green. A desk sat in the corner and on it lay a newspaper and a plate. Her eyes darted to the long hallway beyond, which was shrouded in shadows. When she spun on her heel she found the man looking at her with a frown.

"I'm Agent Amna Nassir," she said in Arabic. "I work with a special unit of the police. What's your name?"

"The police?" He looked suddenly alarmed.

"That's right. What's your name?"

"Omar. What is this . . ."

"A unit within this facility recently took delivery of a shipment from Singapore. It may have been used to smuggle weapons."

Omar's eyes flared. He was taking her seriously but she could also tell that he was playing through the scenarios in his head. One scenario, obviously, was that she was lying.

"Who are you, again?" he asked cautiously. He wiped his mouth with a paper napkin that he folded and put back in his uniform pocket.

She retreated, just a step. "I'm with the police, and this is an investigative matter. I can call in my boss if you need—" She reached into her pocket for her cell phone.

"No!" he said. "I can help you. Any information you need I can provide."

"Thank you," she said, trying to hide the huge surge of relief she felt. "You received a delivery from Singapore earlier this week. I need to confirm the presence of the unit holding the shipment and confirm its ownership." She took out her wallet and flashed some cash at Omar. Her damn hands were still shaking. Omar's eyes lit slightly at the sight of the money.

"I can take you there."

She followed him down a long hallway lined by big, light blue rolling doors. The place looked worn down and barely used. She was increasingly wary as he led her deeper into the dark corridor of units. Was it possible the security guard knew more than he was letting on? As she followed, she reached under her jacket to switch the safety off her gun. Each unit door was numbered. They stopped at a door marked 27.

"It is against the policy of the company to allow anyone other than the owner—"

She handed him five notes. He took them, flashed a smile, and started to root through an extensive collection of keys. Finally, he found the one he was looking for.

After he'd pulled open the door and switched on the light, they entered a space the length and width of two large cars set side by side. It was mostly empty, except for a stack of about a dozen cardboard boxes. Dust marks on the floor seemed to show that there had been more boxes there, recently moved.

Layla strode inside.

"You cannot touch those—" Omar started, but she ignored him. She opened up one of the boxes. It was about two feet on each side. There were about a dozen pieces of hardware inside, each sealed in manufacturer's plastic, labeled in French: *Digital Timer Model CF04*. She peered at one more closely. They were cheap digital timers, a bulk order. She opened up the other boxes and all were identical. She pulled out her iPhone and took photos of the packages.

"What are you doing?" Omar asked.

She glanced at him, held up the phone, and took a photo of his face. He stared at her, mortified.

"Can I see the paperwork for this unit?" she asked. "Who owns it?"

Omar, looking weary and defeated, turned and led her to the office. "I usually do not concern myself with the business matters aside from security, but as this is a police request . . ."

He searched through a file cabinet, found a file for unit 27, then sat at a desk to look through the papers. She tried not to be too obviously anxious as she watched him rifle through the file. The contents seemed to mostly be comprised of receipts showing pickups and drop-offs. After a few minutes, Omar looked up.

"Ghaffar. Mr. Gamal Ghaffar signed these."

"What?" said Layla. She almost grabbed the papers from the desk in front of him. But she didn't have to wait. He handed over three sheets. They were receipts ranging from 2002 to recent months, and they were signed by Gamal Ghaffar.

Layla blinked. She thought of Jehan, of Dreamland, of everything she thought she knew.

And she thought of Pierce at the embassy right now, in a meeting room with Gamal Ghaffar.

LINE OF FIRE

• DIANA RENN •

Layla rushed out of the storage warehouse, dazed and disoriented by all that she'd just seen and learned. Boxes of timers, some of them opened. Transaction records with Gamal Ghaffar's signature. The crates of explosives had been shipped from Singapore to Cairo, then recently moved to who knew where. Back outside on el-Shaikh Rihan Street, these new revelations, combined with the heat, the blinding sun, and the midday call to prayer over the crackling loud-speakers, all hit her at once. She leaned against the cinder block wall of the building and tried to steady her breath.

A group of well-heeled office workers strolled by. They were hurrying to lunch, laughing and talking, ignoring the call to prayer. A group of mothers with shopping bags and strollers hurried past. A cluster of tourists paused to snap selfies with the minarets of a mosque in the background. Through it all, a group of men knelt on prayer rugs on the sidewalk, plastic bottles of water beside them, which they'd used for washing their faces, hands, and feet before the prayer began. All of them were completely oblivious to the deadly secrets on the other side of that cinder block wall.

All these people with different beliefs and backgrounds, of various nationalities. How many of them might die if she couldn't locate those explosives? If she couldn't stop Gamal Ghaffar? It was no longer a matter of which nation she worked for, which she belonged to. Her allegiance in this matter was clear to her, unlike in her investigation of the Rothkopfs. She was on the side of preventing one more tragic event.

She pressed her fingers to her temples, trying to put the puzzle pieces together. According to the transaction records Omar had shown her, Gamal Ghaffar had signed in and out of the storage unit frequently in recent months, and as recently as yesterday. Gamal Ghaffar—Jehan's dad and one of the highest-ranking officials in Egyptian intelligence—was the person behind the shell company Global Relics, the link to the Muharib. An advocate of repatriating lost relics, the spouse of a prominent collector, yet a key link in the money trail linking looted relics to terrorist funding—and now to munitions storage and transport. This was insane. The link had been practically under her nose this entire time.

And yet, it made sense. The increased work hours he'd been putting in at his private home in Dreamland. The intensity with which he pursued his theory about American intelligence operating in Egypt. He could not risk discovery. No wonder he chose a third-rate storage unit in Cairo for his nefarious activities. With no security cameras and at least one bribable guard, he could get away with murder.

Literally.

As soon as the echo of the muezzins died down, Layla sprang into action, running toward downtown and the embassies. She passed a couple of college students wearing T-shirts with Egyptian and American flags, one of the Open Society party shirts people sported at Fareed Monsour rallies. The sight of the American flag shook a realization loose. It was July—July 2, in fact—only two days from the most important date in the American calendar. What more perfect date was there for targeting American interests abroad? A new worry struck her. The American Embassy was known for its lavish Independence Day dinner and festivities. The very building Pierce sat in could be the Muharib's next target. And Gamal Ghaffar was there. Maybe he had used his government position to bypass security and smuggle explosives into the building. He or someone who worked for him could be putting them into place for the Fourth of July. The countdown on those timers could already be ticking away.

Layla quickened her pace. It made the most sense to contact Pierce first. But Pierce did not have her cell. Layla took her phone from her bag and tried calling Pierce's direct office line as she ran. Nobody answered. *Shit.* Pierce's meeting with Gamal Ghaffar and the US ambassador would be wrapping up soon. Pierce was sitting down right now with a man who'd smuggled explosives across countries, and who could be planning an imminent event inside that very building. Layla had to get to Pierce and tell her Gamal Ghaffar had to be confronted before he left the embassy, while he was still under American jurisdiction.

The American Embassy was now within sight: an austere, sand-colored facade standing twenty stories high in the middle of downtown Cairo. Approaching the concrete wall surrounding the compound, Layla noticed soldiers standing at attention. They wore black uniforms and held assault rifles. She recognized the uniforms: Egypt's Central Security Forces. These people protected the perimeter of the embassy. But there were more of them outside than usual; she quickly counted twenty. Why? She hoped something serious wasn't happening already. Maybe she was too late to put a stop to Gamal's plan.

She rounded a corner, sticking close to the concrete barrier wall, then slowed when she saw a crowd of demonstrators at the front of the embassy building. Some held signs and banners declaring "Egypt deserves an open society!" and "Repair our democracy!" in Arabic and English. Others waved pictures of Fareed Monsour—a handsome man in his early forties with light olive skin, close-cropped dark hair, and a smile that exuded both confidence and warmth. His followers must have heard he was giving a talk here today. They never missed a chance to drum up support for his presidential run—and where there were Monsour supporters, counterdemonstrators always turned up, too. Layla felt a catch in her throat. His followers reminded her so much of Rami, who would no doubt be here himself if he hadn't still been in the hospital. She offered a silent thanks for that small mercy.

Her gaze shifted. Sure enough, opposite the Open Society party supporters, a somewhat smaller but rowdier crowd of anti-Monsour protestors was gathering, chanting, and waving signs of their own: "Americans out of our government!" and "A stronger, safer Egypt NOW!"

Some of the soldiers moved into the pathway to keep the two groups separate. She let out an exasperated breath. Now she'd have to cross the lines of soldiers in order to get through the embassy gate. And with the crowd of Monsour supporters pressing in on her, their shouts loud in her ears, she couldn't see a clear path.

The air crackled with tension. The embassy was often a hotbed of anti-American sentiment. Angry mobs had surrounded the embassy during the Arab Spring. And yet, even though she'd been living in America for the past eleven years and fighting for American interests, a part of her understood the anti-Monsour demonstrators, who objected to Monsour's ties to the American president and other Western leaders. She knew why they felt that the American government had a habit of overstepping. Her current mission was evidence enough of that. Americans seemed to insist on seeing the world through their own lens, but did Egypt need the United States to "save" it? Egypt had its problems, but the country's solutions would need to be its own as well.

Layla resumed shoving her way through the crowd of people and signs, inching her way toward the gate. Suddenly, she heard her name called out from somewhere in the crowd of Monsour supporters. "Layla! Layla, over here!" She turned. Waving at her with one hand, carrying a protest sign in the other, was Muhammad.

She froze. Muhammad was still friends with the collectors' kids, even if he was enduring a forced separation from Jehan. How would she explain to him what she was doing at the embassy? All her interactions with Muhammad—clubs and parties, Lake Geneva, Lake Como—seemed to belong to a distant era now. Ancient history.

She didn't want him to see her going into the embassy and wondering why. She didn't want to chat with him and answer difficult questions. So she turned away, pretending she hadn't seen or heard him. She pushed on through the people until she stood at the front of the Monsour supporters' crowd. As two soldiers stepped forward to break up an argument, Layla hurried through the break in the line and came to a guard booth beside the black steel entry gate.

A guard with a name badge that read "Mahfouz" sat there, looking keyed up and tense, darting wary glances at the protestors. "Citizenship?" he asked in English.

"American," she said quickly.

He looked at her with a skeptical expression and held out a hand. "Passport?"

She displayed empty hands. "I lost it. That's why I'm here. I need to get it replaced."

He regarded her a moment longer, then asked to inspect her bag. Fighting to hold back a sigh of annoyance, she handed over her tote bag, remembering at the last second that her Glock, unloaded, was still in there. *Shit.* She should have found someplace to ditch it and the box of ammo before she got this far.

The protestors and counterprotestors behind them grew louder. Some chanted and some hurled insults. Continuing to steal glances at the angry crowd, the guard opened her tote bag and began pawing through it. Layla held her breath. Any second now, he'd see the gun wrapped in her hijab at the bottom and the box of cartridges.

Suddenly, the guard stopped and frowned. Layla braced herself. But his gaze traveled past her to a scuffle in the crowd. His pager crackled.

"It's heating up over there," said Layla, feigning a nervous glance behind her. She knew some police officers and guards didn't need much convincing to join the fray. "I hope it doesn't get completely out of control."

"These things have a way of turning violent in an instant," the guard agreed.

Layla nodded. She knew that all too well. She thought of Rami, peacefully protesting on his university campus, before baton-wielding police had nearly killed him. "I wonder if everything's okay," she said, adding a nervous quiver to her voice. She glanced at her watch. "I hope this doesn't shut the embassy down. I really need to get in there and file those forms for my passport replacement."

The security guard glanced toward the protestors again, then back at her tote bag, then back at the protestors. It was clear where he wanted to be. "Go, go," he said, handing her the bag and waving her forward. "Through those doors to the screening area."

Another screen, another barrier, another delay. But at least she'd gotten past this station. This was real now. She was here to sound the warning. Layla ran across the front plaza toward the tall columns of the building. She entered the embassy lobby and felt a moment of sweet relief in the rush of air-conditioning, the American accents washing over her, and the festive Fourth of July decorations—froths of red-white-and-blue bunting draped across columns, balloons with stars attached to table centerpieces. A group of embassy workers walking past on the glistening tiled floor were discussing an Orioles game. Another employee sipped from a Dunkin' Donuts travel mug. Everyone seemed oblivious to the tensions building outside the compound walls—and no one suspected the dire warning she'd come to relay.

Was this where she belonged? She was a naturalized American citizen, but these weren't her native countrymen. She suddenly recalled how nervous she'd felt the last time she'd stood in that lobby as a gawky teenager, applying for her student visa to study in America. She'd been so terrified, afraid they'd find some reason to turn her down and prevent her escape to a new life.

Another guard spotted her and ushered her toward a screening room. She took her place in line in the hot and crowded room and tapped her foot impatiently as the line inched painfully forward.

Egyptian or American? Layla Nawar or Layla el-Deeb? Her mind raced. Now that she'd entered this building to take action, who did she need to become? The embassy didn't know anything about this investigation. Blowing her cover would blow Pierce's cover, too. But maybe the time had come. Maybe it was now her call.

She watched everyone removing shoes, belts, and jackets for the X-ray machines as if they were preparing to board a flight. Signs around the room announced that cell phones must remain in the locker area. A list of prohibited items in the embassy said "firearms" right at the top, closely followed by "explosives."

This line was way too slow. She wished she could call out her warning, but she mustn't cause a panic, and she couldn't risk scaring off Gamal. But she did need to get to Pierce immediately. She needed the attention of someone beyond a low-level screener. She scanned the room and spotted a Marine, a blond guy who looked barely out of high school. Potentially easy to deal with. She left the line, ignoring curious stares, and strode purposefully over to him. "My name is Layla el-Deeb. Agent el-Deeb. FBI. And I need you to let me through immediately. It's an urgent security issue."

"You're FBI?" A second Marine guard, a young Hispanic man, approached.

Layla felt the distance between her and Pierce widen. The finish line to this bizarre race she'd found herself in seemed ever-receding.

"Where's your badge?" the new guard asked.

"And your passport?" demanded the first one, who seemed to have remembered he was a Marine and not a schoolboy. "We need to see a government-issued identification."

"I don't have them on me," said Layla. "Look. I need to see Ellen Pierce. I need to speak with her immediately." She glanced around her, then lowered her voice so the people in the X-ray screening line wouldn't hear. "There may be explosives in this building. And the man responsible is *also* in this building."

The guards exchanged a concerned look, then stepped to the side and conferred briefly. "Come with us," said the blond guy. Layla fumed as they led her into a small private office off the screening room. Yet another delay. It reminded her strangely of the lieutenant's office when she'd visited Rami in prison. It wasn't as dank or dreary, but she felt imprisoned as the heavy door slammed shut.

"What is with you?" she spluttered, now that they had some privacy. "I come in telling you there might be explosives here, and this is your response?"

"There are no explosives," said the blond Marine.

"How can you possibly know that?"

"Because we just completed a thorough security check, including a complete sweep for bombs," he said.

"Literally, a half hour ago," said the other guard. "The bomb squad and K-9 unit just left. We have Fareed Monsour speaking here today, and with all the recent bombing action in Cairo, every precaution was taken to secure the premises. In fact, you're the last person who got into the building. We're closing to the public during his talk."

Layla stared at them. "Seriously?"

They both nodded.

Layla frowned. She believed the sweep had been performed. That brought some relief. But it still didn't explain where those explosives from the storage unit had gone. Did Gamal have accomplices? How many? Could he have arranged for someone else to bypass security at the embassy and rig the building for an ultimate fireworks display in two days? One thing was certain: she had to get to Pierce. Together, they had to detain Gamal while he was still on US territory. The second he stepped outside that building, he would be beyond their reach.

The door opened, and a third Marine joined them in the office. Layla inwardly perked up at the sight of an African American woman

around her age, wearing the same uniform as the first two guards—
a crisp short-sleeved khaki shirt and tie with navy blue trousers and
a white uniform cap—but more decorations on her shirt and lapels.
She was higher ranking. She could help get her to Pierce.

"I'm Colonel Taylor," said the guard, standing before Layla and
looking her up and down with a critical eye. "I hear you're claiming
to be an FBI agent."

"Layla Naw— I mean, Layla el-Deeb. Agent el-Deeb," Layla
corrected herself. "And yes, I'm FBI." She felt an adrenaline rush
saying her real name and title. She was done with her undercover
work. All the lies she'd told, and all the time she'd spent flitting
around with art collectors and jet-setters, and even her information
from the Rothkopfs hadn't done a damn thing to prevent the next
attack. Time to get real. Layla Nawar was no more.

"You have no FBI badge, no identification at all?" Colonel Taylor
persisted.

"Sorry, no. This was an unplanned visit."

Colonel Taylor raised an eyebrow. "I wasn't alerted that a new
legate was reporting for a post here. And you should never be traveling in Cairo without identification. Surely you're familiar with
the state department's new travel advisory. There's political unrest.
Cairo isn't safe."

"I'm aware. And I'm not a legate," said Layla, her voice rising
with urgency. "I'm here independently. I need to talk to Ellen
Pierce immediately." Panic rose in her throat and she faltered under
the colonel's suspicious stare. Was it possible she'd come this far,
only to find this was the end of the line? She couldn't fail. Not now.
Not after everything she'd been through.

"This woman says there might be explosives here," explained the
blond Marine, turning to talk to the colonel.

"We said it was impossible," said the other. "We just concluded
the sweep and gave clearance to begin seating guests for the talk."

"That's correct," said Colonel Taylor. She frowned and looked
at Layla. "If I told you how many crazies showed up here claiming

to be FBI, or CIA, or diplomats from fictitious countries, you wouldn't believe me. I can't let you in."

As if in response, the two younger guards standing behind their superior officer exchanged a knowing smirk. That smirk inflamed Layla even more than Colonel Taylor's remark.

"Call Agent Tom Monaghan at headquarters," she continued. "He knows who I am and why I'm in Cairo."

"I know Monaghan," Colonel Taylor cautiously admitted, her tight-lipped facial expression relaxing just a little.

"Great. And if you call Ellen Pierce, she can vouch for me even faster," said Layla. "She's in a meeting with some GID officials."

"That meeting's about to end," said Colonel Taylor. "We began seating for the Fareed Monsour event ten minutes ago."

Layla's heart sank. Maybe she was already too late. She didn't imagine Gamal was going to stay for Monsour's talk, seeing as he wasn't exactly an Open Society fan. Gamal was already slipping through their fingers. Her heart began to pound.

"Mr. Gamal Ghaffar, of the GID, is one of the meeting attendees," said Layla. "Do you know if he left already?"

"I don't," said the colonel. She paused. "I'll escort you to the auditorium, and you can look for both of them there. You're not to leave my side, got it? And you'll need to leave your bag and your phone."

Layla reluctantly handed her bag to the two male guards, with an unexpected rush of emotion. This innocuous-looking tote bag had been her lifeline throughout her time undercover in Egypt. It contained her fake ID, her three phones, her hijab, and now her Glock. It had at various points held bribes for Rami's prison wardens, banana bread and medicines for her brother, and stolen keys from Hamadi Essam. It had held Khalid Yasin's phone number. A bronze cat statuette from Bennett Rothkopf. Affectionate little notes scrawled on Post-its from James. The bag still held a photo of Alberto and his family. As she followed Colonel Taylor out of the office and passed by the long line of people at the X-ray machine, she suddenly felt unmoored and exposed.

"Anything in here we should worry about?" Colonel Taylor asked.

"I do have my firearm in there," Layla admitted, with a longing look at the bag. The thought of confronting Gamal without it gave her an uneasy feeling.

Colonel Taylor looked into the bag that the blond Marine was holding open. She reached in and moved some things around. Her eyes widened when she saw the Glock and the box of cartridges. "Run a check on the serial just in case," Layla heard the colonel whisper to the Marine, who nodded.

Her stomach twisted. The colonel didn't entirely trust her—not enough to let her out of her sight. But there was no time to argue. She and Pierce needed to get to Gamal before he, too, slipped through their fingers.

EVEN THOUGH THE GUARDS had said the building had been thoroughly searched, a new worry gnawed at Layla as she followed Colonel Taylor down the hall to the auditorium doors. "How many Marine guards are stationed here?"

"Seven of us."

"That's not very many. How secure is the building? Is it able to withstand attacks?"

"This place is a fortress," replied Colonel Taylor, glancing at her suspiciously. "Both the barrier walls and the outer concrete shell were specially designed to thwart attacks. It's not just the structural integrity of the building, either. The walls have blast-resistant glazing. And while we Marines protect American interests inside, our Egyptian friends keep a close watch on that outer wall."

Unless they're too distracted by mobs of protestors, thought Layla. The dismissive attitude of these Marines astounded her. She'd seen firsthand how explosives, particularly the concoction the Muharib was using these days, caused unimaginable human damage. And she'd been through enough earthquakes in her life, including this most recent one, to be skeptical of structural integrity. In fact, between her childhood and her FBI training, she'd lived most of her life imagining that anything could either fall apart or be blown apart at any time.

Colonel Taylor paused mid-step and gave Layla a long look. "I'm trusting you are who you say you are because I know Monaghan. Should I regret bringing you this far in?"

"No, ma'am," said Layla. She stood up straighter. The colonel had the power to get her to Pierce—or not to.

Colonel Taylor nodded with a skeptical expression. "All the same, I think I'll have you wait here in this alcove, and I'll get Pierce from the conference room. Wait here. Don't move." Colonel Taylor strode the remaining twenty or so yards past the auditorium to what looked like a conference room next door. She nodded at the Marines who flanked the door, and disappeared inside. Guests for Monsour's talk continued arriving and were greeted at the auditorium doors by another two Marines. Less than a minute later, the door to the conference room swung open and the colonel came out with Pierce. Colonel Taylor followed her nearly to the alcove where she'd left Layla, then stood a respectful distance away—far enough not to hear, yet close enough to establish authority.

Pierce walked briskly toward Layla. Between the uncharacteristic black pantsuit and patent-leather pumps, the hair neatly swept back into a chignon at the nape of her neck, Layla almost didn't recognize her at first, but the look of extreme annoyance on her face was definitely familiar.

"This had better be fucking good," Pierce said. She folded her arms across her chest. "You interrupted my meeting. You broke cover. You—"

Layla cut her off. "Gamal Ghaffar. Is he in the building?"

"He's still in the conference room with Youssef," said Pierce. "Why do you—"

"It's Gamal! We can't let him leave. He's the link to the Muharib."

Pierce stared at her as if she'd lost her mind.

"Listen to me," Layla pleaded. "We don't have much time. Gamal is the real owner of the Singapore Freeport unit rented through Masterpiece Fine Arts. He also owns a storage unit just four blocks away from here. Those crates of explosives that left Singapore on June twenty-seventh never made it to DC They came to Cairo, to that storage unit, instead." She explained as fast as she could what Monaghan had reported from DC, and what Omar had showed her in the storage unit. "The explosives could be anywhere now. Maybe even outside this building!" Layla finished. "The protests going on could be used as a distraction, keeping the Egyptian security busy so that terrorists can get the explosives past the barrier walls!" Layla took a deep breath and waited for Pierce to swing into action in her usual calm and effective way.

Pierce scratched the back of her neck. She shook her head. "What you're saying, Layla— This is— This is just—"

"I know. It's a lot to take in," Layla admitted. "But we have to question him about those explosives while he's here on American territory. If he's helping to plan something against American interests, we can legally question him here."

"Layla. Calm down. Gamal Ghaffar is *right on the other side of that door.*" Pierce grabbed her shoulder and pulled her deeper into the alcove and farther from Colonel Taylor's hearing. She pointed down the hallway behind her. "Now, I don't particularly like the guy. You know that. But he's in the GID. He's specifically concerned with matters of international security. We may not agree on exactly how to do that, but we do agree it's our top priority."

"But—"

"Not only that," Pierce continued, as if Layla hadn't made a sound, "think of the ramifications if we accuse a high-level official in the Egyptian government of this kind of crime, without complete proof." Pierce's eyes blazed. "We have a crowd of demonstrators outside this building already. It could inflame both local and international tensions. I can't act on a hunch. There's too much at stake. And Monaghan—"

"There's too much at stake to ignore this," Layla countered, taking a step forward. "I'm convinced Gamal knows where those explosives are. We can prevent the next attack. We can do it right now. And we can't wait to run this by Monaghan. We have to act on our own."

Pierce thought for a moment, then groaned and nodded at Layla. "All right. I'm going to trust you on this," she said. "But it's on my terms. I'll do the talking."

At that moment, the conference room door Pierce had pointed to earlier swung open. Youssef came out, carrying his briefcase, followed by Gamal. The sight of Gamal so close by made Layla shiver. The last time she'd seen him, he'd been standing in front of a closet she'd hidden in, just seconds away from discovering her and destroying her career. And the last time he'd seen her, she was floating in a pool with his daughter. But the jolt of fear at his commanding presence was quickly replaced by anger. This was a man who aided terrorists. He had to be stopped.

Layla and Pierce both watched the men as they made their way toward the auditorium, talking in low, serious voices. They were so absorbed in conversation they did not notice the women in the alcove off the corridor, though Layla, her undercover reflex kicking in, instinctively ducked behind a potted plant just before they passed.

"Go. Now," Layla urged in a whisper.

"Not yet. I want to know what they're talking about," Pierce whispered back. "Their Arabic is too fast for me. What are they saying?"

Layla listened intently, trying to block out all the background sounds of dinging from the nearby elevator bank and guests arriving for the talk. But she caught the gist of the conversation, as the two men paused a few yards away.

"Youssef's asking why Gamal suddenly wants to go hear Monsour's talk," Layla translated. "He says they have meetings booked all afternoon at their office. Gamal said he's changed his mind. He says it's important to hear what Monsour has to say, and he wants Youssef to reschedule the meetings."

"Interesting," Pierce murmured, not taking her eyes off the two men. "But if he stays for the meeting, it buys us more time. We can intercept Gamal as he leaves the auditorium."

"Perfect," said Layla. "Let's go." She stepped out from behind the potted plant but then frowned as Gamal and Youssef parted ways. Gamal was heading into the auditorium and Youssef, his forehead lined with concern, turned abruptly and hurried down a different corridor, to the right. Something about his expression and his sudden haste set off an alarm bell in Layla's mind.

Pierce narrowed her eyes, watching Youssef go. "I don't like that they split up," she said.

"Me neither," said Layla. "You stay on Gamal. I'm going to follow Youssef. At the very least, he probably has some clue as to what his boss is planning."

"You can't just walk around here without an escort. You don't have full security clearance," Pierce reminded her.

Layla looked over at Colonel Taylor, who was giving directions to someone who was lost.

"Watch me," said Layla, and she took off running.

LAYLA FOLLOWED YOUSSEF AS quietly as she could, and at some distance. He passed the elevator bank, rounded a corner, and then pushed open a door to the stairwell. She waited a moment, then followed. She could hear the echo of his footsteps ahead of her. They were not ascending but descending. To the basement.

Her skin pricked with heightened alertness. Youssef did not work in this building. There was no good reason for him to go downstairs.

He opened another door to a basement room. It slammed behind him with a bang that reverberated against the walls and straight into her heart. She counted to ten to allow him a bit more lead, then quietly went to the same heavy door, opened it, slipped inside a cavernous, dimly lit storage and utilities room, and leaned her full weight against the door so that it closed softly.

She immediately ducked behind a concrete pillar, desperately wishing she had her gun.

The sound of footsteps thudding upstairs masked the sounds of her breathing, as did the sound of the ambassador beginning her opening remarks for Fareed Monsour's talk. This basement room must be directly beneath the auditorium. Then Layla became aware of men's low voices, speaking in Arabic, and her skin pricked with a sense of foreboding.

Youssef's voice was audible among them, but because of the echo and the interfering sounds, she could only catch a few words. She had to know what they were talking about. She looked around her. The room was studded with concrete pillars. Her heart hammering, she slipped from pillar to pillar, drawing closer to the voices and deeper into the room.

When she was as close as she dared to get, she peered around a pillar. She saw three men in blue uniforms tinkering with electrical wiring. One man was on a stepladder, working high up near a support beam on the ceiling. The two other men were kneeling and attending to something near the ground, next to two other concrete pillars. Electricians.

But why would Youssef be talking to them?

Then she knew. She felt a rushing sound in her ears, her blood pressure pulsing. They weren't electricians. And Youssef had been in on the plan all along. He was Gamal's lackey. Whatever they were talking about must be connected to the contents of that storage unit, and all the clues that had come before.

"Be silent!" the man on the stepladder snapped at Youssef. "How can we concentrate with all this chatter? You are in the way here!"

The man then stooped to pick up something on a lower rung of the ladder. Layla immediately ducked behind the pillar. When she looked again, her suspicion was confirmed. The man was placing a gray brick up near a support beam. Wires extended out of the brick, and attached to it was a timer. Exactly the kind of timer she had seen in Gamal Ghaffar's storage unit.

Every muscle in her body tensed. She had to warn everyone to clear the building. Now.

Yet she remained fixed to the spot, and forced herself to keep observing, to try to make sense of the surreal scene.

She looked at the two other workmen and noticed, beside them, more gray bricks. C-4 explosives. Exactly like the one that had turned up in the Singapore Freeport raid. She scanned the room again and noticed other bombs already rigged at key structural points. They were going to take the whole place down from within.

Run. Save yourself.

She thought, in a rush, of things that were dear to her. Rami. Sanaa. Badru. James. She thought of morning jogs, strolling in Cairo's busy streets, a felucca on the Nile, the sun on her face. She wanted to live. She needed to live. She wasn't done living, not by a long shot.

Then fury kicked in. So this was what the Muharib spent its relic money on. The bombs. The workmen. The chance to send a message to the United States. This was the very activity that Bennett, James, and that whole circle of collectors were wittingly or unwittingly funding.

Dry-mouthed, her breath coming fast, she looked toward Youssef, who was now speaking to the men in an urgent tone.

"I implore you to reconsider," said Youssef. "Mr. Ghaffar changed his plan. He is still in the building and insists on hearing the talk. You need to change the timers. Delay the explosion until after Monsour's talk ends. I will get Mr. Ghaffar out of the building before then."

Layla put her hands to her mouth, as if to stifle the cry that wanted to escape from her throat.

The man on the stepladder looked at Youssef with disdain, bordering on disgust. "We do not take orders from you," he spat. "You are nobody to us. Nobody. Our orders are to finish this job and then leave this building. It is no concern to us if you and Mr. Ghaffar remain behind to die. "

Youssef slumped momentarily, then stood up straighter and looked at the man on the ladder with hate in his eyes. "This operation would not be possible if it weren't for me," he said. "I helped to transport and store these devices. I let you into the building. Without me, you would never have come this far."

The man on the ladder sneered at him. "The Muharib used you. You are no longer needed. They don't care about you. They never did."

Youssef looked stricken. He opened his mouth as if to protest but did not get a chance to utter a word.

Bang.

Layla jumped. A gun?

No. The heavy basement door, banging shut.

"Hello? Agent el-Deeb? Are you down here?" Colonel Taylor called out.

Shit.

Layla flattened herself against the concrete pillar as she heard the sound of three men drawing weapons.

The three terrorists responded with a volley of gunfire. Bullets pinged and cracked against the concrete and metal. The man on the ladder teetered and then fell as a bullet from Colonel Taylor's weapon hit his chest. He twitched, choked, and then lay still. His revolver skittered across the floor. Layla ran through the gunfire and grabbed it, no longer caring if the colonel saw her. The Marine needed backup, and this was her chance. Colonel Taylor shot Layla a look of surprise, then suspicion. She raised her Beretta and pointed it. At Layla.

Layla's eyes widened. Of course the colonel thought she was one of them. She even looked like these guys.

One of the terrorists lunged toward the colonel, aiming his gun right at her. Layla fired at him, hitting his hand. While he reeled from the hit, Layla and the colonel ran to take cover behind a wall of paint cans and boxes. The colonel quickly reloaded her Beretta. Layla checked the revolver she'd acquired from the dead terrorist. It held nine rounds, but only two were left.

"I'm on your side," Layla panted.

"I believe you. You just saved my ass," said the colonel. Then she reached into a holster on her leg and took out a second handgun. She handed Layla the pistol, then nodded her head as if to say, *Let's do this.*

Both of them ran out from behind their temporary shelter, triggering the return of the terrorists' fire. They ran from pillar to pillar, firing, ducking, firing again, as the two remaining terrorists did the same. Layla looked around for Youssef and found him crawling toward the door, the revolver she'd left behind, with its one remaining bullet, in his hand. She lunged after him, then cried out as a bullet coming from behind her grazed her shoulder. She fired another shot in the direction from which it came, then crouched behind an air-conditioning unit, clutching at her shoulder with one hand to quell the pain. When she pulled her hand away, it was covered in blood. More bullets pinged loudly against the air conditioner. Layla ignored the pain in her shoulder and fired back. A man howled in pain. Then the barrage of bullets stopped at last.

When both the remaining men were down, wounded but alive, Colonel Taylor handcuffed one and tossed a set of handcuffs to Layla, who handcuffed the other man. They patted the men down for weapons and found two additional 9mm pistols on them, and several rounds of ammunition.

Colonel Taylor pulled a pager out of her pocket. "Basement, Room D2. We've had active shooters. One man down, two alive. I need backup. And a bomb squad."

The pager crackled. "Copy that."

The words sounded faint and far away. Layla became aware of the ringing in her ears. But some words stuck. One man down, two alive.

And one, armed, somewhere else in this building, Layla wanted to shout to the colonel, but the words wouldn't come. Breathless, drenched in sweat, and covered in concrete dust, all she could do for a moment was rock back on her heels and try to breathe.

The colonel looked at the terrorists on the ground, her lip curled in disgust. Then she looked at Layla with admiration. "You're a good shot," she said.

"Thanks," Layla managed to gasp out. "You're not so bad yourself. There's another guy, though—" She gestured vaguely toward the door.

"There's no time to talk. We're surrounded by bombs," said the colonel, brushing past her and looking around. "We need to deactivate all of them. We're lucky no bullet set off a detonator."

Layla nodded and sprang into action. Aiming the pistol Colonel Taylor had given her, she approached the two wounded men. "Show me where all the bombs are in this room," she demanded in Arabic.

The men glared at her, rage in their eyes. Their chests heaved with their labored breathing, and blood pooled on the floor.

"Show me!" Layla shouted, shoving the revolver under one man's chin.

He could barely talk, but he gasped out the various locations, pointing around the room. Six bombs.

Layla climbed the stepladder and inspected the one near an air duct. Her stomach lurched. "This timer is set to go off in five minutes," she said, her voice shaking. "Six bombs to deactivate in less than five minutes. I hope you know what the hell you're doing," she added, as she relinquished the ladder to Colonel Taylor.

"I have some experience in this area," the colonel said with a grim expression. She deftly yanked the wire out.

Alarms began to sound through the building. An alarm on the wall flashed colored light around the room, staining everything red.

Layla thought of Gamal, who could now make his escape back to Egyptian territory. And Youssef, unless she could catch up with him. "There's one who got away during the gunfire," she said, when the colonel approached the last bomb. "He's one of the masterminds. I have to go find him."

"I've got this," said the colonel. "I'll wait with these losers until my backup gets here." She cast a disdainful look at the injured terrorists, yanked out the last wire, then wiped her brow and took her Beretta out of her holster. She took the smaller pistol from Layla's hand and gave her the Beretta. She grinned. "Trade you. You'll like this one a whole lot better. And something tells me you may need it."

LAYLA RAN BACK UPSTAIRS only to find more chaos. Deafening alarms blared. Sirens wailed outside. Visitors and employees ran in all directions.

Racing down the corridor by the auditorium, her shoulder stinging from the bullet that had grazed it, Layla spotted Pierce and Gamal. She changed course and ran over to them. If she couldn't get Youssef, she could at least get Gamal. It was a miracle he hadn't fled the building. And what was Pierce doing with him?

"Layla! You're okay!" Pierce cried out when she saw her.

Gamal startled, then did a double take at the sight of Layla.

"What the hell's going on?" Pierce exclaimed. "We heard all these gunshots downstairs, and then the alarms went off." She reached out to touch Layla's arm and noticed the blood dripping on the floor. "You're hurt!"

"Have you seen Youssef? Did he run by here?" Layla demanded.

"No," said Pierce. "Shit. What happened?"

Layla felt rather than saw Gamal's eyes still locked on her. She turned to face him.

"You're Jehan's friend," he said. "What are you doing here?" His eyes shifted to the Beretta in her hand.

"Did you tell him yet?" Layla demanded of Pierce, slowly raising the gun to point it at him.

Gamal took a step backward, his hands raised. Fear crossed his face. "What is this madness? What is going on?" He looked at Pierce in confusion, then back at Layla and the gun.

"I was about to tell you," said Pierce. "Before the gunfire started. This is—"

"I know who she is," said Gamal. "She's my daughter's friend, Layla Nawar."

"I'm not Layla Nawar," said Layla, keeping the gun steadily pointed at him. "I am Layla el-Deeb, FBI agent." Emboldened by saying her real name, she went on, summoning strength and power with every word she spoke. "We know you're storing and moving looted relics and munitions for the Muharib, using a shell company called Global Relics. We also know you received explosive supplies at storage unit twenty-seven at a facility on el-Shaikh Rihan Street. We know you arranged for them to be rigged inside this very building, right beneath our feet."

As she spoke, though, an unsettling feeling washed over her despite her confident tone. Something didn't add up. Why would Gamal Ghaffar arrange for the building to be bombed during Monsour's talk, but insist on staying for that talk? Had he ordered Youssef to delay the bombing, or had Youssef gone rogue and defied some order?

Gamal moved his mouth, but no words came. When he finally spoke, his voice shook. "I don't own a storage unit in Singapore," he said. "I do own one in Cairo. But I haven't set foot in it in nearly a year. And I know nothing about Global Relics." He looked around wildly, and then imploringly at Pierce.

"It's best to cooperate with us, Mr. Ghaffar," said Pierce. "It'll all go so much easier. "We have evidence, too, that your wife has made some illicit purchases from a questionable source," Pierce added. "We can protect her if you cooperate."

Gamal glowered at Pierce. "You leave my wife out of this."

But Layla's mind was racing. New ideas flashed in with dizzying speed. "Did you and Youssef arrive here at the same time today?" she demanded, ignoring Pierce's confused expression.

"What? No. Youssef came in advance to help set up for the meeting." Gamal paused, then stared at Layla. "Are you suggesting *Youssef* brought explosives here? That he somehow bypassed security to bring them into the basement?"

A group of embassy employees hurrying past to find an exit turned abruptly and fled in the opposite direction when they saw Layla holding Gamal at gunpoint.

"I want to know about Gamal's storage unit," said Pierce, glaring at Layla. "Let's stick to the topic, shall we?"

Layla bristled, but bit back her next question. "Fine. Go on. Tell us about the unit," she said to Gamal.

Gamal lifted his chin. "I do own unit twenty-seven at the storage facility you mentioned. I opened it two years ago, when we were beginning to renovate our house. I used to store some of our family's personal items there. But I have not set foot in the facility for more than a year. I had, in truth, forgotten about it."

"Your name is on the log-in sheet," Layla insisted. In a perverse way, she enjoyed this feeling of power over Gamal, of seeing him dance at the end of her string. "I have photographic evidence. And the security guard there, who showed me around your unit, would be willing to testify against you."

"I have not set foot in that unit," Gamal repeated, his voice tinged with acid. "But I know who has. My assistant. Youssef."

"Youssef?" Pierce repeated. She turned to Layla. "That's why you were asking about Youssef?"

Gamal nodded. "He's the only other person with a key."

Layla lowered the gun just slightly. New pieces of the puzzle slid together in her mind. Youssef spoke perfect English and could interact with Masterpiece Fine Arts to authorize shipments and storage, operating as Global Relics. He knew Gamal well and could forge his signature on the log at the Cairo storage unit. And as a government worker, he had access to letterhead in various departments. The requests from the Egyptian Ministry of Antiquities for scholars to write about Faiyum relics—before they were stolen—could have come from him. Well-spoken, well-connected, he made a good front man for the Muharib. Until they were done with him. Today was supposed to have been his last day on the job.

Still, that didn't necessarily absolve Gamal from guilt. "You really expect us to believe Youssef isn't your puppet?" she said. "I heard Youssef mention getting you out of the building before the bombs were set off. Was that the plan before you changed your mind about hearing Monsour speak? Did you—"

Gunfire, three shots, rang out from somewhere in the building and cut off her words. Screams followed. Layla tensed.

"That wasn't from the basement," said Pierce. They all looked down the hallway in the direction of the noise.

"Take cover!" shouted an embassy worker as he ran past them, coming from that direction. "There's a shooter in the building! He just took out a guard!"

"Youssef. He grabbed one of the terrorists' guns downstairs," said Layla. A wave of nausea came over her. If he killed someone, it was partly her fault. She hadn't managed to contain him downstairs. She'd let him get away with a gun.

"I can help you," Gamal said, his voice calm and measured. "Stop pointing the gun at me. I can get to Youssef and calm him down. He will listen to me."

"Okay. Call him," Pierce commanded. She gestured at Layla to lower the gun.

Layla did so, reluctantly, as Gamal took his cell phone out of his pocket. With a surprisingly steady hand he punched in some numbers and activated the speaker.

After five rings, Youssef picked up. "Mr. Ghaffar? Where are you? Are you still in the building?" he asked in Arabic, speaking quickly yet quietly. His voice was muffled, as if he was covering up part of his phone.

"I am in the building," Gamal said, his voice measured and authoritative. Almost paternal. "Where are you, Youssef?" A note of concern, perhaps manufactured concern—Layla couldn't be sure—crept into his voice. "I am worried about you. A shooter is loose in the building. I want to make sure you are safe."

There was a pause, and then Youssef continued, his voice tight and strained. "I am safe, for now. You must get out of the building."

"I am not leaving without you," Gamal said, so smoothly and assuredly that Layla had to admire his control. She relaxed just a little. He seemed to be genuinely trying to help de-escalate the situation and to get her to Youssef. "Where are you?"

"I am hiding," said Youssef. "There are people here who seem to suspect me. And there are people here who want me dead." His voice faltered and grew fainter.

"There is no need to hide, Youssef," said Gamal, his voice so calm he was practically purring. "I will come and get you. We will leave together. Just tell me where you are, and remain there until I come for you."

There was another long pause. Layla held her breath. Then Youssef responded, in a small voice, "The library."

"I am on my way." Gamal hung up the phone and turned to Pierce and Layla. "I will take you to him. I want to help you." He looked tired after his performance, weary. "I am not the man you are after."

"THE LIBRARY'S AT THE other end of this floor," said Pierce, taking off at a sprint. Layla and Gamal followed close at her heels. They ran all along the corridor, through the lobby, and down the opposite corridor, passing terrified people hiding behind furniture or running in random directions.

They came to the library door, which was closed. A repetitive thudding sound could be heard from within. Layla reached for the knob, but Gamal placed his hand on hers to hold her back. "Allow me to go first," he said. "Let me talk to him."

"You can go in first," said Pierce, "but we're not leaving you two alone together."

"As you wish," said Gamal, his voice tinged with sadness. He hesitated for a moment with his hand on the knob, then slowly pushed the door open as if resigning himself to a distasteful task.

Youssef was trying to smash a window with a chair. Tied to another chair nearby was a terrified-looking embassy employee, a middle-aged, red-haired woman in a yellow blouse, streaks of tears and mascara running down her face

Youssef whirled around when he saw Gamal enter and seemed momentarily relieved at the sight of him. But when he saw Layla and Pierce walk up behind him, he dropped the chair in surprise. He looked shocked at the sight of Layla, then confused, as if trying to place her. Then his expression changed to one of sudden comprehension as he saw the gun in her hand.

"Who are these people?" he demanded of Gamal. "I thought you were coming alone!"

"Youssef," said Gamal. "Stay calm. Talk to me."

"Why would you betray me like this?" said Youssef, raising his voice.

"Youssef, I—"

"No. No." Youssef visibly trembled. "You said I was like family. Are you turning me in?"

"Let's talk this out," said Gamal, in his steady, even tone. "I'm sure we can come to some mutual understanding if we—"

Before Layla or Pierce could react or even attempt to restrain him, Youssef lunged forward and reached for a gun he had set on a nearby desk. The gun from the fallen terrorist that Layla herself had used downstairs.

He pointed it at the head of the woman who was tied to the chair. The woman shut her eyes and began to whisper a prayer.

"Let me out of this building, and Mr. Ghaffar, too, without officials apprehending us," Youssef demanded of Pierce and Layla, a wild look in his eyes, "or I will kill this woman." His arm shook, as if with fear, but his chin jutted out in defiance.

Layla raised her gun and pointed it at him. "That's not how we're playing. Drop your weapon, and we can talk."

Youssef glared at her and shoved the gun right up to the woman's temple. "You lower your gun," he retorted. "Or she dies."

The woman continued praying under her breath.

"Let me handle this," Gamal murmured to Layla. "Lower the gun."

Hating herself for it, Layla complied, but she didn't loosen her grip on the handle. She felt the blood from her injury seeping through her shirt and dripping down her arm.

"You are right that I thought of you as family," Gamal said to Youssef softly. "I treated you like my own son," he added with an empty gesture. He let his hands fall to his sides. "I helped you to rise in the department. I was willing to give you my daughter to marry." He sighed, expressing bone-deep disappointment. Then he straightened his shoulders and pointed an accusing finger at him. "You tell me I'm betraying you by coming here with American authorities. But how could you lead me into this situation? How could you turn against me like this, after all I've done for you?"

Youssef met Gamal's gaze. "Your daughter? That shallow whore?" he said with a sneer. "Finally, I saw the light. I know her true character, and I want nothing to do with her. And you have it all backward. I'm the one who's been trying to help you."

Gamal shook his head in disbelief. "Help me? You were working for the Muharib. Using my storage facility. And my good name."

"Only to help you," Youssef insisted. His gaze was dull, as if his soul were already dead. He spoke almost mechanically, beyond a place of emotions—if he'd ever had any at all. "I only worked for the Muharib to make some connections and extra money. At first. Then I realized I could use them, too. To help you. To help our cause."

Layla swallowed hard. If Youssef was telling the truth, maybe Gamal really was innocent. She looked at Gamal to gauge his reaction.

Gamal glowered at Youssef, his thick brows knitting together. "How could aiding the Muharib possibly help our cause?" he asked angrily, folding his arms across his chest.

"I suggested the embassy for the attack," said Youssef, his eyes glassy, his voice completely flat. "I got the Muharib's bomb experts in through the service door, posing as electricians."

"But why?" Gamal spluttered. "Why?"

"An attack on the embassy would justify a government crack-down on America's interfering presence in Egypt," said Youssef, his voice eerily calm now. "It would give you more acclaim, more power. And get Monsour out of the way in the process. You'd not only rise with no difficulty to leader of the GID, you'd have a clear path for a presidential run."

Layla couldn't believe what she was hearing. His words, and his perverse logic, chilled her to the bone. Jehan had been dead wrong about this guy. He was far from unambitious. He was a nefarious schemer.

Youssef gave Gamal a hard look. "I was prepared to do the dirty work for you, for Egypt. I thought you would be proud."

The words struck a chord in Layla. There was something pathetic about them, in this plea for Gamal's approval. It made her think of her own desire for Bennett Rothkopf's approval. This lonely young man had found a proxy family in the Ghaffars. They fulfilled some kind of deep need in him, and it had made him lose his judgment. She hated to admit it, but she could relate to Youssef in that way.

Gamal walked up to Youssef and looked at him as if for the first time, seeing him with new eyes. The hostage held at gunpoint trembled violently, as Youssef continued to hold the gun against her temple. Youssef met Gamal's steely gaze, and the two men stared at each other in silence, both breathing hard. Gamal flexed his hands.

Layla wondered if he might lunge for Youssef and throttle him. She held her breath and tightened her grip on the gun. *Don't do this.* If Gamal pissed off Youssef, or made too hasty a move, that woman was going to die.

"I'm not proud," Gamal said at last, taking a few steps backward.

Layla let out a long breath.

"I am ashamed," Gamal went on, practically spitting the words at Youssef. "Ashamed that I took you under my wing, that I had you in my house, that my wife fed you meals. I am ashamed that I ever knew you at all." His voice rose with every accusation.

Youssef's face clouded over. He looked like a chastised child. His hand slowly released the safety on the gun. The clicking sound echoed loudly.

Layla tensed. Forget letting Gamal play the father figure card. This could not be the endgame here. Layla raised her gun.

Gamal whirled around, knocking Layla's arm. She cried out as he jarred her injured shoulder with unexpected strength. He was bending her arm behind her back, overpowering her. "Layla!" she heard Pierce cry out as she fought to keep hold of her weapon.

Layla grimaced in pain. How could she have fallen for Gamal's act? Of course he was in on the plot. Of course he knew what was happening all along. She tried to kick at Gamal's shins, to get free, but he wrested the gun from her hand and let go of her.

Layla staggered backward.

Gamal aimed the gun at Youssef, whose face registered an instant of surprise before a shot rang out.

OZYMANDIAS

· PATRICK LOHIER ·

Layla recoiled from the shock of Gamal grabbing the gun and the explosive sound of the gunshot. Youssef crumpled to the floor.

"Get the gun!" yelled Pierce.

Layla wrenched the gun from Gamal's grip and pointed it at him. But Gamal didn't resist. He didn't even turn to look at her. He stood with his arms at his sides, staring at Youssef, who lay on the ground. Layla turned to check on the woman in the chair. A mist of blood had sprayed against her yellow blouse. She appeared to have passed out but seemed unharmed.

Pierce brushed by Layla and body-slammed Gamal against the wall with surprising force, given the difference in their sizes. As she twisted one of his arms behind him, Layla stepped in to help her. She leaned her elbow into Gamal's back despite the electrifying pain in her arm. They held him together, each on one side, but he still didn't resist.

"Why did you do that?" Layla said breathlessly.

Gamal looked dazed, almost catatonic. He frowned at Youssef's prone body.

"He was never who I thought he was," he said to himself more than to anyone else.

"Layla, I've got him," said Pierce. She gestured toward Youssef. "Clear his weapon."

Layla went to where Youssef lay, bending to one knee beside him. The gun was nestled firmly in his grip. Layla prized his fingers off it and kicked it aside. Then she set two fingers on Youssef's neck, just to be sure. Blood flowed from beneath him, like ink staining the dark green carpet.

"Is he dead?" said Pierce to Layla, her eyes still on Gamal.

"He's dead." She turned Youssef onto his back and gingerly lifted his jacket, lightly running her good hand over his shirt, searching for a wire, a detonator, explosives. There was no wire, no vest, but she did find the wound. It was in his upper chest, next to his sternum. The bullet must have exited through his back.

"He's clear," she said.

Outside, beyond the library door, Layla heard people running and calling out. The chaos was still raging. They seemed so far away from it all in the suddenly quiet scene in the library.

Colonel Taylor's voice broke through the cacophony beyond the closed door before two Marines burst in, Berettas drawn, and pointed their weapons at Pierce and Layla. Layla instinctively put both hands in the air. She knew she must look highly suspicious, covered in a dead man's blood.

Colonel Taylor entered. She strode toward Layla and knelt beside her.

"Is he dead?"

Layla nodded, lowering her hands, which she noticed seemed to have stopped shaking for the first time since she had witnessed Hamadi's murder the night before.

Colonel Taylor looked closely at her. Layla realized that they had met only half an hour earlier—maybe less—but it felt like a lifetime had passed. Colonel Taylor nodded at Layla and then looked at the blond Marine, who was helping the now revived and weeping woman stand up from the chair. "Help Agent el-Deeb secure this room. Do whatever she tells you to do."

Colonel Taylor gave Layla's shoulder a quick squeeze before rushing from the room. In the hall, Layla spied embassy staff rushing toward exits. Someone had set off the fire alarm. The adrenaline that had flowed through her body all that long day seemed to slow to a drip, and then she had nothing left to give.

"You okay?" said Pierce. She was now only halfheartedly holding onto Gamal, who clearly had no plans to flee or fight. She eyed the wound on Layla's arm. "We need to get you some help for that."

"I'm okay." Layla watched as Marines escorted the distraught woman, and then Gamal, out of the room. She had prevented the attack. Stopped the bad guy. But it didn't feel the way she thought it would. She felt hollowed out. Exhausted.

WHAT REMAINED OF THE day was a blur of debriefs that felt more like interrogations. Finally, she was allowed to return home, to sleep. She woke the next day in the big bed in her penthouse from a sleep that felt as deep as she imagined death must feel.

She padded to the bathroom and sat on the edge of the tub, studying the bandages that covered her shoulder. She carefully unwound them, wincing at the pain. As she showered, the blood from the exposed gash turned the water a dull pink. She watched, mesmerized, as it pooled at her feet and spun around the drain. When she was done she put on fresh bandages and, as if on auto-pilot, dressed and made a breakfast of fluffy eggs and sausage, with good black Turkish coffee, fresh-squeezed orange juice, and toast.

She looked over to the living room, where a sleeping Pierce lay snoring softly on the sofa. It was strangely pleasant to witness Pierce at peace—it was a side of her Layla rarely got to see. The sound of the phone shook Layla from her reverie, and she grabbed it on the first ring to prevent it from disturbing Pierce.

"Hello?"

"Agent el-Deeb?" It was the unmistakable voice of Gamal Ghaffar. Layla hadn't seen or heard from him since he was escorted away in the embassy. But she'd been informed in her debrief that he was no longer under any suspicion of involvement with the attack.

"Yes," she responded quietly, walking into the bedroom to get some distance from Pierce.

"I hope you don't mind my reaching out to you in this way." He paused. "I'm sure you and your colleagues will be leaving Cairo soon, and I felt compelled to talk to you first." There was silence on the line, and Layla wondered if he had changed his mind.

"General Ghaffar?"

"He was like a son to me, Youssef. He showed great ambition, great promise. I admired his patriotism, his passionate belief in the future of Egypt." Layla knew Ghaffar was a military man; she understood that he would not weep but she heard the quaver in his voice.

"Sometimes it turns out that the people we're closest to, we never knew at all," said Layla, thinking of everyone she had loved here in Cairo, everyone she had lied to.

Gamal cleared his throat in what Layla read as a return to professionalism, to their roles as intelligence officers. "The events of yesterday were truly tragic. The fact that they occurred on Egyptian soil is a point of great pain to me, and to the Egyptian government. Despite some tensions in recent years, the United States has been an ally for many decades. An attack on the US Embassy, the security of which is among our highest diplomatic obligations and points of engagement, is an attack on Egypt."

"Thank you, General Ghaffar," said Layla.

"That being said . . ." he continued. "We do not at all appreciate that the United States government appears to have undertaken a rogue intelligence operation on Egyptian soil. Cooperation was always an option. Yet no one reached out to us. You will understand why we are filing a complaint with the United States government and the United Nations. I have already spoken to your Secretary of State, expressing our disappointment that no effort was made to work in partnership."

Layla swallowed hard. This meant that there would almost certainly be an investigation into the mission, and she knew she had not always followed the rules. In fact, she'd broken them many times—to protect James, to see her family. This could spell the end of her career, but somehow she couldn't bring herself to blame Gamal for his actions.

"I understand," she said calmly.

There was a pause and then Gamal said, "Before we say goodbye . . ." There was another pause, rustling noises as the phone changed hands, and then, "Layla?" It was Jehan's voice. She sounded more timid than Layla had ever heard her, and her heart broke. With everything that had happened, she'd had no time to feel guilty about her plan to leave Cairo without saying good-bye to Jehan.

"Layla? Are you there?"

"I'm here. Jehan, I am so, so sorry I lied to you."

There was silence on the line before Jehan responded, "I'm not going to pretend I'm not hurt." She was quiet again, then gave an exasperated sigh. "But I must admit having a secret agent for a friend livened things up around here."

Layla released a hopeful laugh at this perfectly Jehan response.

"Come back to see me soon, okay?"

Layla knew it would be a long time before she set foot in Cairo again, but she agreed anyway.

She hung up the phone as she walked back to the living room to find a tousled Pierce, now awake.

"Who was that?" Pierce asked.

Layla hesitated. How much did Pierce really need, or even care, to know? "Gamal Ghaffar," she said.

Pierce raised an eyebrow, "Oh?"

"He says the government is likely to lodge a formal complaint with the US and the UN regarding the operation. He says we could have been more . . . collaborative."

Pierce nodded thoughtfully. "Not surprising." She yawned, rose from the chair, and raked her fingers through her hair. Her eyes wandered as the implications seemed to sink in. Finally, she closed her eyes and shook her head. "We could be in for a rough ride if anyone looks too deep."

"My thoughts exactly," said Layla. She decided to leave it at that.

She coaxed the sleepy Pierce to the table, sat across from her, and watched her boss wolf down her own plate of eggs and sausage. At some point, perhaps feeling herself observed, Pierce glanced up, took a long sip of coffee, and eyed Layla with a glint in her eye.

"I really needed that."

Layla laughed. "I'm not sure if I've ever seen you eat, let alone eat like that."

Pierce folded her napkin and set it aside. "I'm trying to get back into the habit. The worst part about bad habits is they make you forget the good habits."

They sat quietly for a moment before Pierce spoke again.

"You did great yesterday. I want you to know that."

"Thanks. None of it would have happened without you, though."

Pierce nodded. She looked aside, at the broad window overlooking the city, which shone like a mirage coated with brass dust under the morning sun. Layla followed her gaze. At moments like these the city looked not just ancient, but eternal. Pierce turned to her again.

"You know what's gotta happen next, don't you?"

Layla nodded. All her playacting at a normal morning with coffee and eggs couldn't stop what was coming. "Bennett."

"That's right. State Department's put a real lid on the details around the embassy attack. Reporters are all over it, though. By tomorrow we'll be reading details about our investigation in the *New York Times* that even we don't know. The State Department and our own headquarters will likely want us out of Cairo as soon as possible. I don't think we have much time. We have to talk to Rothkopf as soon as we can."

"But we can't arrest him—not here, at least." Layla hoped Pierce wouldn't pick up on the sliver of hope in her voice.

Pierce set her fork down and sipped her coffee. "You're right. We've got a lot on him, though. And he has a lot to lose stateside if he doesn't cooperate. Bennett used a system of doctored invoices, fraudulent customs and shipping labels, and other tricks to hide the true provenance of millions of dollars' worth of stolen artifacts and smuggle them into the US."

She took a long sip of coffee. "Bennett may not have owned the shell company or been involved in the attack in the embassy, but his role buying and smuggling illegal objects contributed significantly to the Muharib's operations. His house in New York, a property in Idaho, the business and investment assets. We can freeze all of it in an instant after what's happened. We can make it so he'll never be able to enter the US again if he doesn't come with us."

"Jesus," murmured Layla. They sat in silence for a moment. "So I convince him to cooperate."

Pierce's gaze was intense but sympathetic. "It shouldn't be that hard, Layla. I've only described what could happen to his property. If that doesn't convince him, you might need to tell him what can happen to James. I doubt he'd want to put his son's future at risk."

Layla swallowed. She hadn't been ready for that. She took another sip of coffee to buy herself a moment so that she wouldn't reveal how nervous she felt, then looked at Pierce.

"What are his options?"

"The father? Or the son?"

"James," said Layla.

Pierce took a deep breath. "I don't know. I think that's moot. All we really care about is Bennett. We'll use whatever leverage we need."

"Blackmail?"

Pierce raised an eyebrow. "I think the more professional term is 'negotiation.'"

"That's nonsense, James did nothing wrong." She thought guiltily of James's role in Bennett's affairs, which she had so far kept to herself. As far as Pierce or anyone was concerned, he was totally innocent.

"That's not the point," said Pierce. "The point is that we—you—have to convince Bennett to return to the US."

Layla sighed. "So what's the plan?"

Pierce sat up straight. "You'll go. I'll talk to the State Department crew about sending some backup for you. The operation's over. No more hiding in the shadows. After everything that's happened, both the Justice and State Departments want outcomes. For us, it's putting Bennett behind bars. Farwadi did what we asked him to do. He'll get any sentence reduced.

"State wants us to wrap this whole thing up and get out of Cairo as quick as we can. They're thankful for our intervention at the embassy but now they want all this to go away. So keep your eyes open—they've assigned us some security, but I also think those folks are watching us." She looked closely at Layla, who was avoiding her gaze.

"I know Bennett's a real charmer, but he's also a world-class stolen art smuggler. He either comes back with us to see his day in court, or you make it clear that there will be repercussions. As a prosecutor friend of mine once said, give him options, but make it clear he's got no choice."

The words felt like a shadow over love. Pierce's talk of repercussions referred to James, a price that James would pay somehow for the sins of his father—and Layla knew it would be for his own complicity, too. Dread welled up in her. It would be, she understood, the most difficult conversation she had had since the day she stormed out of her family's apartment.

"Do you understand, Layla? What it is you have to do?"

Layla nodded. "I understand. It's just . . ." She eyed Pierce carefully. "They were almost like family." She felt embarrassed at the admission, and expected Pierce to roll her eyes or admonish her, but Pierce just reached across the table and squeezed Layla's hand, giving her the courage to continue.

"You know my family is here, in Cairo. But I walked out on them, after I got into Georgetown. My dad . . ." She looked at the table in front of her, the luxury of it, the room around them . . . She swallowed hard, feeling a shiver ripple through her body. A shiver that felt like mourning. "My father didn't want me to go. He wanted me to stay in Cairo and help the family. But I didn't want to stay. I couldn't imagine staying." She looked at Pierce. "So I left. I walked out the door and I didn't speak to them for years until we came here for this operation."

Pierce squinted. "Until . . . ?"

Layla felt relieved, finally, to confess her contact with her family to Pierce. But saying it out loud also made her feel a tremendous sadness. "I'm sorry," she continued. "I know you told me not to get in touch with them. But I needed to see them. I needed my family again."

Pierce blinked and nodded thoughtfully. "I think that might be one of those things you and I just keep between ourselves." She leaned back in her chair. "Layla . . . remember the night of the *Zephyr* raid? In New York?"

Layla smiled. "Seems like forever ago."

Pierce smiled, too. "That it does."

"What about it?"

"I saw something of myself in you. I saw your ambition, your drive, your dedication." They sat in silence, and in that moment Layla felt as she first had when she'd met Pierce and Pierce had taken an interest in her. She felt lucky.

Pierce looked up. "The deal's this. You can live that way, focused on the job, but you're also going to want to keep your eye on the things that make you human . . ."

"Family," guessed Layla.

"That's right. I've told you my whole sad-sack story. At the end of the day, I figure I've got a decade left in this gig, a little more. Who knows." She smiled grimly. "I could get shot or blown up before then. But at the end of the day, were all the sacrifices worth it to put some bad guys behind bars and nab a pretty statue or two that should be in a museum and not in someone's living room? I hope so, but I'm not sure."

Layla nodded. "I hear you."

Pierce reached back and pulled her wallet out of her pocket. She flipped it open, found what it was she was looking for, and handed it across the table to Layla.

A boy with sandy hair and an innocent smile smiled up at her from a photo. He only looked about twelve or thirteen in the picture. He was holding some kind of stuffed animal, a porcupine maybe, in his open palm, and he had his mother's bright and mischievous smile.

"What's that he's holding? A porcupine?"

"It's a hedgehog." Pierce laughed. "It was his favorite stuffed animal."

Layla looked at the picture more closely. "He's beautiful," she whispered. "What's his name?" She looked up.

Pierce was staring at the photo in her hand and Layla could tell she was holding back tears. "Matthew." She smiled. "That picture must've been taken six or seven years ago. I wanted to show you that, because . . . I don't know. It's just . . . important to remember what you love, who you love. It's hard to be alone in the world. If there's anything I can teach you after all we've been through, it's to try to figure out a way to not go it alone."

Layla nodded. She handed the photo back to Pierce.

"I'm not alone," she said. "I've got you."

Pierce smiled and gave herself a little shake. "Anyway, we've got one last thing to do before you have to deal with Bennett." Her eyes lit up. "I got the call while you were talking to Gamal. The team found something interesting."

LAYLA AND PIERCE STOOD outside a run-down apartment building with an obvious FBI presence out front. Layla threw Pierce a curious look—she still hadn't shared the reason for this sudden detour that was important enough to delay confronting Bennett. Together they climbed the narrow wood steps. Two flights up, Laya heard voices speaking English. A man in a suit stood beside the open door of an apartment.

"Agent Pierce," he said with a curt nod. "In here."

The women followed him through a narrow apartment not much bigger than the one Layla had grown up in. A broad window looked out over the street; a kitchenette contained just a decrepit stove and an old white enameled sink, stained yellow. A TV stood in one corner near a table with two wooden chairs. The room smelled of stale food and of life lived in cramped quarters. One bed stood in the corner under a cone of netting. As they entered, Layla heard sounds from the only other room in the apartment, and followed them to find a crowd of Cairo police and FBI agents clearly gathering evidence.

"What is this place?" asked Layla.

"This is Khalid Yasin's mother's place. She lives here with his sister and nieces," replied Pierce.

"Where's Khalid?"

"Not completely sure. Cairo police are looking for him, though. From what I understand, he's a man of no fixed address." Pierce strode across the room. Layla followed.

"This it?" Pierce asked a young female agent crouched on the ground. The agent stood and stepped aside. "This is it," she confirmed.

Pierce knelt on the floor beside a twin bed and gestured to Layla to kneel beside her. An expensive-looking Nikon camera lay on the floor beside her foot. Pierce set her forefinger in a hole in the concrete floor and pulled up. The panel she pried up was wood. It appeared to have been painted to look like concrete. Pierce set it aside, revealing a square hole. She reached in and pulled back a piece of crimson cloth. Underneath it lay two wooden boxes that looked like antiquities. Beside them lay a square leather case. The hole was big enough to hold three times as many boxes. Pierce glanced at Layla.

"Is any of this starting to ring a bell?"

Layla looked at the boxes. She didn't recognize them. "No," she answered honestly.

Pierce reached in and lifted one of the boxes out. The way she held it, Layla guessed that it was heavier than it appeared. Pierce set the box on the floor between them and opened it. Inside were oval-shaped objects wrapped in white cloth and set in indentations in the box. Pierce pulled one of the objects out of the box and unwrapped it. It was the head of a jackal, set atop a semicircle of solid gold.

"Holy shit," whispered Layla. "Are these Faiyum artifacts?"

Pierce pulled her gaze from the object in her hand and peered into empty space in the hole. "Some of them. I have a feeling he took most of them, wherever he went."

Layla looked at her. "These are some of the most sought-after stolen relics in the world."

Pierce met her gaze. She did not look pleased or proud. "It's just a few of them. Now I've got to find out what that bastard did with the rest."

Layla smiled. "You're never gonna stop, are you?"

Pierce sighed, smiled wearily at her, and shrugged. "What else would I do? You wanna hear something rich? After all these years of begging for budget and resources, the Bureau's finally giving me something I can work with. I'll be doubling the size of the Art Crime Squad starting in December."

Layla grinned. "Congrats. That makes more sense than I thought the Bureau had."

They laughed. Layla's eyes fell on the hole again. "What's that?" she said, pointing to the leather case.

"I was wondering that myself." Pierce reached in and pulled out the black leather case. She undid the latch, frowned, and pulled out a pair of compact and very sophisticated-looking binoculars. "Maybe he's a bird-watcher on the side?"

Layla felt her heart sink. She took the binoculars from Pierce's hands, turned the familiar object over, and looked closer until she found what she was looking for: five letters engraved in the hard black plastic. She shut her eyes and felt a rush of anguish, like falling.

"What is it?" asked Pierce.

Layla opened her eyes. "These binoculars belonged to Alberto Rossi."

Pierce took them, and shook them in Layla's face. "This," she said vehemently.

"This is why we do it, Layla. Why we have to make the hard decisions when it comes to the Bennett Rothkopfs of the world, not just the guys who try to blow up embassies. Do you understand?"

Layla nodded once, her eyes fixed on her friend's binoculars.

FROM THE BACK OF the black SUV, Layla eyed the front of the Rothkopf Gallery half a block away. The last time she'd been on the street she'd run the opposite direction after seeing Mackey kill Hamadi. But now she sat in the back of a US State Department vehicle, behind a driver she had seen place a SIG Sauer pistol into the glove compartment. She also knew that a SIG Sauer 9 was nestled in a holster under the right arm of the man who sat in the seat beside her. She and the men from the State Department had been surveilling the gallery since dawn. She'd spotted Bennett as he entered fifteen minutes earlier. James was nowhere to be seen. She looked at her watch. Pierce and the Cairo police would be on the scene in half an hour. There wasn't much time if she was to talk to Bennett before the planned raid on the gallery. When she looked up she found the man at the wheel watching her in the rearview mirror.

"Let's go," she said.

They drove the length of the block and parked in front of the gallery. Layla approached and knocked on the door. Bennett soon answered.

"Layla!" He grinned. He started to move to hug her, but he stopped short and his smile turned wary and confused at the sight of the two tall men standing beside her. "Hey," he said sheepishly, stepping back. "What's . . . going on? Is . . . is something wrong?"

"Bennett, can we come in? These are some colleagues from the US State Department, from the Bureau of Diplomatic Security. This is Special Agent Cooke and this is Special Agent Covello." She could barely look at him as she spoke.

Bennett flashed a wary scowl at Cooke and Covello and took a deep, weary breath. "Colleagues?" he asked, but he stepped aside to let them enter. They followed him into the gallery and to the offices. Layla felt sick at the memory of the last time she was here, the terrible crime she had seen committed.

Bennett led them to his desk and pulled chairs close to it. "Have a seat here," he said with a stiff smile. "Would you guys like any coffee?"

"No thanks," said Layla, taking a seat between Cooke and Covello. They declined his offer as well.

Bennett nodded and leaned back in his chair. "Okay, Layla. I'll admit, I'm kind of freaked out right now. What's going on?"

Layla couldn't even pretend to smile. Her palms were sweating and her chest felt tight, like there wasn't enough air in the room.

"Mr. Rothkopf . . ." she started.

Bennett's eyes widened and he chuckled nervously. "*Mr.* Rothkopf . . ."

Layla's mouth went dry. She didn't return his smile and continued. "I'm Special Agent Layla el-Deeb of the United States Federal Bureau of Investigation. We've been investigating how profits from sales of stolen artifacts and relics is funding terrorist activity here and abroad, specifically the activities of the Muharib, which is among the organizations on the State Department's Foreign Terrorist Organizations list."

Bennett stared at her. His eyes ranged across her face, as if he were studying its details, as if he were trying to find the seam where the mask met the real flesh. "El-Deeb . . ." His eyes narrowed.

Layla's voice remained even, almost robotic. "We know that you profit from sales of stolen antiquities and artifacts. Several of our contacts have identified you as a buyer of illegal artifacts and as a seller of artifacts on the international market. You purchased some of those artifacts from the Muharib."

He gazed at her steadily. "That is nonsense," he said.

She changed tack. "Bennett, do you know where Hamadi is?"

He frowned and leaned back. The spark of suspicion that she'd seen only seconds before dissipated, and he looked tired and confused. "No. I . . . don't know. He didn't come in yesterday. You know his mom's been sick. I assume he couldn't come in." He shook his head. "Poor guy."

"Bennett, two nights ago, Hamadi was killed in your gallery."

Bennett looked at her, then he laughed, an incredulous chuckle. "Layla . . . I know you speak a bunch of languages, so pardon my French, but that's fucking crazy."

It tugged at Layla's heart that he was still trying to joke with her, trying to charm her. When Bennett saw that Layla and Cooke and Covello weren't smiling, the blood drained from his face and he leaned back.

"It was Mackey, Bennett. On the night of the earthquake, Mackey killed Hamadi, here, in the gallery, in the storage room. He shot him point-blank."

Bennett stared at her. His jaw hung open.

"But what about . . . a body? Police? How do you know this even happened?" He turned to his left and right. "I was here for most of the day yesterday, here this morning. There's nothing anywhere, no . . . signs that anything happened."

Layla folded her hands in her lap. "I want you to listen closely, Bennett. Are you listening?" She was talking to him like he was a child, but she needed him to understand, to do the right thing.

He frowned and nodded.

"We're not here to arrest you. Do you know why?"

He nodded. "You can't. We're not in the US."

"That's right. We can't arrest you here. But we do have evidence against you. And we can indict you in the US. We can freeze everything you've got—your bank accounts, any investments or real estate holdings, all of it. We can also post an international warrant for your arrest. Understood?"

He stared at her pleadingly. "Layla—I'm not involved with the Muharib. This is completely absurd." Layla broke their eye contact—she couldn't stand to see the confusion and pain on his face.

She sighed. "We have evidence tying you to Global Relics, a shell company created and run by Youssef Maghraby, the man who masterminded the attack on the US embassy yesterday."

Bennett's eyes widened. "Youssef? The guy who hangs around the Ghaffars? You're joking."

She looked him dead in the eye now. "I'm not joking about any of this, Bennett. Youssef facilitated the transport and export of stolen relics that you bought. He was also transporting weapons and explosives. We suspect he was trying to figure out a way to get explosives to other countries, including the US, along with the artifacts. Bennett, the connection is . . . clear."

He stared at her, then he scowled and leaned back. "I refuse to believe that you're tying me to some fucking terrorist conspiracy. I may have bought and sold a few things I shouldn't have . . . but I'm not . . . Layla, this is absurd. You know me." He looked wildly around for a moment as if searching for a ripcord. "I sell relics to people who'll care for them. Is that really such a crime?"

Layla heard the echo of James defending his work to her and looked down at her clasped hands. Her lack of response seemed to be irritating Bennett now.

"Anyway, you have no jurisdiction here, like you said. This is not America."

She nodded. She wanted to keep her composure but this was the part she had dreaded most of all. "All that matters is the evidence we have of your trafficking in stolen artifacts. That's all we're focused on, and it's enough. If you choose not to return to the US, we can expand the freeze on your assets. That would include any assets you may have put in trust for James, any accounts overseas to which he might have access . . ."

Bennett's eyes widened.

She took a deep breath. "We can expand the arrest warrant to include James." She struggled hard to keep her voice under control, but it warped and bent. She was looking into Bennett's eyes and he was looking into hers and she was swimming. Every moment they had shared, from the first, flowed through her mind like a dream:

the moment they met, the moment he said yes to her offer to work at his gallery, the dinners in New York.

"Here, in Egypt, we're working closely with the Egyptian authorities. They're hunting for Mackey now. In about fifteen minutes, Cairo police will come to the front door to sweep the gallery and collect evidence about the murder we know happened on the premises. The gallery will be shuttered. James will not have access to anything here."

Bennett watched her, his mouth agape. "Layla . . ." he whispered. "You're talking about James . . . *James*."

"Yes," she said. She thought she might drown in the pain. "You have five minutes. Do you want to come with us now? Or do you want to involve him in the mess you've made?"

Bennett sat back and blinked. He gazed at her steadily but she could tell that he wasn't really seeing her. Something had left him. After a minute he spoke. "I won't let James be pulled into this."

She nodded. She thought for a moment to thank him, to say something about the good decision he had made, but she knew that those days were over. He had made the decision for James, not for her. She was no longer part of any equation. "If you need a few minutes, we can wait. Agents Cooke and Covello can take you to your place. You can collect what you need, and you'll be escorted back to New York under our protection. There, as soon as you arrive, you'll be in FBI custody and you'll be read your Miranda rights. Do you understand?"

He nodded. Layla stood. She felt a vast and nauseating emptiness. "Thank you, Mr. Rothkopf."

Outside, Layla climbed into the waiting SUV. Cooke and Covello could manage the rest. She couldn't bear to see Bennett escorted away in handcuffs.

"Where to, Agent el-Deeb?" asked her security guard, Agent Alice Greene.

"Do you know where Manshiyat Naser is? The neighborhood?"
Greene shook her head. "Do you know the way?"

"Yeah," said Layla. "I'll tell you how to get there. For now, just head east."

Layla leaned against the door, rested her face in her hands, and began to weep. The tears flowed as easily as they ever had, and she did not know exactly what she was mourning but the loss felt great and boundless, like her whole soul howling in silence. She bent her head and stifled the sound of her weeping, pulled her sunglasses out of her jacket pocket, and put them on. She checked to see if Agent Greene had noticed her quick breakdown. Their eyes met in the mirror. "What's in Manshiyat Naser, Agent el-Deeb?"

Layla looked out the tinted glass at the quickly passing streets.

"Home," she said. "My family."

WHEN THE SUV WAS within sight of the sprawl of Manshiyat Naser along the base of the cliffs east of the city, they entered a stench like an enveloping fog. Layla understood almost immediately that she had put Agent Greene in an awkward position, as she watched her fumble with the air-conditioning to try to stave off the smell. Piles of burst garbage bags spilled from alleyways and the edges of the redbrick apartment buildings.

Greene turned her head this way and that in obvious, stunned disbelief. "Agent el-Deeb, are you sure this is the right way?"

"Yes," said Layla. "I grew up in this neighborhood. It's called Garbage City. And yes, it's a bit of a maze. Take a right up here . . . just a little farther." Although she spoke calmly, Layla also felt impatient with the driver. Greene's visit would be a matter of an hour or two. Most of the people who lived here were fated to smell that stench for the rest of their lives.

The SUV came to a stop at the curb and Layla stared out the window for a few seconds, up at Sanaa's apartment building. Greene turned off the car.

"No need to come with me," said Layla. "I've got it. Thanks." She stepped out and stood on the sidewalk.

"I'll wait here for you," Greene said through a crack in the window, which she quickly powered up to close.

"Thanks," mumbled Layla.

It had been weeks since she'd visited Sanaa and Badru with Rami. But she remembered the way. She entered the apartment building and climbed up the two flights of stairs, slowly making her way down the hall to Sanaa's door.

Her sister answered when Layla knocked. She stood silently for a moment, and then they embraced. It felt less awkward than the time before, when things had ended so badly.

"Sister . . ." whispered Sanaa into her ear. "Layla."

Every tense muscle in Layla's body seemed to relax in her sister's arms.

They entered the apartment together. She found Rami seated on the couch in the far corner with his feet up, holding baby Badru in the crook of the arm that was not encased in a cast. A small TV was propped up on a table in front of the couch. On the screen Layla spotted flashing images of the US embassy.

"Layla," he said, his voice urgent. He rose and came to the entrance. "We've been trying to reach you." Sanaa took the baby and Rami and Layla embraced.

He looked much better than when she had last seen him. His broken arm was in a clean cast, and he wore jeans and a yellow polo shirt. His face was clear of the bruising she'd glimpsed when he first got out of prison. The three of them sat at the small kitchen table. Badru was barely awake. Sanaa, seeing Layla's eyes fixated on her nephew, handed him to her. The baby squirmed sleepily. Layla gazed at his face with a smile and felt a moment of calm.

"Layla, we've been watching the news about the embassy, calling, trying to get through. It's so good to see you're okay," Rami said.

"It's good to see you both, too."

"Are you hungry, sister?" asked Sanaa

"No, I just wanted to be with you," she said.

She smiled down at Badru and she felt, if not complete, at least close to something like peace. She felt like she was in the right place, although it pained her that it would not be for long.

"Were you at the embassy?" asked Rami, "When it was attacked?"

"That's part of why I'm here. There's something I have to tell you."

"What is it?" said Sanaa.

"I have to confess something. While I've been here, I've been telling you both that I work at the embassy. But that's not entirely true. I work for the FBI."

Rami and Sanaa stared at her with identical, puzzled frowns.

"I'm a Special Agent, based in New York, and I've been here in Cairo for a few months, but . . ." It was this last part that hurt the most to say. "Now I have to go. I have to go back to New York." She looked down at Badru. In a few months' time he would be one. She would miss his first birthday. She would miss watching him grow up.

The three siblings sat in silence. Badru breathed heavily in his sleep. Finally, Rami spoke.

"What about Mama, Layla? Won't you see her before you go?"

She had hoped that neither of them would bring up their mother, but that wasn't realistic. Now, confronted with how little she herself had done to mend that broken bridge, she found herself overcome with sadness. Sanaa leaned forward and wiped a tear from her cheek. "It's okay, Layla. Everything will be okay."

Layla rubbed her eyes. "Listen I . . . I really wish I could figure out a way to stay longer, to be with you longer. But I have to go. I won't be able to see Mama. And I don't think Mama is ready to see me."

Rami closed his eyes and shook his head mournfully. "I'm so sorry about what happened, Layla," he said. "I didn't mean for you to feel like it was an ambush. Sanaa and I . . . we just got so excited about all of us being together again."

"We missed our big sister," said Sanaa.

"Shhh," hushed Layla. She touched Sanaa's face, and Rami's face. Their eyes looked the same as they had when they were little children. "It's okay now. And I'm the one who should apologize. I don't know why I exploded that way."

"You felt cornered," said Sanaa.

"Maybe," said Layla.

Rami grinned. "At least it reminded me of the good old days . . ."

Layla smiled, embarrassed.

They sat in silence for a moment, but when she had summoned up the courage she spoke again. "I have to go. I want to come back sometime soon, though. Maybe in a year or so."

"Or so?" said Rami.

"Maybe in a year," she said, to console him.

"Won't you stay and have a meal with us?" said Sanaa. "I have bread, we have chicken—"

"I'm so sorry. I really have to go."

They embraced again. Rami looked sad but resigned.

She handed the sleeping baby to her sister and hugged her. Now Sanaa was crying. "My sister . . . My big sister . . ." she repeated. The reverence in Sanaa's voice, and Layla's own feelings of protectiveness for the little girl she remembered and the woman and the baby she now knew, were overwhelming. Layla fought back tears as she held Sanaa close.

Finally, she pulled away and kissed Sanna's forehead, then Badru's. "I have to go," she said again. "There's someone waiting for me downstairs."

She opened the door, turned for one last look at the three of them, Sanaa and Rami and the baby, then she closed the door behind her.

Layla stood in silence for a moment, pausing to reflect. When she turned, she glimpsed the taller buildings of Manshiyat Naser, the upper balconies of some of the buildings packed with garbage. She glanced down from the balcony. Below, the street was quiet; farther down, at the corner, she saw the rear of the waiting SUV. Layla sighed and walked the length of the balcony to get to the stairwell.

It was at the corner of the second-floor balcony, leading to the stairway, that she found Mackey peering down at the street below. He heard her, turned, and his face lit with a possessed smile.

Layla blinked. Mackey couldn't be here, at her family home. She backed away. In only three steps her back was against the balcony wall.

"What do you want?" she said.

Mackey sighed. He looked her up and down, like he was taking the measure of her.

"I wanted to make sure you understand what you've done."

"How did you find me?"

He raised an eyebrow. "I followed your friend in the car down there, the other young lady. It's not hard to keep track of a big black car with a diplomatic license plate." He smiled a little. "Wherever you go, she goes."

"I've done nothing wrong," Layla said. She was breathing hard. She glanced to her left but the doorway to Sanaa's was closed and the balcony was silent. Only the sounds of the street below penetrated the tense silence on the balcony.

Mackey took one cautious step toward her. "That's not true. You did many things wrong. Most important, you did not listen to me." He glanced over his shoulder, down at the street, then turned back to her. From his pants pocket he drew a switchblade. He flicked the catch and a slender, double-edged blade appeared. He held it casually. Like he knew how to use it.

"You don't have to do this," she said, her heart pounding. She was afraid for her own safety but she was more concerned with keeping him away from Sanaa's apartment. "It's all over. Bennett's going back to the States. I don't know where James is. It's not worth it. Everything is done."

"But don't you understand?" Mackey said. He cocked his head and peered at her with real curiosity. "Not everything is done. You're still here. You're walking around. For everything to be done, you must also be done." He took two fast steps toward her with the knife held over his head.

Layla brought her hand up to grab Mackey's wrist and the blade stopped an inch from her eye. They stood like that for seconds, like a statue of two mortal combatants. Layla struggled with all her strength to keep the shivering blade from plunging into her face. The wound in her shoulder felt like it would burst open. Although she could hear herself breathing hard, she was unnerved by Mackey's perfect silence. He made no sound at all—even his expression seemed indifferent. He was taller. Stronger. The knife slowly moved toward her face.

"There's nothing to gain by this. Are you really going to kill an FBI agent?" she protested.

He stared into her eyes. She felt no feedback from him, no human warmth. His gaze was almost reptilian in its coldness.

"You've destroyed everything I had. You destroyed my family."

Layla swallowed as the blade insisted on moving toward her. But Mackey's mention of family lit a fire in her. Her family was just down the hall, and she would not let this monster hurt them. She brought her right foot up and kicked hard at Mackey's shin. He didn't react. She did it again, harder, and twisted his wrist around, but then the blade threatened her belly and her thigh. They were leaning now against the redbrick wall of the building. The tip of the blade quivered in their almost mutual grip, so close to her side that she felt sure this was it. She thought to cry out, to scream and make a commotion, but Badru's face loomed in her mind. She didn't want anyone to get hurt . . . except for Mackey.

She brought her knee up into his groin and he grunted. The seconds of his distraction let her twist his wrist back again so that the blade hovered horizontally over both their heads. Realizing that Mackey was top heavy, Layla put all of her strength into pushing him. The balcony wall was low and she forced him against it, so that he hung with his back over the ledge. His eyes were obsessively fixated on the blade clenched in his grip and hers above his face. Layla held on, the muscles in her arms burning with the effort.

And then she gave a final thrust forward, and immediately pulled back to escape Mackey's flailing grasp as he flipped backward off the balcony.

She gasped and watched in horror as he landed headfirst on the hood of the waiting SUV. The sound was like a piece of heavy fruit smashing onto concrete from a great height. Mackey spilled over onto the street faceup, the blade clattered feet away, and Layla watched numbly as a halo of blood spread around his head onto the garbage-strewn street below.

Breathless, she leaned against the balcony. Agent Greene threw open the car door and rushed out with her gun in hand. She stood over Mackey and looked up at Layla, her sunglasses reflecting the sunlight.

"What the hell just happened?" she called up. "Who the hell is this?"

Layla felt like she was going to throw up. "He's a fugitive," she called. "Make sure he doesn't stand up again."

People were now rushing down the street to the scene. The commotion rose into the air like a flock of pigeons. Sanaa and Rami came to the balcony and stood on each side of Layla.

"Oh my God," gasped Sanaa when she saw the body in the street. She held Badru closer to her chest.

Rami peered down. Agent Greene knelt over Mackey's body in the middle of a thickening circle of onlookers.

"Who is that guy?" asked Rami.

Layla, still catching her breath, looked at him.

"Don't tell me," said Rami. "You *can't* tell me."

Layla nodded. "That's . . . right."

Layla stared down at Mackey's prone body. She felt the tension of the struggle she'd had with him course through her like a nauseating electric current. When Rami touched her shoulder and she looked into her younger brother's eyes, she understood that she wasn't alone in the world anymore. She, too, had family to protect, and who wanted to protect her. Rami hugged her close, and after a few minutes they led Sanaa and Badru back to the safety of the apartment.

• • •

LAYLA CARRIED THE LAST of the cardboard boxes from the penthouse down to the sidewalk, where Agent Greene stowed it in the back of the SUV. Just as they were about to leave, a young boy in dark blue slacks and a white Chicago Bulls T-shirt ran headlong into Layla. They tumbled to the ground.

"Jesus, kid, watch it," yelled Greene, as she bent to help Layla up.

"I'm *sooo* sorry, madams!" called the boy. "I'm *sooo* sorry!!"

Greene and the boy each took one of Layla's hands and helped her stand. "Please forgive me miss. I'm so sorry. I didn't mean to do that."

"It's okay," said Layla, brushing herself off.

"Thank you, miss. Thank you for your forgiveness." He took her hand in one of his, brought it to his lips, and kissed the back of it like a noble courtier. Then he winked at her and bolted. Layla and Greene watched him run off.

"Little shit," muttered Greene. "It's all right. It wasn't on purpose. Let's go."

They climbed into the car. Greene pulled away from the curb and Layla opened her fist to see what it was the boy had squeezed into her palm. It was a folded piece of paper. She unfolded it. It read simply: *Meet me at the café tonight at 8.* She recognized James's handwriting, and she knew exactly the place he was talking about. As soon as she read it she turned this way and that, wondering if he might have been watching the whole time. But she didn't see anyone on the sidewalks or street who looked like James.

That evening, after dinner, she took the elevator downstairs. Greene was sitting in a leather chair in the lobby, reading an old copy of *Time* magazine.

"You must get bored hanging out here all the time," said Layla.

Greene smiled. She looked exhausted. "I'm okay. Things've been a little tense since the embassy attack, I'll admit. It'll be good to get you and Agent Pierce on your way home safe and sound."

Layla pulled the keys to the penthouse out of her pocket and handed them to Greene. "Why don't you go rest upstairs? I'm embarrassed I didn't think of it before. Go up and you can lie down on the couch."

Greene smiled and shook her head. "That's really nice of you to offer but . . . you know, procedures and all."

"Well, what if I come up with you? That's no big deal, right?" Layla stepped toward the elevator and pushed the button. "You can have a snack or watch TV if you want." She grinned. "You'll be doing your job *and* getting some rest."

The elevator chimed and the door opened. Layla stepped in. Greene stood, hesitantly, in the hall. "C'mon. Get a load off. I won't tell," said Layla, smiling.

Greene sighed and smiled back. "You're really nice, you know that?" She hopped onto the elevator. Layla pressed the penthouse button to send them to the top floor—then, just as the doors were closing, she leaped out and spun on her heel.

Greene lunged for the closing doors but she wasn't fast enough. The doors snapped shut.

As soon as Layla was out of the building, she ran up the street. She was late, and it took ten minutes to get to the café on the south side of Tahrir Square by cab. The fronts of the two buildings adjacent had massive blue tarps covering them. She wondered if that was because of the aftermath of the earthquake. She entered, peering about the busy café, and spotted James in a corner. He had on a baseball cap, and he nodded to her when their eyes met.

She walked toward him, her heart racing. She wasn't afraid of James, but she was afraid of his anger, of the possibility that he would lash out at her for all her lies and the ultimatum she had given Bennett. She sat across from him and they gazed at each other wordlessly for a moment. What could she say? What did she expect him to say?

"Layla," he started. "I . . . I spoke to my dad. He told me everything."

"I'm sorry," she said. "I'm not who I said I was."

He frowned. "I know that, in a way, but I still find it hard to believe." He sat back and studied her face. "Who are you really?"

She hesitated. "That's a hard question to answer," she started. "I—"

"How *hard* can it be?" he cut in. "I mean, you're a pro, right? You're an FBI agent who's spent months fooling us all. Telling me who you are seems like it would be easy compared to all that."

"James—" She felt like he was sliding a dagger into her heart.

He looked down at the table and took a deep, audible breath. When he looked up, his eyes were shadowed by anger. "What am I supposed to say?" He stared at her. "I've never known anyone like you. I've never felt that way about anyone before." His eyes were pools of pain and confusion. "But it was all lies."

She wanted to protest, but he pressed on. "Listen, Layla, I've run this through my head dozens and dozens of times now. What you did may have saved my dad's life. If he'd gotten in any deeper who knows how this might have ended up." He shut his eyes and squeezed the bridge of his nose. "I still can't believe that Mackey killed Hamadi." When he looked up she saw that tears had welled up in his eyes. "Is that true?"

"That he killed Hamadi?" She nodded. "Yes. He also tried to kill me."

His eyes filled with terror and tears as he put his hand to his mouth. "This has been . . . such a nightmare," he said.

Seeing him weep brought tears to her own eyes. She looked about but the other people in the café were minding their own business; the place felt calm and hushed.

"I wanted to see you before I go to the embassy," he said.

She brushed away her tears. "Why are you going there?"

"They took my dad on a flight yesterday, back to New York. I can't let him go through this on his own. I'm gonna turn myself in, tell them about my part in all of this. Maybe I can cut some kind of deal, get whatever they're planning to do to him reduced or something."

She felt a rising anxiety. "That's not a good idea."

"What are you talking about? I thought you of all people, after what's happened—"

"You won't make a real dent in his prosecution. They only really want your father."

"They? Don't you mean . . . you?"

She sat back, stung, before trying again.

"James, your dad is ready for this. He's resigned to it. He made his choice. Don't do this. Just . . . go. Go anywhere." She was pleading with him now.

James looked at her as if he didn't understand what she was saying. "I thought you'd be telling me to turn myself in."

Layla took a shuddering breath, "I'm not. That's not what I want."

They stared at each other.

"That job offer in Australia—" she started.

"What about it?"

"Take it. Start over."

He sighed and his eyes fell to the table in front of him. When he looked up again she had guessed what he would say. "Come with me. If any of it was real, come with me."

"I can't." She looked at her lap. "The Bureau is focused on your dad right now, but there's no guarantee they won't eventually come after you, too. Just go quietly. Maybe one day . . ."

They gazed into each other's eyes. The memory of their first kiss flooded Layla's mind.

"What's your real last name?" he asked.

She hesitated. Professionalism dictated that she remain silent, but she knew why he was asking. He intended, one day, to look for her. She wanted to be found.

"El-Deeb." She spelled it for him.

He nodded, rose, and picked up a backpack. "Layla," he said.

She had no words. The tears welled up in her eyes again.

He leaned over her, kissed her deeply, and ran his thumb along her cheek.

"I'll see you," he said.

He backed away, then turned and left the café.

ON THE MORNING LAYLA flew out of Cairo, she flew alone. Pierce would leave later that evening on a separate flight.

As the plane sat at the gate, Layla leaned forward and drew from her bag the cheap spiral notebook in which she had kept notes during the past months. From the middle of it, she retrieved the photo of Alberto and his family. She gazed at Alberto's smiling eyes, the joy apparent in all their faces. They were a family, luckier in many ways than hers, but also tragically torn apart. She remembered Khalid and her brief meeting with him at the Hanover Club, and felt a pang of frustration that she had been so close.

Layla set her head back against the seat. When she had flown out of Cairo as an eighteen-year-old girl, she had anticipated a whole new life. She had hoped to become something different and strong, the woman she wanted to be. This time, as she looked out the window and squinted at the morning sun, she understood that she was closer to being that woman than she ever had been, and she had Cairo to thank.

She vowed to herself that she would return to Egypt to find Khalid and avenge Alberto. That is, once she had made it through the investigation into her role in the mission back in New York. She knew the thought should fill her with fear, given her many missteps and disregard for protocol, but she couldn't shake the strange sense of peace she had found.

The plane sped down the runway of Cairo International Airport, banked in a stomach-churning turn, and arced northward, toward the Mediterranean and, eventually, toward the Atlantic and to a country she loved and called home, but which she knew was not the setting of her whole life's story.

She leaned forward and slipped the notebook back in her tote, casting a wary glance to her side. But the woman across the aisle was reading, not paying her any mind.

She left the city of her birth as she had left it once before, with no witnesses to her departure. Her only companion was the ancient and priceless—but very ugly—bronze statue of a cat in her carry-on tote.

ABOUT THE AUTHORS

LISA KLINK started her career writing for the series *Deep Space Nine* and *Voyager* before coming back to Earth for shows such as *Martial Law* and *Missing*. She's also written short stories, graphic novels, a theme park attraction and three books in The Dead Man series, as well as co-authoring the novel *All In* with Joel Goldman. Lisa is also a five-time champion on *Jeopardy!*

PATRICK LOHIER was born in Montreal, Canada, grew up in Philadelphia, and graduated from the University of Chicago. His stories, book reviews, and essays have appeared in *African American Review*, *The Georgia Review*, *Callaloo*, *The Globe and Mail*, Boing Boing, and other publications. He lives in Toronto with his wife and two kids.

DIANA RENN is the author of *Tokyo Heist*, *Latitude Zero*, and *Blue Voyage*. Her essays and short fiction have appeared in *Publishers Weekly*; The Huffington Post; *Brain, Child*; Literary Mama; *The Writer*; YARN (Young Adult Review Network), and others. Diana grew up in Seattle and now lives outside of Boston with her husband, her son, and a spooky black cat.